→ THE

MADRONA HEROES
REGISTER

BOOK Nº. 5: UNDERNEATH IT ALL

BY

HILLEL COOPERMAN

ILLUSTRATIONS BY CAROLINE HADILAKSONO

ISBN 978-0-9899905-6-1

Typeset in Athelas by TypeTogether and Luxury Diamond by House Industries.

For Sivan.

Books by Hillel Cooperman

The Madrona Heroes Register

Book No. 4: Echoes of the Past

Book No. 5: Underneath it All

The author recommends that you read The Madrona
Heroes Register series in the order listed above. When
asked "Why start with Book No. 4?" the author invariably
responds, "Because Star Wars."

The Experience of Being Alive

CONTENTS

Chapter One

The Shopping List 1

Chapter Two

The Sudden Rain 15

Chapter Three

The Missing Cheese 29

Chapter Four

The Accidental Summer Camp 42

Chapter Five

The First Walk 53

Chapter Six

The Caramel Apple Pancakes 64

Chapter Seven

The Sandbox Kiss 75

Chapter Eight

The Robotic Milkshake **86**

Chapter Nine

The Broken Pieces **96**

Chapter Ten

The Fiftieth Digit **107**

Chapter Eleven

The Mango Mural **119**

Chapter Twelve

The Almost-Finished Portrait **133**

Chapter Thirteen

The Hole in the Wall **150**

Chapter Fourteen

The Awful Smell **165**

Chapter Fifteen

The Hungry Hero 178

Chapter Sixteen

The New Headquarters 186

Chapter Seventeen

The Unexpected Visitor 205

Chapter Eighteen

The Lunch Date 216

Chapter Nineteen

The 1911 East Cherry Sewer Tunnel 228

Chapter Twenty

The Tunnel People 235

Chapter Twenty-One

The Papaya Break 248

Chapter Twenty-Two

The Gift 261

Chapter Twenty-Three

The Books on Reserve 273

Chapter Twenty-Four

The Broken Generator 289

Chapter Twenty-Five

The Fixer 305

Chapter Twenty-Six

The Picture Frames 317

Chapter Twenty-Seven

The Packages 332

Chapter Twenty-Eight

The Last Walk 347

Chapter Twenty-Nine

The Seattle Police Department 360

Chapter Thirty

The Isle of Man 375

Chapter Thirty-One

The Lone Walk 391

Chapter Thirty-Two

The New Patient 400

Chapter Thirty-Three

The Harvesting 411

Chapter Thirty-Four

The Posters 425

Chapter Thirty-Five

The Ice Cream Break 437

Chapter Thirty-Six

The Speakeasy 449

Chapter Thirty-Seven

The Places You Shouldn't Be 461

Chapter Thirty-Eight

The Linden Tree 473

Chapter Thirty-Nine

The House in the Weeds 487

Chapter Forty

The Long Way Around 498

Chapter Forty-One

The Way Out 512

Chapter Forty-Two

The Secrets that Bind 523

Chapter Forty-Three

The Change in Plans 536

Chapter Forty-Four

The Elusive Truth 548

Epilogue 559

⇥ 1 ⇤

THE SHOPPING LIST

"**B**ut how are you going to remember everything if you don't write it down?"

"I'll remember."

"There's no shame in admitting you're not superhuman you know." Zach's father admonished him gently.

"I said, I'll remember."

"I always suspected you were part elephant. And you're stubborn like an elephant too."

Zach Jordan thought of a sharp retort but swallowed it as he knew that once his father was making dopey jokes, any response would only encourage him further.

"I'll admit that your skin isn't nearly as leathery as I would have expected for an elephant but I suppose that will come with time."

"Dad!" Zach was getting annoyed.

"Fine, but don't' forget the parmesan cheese. We're out."

"Uh huh." Zach was already moving towards the back door to collect his bike and head uphill to the neighborhood market.

On his bike Zach was free. Free of his father's constant requests and free to think. Zach didn't mind helping, it just felt like he was always the one being asked to help, while his younger sisters were getting away without lifting a finger. Zach knew that the increase in his responsibilities was somewhat due to his parents no longer living together, but he didn't like to dwell on that too much. And besides, there were so many other things to think about as Zach biked up the Madrona hillside.

It had been almost exactly a year since the adventures of the previous summer. Once he and his siblings had narrowly escaped the scrutiny of the scientists at Luce Laboratories, the Jordan kids' main challenge, other than schoolwork, had consisted of keeping their powers a secret.

For Zach it meant not doing *so* well at school as to raise eyebrows, but still getting good enough grades to keep his parents happy. For Binny it meant not being nearly as nosy as she could be. And for Cassie it meant near constant admonishment from Zach and Binny that she was not to show off about her power no matter how desperate she was to tell someone - anyone. Luckily Cassie still couldn't disappear on command but Zach and Binny still kept a close eye on her and on a couple of occasions had needed to resort to discrediting Cassie's statements or distracting people from Cassie's sudden exits.

Zach wasn't sure that his extraordinary memory skills were really that much of a "super power" anyway. Not compared to mind-reading and invisibility (if Cassie ever figured out how to do it on command). Even Penny, could break stuff just by touching it. Zach imagined there were more uses for that kind of thing than his ability to retain pretty much everything he saw. His powers definitely made school easier, and he was pretty sure he could be the world record holder at memorizing Pi, but the relative uselessness of his skill was another topic Zach didn't like to think too much about.

Zach consoled himself with the fact that being one of only four people on Earth with an actual super power was better than being one of the remaining almost seven billion without one. Even more importantly, school was out for the summer. Other than doing chores for his father Zach could spend his time hanging out in the woods, or riding his bike with the summer sun on his back. On his bicycle, Zach shed his worries about revealing his super powers. And as far as whether his power was as good as the others, for the moment, it just wasn't that important.

§

Angel Hair pasta – two packages, one bunch of fresh basil, and a block of parmesan cheese, Zach recited Jay's shopping list word for word in his head. Zach collected the ingredients one-by-one as he walked the handful of aisles of Madrona Dry Goods – the small neighborhood market located in the commercial heart of the neighborhood.

Zach approached the register spreading his items on the counter for the cashier when something caught his eye through the market's glass door. More someone than something really.

Bobbing, well, no, floating really, was this hair. Mahogany curls. A huge spherical mass of shiny hair sprouting upward like water from an ornate outdoor fountain. The curls reached their apex and then headed down tracing countless gently curving paths around a face. A girl's face. An absolutely beautiful face. Zach had never seen anyone like her.

Zach's mother liked to buy him word-a-day calendars at the beginning of each year. Zach would chew through one of them in a half-hour. He would then move on to the thesaurus memorizing synonyms for the words he'd just learned. And despite the fact that striking, gorgeous, stunning, appealing, alluring, enthralling, and captivating, were available choices in

Zach's mental database, "beautiful" was the only word that came to mind.

But Zach knew instantly that "beautiful" was way too simple a word to capture the face he was looking at. Even from across the street Zach could see the eyes glinted with intelligence and confidence. And the lips were pursed in the most adorable way. They looked curious. *Could lips look curious?*

"Um, did you hear me? That'll be $16.27."

1627. 1627. What was 1627? Zach thought.

And then suddenly the voice of the teenage cashier brought Zach out of his reverie. The cashier leaned forward, peered around the register, and followed Zach's gaze. A moment later she turned back to Zach, a wide grin on her face, "Oh yeah, she's *very* cute. You've got excellent taste."

Zach flushed a sunburn shade of red, fumbling to get the twenty dollar bill his father had given him out of his pocket as quickly as possible. It seemed like forever. Zach kept fishing around in his pocket and the cashier kept grinning. Zach was so desperate to leave he almost left without his change.

The cashier delivered her "Thank you for shopping at Madrona Dry Goods" with an extra big knowing smile.

Zach felt the early summer evening air brush over his hot face as he finally made it outside and walked towards his bike with his bag of groceries.

There was nothing in Zach's photographic brain that prepared him for what he'd felt when he'd laid eyes on the curly haired girl in the park. In fact, his mind was now adamantly repeating the instruction "Don't look!" over and over. The rest of Zach either didn't hear the instruction or was ignoring it outright because before he could stop himself Zach was looking directly at the girl again.

Zach breathed a small sigh of relief that the girl hadn't noticed his gawking. She was still crouched at the edge of the park peering intently into a bush.

Ten minutes earlier Zach's route home had not been through the park. But now that was clearly the most efficient way to get home. Zach walked his bike across the street trying not to stare too hard. He had just enough sense to make sure no cars were coming.

As Zach approached the spot where the girl was crouching, he suddenly realized that he wasn't sure what he was going to do when he got there. Say "Hi"? Introduce himself? Ignore her? Zach didn't have time to come to a conclusion as a sudden screech was followed by a cat shooting out of the bushes at top speed.

Before Zach knew what was happening, the girl had jumped up out of her crouch, and was standing hands on hips in front of him. She said "What is wrong with you? You scared her away!"

Oh wow. She was angry. Zach mumbled something incoherent.

The girl continued, "I was trying to get her to come to me and *you* scared her off."

The lips were a different kind of pursed now. Their shape looked, exasperated. And still adorable. Her hair was gently bobbing back and forth as the girl waited for Zach to explain himself. It took Zach a second to replay the sounds the girl had made and hear them as words instead of a jumble of random snippets.

"Uh, sorry. I didn't, uh, see the cat."

The girl kept shaking her head slowly.

"Zooooooooooooeeeeeeeee!" the wail came from the playground on the other side of the park. In a flash, the girl was gone, running towards the source.

That hadn't gone as planned, Zach thought to himself. While he didn't have a plan exactly, making the girl extremely angry was definitely not it. But there was one silver lining – Zach knew her name. Zach repeated the name over and over in his mind making extra sure that he would never forget it. *How did she spell it? Was Zoe short for something?* Zach liked it.

Not knowing what else to do, Zach hurried after the girl.

§

"Zoooee! Zoooee! Zoooee!" The yelling was coming from a little boy, Zoe's little brother, Zach guessed by the family resemblance and the way he called for her. The boy was perched atop the jungle gym. To Zach the boy looked even younger than Cassie – maybe six or seven, and he was small at that. The boy whimpered, "I can't get down."

7

"Take it easy little guy." A few feet from the jungle gym, another boy, about 9 or 10 by the looks of him, with pale skin, and short cropped hair so blonde it was almost white, sat at a picnic bench. He was holding some sort of notebook and a pencil.

Zach no longer felt hot. The evening had turned decidedly cooler.

"What did you *do* to my brother?" Zoe demanded of the white-haired boy.

"I'm not little." Zoe's brother protested from above.

"What did you do!?" Zoe repeated in the direction of the boy on the bench. Each word got its own distinct emphasis.

"I didn't *do* anything." The boy repeated Zoe's accusatory inflection. "He was playing on the jungle gym, and I was drawing. He asked me to draw him on the jungle gym posing like some sort of superhero. He shouldn't have climbed up there if he's too scared to get down."

"I'd like you to not tell me what my brother should or should not do." Zoe responded icily.

"I'm not too scared to climb down. It's just very high up." The little boy repeated.

If Zoe or the white-haired boy heard Zoe's little brother's protest, they showed no signs of it. They just stared at each other. To Zach it seemed like it went on for a very long time.

Finally the white-haired boy broke the silence. "I'm outta here." He picked up his notebook and writing implement, and stormed away across the park. Zach saw Zoe slowly shaking her head as she watched the boy get further and further away. The same head shaking that he'd received a minute earlier. That was not a good sign.

Finally, satisfied that the white-haired boy was far enough away, Zoe turned her angry attention to her little brother. "You shouldn't be talking to strangers."

"It was just another kid. Not a stranger."

"Well, kid or not, he was a stranger. And a jerk. Come on Gabe, get down from there. It's time to go home."

"I can't." her brother said in defeat.

The jungle gym was cone-shaped and made up of metal triangles. The base was only six feet across but it rose at a steep angle with the top being ten feet off the ground. To Zach it seemed like an easy climb down across the face of the structure. But to Gabe it seemed much more difficult.

He *was* a little guy, Zach thought to himself, though Zach knew better than to mention that aloud. Maybe this was an opportunity to redeem himself with Zoe. "I can climb up and help him down if you like."

"Don't you have some more cats to scare off?" Zoe shot Zach a look that made it clear his help was not welcome.

"Zoe, can you *please* climb up and help me down?"

"Seriously? You got up there. You can't get back down?" Zoe sounded irritated.

Two large wobbly tears slowly made their way down the little boy's cheeks.

"Gabe. Gabe. It's fine. I'm sorry, I'll help you down."

A quiet "Thank you." floated down from above.

Zoe climbed onto the first rung of the jungle gym and reached out her hand.

"I can't reach you. Climb up higher." Gabe instructed.

"Don't tell me what to do!" Zoe snapped.

Zach thought Gabe was being reasonable but knew better than to say anything.

"Ugh. Gabe you're really making this hard." Zoe complained.

"Just climb a little higher. Please Zoe?"

"I don't feel like climbing higher. You need to meet me half way!"

"I don't think I can do it."

Zoe climbed down and through the jungle gym so she was standing in its center directly under her brother. "Fine, just hold on up there while you slide your body through one of the holes and drop down to me. I'll catch you."

Gabe shook his head "No. No. No. No. No." Tears were threatening again.

Zach bit his lip even though he didn't think it was really that high. He understood why Gabe was scared. Gabe was pretty young after all. What Zach *didn't* understand was why Zoe wouldn't climb up and get him. Zach wondered if maybe she was trying to teach her little brother a lesson?

"Do it Gabe!" Zoe's voice was rising with frustration.

"Noooooo." Gabe wailed. The tears were coming now.

"I've had enough Gabe. Stop being a baby." Zoe was really upset. "It takes at least ten minutes to walk home, and we're already late. I need to get you home for dinner now or *I'm* the one who's gonna be in trouble."

Gabe sobbed.

"Gabe now!" Zoe's voice was commanding. As she yelled, she stamped her feet on the ground out of frustration.

Zach replayed the scene repeatedly in his mind later that night and in the following days. The exact moment it had happened was still a little fuzzy. But the result was unmistakable. The ground around where Zoe stamped her feet had caved inward. The earth seemed to disintegrate in a circle around her and the effect radiated out just beyond the perimeter of the jungle gym.

As the ground gave out beneath her, Zoe fell backward. The jungle gym followed quickly moving downward into the hole that had formed. Gabe held on for dear life screaming as it descended.

When the dust had settled – and there was actual dust everywhere – Zoe was on the ground brushing the dirt off her clothes and out of her mass of hair, Gabe was sprawled flat across the top of the structure which was now at least three feet lower, and Zach just stood staring, mouth agape.

Everyone was silent for a moment except for the small coughs coming from Zoe as she tried to get dirt out of her mouth.

"Zoe, it happened again." Gabe said, his tears gone.

"Quiet. Nothing *happened*."

Zach started to open his mouth to say something but nothing came out. He closed it trying to think of what exactly to say.

Zoe climbed up over the lip of the large depression and through the gaps in the now sunken jungle gym. "Now can you come down?" She asked Gabe, still sounding annoyed as she reached out a hand in his direction. The jungle gym had lowered enough that Gabe could reach Zoe's outstretched hand as she stood on the lip of the hole.

"You did that." Zach finally mustered.

Zoe looked up at Zach glaring as she continued to wipe the dirt off her clothes. "You don't know what you're talking about."

Gabe was now safely on the ground looking as if nothing remotely out-of-the-ordinary had happened.

"I know what I saw." Zach said quietly for the first time not at a loss for words in front of Zoe.

"Forget what you saw." Zoe replied with equal force.

"I *never* forget things."

"Never?" Gabe piped up cheerfully.

Zach took his eyes off Zoe momentarily and gave her little brother a half smile. "Never."

"Wow. That's cool." Gabe said.

"Thanks. You okay now?" Zach asked concerned.

Zoe cut off the discussion, "We're going home now. Come."

Gabe seemed to know who was boss and let Zoe take his hand and lead him away from the playground without another word.

Zach stood rooted to the ground watching them walk off into the distance, getting smaller and smaller. Gabe periodically looked back over his shoulder at Zach, but Zoe never did.

It didn't matter. Zoe was the most amazing and beautiful girl Zach had ever seen. Amazing, beautiful, and powerful. Literally. Zoe had a super power, like him, Binny, Cassie, and Penny. Zoe was one of them. Zach knew it.

Zach picked up his bike and the bag of groceries, both of which had fallen over in the tumult. Zach didn't notice that his grocery bag was a little lighter. He had other things on his mind.

As Zach biked slowly home through the quiet lakeside neighborhood of Madrona, he marveled to himself about how his world had just changed so significantly. *They weren't the only kids with super powers.*

One thought kept coming to the foreground of his mind over and over – *Wait until Binny hears!*

❧ 2 ❧

THE SUDDEN RAIN

I am so sick to death of other kids, the boy with the blonde hair thought to himself. The light from the low setting sun was making his hair look almost white. His cheeks were scarlet for the moment in deep contrast to his typically pale skin.

The boy fumed. *It's no more my fault that her little brother climbed too high than that girl at camp today can't draw.* The girl who sat next to him at art camp was struggling with her painting of a panda. When she asked for help, he had helped. But the moment he finished painting a superlative panda over her original awful rendition, the girl had wailed to the teacher that he had ruined her painting.

The boy could still hear the teacher's words ringing in his head, "Ollie, you can't just paint over someone else's painting."

"But she wanted me to show her how to improve her panda."

The teacher had a pitying look on her face that confused and angered Ollie. "You ruined her painting."

"Ruined?" Ollie was almost yelling now he was so upset. "Ruined? I improved her painting. Her panda was awful."

"Ollie, please lower your voice." The teacher said.

Ollie had fumed then too. In fact, Ollie hadn't really stopped fuming since camp had ended that day. Ollie loved to draw, but how was he expected to do his best when the teachers cared more about not hurting anyone's feelings than they did about great art? Not that painting a panda from a poster was so 'great'. Nothing was as beautiful as drawing an actual living thing.

Ollie remembered the first moment he'd understood this. Ollie had never been particularly inclined towards drawing or anything artistic, but at the age of six he'd sat in the back seat of his mother's car when they'd come to a stop light. Ollie wasn't sure why he looked out the window at that moment. Maybe some motion caught the corner of his eye. Out the window Ollie saw the most striking bird.

It was a small bird, perched on the trunk of the tree but sticking straight out at a right angle. The bird appeared to be able to stand sideways from Ollie's perspective. Its chest and face where white. A black stripe started between its eyes and stretched over its head to the top of its back. Shades of bluish gray intermingled with slightly darker stripes of the same color spreading down the bird's back and to its wings. The tail was black. The lower part of the bird's stomach almost concealed a small yellow glow. Ollie noticed every tiny detail.

Ollie was struck, not so much by the bird's beauty, but by the notion that the bird had something to give him. The bird had a gift, and it was Ollie's to receive. The image of the bird stuck in Ollie's mind. Ollie collected his gift the only way he knew how. When he and his mother arrived home Ollie rushed to find colored pencils and paper and transferred what was still fresh in his mind to paper.

When Ollie's mother took a moment to glance at his drawing as she scooted away from the soon to be set kitchen table, her jaw dropped. "Ollie, where did you get this?"

"Get what?"

"This drawing. Where did you get it?"

"I drew it."

"Don't tell fibs young man. You did not draw this."

Even at the age of six Ollie's temper had been quick to rise. "I drew it! I drew it! I drew it!" Ollie screamed at his mother.

"Show me."

Ollie's little fist was clenched around a gray-blue colored pencil. He slowly unclenched it tearing his angry look away from his mother and reproduced the original drawing in painstaking detail.

Ollie's mother was speechless. The drawing was exquisite. Perfect in proportion. Vividly colored. And the eyes. Ollie's rendition of the eyes made it seem like the bird could jump right off the page. They were alive. Sad or afraid maybe, but somehow, alive.

Ollie stood for a bit with his arms crossed waiting for an apology from his mother. It never came. He soon tired of waiting and harrumphed out of the kitchen. Since that day Ollie had tried to find more living things to draw. And while he was fine drawing from photographs of animals or from TV shows, it just wasn't the same.

Ollie didn't know quite how, but while his drawings were rendered with incredible precision, he wasn't picturing the way an animal looked when he drew. In Olli's mind, he was drawing how the animal felt. There was an energy that spoke to Ollie, that was begging to be captured, and he was doing his best to put it on the page. Painting pandas from a poster at art camp just wasn't the same thing.

A black streak roused Ollie from his simmering anger. It was a cat. A sleek black cat. It looked curious but wary. Ollie squatted slowly where he was standing on the sidewalk that ringed the park. Apparently he had caught the cat's attention just as it had caught his.

Ollie reached his hand out towards the cat. The cat didn't move. It looked like it was considering Ollie's offer. Ollie and the cat stared at each other for awhile. The cat inched slowly closer. Ollie's hand was outstretched, his palm facing upwards. The cat came a little closer. Ollie didn't dare move closer knowing the cat had to make the decision to come to him, but he made what he thought might be friendly sounds with his tongue against his teeth. The cat came a little closer.

When the cat was just inches away, Ollie slowly moved his hand toward the cat to pet its head. But just as Ollie made the barest contact, the cat seemed to change its mind all at once. It lashed out with its paw, claws extended, giving Ollie's hand a sizable scratch.

"Owww!" Ollie drew his hand back shocked and in pain. The cat now had its hackles up, its hair on end and was hissing at Ollie. Ollie was so surprised he fell back on the sidewalk from where he'd been squatting.

What a horrible animal? What did I do? The thoughts bounced in Ollie's head. His cheeks reddened in shame. The sting of the cat's rejection was worse than the pain in his throbbing hand which had started to bleed.

For its part, the cat had apparently decided it had enough and walked away from Ollie, not glancing in his direction again. As the cat left, Ollie felt a light wind on his face. Clouds had rolled in over Madrona.

Just my luck, even the animals I run into don't understand me. And now it looks like it's going to rain. Ollie stood up brushing off his pants and wiping the droplets of blood from his hand on his shirt. Luckily the cut seemed shallow, but it stung badly. Ollie felt tears coming to the surface, propelled by white hot anger and shame. The prospect of rain only made things worse. He would be soaked before he got home.

Suddenly Ollie felt a tap tap tap on his shoulder. Someone had been watching him. Watching the cat hiss at him and scratch him. "What!?" Ollie turned on the tapper, his rage, and shame, coalescing into a hard ball in his stomach.

But as he turned, all Ollie saw was a tree hurtling through the air, away from the spot where he was standing. It was roughly eight feet tall with a skinny trunk. It couldn't have been planted in the spot more than a year or two ago. But it wasn't planted any more. The tree landed 20 feet away. And at Ollie's feet was the hole where the tree had been rooted to the ground. It was empty now.

At that moment, all the anger, and humiliation drained out of Ollie and his jaw dropped. The uprooted tree just lay there. Like a corpse. The branches that were pointing toward the sky were swaying in the wind. *What had just happened?*

The darkening sky pushed Ollie into action. He started running home. Later he would wonder whether he ran so fast to escape the rain, or to escape mean kids, hissing cats, and flying trees.

§

Caleb Adams rarely stopped to gawk on his way home from a day of tending to the Madrona Woods. No matter which route he took out of the small forest in the heart of the lakeside neighborhood, he ended up walking by the park. Caleb's house sat on the edge of the park in a row of old homes. Caleb knew most all of the kids in the neighborhood, and the blonde boy was no exception. The boy's name was Ollie.

There was a look of sadness and pity on his face as Caleb watched Ollie waiting patiently to pet the cat. In the sky above them, clouds were rolling in. Suddenly, the boy yelled and the tree flew up into the air, roots leaving the ground. Caleb's eyes went wide. Caleb didn't know if it was because the boy had yelled in the otherwise quiet park, but suddenly the quiet felt heavy, like the clouds above. Caleb suddenly felt heavy too.

As the rain started to fall, the boy ran home. But Caleb stood still. Immobile. Thinking. For a long time.

§

"Gabe, are you listening to me?"

Zoe's little brother had been chattering away as they walked home.

"I'm not going to let you screw this up for me."

"What do you mean?" Gabe whined to his sister.

"Do not tell Mom or Dad, or PopPop either." Zoe insisted.

"Tell them about what?"

Zoe stopped in her tracks as they approached the steps to their grandfather's house and turned to face her brother. She kneeled as she addressed him. "I'm going to say this one more time. Do not tell them what happened at the park. I'm supposed to be taking care of you. And if they think that I let you get into trouble they'll think I'm doing a bad job."

"But you didn't do a bad job. You tried to get me down. You even made that hole. Just like the one you made in the basement."

"Gabe, do you think someone who can make huge holes in the ground is doing a good job or a bad job taking care of a kid?"

"A good job?" Gabe asked earnestly.

"Okay, do you think Mom and Dad will think someone who makes huge holes in the ground is doing a good job?"

Gabe thought for a moment. "Probably not."

"What happens at the end of the summer when I do a good job taking care of you?"

"You get the camera you want?"

"Exactly."

"If you tell them what happened today they might not give me the camera." Zoe explained.

Gabe nodded to his sister.

"And if I don't get that camera, neither of us is going to be very happy."

"Will you let me take pictures on it?" Gabe asked.

Zoe thought for a moment knowing full well there was zero chance she would ever let her brother even breathe near the expensive camera her parents had promised her as a reward. But the end of the summer was two months away and she needed to keep her brother in line. "Of course I will."

"As many as I want?"

"Yes. Of course."

§

"You're late." Zoe and Gabe's mother Melissa was all business.

"I..." Zoe started.

"I'm not interested in excuses young lady. I'm interested in you being on time. This summer is not a party where you get to waltz in and out of this house whenever you please."

"You can all feel free to waltz right out of my house if you like." Zoe and Gabe's grandfather grumbled from the large chair by the window where he spent most of his time.

"Dad. Stop that." Melissa Flowers chided her father slightly more gently than she'd admonished her daughter. She continued, "Zoe, being on time for dinner is part of being responsible. And we're not buying a camera for someone who does not fulfill their responsibilities."

"If she gets a camera for watching the boy, what do I get for watching the both of them?"

"Dad, shhhh." Melissa said.

James Flowers, Gabe and Zoe's father came trundling down the stairs. "Hey kiddos. Looks like you just beat the rain. Anything interesting happen while you were out and about?"

Zoe shot her little brother a look.

"You come down those stairs like a herd of cattle you know." Zoe's grandfather grumbled from his chair.

"I know PopPop. Sorry about that. I'm just excited to get to the restaurant. We start painting tonight."

PopPop looked like he had a comment to make and then chose to keep it to himself. He harrumphed a bit and went back to his crossword puzzle.

The sixth resident of the house ambled in and rubbed up against Zoe's ankles. "Tango!" Zoe bent down to scratch behind her cat's ears and give it a protective kiss on the mouth. "Aren't you a sweetie."

"He is definitely not a 'sweetie'." PopPop mimicked Zoe's tone. Look what he did to my puzzle. There was a tear in the newspaper that looked like it could have been made by a cat.

"Tango is a *she* PopPop." Zoe corrected her grandfather.

"He. She. I can't keep track." PopPop muttered. "I thought you had a he cat."

Zoe frowned, but said nothing.

"Maybe she was trying to do the puzzle?" Gabe offered.

"Dad, the fish is on the table, please come and eat. And make sure the children eat their vegetables." And then in a quieter voice Melissa addressed her daughter, "And please make sure your grandfather gets up from that chair and eats *his* vegetables."

"I heard that! How much longer is my home going to be overrun with all of you." PopPop said.

"Can we go swimming after dinner?" Gabe interjected.

Melissa Flowers winked at her daughter as she joined her husband at the door. "Dad, we're working as hard as we can, days, nights, and weekends, to get this restaurant open by the fall. Restaurants take time to get going. But I'm sure your food will help this one get over the hump quickly."

"Exactly. *My* food. It's my house and you're living in it. They're *my* recipes, and now you're gonna cook 'em at your fancy restaurant."

"What about swimming?" Gabe repeated.

"We've already covered this." James Flowers said to his son. "They're renovating the Madrona pool this summer. It won't be open until the end of the year."

"What about the lake?" Gabe wheedled.

"Tonight? It's getting dark out. Maybe in a few days after we've caught up with the work at the restaurant." James gave his son a squeeze before he went out.

"I love you Dad." Melissa said as she headed out behind her husband.

As the front door clicked shut, Gabe crossed his arms and furrowed his brow. "I'm never going to get to go swimming again."

"You and this fish both." PopPop joked as he started serving the dinner his daughter had left on the table.

§

Ollie was wet. He didn't make it home before the rain started. But it wasn't all bad. The rain had washed the blood from his scratched hand. His sketchbook had been tucked under his arm and remained mostly dry. His anger was gone for the moment, but his confusion wasn't. *How had that tree flown across the park?*

"You're getting water all over my kitchen floor." Ollie's mother was not pleased. "Please take off those wet clothes."

Ollie moved towards the stairs to head up to his room to change.

"Not up the stairs, you'll make a river throughout the house." Change down here.

"Mom!" Ollie complained.

"You can change in the bathroom if you want."

"Into what?"

Ollie's mother walked over to the laundry room that abutted the kitchen and pulled a fluffy pink bathrobe out of the dryer. "Here, you can wear my robe."

"Mom!"

"Stop being a baby. It's just a robe."

"Did something happen at camp today?" Ollie heard his mother through the door as he changed out of his wet clothes.

"Uh no."

Ollie opened the door to see his mother with her hand out waiting to collect the wet clothes he'd been wearing.

"Are you sure? Because the camp called."

"What did they say?"

Ollie's mother turned to face her son, "Well they didn't have anything good to say."

Ollie stayed silent.

"They said you ruined another child's artwork and that they'd prefer if you didn't come to camp tomorrow. So I'll ask you again, did something happen?"

"The other kids are lousy artists."

Ollie's mother put on as conciliatory a voice as possible, but to Ollie she just sounded far away. "Great or lousy, it was *your* behavior that has made you unwelcome at camp."

"I'm never going back to that lousy place." Ollie fumed. This new round of criticism reignited Ollie's frustration. His earlier anger was now starting to spark and smoke.

"What exactly do you expect me to do with you? It's too late tonight to find something new for tomorrow." Ollie's mother complained.

"Leave me here?" Ollie suggested.

"Yeah right." Ollie's mother's words dripped with sarcasm. Samantha Trace looked at her son and thought for a moment. "Until we figure out an alternative, you're just going to have to come to work with me at the lab. That'll be a *treat*."

Ollie didn't believe that his mother thought it would truly be that much of a treat for anyone.

ᕽ 3 ᕽ

THE MISSING CHEESE

"**D**id you go all the way to one of the islands to get the groceries?"

"Huh?" Zach had piled the food he'd bought on the kitchen table.

"I think you forgot something." Jay's eyebrows had an 'I-told-you-so' look to them.

"I didn't forget anything."

"And the Parmesan cheese is where?" Jay said.

Zach scanned the groceries again. The cheese was nowhere to be found. "I didn't forget it. I definitely bought it."

"Did you feed it to some mice along the way?"

"Dad, stop. It's not funny."

"OK. You're right. It's not funny. And now I'm being serious. I depended on you to get this done, and you promised you would get it right. I know it doesn't seem like a big deal, but it's important. I'm trying to make a nice dinner for everyone, and I can't do this all alone."

Zach mumbled something that sounded like "And that's my fault?"

Jay's brow furrowed. "I guess we'll be cheeseless tonight."

"I don't want to be cheesles." Cassie announced as she walked into the kitchen. "It sounds like measles."

"Cheese-less. Not cheese-ells." Jay corrected.

"I don't want to be either." Cassie proclaimed. "Wait, what does it mean to be cheeseless?"

"It means your brother forgot the parmesan cheese for the pasta tonight."

A wounded look crossed Zach's face. Jay didn't notice as he was tending to the cooking and his back was turned.

"Zaaaaach." Cassie whined.

"I don't know what happened. I bought it, and it's not here. It must have fallen out at some point."

"What fell out?" Binny asked as she joined the fray in the kitchen.

"Next time, say the dog ate it. That's a classic." Jay suggested smugly.

Cassie lit up. "Dad can we get a dog?"

"Yeah. I want a dog." Binny chimed in.

"I'm not quite sure how many times I need to repeat myself on this topic, but let's do it one more time. I can barely take care of the three of you on my own. I certainly couldn't take care of a dog on top of that." Jay said.

"But we'll take care of it." The girls chimed in.

Zach was happy the subject had changed.

Cassie peppered Jay with 'please's.

"What are you begging for now?" Julie smiled at her daughters. She had just arrived in time for dinner.

"Daddy won't let us get a dog." Cassie informed.

Julie smiled at her ex-husband. "Thanks for having me over for dinner." And then back at her daughters. "Do you realize that having a dog is a huge responsibility?"

"Yes. Absolutely."

"Maybe a small dog?" Julie winked at Jay.

"Hey, stop causing trouble." Jay protested.

"A puppy maybe?" Julie continued.

Jay feigned anger.

"You could call it Krypto." Julie was having fun.

"You know me too well." Jay conceded.

Julie turned back to her daughters. "Your father is right. You guys don't even pick up your clothes off the floors. You're definitely not going to want to pick up what the dog leaves on the ground."

Even Zach managed a smile at that remark. "Yuck."

"You don't want a dog because you're afraid of dogs." Cassie piped up.

"That's not true." Zach said.

"Yes it is. You're afraid of dogs. There's nothing wrong with telling the truth." Cassie said.

"Absolutely true. The truth will set you free." Julie beamed at her daughter.

"Though it's possible sometimes you overdo it a touch?" Jay added with a grin.

Cassie ignored Jay's comment, "I'm afraid of spiders and I don't care who knows it. Except for maybe the spiders. But I'm pretty sure they don't understand English and I don't speak Spiderish."

"Not wanting a dog doesn't mean that I'm afraid of dogs." Zach insisted.

Cassie pressed, "Zach, you're good at saying all sorts of things you read in books," Binny and Zach's eyebrows inched upwards, "but you don't like saying how you feel."

Now it was Jay and Julie's turn to raise their eyebrows at their eight-year-old's insightful comments.

"There is a dog nearby that you could probably spend some time with." Julie changed the subject sensing how uncomfortable her thirteen-year-old was getting with the direction of the discussion.

"There is?" The girls asked.

"What about Rembrandt? Dr. Huitre's dog?"

Cassie lit up. "I love Rembrandt."

Binny frowned. "He's a nice dog."

I have to return a book to Dr. Huitre anyway. Why don't I take you over there tomorrow before dinner and I bet he'll be ok with you guys taking Rembrandt out for his walk.

Cassie nodded her head up and down vigorously, excited at the prospect.

Binny kept her thoughts to herself.

§

It was after dinner and the kids had spread throughout the house leaving Jay and Julie to clean up.

Julie emptied the dishwasher. "Really, thanks for having me over."

"It's good for the kids that we can still spend time together as a family." Jay was wiping clear the table.

"Yeah. I know. You're right. It's good for them." Julie started to put a bowl in one of the cabinets.

"Oh, wait, that doesn't go there." Jay took the bowl and deposited it in a different cabinet.

"It doesn't? Since when?" Julie had a look of surprise on her face.

"A few months ago?"

"Oh."

"I moved some stuff around."

"Of course."

§

"What?" Binny responded to the gentle knock at the door.

"It's me." Zach responded from behind the closed door.

Binny paused the skateboarding video she was watching and got up to open the door. Her eyebrow was raised as if to say *what could possibly be more important than Eliana Sosco about to crooked grind.* Zach ignored the eyebrow, went into Binny's room, and closed the door behind him. The look on Binny's face changed subtly from annoyed to slightly nervous. Zach never came to Binny's room to talk like this.

Zach opened his mouth to talk and then seemed to think better of it and closed his mouth, brow furrowed.

Binny was getting fidgety but kept silent in a rare case of not wanting to interrupt Zach's thinking. A little voice in Binny's head wondered if she should just find out what was on Zach's mind on her own. Binny ignored that idea for the moment.

Finally, Zach looked ready to share. "I went to do the shopping for Dad and I saw these kids in the park." Zach paused still not quite sure how to approach the subject. "It was a brother and sister. The sister was older. And there was this third kid too. He was really blonde and pale. And, well, I guess he doesn't matter, but the point is, the younger brother got stuck up on the jungle gym, and his sister was trying to get him down, and well, she got really upset that he wasn't coming down and suddenly she'd made an enormous wide hole in the ground where she was standing."

Binny stared at Zach.

"The hole was several feet across."

Binny remained motionless.

Now it was Zach's turn to raise his eyebrows expectantly.

"She made it? She dug it? Binny asked.

"It just appeared."

"You mean she found a hole? It was covered and she fell into it?" Binny was trying to reconstruct the scene in her mind.

A bit of frustration crept into Zach's voice. "No. There was no hole, and then suddenly there was a hole.

The entire jungle gym lowered itself by a couple of feet into the hole."

"That's impossible." Binny crossed her arms.

"Impossible? Like mind reading? Or turning invisible? You mean, *that* kind of impossible?"

"That's different." Binny said.

"I don't think so. I think it's the same. I think this girl has a power. Just like us."

"How would she get it? She's not in our family." Binny said.

"Neither is Penny. But she has a power."

Binny seemed stumped for a moment, and then continued, "Well, it sounds stupid. What good is making a hole? I don't even believe it's a real power. Maybe the ground was weak."

"Weak like things that Penny touches right before they fall apart?"

Binny and Zach sat for a few minutes, each thinking on this news. Binny finally broke the silence. "What did she say?"

"Who?" Zach answered.

"The girl. Hole-maker." Binny's expression was one of impatience.

"Oh, Zoe."

Something about Zach's tone was curious to Binny. And before she could consider whether it was a good idea or not, Binny found her mind's eye looking upward.

Upward to the part of her mind where she saw things. Things that other people were just thinking. And there in Zach's mind, vivid, was this Zoe girl. She looked annoyed. Presumably she was annoyed with Zach as these were Zach's thoughts Binny was watching. The image of the girl was bathed in a pink light. A deep saturated pink.

Over the past year, Binny had tried very hard to refrain from using her powers. It made her feel weird to know what people were thinking, to invade their minds without their knowledge. Sometimes it had been a help like when Binny was having trouble understanding how Mr. Puleo had wanted her to tie a knot in Art Class. Once she could see the picture of the knot in his head, Binny picked it up quickly.

But sometimes Binny found out things she didn't want to know. Like the time Hannah lied to her about having a birthday party. Binny suspected she'd not been included. She had watched the details of Hannah's slumber party with her friends unfold on the screen in her mind bathed in yellow. Listening to Hannah insist that she'd only had some cake with her family was incredibly disheartening.

The previous summer Binny had realized that the colors she saw meant something. She didn't know what most of them meant, but she knew yellow. It was the yellow of a lie. The yellow of untruth. Binny hated yellow.

As often happened when Binny's instinct took over and she looked into someone's mind, she immediately chided herself for breaking her own rules. But that pink.

37

She'd seen light pink before when she was being particularly charitable towards her sister. Or from her parents. But this darker pink was new to Binny.

"Are you doing what I think you're doing? You know how I feel about that." A touch of anger crept into Zach's voice.

"No no." Binny lied.

Zach looked skeptical.

Binny tried to change the subject. "How would Zoe," Binny rolled her eyes a bit as she said the name, "have gotten a power anyway? We know her mother wasn't in the Luce Labs study that Mom was in. Nobody was."

"Penny's mom wasn't in the study either."

"Right. Well I guess we still don't know *where* the powers come from."

Zach's eyes looked far away, "I think there's someone who does know."

"Who?" Binny demanded.

"Caleb." Zach paused. "And there's something else."

"You're stressing me out." Binny said.

"I want to tell Zoe about our powers."

"No way! Look, I don't know this girl, or her brother. We agreed that telling people was a bad idea. Don't you remember how hard it's been to keep Cassie from telling people? We don't even really know if this girl has an actual power."

"She does." Zach insisted quietly.

"So you say."

"We could tell her in the hideout."

"Now you want to show her the hideout?" Binny was almost yelling.

"I..." Zach was taken aback by the ferocity of Binny's negative reaction.

"Listen to me. You don't get to just decide who's in the group and who isn't."

"And you do?"

"Well." Binny stopped short of voicing her answer.

Even without the ability to read minds Zach knew exactly what Binny thought. Zach had had enough. Without another word, Zach left Binny's room.

§

"I'm not tired." Cassie was being shuttled up the stairs by her father.

"But I am." Jay offered as he tried to direct Cassie to the bathroom to brush her teeth.

"Why do I have to go to bed because *you're* tired?" Cassie wheedled.

"Someday you'll understand." Jay said, and then trying to change the subject, added, "Zach, it's late, have you brushed yet?"

Zach nodded yes. But Binny had popped her head out of her room adding, "No he didn't."

"Binny, mind your own business." Jay and Zach said at almost exactly the same moment.

"Just sayin'." Binny retreated back to her room.

"Zach, please go brush your teeth."

"I did."

"Then do it again please. For me." And then after a moment Jay added, "You're thirteen years old. Do you think you're old enough to stop lying to me about little things like this. I expect more grown up behavior from you frankly."

"Fine, I'll only lie to you about big things from now on."

Jay frowned.

§

As the Jordan family settled down for the night, a large man sat in a black car. One would be hard pressed to see the floor of the man's car given the heap of fast food containers, cups, and junkfood wrappers that covered every inch. The man didn't seem to pay them any attention as he was focused entirely on the phone outstretched in front of his face. The light from the phone's screen reflected on the man's thick features highlighting every crag and pore.

At one time the man had been more fit, but the steady diet of junk food and sitting for hours at a time had made the man significantly overweight and given him an unhealthy pallor.

The man stared intently at the screen of his phone. He was using it to record a video. From the man's vantage point he could see two windows on the second floor of the home. They were far away, but he could still make out some details. The father came into view in one and kissed the girl. Then the light went out. Next the father appeared in the second window, and after what appeared to be some negotiation and a hug, the second light went out. The Jordan family had gone to sleep for the evening.

The man stopped recording. He stretched his arms. And deposited the phone in the chest pocket of his black shirt. Embroidered under the pocket were the words "HEAD OF SECURITY". On the other pocket was the man's name, "G. GRATER".

THE ACCIDENTAL
SUMMER CAMP

"I want you to sit here and not move."

"For how long? What am I supposed to do?" Ollie fidgeted on the black leather couch.

Gore Grater stood a few feet away inside Samantha Trace's office doing a fair bit of fidgeting of his own.

"I thought you brought your sketchpad?" Samantha asked her son impatiently.

"I did, but what am I supposed to draw?" Ollie whined.

Samantha scanned the outer area briefly lighting on a potted plant a few feet away. "What about that plant?"

"It's fake."

Grater cleared his throat.

"It's gonna have to do for now. I need to start my first meeting. Stay put until it's done and then we'll see if we can find a better spot for you." With that, Dr. Samantha Trace entered her office and closed the door.

§

"What if I sit very very quietly? I'll be invisible." Cassie pleaded with her brother giving him a knowing raise of her eyebrow.

Zach laughed a little despite himself, "Isn't there anything else you can go do right now?"

"Nope." Cassie shook her head giving her best earnest look.

Zach looked at his sister for a few moments before he let out a resigned sigh and turned back to his computer screen. Zach took a deep breath and seemed to recommit to whatever task he had in mind.

Zach loaded a mapping program. It showed a map of most of the planet. He typed in the Jordan's home address. The program zoomed with lightning speed to an aerial view of the Madrona neighborhood in which the

Jordans lived. Zach used his mouse to move up the hillside until he could see the Madrona park where he'd met Zoe and Gabe and the white-haired boy the previous evening.

Zach dropped a virtual pin on the spot where he'd seen Zoe create the huge hole in the ground. Then Zach drew a line from the pin outwards on the screen. The line was the radius of a circle that kept expanding as Zach drew the line. The circle grew until a little figure of a person in the upper right hand corner of the screen read "5 min". Zach thought for a moment and then extended the circle further until the readout said "10 min".

§

Victor Barrios was no closer to understanding his supervisor than he had been at any time in his several years of employment as a security guard at Luce Labs. It wasn't that Grater was a particularly complicated man. Quite the opposite. He was overly simplistic; viewing the world in only black and white. And often, mean. In Victor's mind, the combination was dangerous.

Victor couldn't help but think back to the incidents of the previous summer and the venom that had possessed his boss when they had failed to capture a little girl running around the campus. While Victor didn't think kids should be running around Luce Labs, he was relatively certain that a few children didn't represent a real threat to the proprietary research of a big company.

Maybe it was the thought of Victor's own young daughter's face judging him, or maybe it was Victor's appreciation of the steady job, or maybe it just wasn't in Victor's nature. Whatever the reason, Victor had a hard time feeling that kind of anger at anyone. Especially at a little girl.

So when Victor saw what looked like a young boy with almost white hair sneaking into the Greenhouse on the Luce Labs campus, he wasn't angry, but he was eager to make sure that this boy didn't end up on the receiving end of his boss' rage. Avoiding that outcome would be best for all involved.

§

"Why does it say 'ten min' next to the little man?" Cassie's bright face loomed over Zach's shoulder.

"Cassie, out!" Zach barked.

"I'm sorry. I just got curious."

"You said you'd be invisible."

"I still don't know how to make that happen exactly." Cassie gave a sheepish grin.

"I would have settled for silent." Zach grumbled.

"Why does it say 'ten min' next to the little man?"

For the moment, Zach's enjoyment of explaining things superseded his desire for privacy. "It's not 'ten min', it's '10 minutes'." Zach waited for some recognition in Cassie's face, and continued when none was forthcoming.

"See this pin?" Zach pointed at the screen. "That's the park where you like to play. This circle shows all the area that's within a 10 minute walk of the park. The area is drawn as a circle because you could walk in any direction from the park. All these houses in the circle could be reached from the park in ten minutes or less. Most are in Madrona, but here on the edge a few are in the Central District."

"Why do you want to know which houses are a ten minute walk from the park?"

A nervous look crossed Zach's face and he took a moment before he answered his sister's question. "No reason. Just curious."

Cassie didn't seem to notice Zach's evasiveness and had already moved onto her next question. "What does that button there do?" Cassie pointed at an icon on the screen that looked like a stack of maps.

Zach seemed relieved at the subject change. "That brings up alternative maps that can be laid over this one. For example, here's a map of all the underground utilities under our neighborhood."

"Utlities?"

"Water, sewers, stuff like that. This map shows where all the pipes and tunnels are under the ground in our neighborhood." As Zach spoke the map lit up with colored lines of different thickness criss-crossing under the streets and under some of the homes as well.

"Why do you want to see where the pipes are?"

"I got this map from the city. I wanted to see if our hideout was on it." Zach zoomed the map into the Madrona woods.

"And?" Cassie craned her neck to get a good look at the map of the woods. The colored lines came to the edges of the woods. One gray line even dipped into the woods for a little bit. But most of the woods were devoid of any lines.

"And nothing. Our hideout is just not there."

§

"That was a long time to spend. All *I* see is three bratty kids who spend way too much time indoors." Dr. Trace looked up from her screen at Gore Grater who was standing over her shoulder.

"But don't you see, the video is uploaded as I shoot it. Right to our servers. So you could even watch what's happening there in realtime."

"Yes, that's truly amazing." Trace didn't make any effort to mask her sarcasm.

"OK. I realize that I haven't caught them doing anything particularly interesting yet, but I will. They usually play outside more. There was sudden rain last night."

"I know it rained last night." Trace observed dryly and then seemed to relent a bit. "I know you're putting in a lot of extra hours. I appreciate it. And I appreciate that you've kept this particular task just between us."

Even the slightest compliment from the usually icy Dr. Trace was cause for a smile on Gore Grater's swollen sallow face. "Thank you Dr. Trace."

"I'll let you get back to it then while I figure out what to do with another unruly child." Dr. Trace changed the tone of her voice only slightly as she rose from her chair and headed towards the door. "Ollie, I'm done now. Thank you for waiting patiently."

But when she opened the door, the black leather couch was empty.

§

"I was just looking for something to draw." The white-haired boy said with less fear than Barrios would have imagined from a trespassing child.

"And what made you think that ignoring the Employees Only sign on the greenhouse door was a good idea?" Barrios responded.

"My mother works here."

"I've heard that one before." Barrios smirked.

Beeeep beeeep beep beep. Before the boy had a chance to respond, the walkie-talkie on Barrios' company issued phone started crying out urgently. Grater had made all the security guards memorize a series of signals. Two long and two short meant 'emergency'. Why Grater couldn't just start talking and say there was an emergency Barrios didn't know but he'd learned long ago to not ask those kinds of questions.

Grater's short clipped words followed the urgent beeping. "Attention all teams: Dr. Trace's son has wandered away from the Epaphus building. The child is ten-years-old with fair skin, and bright blonde, almost white hair. He's wearing a red t-shirt, jeans, and sneakers and most likely carrying a drawing pad.

Now it was Ollie's turn to have a smirk on his face. "Told ya."

Barrios shook his head in disbelief. "Indeed you did." Then turned and spoke into his phone, "Sir, I've got the boy here at the greenhouse. He's fine."

"We're on our way." The walkie-talkie crackled.

§

"What part of stay on the couch did you not understand?" Dr. Trace said in a low voice to her son once she and Grater had reached the Luce Labs greenhouse. Dr. Trace had intended it primarily for her son, but it was impossible for Grater and Barrios not to hear her admonishment. Grater tried to suppress a grin. Barrios looked embarrassed.

An older man with a thick crop of white hair that extended to his trimmed beard and mustache, strode into the entry area of the greenhouse, and announced, "Sorry I'm late for the tour." The man was wearing work clothes appropriate for the greenhouse. He chuckled to himself, "I'm not quite as fast as I used to be."

Dr. Trace looked up, her face a tight mask, trying to conceal her embarrassment, "I'm so sorry to bother you we'll get out of your way."

"The tour?" Ollie spoke up in a bright voice.

"Why yes son. I assume that's why you found yourself here. I'm always eager to show inquisitive future scientists around my greenhouse."

"I'm going to be an artist, not a scientist." Ollie proclaimed.

Samantha Trace was looking more and more uncomfortable.

"Is that so." The old man said more than asked, a big smile spreading across his face. "The tour is great for budding young artists as well. We've got plenty of beautiful and exotic plants for you to draw to your heart's content."

"Oh no, we couldn't." Dr. Trace insisted.

The old man put his hands up cutting off Dr. Trace's protestation. "You can and you will. It's already decided." The man's smile got even wider. He motioned to Ollie, "For the rest of the day, the young gentleman will stay with me cataloging some of my most visually interesting plants on his sketchpad."

"My name is Ollie."

"This is – " Dr. Trace was about to introduce the greenhouse's caretaker but was interrupted.

"Nice to meet you Ollie. Please call me Xander."

And just like that, it was decided.

§

Samantha Trace had to restrain herself several times throughout the day from marching over to the greenhouse to retrieve her son. She was a private person and didn't want to impose her challenges with Ollie on the people at Luce. But even more, she fretted that Ollie would cause trouble and wanted to pull him from the greenhouse before things went sour. And those weren't the only reasons she didn't want her son spending the day at the greenhouse.

The dreaded call to retrieve her misbehaving son never came. At 4:58pm there was a knock at her door. She recognized the laugh and before she could get out a greeting Ollie was on her.

"Mom, mom, mom, look." Ollie started leafing through the numerous drawings he'd made during the day. "See this one? And this one? And this one?"

The old man ruffled Ollie's hair. "Could I interrupt the exhibition for a brief moment to talk to your mother?"

"Oh, yeah, sure." Ollie planted himself on the couch outside the office.

"I'm not trying to pry, Dr. Trace, but I'm assuming that you didn't have a place for Ollie to go today?"

Samantha Trace's face, usually a carefully composed mask of discipline and authority, had a rare look of helplessness.

Before she could answer, the old man put his palms together in front of him, and continued in a low and serious voice, "Samantha. The boy has talent. And sometimes people with talent are misunderstood. But luckily, I understand people with talent." The old man gave Dr. Trace a look that was meant just for her, and added with his typical mirth," It would be my honor to have the boy spend some time with me at the greenhouse. I could use the company. You can avoid feeling pressured to find other arrangements and can focus on your work knowing he's well taken care of. It'll be like summer camp – Camp Luce!"

❧ 5 ❧

THE FIRST WALK

It's not clear when the knock became more of a formality, but at some point over the past year Penny's presence at the Jordan house became so ubiquitous that her knock turned into something that came after she was already halfway through the front door.

"Is it time to walk the dog?" Penny announced as she strode into the family room.

§

Julie led the chattering girls, Binny, Cassie, and Penny down the Madrona hillside towards Dr. Huitre's house. Apparently Binny had informed Penny about tonight's dog walking plans mere milliseconds after they'd been formed the previous evening.

Julie looked down at the book she was holding in her hands. *A Distant Mirror* – just your average historical account of the black plague in the 14th century. As she read, Julie had imagined herself in the book, trying to calm people and teach them how to protect themselves using tested techniques instead of depending on superstition and fear.

Cassie had run ahead and had reached the door of Huitre's modern house at the end of the road just before the woods took over the side of the hill. Julie made it to the door just as a smiling Dr. Huitre pulled it open.

"You sure you're okay with this?" Julie smiled motioning towards the kids with her eyes.

"Rembrandt!" Cassie shot through the empty space between Huitre and the door to pet the big dog excitedly.

"Cassie! You don't just walk into people's houses." Binny reproached her sister.

Huitre laughed. "I think it's already been decided." And then to the kids he added, "Come in. Come in. I think Rembrandt is even more excited than Cassie."

"Thanks for doing this. It's very kind of you. The kids really want a dog, and Jay's not, well – *we're* not sure they're ready for that kind of responsibility."

"Are you kidding? They are doing me a favor." Huitre laughed.

"Let's go! Let's go!" Cassie urged.

Binny rolled her eyes at Cassie's eagerness.

"Okay, let's go then." Julie said.

"Wait! You're coming?" Cassie pointed an accusatory finger at her mother. "No you're not."

"Of course I'm coming."

"I thought we were going to show you how we can do this *on our own*." Cassie emphasized the last words to make it clear she wanted zero assistance from the adults in the room.

"That's true Mom." Binny added.

"If your mom is ok with it, I think you three will do a great job walking Rembrandt." Huitre said.

Everyone looked at Julie.

"Are you sure?" Julie's raised her eyebrows at Huitre.

Huitre smiled, "I think these young ladies will be incredibly responsible. Rembrandt on the other hand, I am not so sure about."

§

Binny kept looking over her shoulder as Dr. Huitre's house started to disappear around the corner. When she wasn't looking back she was barking at Cassie to "Slow down."

"I can't slow down. Rembrandt is in a hurry." Cassie had found her partner in crime.

"Why do you keep doing that?" Penny asked her friend.

"Huh? What?" Binny said.

"You keep looking over your shoulder." Penny prodded.

"Oh. Nothing. Sorry."

"I'm sure they're just friends." Penny said gently.

Binny breathed inward sharply, about to say something, and then closed her mouth. After a moment Binny gently teased her friend, "I thought I was the one with the mind-reading powers."

Penny smiled.

"It's just, that, I wish..." Binny's sentence trailed off as her eyes followed Cassie and Rembrandt's looping trail through the neighborhood.

"But isn't the divorce final?"

Binny's shoulders slumped. "Yeah."

"At least your parents are both here." Now it was Penny's turn to focus off in the distance.

Binny turned to face her friend. "Oh, I'm so sorry. I didn't mean to be insensitive."

"It's okay." Penny said.

The walk continued with Rembrandt and Cassie enjoying themselves thoroughly. The two older girls tried their best to do the same.

§

"I'm impressed with your book recommendation skills." Julie said.

"Oh good. Who doesn't love a good plague account?" Huitre joked.

Julie found herself slightly embarrassed at how much she was laughing at Huitre's jokes. The armor she wore at her job every day was nowhere in evidence as she sat on Huitre's couch.

Huitre broke the silence. "So, how are you doing?"

His question was generic, but Julie understood what he was really asking. "It's fine. A little lonely. But fine. Good even. I read a lot."

"You enjoy books more than people?" Huitre smiled gently.

"Is that so bad?"

"No. Not at all. I have spent more time than I can count with only books to keep me company. And Rembrandt of course."

The conversation lulled again. Julie screwed up her courage to ask this next question. "How long has it been?"

Huitre understood what she was really asking. "It's been fifteen years."

"Zach is thirteen." Julie started doing the math in her head. "So when I was your patient..."

"Right before that, in fact." Huitre said.

"That must have been a terribly difficult time." Julie observed.

"Well, she and I had adopted Rembrandt together just before she... So between him and my work, I was able to stay pretty distracted."

Julie put her hand on Huitre's and gave it a gentle squeeze.

Huitre seemed to gather up his stray emotions and continued, "In fact, these days he's my main concern. Bernese Mountain Dogs aren't supposed to live this long. He seems energetic still, but all I can see is how he's slowed down. I fear it is just a matter of time."

"We're back!" The knock came only after the door had opened.

Julie and Huitre pulled their hands back from each other hastily.

The three girls and the big dog stood in the doorway.

Huitre stood and smiled, "How was the walk?" And then crouching he took Rembrandt's face in his hands and asked, "And you? Were you well behaved?"

"Yup! He was great." Cassie's statement left no room for argument.

Binny kept looking at her mother. She didn't seem to notice anything else in the room.

Penny held up the plastic bag she'd been holding. "And what should we do with *this*?"

§

"I think he peed five different times." Cassie said.

"I think you've said that five different times." Binny criticized.

Jay frowned at his eldest daughter. "Can't you see she's excited? Did *you* have a good time walking the dog?"

"Yeah." Binny muttered.

Julie rolled her eyes at her daughter's brevity.

Jay tried another avenue. "What about you Penny? Maybe you could give me just a bit of detail?"

"Well, we got a lot of exercise." Penny smiled.

"Then I bet you're hungry?" Jay said.

Ding dong. The doorbell rang just as Jay was about to rally the kids to set the table for dinner.

"I'll get it." Cassie yelled. She scurried out of the kitchen before anyone could disagree.

Cassie was already opening the door when Jay had caught up. A woman stood just outside the door. Her angular face was framed with long wavy black hair with shiny red streaks that shifted slightly in color depending on how she held her head in the setting sunlight. The woman's movements were slow and deliberate, like a ballet dancer. But her eyes were sharp and moved quickly and with purpose. The beginnings of very small lines were visible at the corners of the woman's eyes. Instead of making her look old, the lines just made her look more observant. The woman smiled gently as she looked up from Cassie and said to Jay, "Hi. Is Penny here?"

"Where else would she be?" Jay responded, and they both laughed. Jay looked over his shoulder and yelled to the kitchen, "Penny, your mom is here." And then turning back to the woman, "We were just about to have dinner. You should stay."

"That's very kind of you. But you're always having Penny over for dinner. You're too generous."

"Oh please, it's no bother. We love having her around. And as a bonus, she distracts Binny from fighting with her brother and sister."

"I do not fight with them. They fight with me!" Binny interjected. Binny and Penny had just poked their heads into the conversation. Julie stood just behind them.

"Can I stay for dinner Mom?" Penny implored.

After a moment, Julie spoke, "Hi, I'm Julie. I'm Binny's mom."

"Oh, I'm so sorry. I forgot you two hadn't met yet. Julie this is Penny's mom Serena."

Serena gave a little wave from the door, "Hi. Sorry. I know it's been overdue. Jay and I have chatted about the girls in passing outside, but I've never really formally thanked you both for welcoming Penny into your home so often. Penny really loves your family."

"Penny's great." Julie added. "But Jay is really the one to thank. I live just up the street." Julie forced a smile.

Binny frowned in the brief pause after her mother's clarification.

"Well, you've all been very welcoming. And I'm grateful. So thank you." Serena said to both Jay and Julie.

"Come in, come in." Jay waved Serena into the house.

"Can I stay for dinner Mom?" Penny repeated her request?

Cassie appealed to Serena as well on Penny's behalf.

"How about tonight we give the Jordans a night off and let them have their dinner to themselves. I'm sure there will be a *million* other opportunities. OK?"

Penny gave in and retreated into the house to collect her things with Binny in tow. Cassie toddled after them.

The adults were left to themselves for the moment when Zach came through the front door wiping the sweat off his brow and his long hair out of his eyes.

"Late again?" Jay raised his eyebrows.

"Sorry. Hi Mom. Zach pushed past the adults to head upstairs to his room."

"Clean up for dinner please?" Jay said to Zach's back as he disappeared up the stairs.

A mostly positive sounding grunt came from the top of the stairs. All three of the adults laughed.

"I swear I don't know what's going on in his head. The only kid that is still willing to tell me what they think is Cassie."

"And she's a little *too* willing." Julie added.

They all laughed when something caught Serena's eye. She had wandered over to the wall in the study. "These are the kids, right?" Serena was pointing at an illustration Jay had drawn and framed. Cassie, Zach, and Binny stood in a tight knit circle, backs to each other, facing menacing villains.

In the drawing, each wore tight fitting superhero costumes. Zach, a big "DS" on his chest, was disabling villains with sarcastic comments, *Of course I'm fine with you walking off with that money.* Binny, wearing judge's robes, was throwing books titled "The Rules" at villains with deadly accuracy. And Cassie was dazzling in pink sparkles, mesmerizing the villains into submission with her singing.

"This is really quite great." Serena looked back at Jay taking her eyes off the drawing momentarily. "You drew this, right?"

"Yeah." Jay suddenly didn't know where to look and started shuffling his feet a little.

"No really, you've captured them so well. Their personalities just jump off the page. I bet they love it when you draw them."

"Well, uh, you'd be surprised. Not so much." Jay said.

"Well, count me impressed." Serena's eyes sparkled as she smiled.

§

"Why couldn't we stay for dinner Mom?"

Penny and her mother were making the short trek across the street back to their house.

"Well, Binny's mom was over and I didn't want to interrupt their family time."

"Julie is over there all the time." Penny thought for a moment, and then asked. "Mom, if Binny's parents spend all that time together even though they're divorced, why does Dad live so far away? Why can't we be more like them?"

The lines at the corners of Serena's eyes seemed to lengthen a bit as she sighed and put her arm around her daughter.

"Every family finds their own way my shiny Penny. I think we're still finding ours."

⇥ 6 ⇤

THE CARAMEL
APPLE PANCAKES

"I'm making caramel apple pancakes for breakfast if you can hang on a bit." Jay Jordan pulled ingredients from the cupboard, setting them on the counter.

"Can't. Gotta go." Zach responded through a mouthful of granola bar.

"What's the hurry? Did you get a job and not tell me? I was thinking maybe it was time for you to start earning a living anyway." Jay joked.

"It's a girl." Binny stood in the doorway wearing pajama pants and a tank top and rubbing the sleep from her eyes.

Zach shot Binny a look.

Jay raised his eyebrows. "Oh?"

"As usual, Binny doesn't know what she's talking about and is sticking her nose where it doesn't belong." Zach spoke to his father, but didn't take his eyes off his sister.

"Is she wrong or nosy?" Jay joked. But after seeing the expression on Zach's face he decided to change the subject. After some mental calculation, Jay asked, "Did you fold your laundry like I asked?"

"Yes."

"What about taking out the garbage cans?"

"I'll do it on my way out."

"And wasn't today the day you were going to help me clean out the shed?"

Zach was getting more and more frustrated. Having this scene unfold in front of Binny didn't help. "Can we do that one later? Please?"

Jay had exhausted his list of tasks for Zach. "Yeah. OK. But right after lunch, alright?"

Jay heard another affirmative grunt as Zach barely made his escape out the back door.

§

"I need you to take this very seriously Ollie. This is my workplace." Samantha Trace was walking the curving paths of the Luce Laboratories campus making her way with her son to the greenhouse complex that sat next to the records room with its signature curved roof.

"I *am* taking it seriously." Ollie whined.

"I'm out of options for art camps. The only camps left I could find with availability are for tennis and canoeing." Dr. Trace let the implications hang in the air.

Ollie shuddered. "I promise. I'll behave."

Dr. Trace held the door of the greenhouse open for her son as he went through clutching his sketchbook in one hand and a bag lunch in the other.

"Young Master Trace." The old man with the white beard from the day before was waiting for them with an expansive smile on his face.

"I promise it won't be for long – " Dr. Trace began.

"Oh shoo. We'll be fine. You're doing *me* a favor. I never get company in here. It will be nice to have a young apprentice for the summer.

§

"PopPop, Where's Mom and Dad?" Gabe asked expectantly.

"Already off to work at the restaurant I believe." Gabe's grandfather said from behind his newspaper.

"What about breakfast?" Gabe whined.

"I made you a bowl of cereal. Here. Eat." Zoe said as she directed her brother to the dish in which she was currently pouring milk.

Gabe made a face but sat down to eat.

Zoe sat down to eat her own cereal as well.

"PopPop, why don't you ever make us breakfast?" Gabe asked between mouthfuls of cereal, a little milk dribbling at the corner of his mouth.

"Don't talk with your mouth full." Zoe gently chided her brother.

"What do you need me for? You can make your own breakfast." PopPop said.

"But weren't you a chef or something?" Gabe continued his line of inquiry.

"Or something."

"Not *or something*. You were a chef. Mom always says so." Zoe corrected.

Exasperated, Gabriel Walker lowered his newspaper to give his full attention to his seven-year-old namesake.

Zoe braced herself for a lecture knowing that her grandfather only lowered the paper when he was annoyed.

"First of all, if you knew I wasn't *or something* then you shouldn't have given me that choice of an answer. Second, I was not a chef. My food wasn't fancy enough for that. I *was* a cook. But now I'm an old man who is trying to enjoy reading his newspaper without interruptions. Am I done answering your questions?" PopPop's eyebrows were raised.

"Yes PopPop." Gabe kept eating his cereal.

Zoe caught sight of her grandfather shaking his head just before the newspaper went back up and she could no longer see his face.

§

"What's this one for?" Ollie pointed at the last plant on the tour. They'd spent most of the last hour going through all the different sections of the greenhouse with the old man giving the plant names, and Luce Labs' goal in growing them. The purposes varied. One was for pain relief, another might help people quit smoking, and a third might someday help replace an annual flu shot. Per his mother's instructions, Ollie was doing his best to stay interested and polite.

"That one cures hunger." The old man's eyes sparkled.

"It does?" Ollie couldn't help but feel there was a joke coming.

"They're mangoes. My favorite." The man plucked a ripe fruit from one of the small trees he had growing in a particularly humid sub-section of the greenhouse.

"So does anything here pique your interest?" The old man asked after the mango slices had been distributed.

"The one with the pale yellow leaves that looked bloodshot. That one was interesting."

"Rumex Vesicarius?"

Ollie had retained exactly *none* of the latin names for the plants.

"Oh, I'm being silly. Yes, the pale yellow leaves with the red capillaries. I know what you mean. The most interesting part of that plant, the part that we're interested in, is actually the root. It might be a good anti-oxidant or anti-bacterial agent."

Ollie nodded as if he understood.

"But you're not interested in the plant in the same way we are. Are you?" The old man's question came out as more of a statement.

"Not really?" Ollie said hesitantly. He didn't want to mess this up. While spending his days in the greenhouse wasn't his idea of a great time, it sure beat canoeing or tennis. Ollie couldn't help but eye his sketchbook.

"Would you mind drawing a picture of the Rumex Vesicarius?"

"Really?" Ollie's eyes lit up.

"Yes please. Take your time. I really want you to capture all the details."

§

Zach knew that what he was doing was a little bit creepy, but what choice did he really have. The previous day had been a complete waste, but he wasn't ready to give up yet. Not even close.

Zach had gone over in his mind all the things he could have said at the playground a couple of days earlier. Things like: *Hey Zoe, how are you spending your summer? Do you come to this playground often? Do you want to hang out some time?* The thought of saying any of these things made Zach's stomach turn. If he was going to humiliate himself, he thought, why not just say *You're the coolest person I've ever met. You are a hurricane of strong and smart and funny and I want to be your friend.*

Zach couldn't imagine a place on Earth that would be far enough from Madrona that he could slink off to die quietly from the embarrassment he would experience if he ever uttered that sentiment. Since the truth was obviously not an option, Zach had to find a way to 'accidentally' run into Zoe.

The previous day had been spent canvassing the entire neighborhood. Zach remembered Zoe saying it would take ten minutes to get home from the playground. Using his mapping software Zach plotted out every possible neighborhood hangout within a ten minute radius.

It was roughly 12 or 13 blocks in any direction. A handful of parks, some small grassy areas, and three little shopping areas, not to mention the Madrona woods themselves were all in the searchable area. And that was assuming Zoe would even spend any time outside. Maybe she was holed up in her room reading a book. Zach wondered what kind of books Zoe would read. Definitely something advanced and literary. Maybe Animal Farm by George Orwell. She seemed to like animals. Zach wasn't sure he really knew what that book was about.

Yesterday he'd covered the entire neighborhood five times on his bike. Zach was already on his second circuit and starting to wonder if this was really the best way to spend his summer.

§

"Mind if I take a look?"

Ollie had made quite a bit of progress filling several pages already with intricate sketches of the plant with the pale yellow leaves laced with blood red capillaries. His drawings were all in black and white, but the plant looked almost as alive on his page as they did sitting on the table. "Sure." Ollie showed off his work.

"These are marvelous drawings Ollie." Xander said. "You really have the makings of a great scientist!"

"Uh –" Ollie wasn't quite sure how to respond. "Did you mean artist?"

"That too of course, but I meant scientist." The man raised his eyebrows at Ollie. When a response didn't come, he continued. "Do you know what a scientist's job is Ollie?"

"To conduct experiments?"

"That yes, but that's not a scientist's true purpose. Our true purpose is to discover the truth. And in my case, in the biological sciences, it's to discover the truth inside living things." The old man was now animated waving his hands and getting excited. "We observe and see things that others don't. And we see the power in things that others don't. We capture it and repurpose it. When we find a plant with a medicinal property that nobody has discovered, that's understanding the gift the plant has to give us. We learn how to use that gift to improve the lives of other living creatures. Do you see how this connects to your masterful drawings?"

Ollie wasn't sure what to say for fear of disappointing Xander.

"You Ollie, are an amazing observer. You see the truth in living things and capture that truth. You capture it in your sketchbook with your pen. Anyone who sees your drawings has their lives improved. You and I Ollie, we do the same thing."

The old man continued. "And it's not just plants, is it Ollie. Your favorite subjects are *all* living things. Not just plant life. Yes?"

"I like drawing animals." Ollie said.

"Yes of course. I bet human beings too."

Ollie thought for a moment. "Humans too I suppose, but I really do like to draw animals. They have something inside them, something beautiful." Ollie was staring off into the distance considering something. "But it's hard to keep them still."

"That's what cages are for." The old man said in what seemed like a serious tone. And then after a moment he smiled.

Ollie thought Xander was serious for a moment. "You don't have a zoo here do you?" Ollie tried to joke back.

"A zoo? No. But we do have labs where we have animals that are used as experimental subjects."

"That seems sad."

"Sad? I think it's noble Ollie. Honorable if you will. These animals have the ability to help improve humanity's existence by participating in our experiments. And I am grateful for each and every one."

Ollie fidgeted, his next question trying to figure out a way to present itself. Finally in a quiet voice he asked, "Do the animals ever die during the experiments?"

"Sometimes. Yes. Sometimes they do." Xander answered somberly.

Ollie processed that for awhile and then uttered, "Okay, but you don't experiment on humans, do you?"

"We don't?"

"You do?" Ollie's eyebrows were raised, hoping the old man was joking again.

"They're called clinical trials Ollie. Approved by the government and everything. Again, the people who participate are willing to be part of an experiment in the hope that they can help whatever disease they're fighting and in the process help us bring new medicines to the world."

"Oh, right." That answer seemed to satisfy Ollie. "Well, I'm stuck drawing mostly plants. I don't have a

73

bunch of friends that I can draw, and the animals I run into" Ollie paused for a moment reflecting on some inner thought, "don't stand still long enough for me to draw them."

"Well, I've got plenty of beautiful plants here for you to draw, so maybe we could start there for now. Sound good?"

"Thanks."

Xander ruffled Ollie's hair. Ollie thought to himself, *maybe this won't be so bad after all.*

7

THE SANDBOX KISS

Zach needed a break. He'd stopped at Madrona Dry Goods for a drink and was sitting in the park weighing his options. *This was insane wasn't it?* Biking around the neighborhood in the faint hope that he'd meet Zoe again. *Who did things like that?* But what were his options? What other pressing activities did he have this summer?

He could spend the summer evading chess camps and island outings for blackberry picking, and play video games all summer. For some reason, what usually sounded like a great option to Zach, suddenly seemed kinda lame. He could spend the summer chasing after a girl he'd met for ten minutes and never finding her or stay locked in his room.

Even if Zach did find Zoe again, he wasn't entirely sure she would agree with his assessment. Maybe she would have wished he'd stayed locked away in his room playing video games? Really what was the point of all this?

From his vantage point on the bench Zach could see the geodesic jungle gym where Zoe had made the wide hole appear in the ground. That just reminded him of his futile quest. Zach put his head in his hands trying to decide what to do next.

§

"You know I can't buy you candy."

"I have money." Gabe raised his eyebrows hopefully.

"Where did you get money?" Zoe continued exasperated, sounding like she was repeating something she'd said a thousand times, "Money is not the issue. Mom and Dad don't want you eating candy. If I get you candy, I'll get in trouble."

"I won't tell."

"You always tell."

"I promise this time."

"You promise every time."

"I'm not a little kid anymore." Gabe challenged his big sister.

"You are *exactly* a little kid." Zoe snapped.

Gabe squinched up his face in anger, having run out of arguments for the moment.

Zoe was resolute in not wanting to get into trouble. The camera she desperately craved hung in the balance. But she was still somewhat sympathetic to her little brother. "How about we stop at the park. I'll push you on the swings."

Gabe didn't respond, but Zoe could tell her suggestion made him feel a little better when he followed her in the direction of the park. She even thought she saw his face relax a little bit. Just a little though.

§

Zach made up his mind. He couldn't sit here all day. He needed to do *something*. He was going to forget about this crazy search for a girl he barely knew, head home, do some reading, and start his summer fresh. He would do that right after he did one last circuit of the neighborhood to make triple sure he hadn't overlooked any small spot where she might be hanging out.

"I knew this would make you feel better."

Though he did his best to stay angry, Gabe couldn't suppress the fun he was having on the swing. He said "No it isn't" through clenched teeth. But his budding smile was unmistakable.

I knew this would make you feel better. Where did that come from? And he *was* feeling better. The voice. He recognized it. Zach looked up from the palms of his hands where he'd been doing his thinking, and standing at the swings were Zoe and her little brother. All that searching the neighborhood for nothing. All he'd needed to do was wait at the original spot where they'd met. Why hadn't he thought of that?

Zach's relief was short-lived when he suddenly realized that he'd spent so much time trying to find Zoe, that he'd given zero thought on what he would say to her if he actually did. Unfortunately Zach had already started walking towards the swings when this thought had occurred to him, so he needed to come up with something quick.

"Hey. Look. It's that boy." Gabe yelled from the swing.

Zach saw Zoe look up. He wouldn't characterize her reaction as full-fledged disappointment but she didn't look exactly thrilled either.

"Hi." Zach waved a small wave as he approached.

"Hey." Zoe responded.

"We saw you the other night. When Zoe made the hole." Gabe said.

"Gabe!" Zoe hissed at her brother.

"I don't remember anything about someone making a hole, but I remember seeing you." Zach replied cheerily.

Zoe looked back at Zach, relief washing over her face. Gabe was about to continue the discussion about the hole when a look from his sister cut that short.

"Do you come to the park often?" Zach regretted the words mere milliseconds after they'd left his mouth.

"I'm watching my brother all summer. So yeah. Probably. I need to do *something* with him." Zoe was now pushing Gabe a little harder so he could only hear every other sentence in her conversation with Zach.

"Oh?"

"Yeah. My parents are working on opening a restaurant so they're really busy." Zoe said between pushes.

Zach was working hard trying to come up with a not totally stupid sounding response when Gabe interjected, "Stop pushing. I want to climb on the jungle gym."

"Only if you promise not to climb too high this time."

"I promise. I promise." Gabe insisted.

Gabe raced over to the now sunken jungle gym. Zach and Zoe followed slowly.

"Do you have any other siblings?" Zach asked.

"He's plenty." Zoe laughed a gentle laugh. "You?"

"Two younger sisters. They're *more* than plenty."

Zach and Zoe sat on the bench while Gabe climbed.

"We just moved to this neighborhood. My PopPop – I mean, my grandfather lives nearby. We moved in with him."

"Well, this is a cool neighborhood, I think."

"I think it sucks." Zoe declared.

"You decided already? You just moved here."

"My room is smaller. My parents are never around. And I'm stuck watching the brat."

"OK. That does suck. But that's not the neighborhood's fault. Give it a chance." Zach reasoned.

"I'm not a brat." Gabe had walked over from the jungle gym. "Can we get candy now?"

"No." Zoe refused her little brother and then turned back to Zach, "Even though we just moved here, I've been here many times. My grandfather used to bring us to this park to play."

"Please?" Gabe wheedled.

"In fact," Zoe raised her eyebrows. This is where Gabe got his first kiss."

"Zoe!" Gabe had been successfully diverted from his candy mission.

Zach listened politely trying not to get involved in the sibling squabble.

Zoe continued over her little brother's protests. "Well, three years ago, Gabe was over there playing in the sandbox with a little girl with curly hair. I wasn't watching closely. But all of a sudden, Gabe was crying. Apparently she had kissed him."

Gabe was starting to make his angry face again.

"Oh stop. You were four." Zoe reassured her brother.

"I think I know this story." Zach finally said.

"You do?" The siblings exclaimed at the same time.

"Little girl, blonde curls, big smile, kinda living in her own world?"

Zoe and Gabe nodded.

"That was my youngest sister Cassie. We tell that story in my family too."

§

As a secret hideout, the bomb shelter in the middle of the woods was way cooler than the abandoned car Binny used to frequent. When Penny and Cassie referred to the shelter as the Madrona Heroes headquarters, Binny still snorted.

Unlike the previous year, Binny had a new best friend in Penny that she loved spending time with. But like the previous year, Binny still periodically needed her alone time. Especially when Cassie was getting on her nerves. The bomb shelter was her refuge.

But while she used to mostly read in the now defiled rusty car shell, in the bomb shelter she now mostly wrote. The stack of ancient notebooks still sat in an old milk crate, as she'd first found it.

Binny had written on and off all year. She'd written about her parents, she'd written about her friends, but mostly she wrote about their powers. And in many cases she wrote about their efforts to keep them secret.

There was the time Cassie turned invisible in the middle of the school play. Zach had to creatively do worse on one of his exams so as not to arouse suspicion.

Penny's desk had fallen to pieces in the middle of class. Binny too had run into all sorts of issues. Though hers were more ethical quandaries than scrapes. She still wasn't sure when if ever it was okay to use her powers. She did have one incident where an annoying teenager had cut her in line at Soul Repair, the neighborhood's hot chocolate and ice cream cafe, but that had turned out okay in the end.

And while the children had learned scant bits and pieces about their powers, Penny still sometimes broke stuff accidentally, Zach still remembered way too much of everything, Cassie still couldn't turn invisible on purpose, and Binny still knew more than she should about what was in people's secret hearts.

Binny finished this day's entry in the register as follows: "One more thing. Zach thinks a girl he met has a power. I think her main power is over him. As far as I'm concerned, we're still the only four people on Earth with powers. And I hope it stays that way."

Binny's last paragraph took her to the end of the page. Even though she was done writing, she took a peek at the next page, but there wasn't one. After a full year of documenting the highs and lows of their exclusive club, she had filled an entire book. Well, a 'Daily Register of Pupils' to be exact.

Binny stood on her chair to retrieve a new blank journal off the stack and returned the finished one to the crate. Why a stack of old school supplies from a million years ago were being stored in an abandoned bomb shelter, Binny had no idea.

Binny still scoffed at any "Madrona Heroes" mentions, but she was more of a stickler for consistency than she was self-conscious about the kids calling themselves super heroes. Much as she'd done almost exactly a year earlier, Binny crossed the word "Daily" off the cover and wrote in "Madrona Heroes" so now the title read "The Madrona Heroes Register".

§

"We should probably get going." Zoe and Zach had been talking for some time only periodically interrupted by Gabe's pleas for candy and attention.

"Sure." Zach wondered how he was going to run into Zoe again.

Zoe gathered Gabe and they started heading out of the park. "Are you heading in this direction?"

Zoe was in fact walking in the exact opposite direction that Zach needed to go. He answered her, "Yeah." They walked for a bit heading to the edge of the park.

Zoe stopped in her tracks. "What's that?"

"What?" Zach asked.

"Shhhh..." Zoe put her finger to her lips.

Zach and Gabe waited.

After a moment, they heard a pitiful whine coming from behind a nearby bush that was up against a fence.

Zoe crouched down approaching the bush. The sound got louder and to Zach sounded even sadder.

Zoe made all sorts of comforting sounds, while Zach and Gabe crouched behind her not wanting to disturb her efforts. Zach was able to make out a black cat, cowering behind the bush. Zoe got closer and closer until Zach heard a hiss. And then the cat shot out of the bush.

But something was clearly wrong. The cat was moving as fast as it could, but it was dragging its front left foot.

Zoe stood up, her hands going to her face. "Oh no!"

Even though the cat was limping, it was still moving faster than the kids could give chase. And seeing how scared the cat was, none of the kids wanted to do so and make it more upset. They watched helplessly as the cat lamely crossed the street and disappeared down an alley.

"What are we going to do?" Zoe said desperately. A tear ran down her cheek.

Zach wasn't entirely sure what to say. "I'm sure the cat will be okay." But he wasn't sure at all.

§

She's crying over a cat? Gore Grater thought to himself. He was parked a block away from the park. His right hand was propped up on the car's steering wheel holding his phone, videotaping the scene before him. His left hand held an super-sized popsicle which he absent-mindedly licked. The popsicle was melting faster than he was able to eat it and had dripped onto his fingers making them sticky.

⇒ 8 ⇐

THE ROBOTIC MILKSHAKE

Jay was pretty sure that the client that had hired him to draw an illustration explaining how to install their new heart monitoring device, would not find the current drawing he was working on a satisfactory substitute.

In *this* drawing, a giant robotic milkshake was threatening the neighborhood. A shriveled bald old man with an egg shaped head and wraparound bomber goggles sat in the robot's cockpit shooting milkshake at the homes and people. Jay had wrestled with his villain's choice of weapon, as *wasn't a milkshake that large really a blessing?* But in the end Jay decided that this was the villain's ironic twist. He took things that people loved and used them as weapons.

As usual, Zach, Binny, and Cassie were fighting evil wielding their super powers, sarcastic barbs, deadly flying rule books, and mesmerizing singing respectively. But for the first time there was a new addition to their little group – the girl from next door, Penny.

Illustrated Penny was also barefoot. And it seemed from the drawing that her feet could grow extra large and strong. She was using them to kick a hole in the robot's side. A hole had started to form. How letting the contents of the giant milkshake leak out through the hole was better than letting the villain shoot it out through the robot's enormous straw, Jay wasn't entirely sure. But it was just a doodle after all. It didn't all have to make exact sense.

After putting the finishing touches on his drawing, a small voice in the back of Jay's mind started reminding him that his actual paid illustration work awaited for the people that hired him. At that moment Jay would have paid *them* to let him off the hook.

While Jay loved to draw, there was just something profoundly uninteresting about spending his days drawing images of things he didn't care about – a heart monitor, a logo for a small bank, a new type of industrial screw.

Once he'd had to draw a sick cruise ship for an article in a magazine about how people were getting sick on cruises. At least there he got to be a little bit funny though the client had made him remove the vomit from his drawing. It was especially sad as the passengers of the ship were actually in the puke he had drawn. He thought that was particularly *on point*.

Jay was good. He knew it. Penny's mother Serena had said so. She had said she was "impressed". Jay recalled her words with precision. That's what he needed to do – show Serena that he'd included Penny in his latest drawing. She would get a kick out of it. The voice in the back of Jay's head reminding him to get back to the paid work was mute, for a little while anyway.

§

"Oh, hi." Serena smiled politely as she opened the front door.

Suddenly what had seemed like such a good idea a few minutes earlier seemed juvenile and silly to Jay, but now that he was here, there was no choice but to press on. "I wanted to show you something."

"Of course. What is it?" Serena said.

"To be honest, I'm also procrastinating a bit, so I appreciate you helping me on that front." Jay admitted sheepishly.

"I don't like to boast, but you're talking to a procrastination black belt. Nobody can touch a writer in that department."

"You write?" Jay smiled.

"Only when I've run out of gardening, cooking, cleaning, TV watching, and reading every single thing on the internet." Serena looked down at Jay's hand. "Is that what you wanted to show me?"

"Uh, yeah." Jay handed her the drawing. "You liked the one on the wall, and this time, I put Penny in the action."

"Oh. Her bare feet. That's so great. I'm guessing her powers only come when she takes her shoes off?" Serena didn't wait for an answer. "You really captured her."

Jay uttered a quiet "Thanks."

Serena pondered the drawing for a moment and continued, "Would it really be bad to have that much milkshake? I wonder if instead of fighting this guy shouldn't we be lining up with straws?"

"Yeah, that occurred to me too." Jay admitted. "Is it wrong that I keep coming up with villains who just make everything really messy?"

"Maybe his motto should be 'You *can* have too much of a good thing.'"

"That's really good. You're a great writer."

Jay's compliment caught Serena off guard and now she was the one uttering a quiet "Thanks".

§

Zach wasn't usually at a loss for what to do. If his father was bugging him, he would placate him by telling him what he wanted to hear and getting away as quickly as possible. His mother could be bought off with a hug.

With his sisters it was either ignore them or mess with them. Especially Binny. But Zoe was another situation altogether.

Zach hadn't realized how much he'd gotten used to having all the answers. There was no guide to Zoe that he could read and memorize. No playbook. There was just this really cool person crying over an injured cat. And Zach felt entirely helpless.

"I'm sure he'll be okay." Zach repeated.

Zoe ignored his statement. "Remember that kid with the white hair. I bet *he* did this."

"Why do you say that?" Zach asked, curious.

Zoe whirled to face him. "Why? Because *somebody* did it. And something was wrong with that kid."

Zach agreed that there was something strange about the boy from the other evening, but he also thought that it was most likely the cat had been in a fight with another cat. Luckily Zach also thought better of sharing either of those thoughts with Zoe who looked ready to have a fight of her own. Zach shifted gears. "Maybe we can find the cat and get him help."

"How do you propose doing that?" Zoe's hands were on her hips.

"I found you didn't I?"

"You what? You *found* me?"

Zach desperately searched for another way to shift the conversation, but he didn't see a smooth way out of the hole he had just dug for himself. It occurred to Zach that Zoe wasn't the only one who could magically dig herself into a hole in the ground. Zach kept that thought to himself too. Instead he offered a meek, "I meant, I ran into you. And that's the second time we've run into that cat. I'm sure if we hang out here we would run into it again."

Zoe looked unconvinced but seemed to decide to let it go as she was more concerned about the cat than she was creeped out by Zach's declaration. "Hmmm... Maybe." Zoe's eyes widened and angry tears started coming again. "I just feel *so* bad. It's hurt and there's nothing we can do." Zoe wandered over to the bench and sat scrunched up letting her knees catch most of her tears.

"This is the point where I usually leave her alone." Gabe offered.

Zach turned to face Gabe who had a wiser-than-his-years look on his face.

Gabe continued, "She'll eventually be okay. It just takes her awhile."

"She's really upset." Zach said.

"My sister cares about two things. Her cat, and all cats I guess, and getting a new camera at the end of the summer."

"That's three things. Or millions of things depending on how you count." Zach responded absent-mindedly.

"Huh?" Gabe looked confused for a second.

Zach looked down at Gabe and realized he was talking to a little kid. "Uh never mind. Thanks for the tip."

Gabe's smile returned.

"A new camera? She likes to take pictures?" Zach asked.

"My sister *loves* to take pictures. My parents told her they would buy her a new camera if she took care of me this summer. Zoe said maybe I could use it too." Gabe's smile turned hopeful.

§

"What are you guys talking about?" Penny walked tentatively into the room where Jay and Serena were chatting.

"Hello Penny." Serena chided her daughter for her brusqueness.

"I was just showing your Mom this new drawing I made. See someone familiar?" Jay handed Penny the illustration.

"Hey. That's me! What am I doing?"

"You're breaking the villain's milkshake robot." Jay explained.

"With my feet?" Penny didn't wait for an answer. "And also, is an enormous milkshake really a bad thing?"

Jay and Serena shared a laugh.

Knock knock. "Hellooooo…"

Penny froze at the sounds coming from the front door, rabbit-like. Jay thought he could almost see her ears perk up.

Penny ran to the door. "Daaaaaaaaaddyyyyyy."

§

Cats. Cats and photography. The gears in Zach's mind were turning and turning. These were two topics where his knowledge was relatively meager. Less than meager. Zach thought more as he watched Zoe wipe the last of the tears from her cheeks.

Zach's mind wandered back to the injured cat. Zach wasn't in tears but he could empathize. It was sad. The cat was clearly hurt, and all alone. Zach just didn't know how to help. They could try and catch the cat, but it was so scared. Zach suspected that he and Zoe would only make the cat more anxious and the odds of catching it and getting it help were extraordinarily low. This was really a task for more than two people.

Zach had an idea.

§

Serena smiled at how happy her daughter was. Penny wrapped tightly around her father's waist.

Penny's father raised his hand in hello and then stuck it out towards Jay. His button down shirt cut crisp lines on his tall frame. His jet black hair was spiky and cut smartly. "I'm Quincy. Penny's dad."

93

Jay shook off his momentary confusion and stood up to shake the proferred hand. "Oh, hi. I'm Jay. From next door. We were just chatting."

"Remember I told you about my friend Binny? That's Binny's dad. He and Mom were just looking at one of his drawings."

"I should go." Jay stood up to leave, sliding the folded drawing into his pocket.

"Nice to meet you." Quincy said, while being pulled in another direction by his excited daughter.

"You too." And then turning to Serena. "Thanks for the distraction."

Serena smiled and responded. "Anytime. I may need you to return the favor one day."

§

"I should probably get Gabe home for lunch."

"Of course." Zach agreed. I've got to go too. "I'll probably be back here later this afternoon. My Dad always sends me shopping for stuff he forgot." Zach rolled his eyes.

Zoe managed a small knowing smile despite still recovering from her emotional reaction to seeing the injured animal. "Yeah. I think we'll be around."

"Cool."

"Cool."

Zach watched them walk away for a few seconds. Gabe looked back over his shoulder as they walked, "Bye Zach. See ya later."

Zach smiled, "See you later Gabe."

Zach was counting on seeing Gabe and Zoe later. In the meantime, Zach knew just what he must do.

⇒ 9 ⇐

THE BROKEN PIECES

The sun was high in the sky as Zach rode down the Madrona hillside towards home. Zach rehearsed his arguments during the entire bike ride. It wasn't like him to be nervous, but he knew Binny could be prickly on this issue, and he wanted to handle it just right.

"Absolutely not!" Binny didn't even let Zach get through his first sentence before cutting him off.

"Can you please just listen to me before – "

"You would tell our secret to someone you just met two days ago to find some stray cat?" Binny demanded.

"That's not what I was saying". Zach wasn't even a minute in and things were going even more poorly than he had feared. "I told you, she's like us."

"She is nothing like us. She does not have powers. There was only one name in that study. Mom's."

"But you know that study didn't give us our powers. And Penny is the proof." Zach was using every ounce of his focus to stay calm. He knew from experience that escalating would only make things worse.

"It doesn't matter. I don't know where our powers came from. I just know that we're the only four people that have them."

"I know what I saw." Zach said.

"I know what I'm seeing." Binny said acidly.

"What is that supposed to mean?" Zach let some of the frustration he was feeling creep into his voice.

"You know what it means." Binny gave Zach a knowing look.

"No, I don't know. Please illuminate me." One of Zach's' eyebrows rode high on his forehead. His eyes were wide getting ready for whatever blow Binny had to administer.

"Well," Binny paused looking like she was wondering whether to follow through, "I think you want to include this girl in our group for reasons you're not admitting."

"Like what?" The edge in Zach's voice was now unmistakable.

"Like that you like her."

Zach looked at Binny hard.

Binny raised her eyebrows in defiance.

"You don't get to make all the decisions in this group. I can do whatever I like." Zach finally responded.

"Maybe I don't get to make all the decisions, but this decision affects us all."

"I don't need your permission. I'm older than you." Zach knew he was on thin ice trotting out his two year age advantage, but he was frustrated and angry.

"You may be older than me, but the older we get, the less that will matter. But my power is better than yours. And that will never change no matter how old we get."

Some of the color went out of Zach's face. It was clear that Binny had poked a tender spot.

Binny didn't stop. "We both know that the most powerful person in the group makes the decisions. Like Superman."

"Batman makes most of the decisions in that group and he has no powers."

"Your new *friend* doesn't have any powers either. Your crush on her is affecting your judgment."

"That's ridiculous."

"No. It's not ridiculous. It's the truth."

"How would you know that?"

"You know how. I can tell these things. It's not just that I can see thoughts, I can see how people are feeling."

It was all too much for Zach. He'd been so thoughtful, and so careful. Maybe he did like Zoe. So what. He didn't even know himself for sure. He knew that he really wanted to make her feel better. Was that 'liking' someone? Being nice to them?

What Zach was certain of was that Zoe had a power. His judgment wasn't off on that issue. And as far as Zach's power, it was just fine thank you. So what if Binny could read minds. She was so proud of herself. Her power was obnoxious. His was useful in all sorts of everyday activities. Zach tried hard to convince himself that Binny's comment about his powers didn't matter. But his heart had started to ache.

Zach lashed out, "I don't need your power to know what you're thinking Binny."

"Oh really? What's that?" Binny's hands were in one of their familiar positions on her hips.

"You think you're gonna get Mom and Dad to get back together. And guess what? You can read every mind in the world and it's never ever ever going to happen. So stop being such a baby."

Binny looked like she'd been punched in the stomach.

Zach knew the moment he saw her face that he had gone too far.

Binny burst into tears as if she was made of water and the floodgates had been opened. Hands up to her face, she ran sobbing from the room.

Zach just stood there, shaking in anger, and feeling awful.

§

"After that, I think we should eat lunch at the Space Needle. I've never been, but the restaurant at the top spins. I hope it spins fast enough that it makes me throw up." Penny tugged at a latch on the bottom of the coin bank she was holding as she spoke. The bank had transparent walls so you could see deposited coins sliding around inside until they found the right sized slot in which to descend.

Serena watched her daughter with a slightly strained smile on her face.

"Penny – " Quincy tried to get a word in.

"And then, I think we should go to the place with the donut robot in the market. I like the ones with cinnamon and sugar. You would think I wouldn't be hungry after all that lunch, but remember, I'll have just thrown up cause the restaurant spins." The latch opened, and dozens of coins spilled out onto the table. "And I'll buy the donuts. Look, I've saved lots of money."

"Penny – " Quincy said more insistently this time.

"Of course, we will have to wait a bit before we leave the restaurant to make sure anyone who got puked on isn't hanging around still."

"Penny, darling, – "

Penny finally looked up at her father, "What?"

Quincy took a breath. "Sweetheart, I'm only here for a day or so. I don't know if we'll have time for all that on this visit."

"What?" Penny erupted.

"Sweetheart, I'm only driving through right now. But I'll be driving back through in a few days and I'll be able to spend a bit more time then. And then at the end of the summer, you'll come visit me and – "

"A few days? The end of the summer? Visit you?" Penny was shouting now.

Penny's father continued in a steady tone, "It's just a few days. We're going to spend lots of time together. I promise."

Penny slammed her hand down on the table. "I'm sick of your promises." The coins jumped. A few started rolling towards the edge of the table. Penny was now standing at the edge of the table clutching the coin bank in one hand. "I'm never going to get to spend any time with you! Why don't you just leave now." With that, Penny walked out the front door of the house.

§

The branches that swayed in front of the windows to Binny's room were especially lovely on summer days. The leaves stretched out as much as they could absorbing every ray of sun as if to make up for the months they spent under a thick blanket of clouds. The sun glinted brightly off some of the leaves, but out of the corner of her eye Binny noticed her best friend Penny sitting on her stoop, pieces to something now broken strewn about her bare feet.

§

"What was it?" Binny was making much the same sympathetic smiling face that Serena had made at Penny a few minutes earlier.

"A coin bank."

"Where are the coins?"

"My dad gave it to me."

Binny put her hand on Penny's shoulder.

Penny continued, "He's inside."

"Oh. Let me clean it up. He doesn't need to see it now. I'm sure we can put it back together with some time." Binny crouched and started collecting the pieces.

Penny didn't seem to notice and kept staring forward and out to the lake. When Binny had collected most of the pieces, Penny finally added, "It's never going to get put back together. Nothing ever does."

§

"Seems like you're not feeling good about something, Mr. Jordan."

Zach thought that Caleb had a way of getting straight to the heart of the matter. It made him uncomfortable. But after his fight with Binny, he supposed that his guilt was written all over his face. Maybe knowing how someone was feeling wasn't such a difficult skill after all. "I guess not." Zach replied.

Caleb didn't say anything as he went about carefully removing a series of weeds from around a wild flower that had grown in the forest.

They continued in silence for a bit. Zach thought about the look on Binny's face as he'd said those last words. It reminded him of the look on Zoe's face when she saw the injured cat. Zach said, "I'm not sure how to fix things."

"What needs fixing?"

"Well," Zach started slowly, "we found a neighborhood cat with a hurt leg."

Caleb raised his eyebrow slightly at the mention of *we* but Zach didn't notice.

"Anyway, we wanted to help it somehow, but I'm not even sure we could catch it. I'm also worried about scaring it. It's probably already pretty scared and I don't want to make things worse."

"Sometimes animals get into fights with other animals." Caleb said.

"That's what I said, but Zoe thinks that this cat was hurt by a kid."

Caleb stopped what he was doing for a moment and turned to Zach. "Zoe Flowers?"

"Huh?" Zach looked puzzled.

"Zoe Flowers. Young lady, about your age. Sizable hair."

One of the things Caleb could tell by the look on Zach's face was that they were talking about the same girl. "So if Ms. Flowers doesn't think the cat was hurt by another animal, who does she think hurt the cat?"

"Some kid we met in the park. A couple of years younger than us. Very light blonde hair. Seemed kind of angry."

If Zach had been paying closer attention he would have seen Caleb's shoulders sag as he processed the information.

"Well Mr. Jordan, you can't play baseball with one player."

Zach knew that talking to Caleb was a bit of a bet. Caleb was always willing to talk, but Zach wasn't always sure he understood what Caleb was saying.

Caleb continued, "Helping that injured animal, and figuring out what happened is not a one person job. You need a team."

"That's what I said!" Zach's words tripped over each other as he responded eagerly. "But Binny wouldn't listen."

"You can't just throw nine players on the diamond who don't know each other. The players have to trust each other before they can truly play together. They need to be friends first, teammates second."

"How am I going to get everyone to be friends?"

"Well one thing I know, don't try and force it. People have to become friends naturally. If you push them, you'll only end up with more hurt feelings and more sad-faced walks to the woods. And while I enjoy your company, I do have more weeds to pull."

§

The pieces of the coin bank were laid out on Binny's desk now. Binny's head was lowered examining them closely as much to try and see if she could fit them back together as to give her friend some space.

"He said he's only here for a day. I don't know why he even bothered to come at all." Penny said from her prone position on the bed.

"But didn't he say he'd be back soon?" Binny responded without taking her eyes off the pieces.

"He *always* says that." Penny complained.

Minutes passed, Binny gave up on her coin bank investigation and lay down opposite Penny on the bed. Binny was turned the other way so they each had their heads at different ends.

Binny's conversation with Zach, and watching Penny's spiral into sadness were a thick gray blanket, pinning Binny in place. Staring up at the ceiling, Binny said, "Maybe you and Zach are both right."

"About what?"

"Maybe sometimes, things stay broken."

❖ 10 ❖

THE FIFTIETH DIGIT

"Look, Mom, I made these." Ollie announced to his mother.

Dr. Samantha Trace followed her son's outstretched finger to a small sign that read *Serenoa*. On the sign was a hand-drawn spiky fan of a plant identical to the actual plants that sat above it. "Nicely done Ollie."

"I've done lots of them." The new signs stretched down the row they found themselves in. "We're cataloging the whole greenhouse."

Sam Trace had seen countless drawings done by her son. She didn't usually give them more than a casual glance. But seeing Ollie so excited, she took a longer look than usual – something she hadn't done in a long time. They were exceptionally well done. With only a black and white pen, Ollie had rendered unbelievably lifelike plants. The drawings were almost photographic. Bristling with life. For a moment, Dr. Trace was at a loss for words. "Ollie, These drawings, they're – "

"Very impressive, no?" The caretaker of the greenhouse finished her sentence. A big smile on his face, his hand ruffling Ollie's hair in approval.

"Why yes. It's more art than science, but impressive nonetheless." Dr. Trace made a thin smile.

"Oh, but I'm not so sure about the distinction you're making. So much of science is keen observation and description, and isn't that what young Ollie has done here with remarkable precision?"

Ollie's smile widened briefly before he looked up at his mother, eyes expectant.

Dr. Trace paused, locking eyes with her son, and then said, "Why, yes. I suppose so. Keen observation and description are critical pieces of the scientist's toolkit."

Ollie allowed himself to smile more broadly.

"I think that's enough for today though, no? It's getting close to dinner time and you can do more tomorrow."

Ollie looked back over his shoulder as he followed his mother out of the greenhouse only to see Xander, Ollie's impromptu camp counselor with his characteristic big smile, waving goodbye.

As Dr. Trace and her son exited the humidity, the old man turned to examine Ollie's handiwork. The man thought to himself that the drawing was even more impressive than when he'd seen it earlier in the morning when Ollie had drawn the Serenoa. The drawing looked like it was straining to get off the page and pop into existence.

His eyes drifting off the sign and onto one of the plants behind it, the man noticed something he hadn't before. He said aloud – he had come into the habit of talking to himself since he spent so much time alone – "Why you're looking a little unhealthy."

The man rubbed one of the spiky leaves between his thumb and forefinger. It felt rough and it was pale in color relative to some of the other leaves on the plant. "Are you not getting enough water?"

The man pulled a small device out of his pocket, and tweaked the programming on the automated irrigation software that kept the plants in the greenhouse hydrated. With that done, he walked slowly down the aisle, admiring Ollie's signs and the plants they referred to.

§

"Befuddled. Honestly, I am befuddled."

"That's a stupid word." Zach informed his father.

"Stupid or not, it's the right word. It means I am confused and unable to think clearly."

"I know what it means."

Jay Jordan ignored his son's snarky response. "I simply don't understand where all the food in this house goes. I know the three of you are growing, but this seems ridiculous."

"What do you need?" Zach knew by now that his father's observations on the speed at which they ate the food in the house were almost always followed by a request to run to the market to get an ingredient or two for dinner.

"Aren't you considerate." Jay smiled at Zach's request as if he hadn't heard the exasperation in his voice. "And now that you mention it, yes, I could use some broccoli and some firm tofu. We're having stir fry tonight!"

"Oh and Zach," Zach stopped on his way out the door waiting for his father to finish, "don't take too long please. Your mother took your sisters over to walk the Doctor's dog again, and I want to have dinner going before they get back."

§

"You're not coming with us?" Binny said to her mother, her forehead furrowed.

"You guys did great last time, and Henry has a bottle of wine he wants to show me."

"Wine! Are you getting drunk?" Cassie interrupted loudly.

"We will not be drinking the whole bottle Cassie." Dr. Huitre said with a wink.

"I guess you'll just have a good time with *An-ree*." Binny muttered this under her breath mimicking the way her mother pronounced Dr. Huitre's first name.

Julie and Henry had already turned to analysis and discussion of the label on the bottle and didn't notice.

§

Zach had a feeling Zoe and Gabe might be at the park. And sure enough he was rewarded when he saw the big cloud of tight curls swinging back and forth on the swingset.

"Don't get on that thing." Zoe said to her brother as he approached the now sunken jungle gym. It had been cordoned off with tape, apparently by some city official, until it could be restored to its rightful height. Zoe wondered what explanation that person had conjured up in their mind for the huge hole underneath the play structure. She was relatively sure it was nothing even close to the truth.

Zach had thought he was over most of the jitters he had felt when talking to Zoe, but as he approached her, the butterflies in his stomach took flight in large numbers. All he could muster was a sheepish "Hey".

"Hey." Zoe seemed unsurprised at Zach's sudden appearance in the park. "Whatcha up to?"

Gabe came over, just slightly out-of-breath. "Hey Zach." He'd dropped whatever he was doing as soon as he saw Zach.

"My Dad's daily request that I get ingredients for dinner." The butterflies were making quite a ruckus at this point.

"What's for dinner at your house?" Zoe asked.

Dinner. House. Zach knew he recognized those words. He was even pretty sure he knew what they meant. But strung together they just felt kind of foreign. Zach could tell he should say something soon as Zoe's eyes were widening and her eyebrows rising. But somehow the bigger eyes just made Zach feel more flustered. "I can't remember." Was all Zach could muster.

"You can't remember what you were supposed to get?"

"Zach remembers everything. He said so." Gabe chimed in.

"Not today apparently." Zoe said to her brother.

Zach managed to take his eyes off Zoe long enough to collect his thoughts. "Oh no. I am good at remembering stuff. Really good."

"Uh. OK." Zoe sounded neither interested nor impressed.

"I can recite Pi."

"Pie?" Gabe's grin got large.

"Not pie dummy. Pi. P. I. No E. It's a number."

"Oh." Gabe tried to hide his disappointment. "I guess that's good too."

Zach retreated momentarily up into his brain, mentally floating at high speeds down aisles of file cabinets until he found the one with the information he needed. He could picture the computer screen where he'd looked up Pi one day the previous March when he was bored. It floated in front of him just as it had months earlier.

Zach read aloud. "3.1415926535897932384462643"

Zach took a moment to breathe and looked down from his mental computer screen. Zoe's look of indifference had faded. Zach decided to look back up at the screen and keep going before he totally lost his place.

"38327950288419716693993751"

Zach couldn't help but steal another glance. Zoe's head had turned ever so slightly and her lips were slightly apart now. What had he been doing again? *Oh right. Pi.* Zach tried to look away from Zoe's face but no matter where looked the computer screen was gone. Maybe that was a good place to stop anyway.

Zoe kept staring for a moment. Then as if realizing that she had been staring she looked down, anywhere but at Zach. "Uh, cool. I mean. Very cool."

Zach thought at first that Zoe was trying to hide her excitement, but then he wondered if maybe he had fantasized that she was impressed.

"That was like a million numbers." Gabe said.

Welcoming the interruption Zoe creased her eyebrows at her brother. "Don't be ridiculous."

"Fifty actually. I..." Zach was going to say *I could keep going* but he wasn't entirely sure that he could keep going, and more importantly he wasn't sure that he *should* keep going. He wanted more than anything for Zoe to confide in him about how she had created the huge hole in the ground the other day. And he thought that the best way to do that was to share his secret with her. Caleb even seemed to agree. But Binny was dead set against it. And the guilt he was feeling about what he'd said to her earlier was still bitter in his stomach.

Zach switched gears, "...I think it was 50 anyway. I'm not exactly sure."

"That's cool." Zoe said.

"That's *way* cool." Gabe echoed.

"Anyone could do it with enough time and practice Even you." Zoe's eyebrows were furrowed again.

Zach bit his lip.

§

"So what do you talk about with him?"

"I dunno. Art and science and stuff." Mostly I got to draw all day. Ollie pushed the piece of fish with a fork, chasing an errant pea around his plate.

"He hasn't said anything to you?"

"Nope."

Samantha Trace grabbed the fork from her son's hand and placed it on the table. "The fork is for eating your food, not playing with it."

"I *am* eating it." Ollie whined.

"That's not what it looks like from here."

"Well maybe you don't know what you're looking at." The words left Ollie's mouth before he realized he'd probably crossed a line with his mother. But the sharp words didn't come. His mother was looking at him. Hard. But she seemed to be thinking intently about what to say next.

"Has he asked you to do anything other than draw signs for the plants?" Ollie's mother asked him.

"He didn't ask me to do that. That was *my* suggestion!" Ollie was relieved that his mother had decided to ignore his impertinence.

"Are you at least learning something about what we do at Luce Labs?"

"You do experiments on plants and animals to find medicines. And sometimes the animals die. But he said it's noble for them to die. Because they're giving their lives to save the lives of others." Ollie said between mouthfuls of fish and peas.

"He used the word 'noble'?"

"Yes. 'Noble'."

Samantha Trace's expression changed as if a cloud had passed over head, "Well we should probably start thinking about getting you into some sort of real camp in a few days."

"Noooo. I like it there. It is real camp. But just for me. No other kids to deal with."

Lips pursed into a thin line, Samantha Trace just looked at her son for awhile, "Eat your dinner."

§

"I'm getting tired." Cassie whined. "It wasn't as hilly last time."

"I decided to take a different way." Binny replied.

"Want me to take a turn holding the leash?" Penny offered?

"But I get it back as soon as we get to the park." Cassie waited for agreement before she handed over the leash.

"Come on. We're almost there." Binny said.

Binny had been taciturn on the way up the hill from Dr. Huitre's house. What she was seeing now was giving her even more to stew about. Off in the distance she could see her brother. Even though he was a fair ways away, she could tell it was him from the gawky way he moved. Sitting in the swing next to him was someone she'd never met before, but Binny already knew who it was.

§

"Zaaaach." Cassie ran over to her brother almost dragging Rembrandt along with her. "Look. I brought Rembrandt."

Rembrandt barked loudly making sure he was heard. Surprised, Zach almost jumped out of his skin, stepped backwards, and tripped over a tree root falling backwards in an embarrassing, and painful, thump.

"Are you afraid of the dog?" Gabe asked absent-mindedly as he gave the large creature a good head scratching.

"I'm Cassie." Cassie interjected.

"Of course not." Zach replied, feeling the red rising in his cheeks.

"Gabe, introduce yourself." Zoe instructed her brother. "You've already met anyway."

"I'm Gabe."

"We have?" Cassie asked with excited surprise.

"Of course Zach's not afraid of dogs. He's always tripping over himself and landing in the dirt whether there's a dog nearby or not." Binny said, referring to her brother as she and Penny arrived on the little gathering.

Zach made a face as he gathered himself up from the ground and brushed off his pants.

"Aren't you going to introduce us to your friends Zach?" Binny continued in a haughty tone.

"Zoe this is my sister Binny and her friend Penny. Binny, and Penny, this is Zoe and her brother Gabe."

Small waves were exchanged while Zach contemplated how things might get worse.

"Is this your dog?" Zoe asked.

"It's Dr. Huitre's dog. He's our mom's friend." Cassie offered.

"Their mom. Not my mom." Penny added to no one in particular.

Lines formed at the corners of Binny's already pinched mouth. "He's not her friend. He was her doctor. A long time ago."

"He lets us walk Rembrandt whenever we want." Cassie continued, blithely ignoring her sister's discomfort.

"He's beautiful." Zoe got down on a knee to commune with Rembrandt, petting him, and rubbing his cheeks with hers.

Zach tentatively approached Rembrandt, hoping to rescue his reputation. Standing as far away as he could while still being able to reach the dog, Zach extended a stiff arm and stroked the dog's mane.

That Rembrandt's bark was cheerful was open to interpretation. And while Zach managed to keep his balance, at the sound Zach cut short his petting activities and shuddered. Zach's discomfort didn't go unnoticed by the others. Zach wondered if Zoe could produce another hole in the ground, this time for him to crawl into.

✦ 11 ✦

THE MANGO MURAL

"**H**ungry?" The old man had a way of surprising Ollie.

This was a pattern they had gotten into. Sometime in the middle of the afternoon Xander would appear out of nowhere with a mango in one hand and a large kitchen knife in the other. He would slice chunks of fruit onto a plate. Ollie always worried the man would cut himself but despite his age his hands were steady.

"Thank you." Ollie responded as he always did.

It had taken most of a week but Ollie had finally worked his way back to the area of the greenhouse where

119

the mango tree was located. Ollie had assumed that the fruit was bought at the supermarket, but the man had taken special pride informing him that he grew it himself right there in the greenhouse.

Row after row in the sprawling greenhouse now had beautifully illustrated signs courtesy of Ollie. He hadn't realized how large the structure was, but it seemed to stretch on forever with lots of different sections, each walled off from the next. This section was different though. It wasn't just the mango trees. It had a windowless door marked "PRIVATE". Ollie had seen the old man disappear through it periodically.

"What's in there?" Ollie said between mouthfuls of mango.

"Behind the door marked private?" Xander asked.

Ollie suddenly felt self-conscious and wondered if he had been impolite to ask.

"Curious?" Xander prodded.

Ollie had no idea what the right answer was at this point, and decided silence was the best policy for the moment.

The man continued as if Ollie had responded in the affirmative. "Curiosity is good!" The man said and let his stern mask turn into a smile.

Ollie smiled out of genuine relief. He was actually enjoying his time in the greenhouse and didn't want to get in trouble.

"Those without curiosity are like boats without rudders. They float on the ocean, but they have no direction." The man leaned in close. "You're not a rudderless boat, are you Ollie?"

Ollie shook his head.

"I didn't think so."

Ollie thought for a second. "What should I do next? It looks like I'm gonna be done soon with drawing signs unless you have a secret underground level of the greenhouse." For a fraction of a second Ollie thought he saw the man's eyes flicker, but the moment passed and Ollie decided he'd imagined it.

"More curiosity. I like it. There's always more to do."

Ollie let himself smile out of relief once again. His one positive summer camp experience wasn't going to end anytime soon.

"What would you like to do?" Xander asked.

"Well, I do love drawing." Ollie answered.

"Have you ever heard of etching?"

Ollie wasn't sure.

"Etching is a process whereby the artist uses a pointy tool to make scratches in a black coating that reveals the white canvas underneath. There are some positively beautiful etchings."

"That sounds more like erasing than drawing." Ollie laughed.

"Yes. Exactly." The old man was getting excited. Sometimes we make art by removing, rather than adding."

"You want me to etch?" Ollie said.

"Sort of." The man led Ollie over to a nearby table. "See this Chondrodendron Tomentosum? And I know it's Chondrodendron Tomentosum because of the beautiful label you drew yesterday." the man said conspiratorially before he continued. "All told we have about three dozen separate versions of this species growing right here. But see this one here?"

Ollie's eyes followed the man's finger. "It looks different. Some of the leaves are brown. It wasn't like that yesterday."

"This happens periodically with plants. Leaves die, flowers grow when we're not quite ready. Our job is to guide them by pruning back parts that are hurting the rest of the plant."

"I understand cutting off the dying parts. But why the flowers?" Ollie inquired.

"Excellent question! While flowers may be beautiful, in some cases they signify that the plant is going to stop producing fruit. And when we need the plant to produce fruit, this is counter to our goals."

The man leaned in even closer. "Never let superficial beauty distract you son. In nature we often think beauty evolved for attraction. But I believe that often it's evolved for *dis*traction. What better way to stop us from using the parts of the organism we need than by mesmerizing us with a pretty face."

§

Time passed. Xander left Ollie to his own devices as he usually did and Ollie drew more signs. Ollie's thoughts mulled over the new task Xander wanted him to do. He wasn't sure that pruning plants was nearly as fun as drawing, but it was better than going canoeing with other kids. Ollie tried to think of ways he could find art in cutting things away. But he kept getting distracted.

Ollie wasn't entirely sure how they'd gotten in, but periodically a bird or two would fly around the greenhouse. The old man had grumbled about having to do something about them but apparently hadn't gotten to that task yet.

FLAP. FLAP. FLAP. Even just a section of the greenhouse was very large, but Ollie imagined it felt tiny for a bird. *FLAP. FLAP. FLAP.* And then silence. Ollie imagined the bird was watching him now. If he just turned around he would see the bird staring at him.

Ollie turned around, and there by the wall with the door marked PRIVATE was the source of the flapping. Perched on a ledge and watching Ollie, its pointy-crowned black head was moving back and forth on its deep blue body. It *was* watching him.

Ollie tore the current sheet off his drawing pad and started sketching the bird. Ollie stared at the bird as he sketched. At first Ollie saw geometry. Curves. Intersecting lines. Shading filling in each little polygon. The bird's feathers looked like a mesh in Ollie's mind. And Ollie saw even more inside.

When Ollie would draw the plants he could see where the plants were going to grow a branch or a leaf even before it was there. It wasn't that he could see into the plant. It was more that he could see a second shape inside the plant. He could see the energy coursing within it. And that life was what he was trying to capture and imbue in his drawings.

But the life, the electricity running through an animal, even this small bird dwarfed what he saw in the plants that he drew. That's why he liked drawing animals so much more. They were just easier to *see*. But then something changed.

It was as if the bird had changed its mind. Where Ollie had been a curiosity with his intense stare and his furious sketching, Ollie had looked too deeply and the bird felt Ollie tugging at something that it kept inside, something private. Something that it most definitely did *not* want to share.

Ollie knew he had to draw fast. It was always this way with animals. They wouldn't sit still. It was just so frustrating. *This* was why he didn't want to go back to camp. He just didn't like dealing with other living creatures. They wouldn't listen. They wouldn't play along. And eventually they turned on him. Hissing at him. Complaining to the counselors. Or just running away altogether.

Ollie had had enough.

The bird was going to sit still for once and let Ollie finish his drawing. *FLAP. FLAP. FLAP.* The bird started flapping to leave, and for a moment it rose an inch or two into the air, but then it was back where Ollie wanted.

Ollie drew faster. But his drawing wasn't even half done.

FLAP. FLAP. FLAP. Ollie was getting even more frustrated. That stupid bird was going to ruin everything.

The bird flapped harder. Ollie could feel it slipping away. Ollie's drawing was getting ruined. Not only was it not complete, but it was frenzied and sloppy. The bird was now hovering a foot in the air and flapping furiously. Ollie felt the bird slip away completely and then *CRACK* Ollie's pencil snapped in two.

Ollie knew exactly what would happen next. The bird would leave. It would fly away as fast as it could from Ollie. And it would never return. But that's not what happened.

The bird flew straight at Ollie, its beak aimed at his head like the tip of a spear. Ollie put his hands up to cover his face but the bird made contact. It squawked and squealed, pecking at Ollie's head and hands in a rage. Ollie batted wildly at the bird, but he didn't connect. He couldn't see what he was doing as he was covering his face from the bird's attack.

Then *THUNK*. And *THUNK THUNK*. And a dozen more *THUNKS*. And then silence. The bird was gone. Ollie was crouched on the ground in a ball. He had tried to make himself as small as possible to avoid the bird's attack. With the bird apparently gone Ollie dared to take his hands away from his face. Long scratches crisscrossed the recently healed cat scratch Ollie had received at the park. A thin line of blood had formed in each one. Ollie burst into tears.

"What the hell is going on here?!" Gore Grater boomed.

Ollie had stopped crying but was still sitting on the ground knees up to his chest, not entirely sure what to do next.

The area where he had been sitting was a shambles. Planters were up ended. Some plants had fallen to the ground. Many of Ollie's drawings were ruined. His notepad was covered in dirt. But something more fundamental was amiss. The mangoes that were usually the old man's afternoon snack were everywhere but on the trees. It was a huge mess.

"Oh boy. You're trouble kid. You know that? You're not just in trouble, you *are* trouble." Luce Laboraties head of security pulled out his walkie-talkie cell phone, "Dr. Trace. Yes, It's me. Your son has vandalized the greenhouse. You're gonna want to come over here."

It normally took at least five minutes to get to the greenhouse from Dr. Trace's building. She made it in under three. But they were the longest three minutes of Ollie's young life.

Samantha Trace's eyes flashed with anger as she surveyed the scene. "What have you done?" she hissed at her son.

The door marked PRIVATE opened and out came the old man. As much as Ollie dreaded his mother's reaction, it was the old man he was truly afraid of disappointing. Ollie knew his mother could punish him, but somehow letting the man down felt much worse than anything his mother could have done to him.

"I see we have visitors." The old man smiled.

"I'm so so sorry for this. I knew this was a terrible idea. I promise you Ollie will be here all night cleaning up if he has to. Isn't that right Ollie?"

"I was doing my rounds nearby and I heard the noise and got here as soon as I could." Grater actually looked happy at the situation.

The old man knelt down by Ollie, and put his hand on his shoulder. "Ollie, what happened?"

Ollie took a breath, not entirely sure what happened himself. Though he was quite sure that no explanation, truth or otherwise, would satisfy his mother.

As if reading his mind, the old man looked Ollie in the eye and said, "Just tell me."

Ollie recounted what had happened, more or less. No, Ollie had no idea why the bird had attacked him. No he didn't do anything to the bird other than try to draw it. Yes, the scratches on his hand were from the bird. Yes, the huge mess on the wall was the remnants of the mangoes. And, *yes* he'd thrown the mangoes at the bird in self-defense.

Ollie knew he was in trouble. But punishment for throwing mangoes at a crazed bird seemed less worse than a trip to the psychiatric hospital. If Ollie had insisted that the mangoes had thrown themselves, he was pretty sure he'd be entering a whole new stratosphere of trouble. *Best to lie on this one small point.*

"Amazing! Just amazing!" Xander exclaimed.

Dr. Trace, Ollie, and Grater were speechless as they watched the old man start examining the mess on the wall. Mango juice was slowly sliding down the wall in long drips all along the face of the concrete. Chunks of fruit had lodged themselves in the porous material at various spots. And in one spot three mango pits had buried themselves in the wall exactly next to each other forming a black circle in the wall.

"Ollie, maybe baseball is your thing. You've got quite an arm on you." The old man smiled.

"I'm so very sorry for this. I don't know what got into him."

"Dr. Trace, I appreciate the sentiment, but I'm not quite sure why *you're* sorry. *I'm* the one who should be sorry."

Grater sputtered as if his winning lottery ticket had just been torn in half.

The old man continued, "Your son has been nothing but gracious and helpful to me. I've truly enjoyed his company and he's been a model Luce Laboratories citizen. He was in my care and was attacked by an unruly bird. Thankfully he had his wits about him and used the mangoes to defend himself before the bird did him any further harm. I knew these birds were a nuisance and should have done something about them sooner. This is completely my fault. Please accept *my* apologies."

Ollie straightened a bit.

"But Dr. Luce – at least let us clean up this mess."

Dr. Luce? Ollie thought. *As in Luce Laboratories?*

"Sam, the one thing you can do for me is call me Xander. You know I prefer that. We're a big family here. As for cleaning up, I'm perfectly capable of doing that myself. Who do you think cleans up the messes around this place?"

Realizing he had avoided the worst of it, Ollie's curiosity got the better of him. "Your name is Xander Luce? Your name is the same as the name of the company?"

Luce turned his gaze at his young charge, "Why yes. Naming your company after yourself is either the height of ego, or sign of a distinct lack of creativity. I'll let you decide which." Luce laughed at his own joke.

"Your cuts look pretty shallow but you need to wash them out properly. Why don't you head to the washroom and clean up so your mother can take you home." And then Luce added to the Head of Security, "Grater, help the boy. Then you can focus your myriad talents on finding the winged perpetrator of this assault. That seems like a security task to me."

With Grater and Ollie off to the bathroom, Luce and Samantha were now alone. Luce turned to Ollie's mother, "Dr. Trace. What of your task?

Samantha Trace had been uncomfortable when she thought her son had vandalized the company founder's workspace. But now she was positively twitchy. "Well, thank you for asking. I have Grater observing the children per your specifications."

"But he hasn't found much has he."

Trace pursed her lips but pushed forward determinedly, "No. He hasn't. But I'm hopeful. At some point he will document them demonstrating their abilities. I also have some other ideas for how to get what we need."

"I certainly hope so. I'm an old man Sam. I can't wait forever."

§

"I need to head out. I'm already late to start tonight's monitoring." Grater shot a sideways glance at Ollie as the three of them walked from the greenhouse back to the Epaphus building.

"You've been doing this for months now and what do you have to show for it." Samantha said.

Grater answered even though Trace's statement hadn't sounded like a question. "Yes. You're right of course Dr. Trace. But keep in mind that summer vacation just started recently and the weather's gotten nicer, so they're spending more time outside."

"I'm disappointed." Trace said without looking at Grater who was working hard to keep up with her brisk pace.

"I have some ideas for how to *spark* the activity you're looking for." Grater said.

"Let's hope that you do."

If Ollie noticed the discussion between his mother and the head of Luce Laboratories security, he gave no indication of it.

§

Xander Luce, founder, Chairman, and single largest shareholder of Luce Laboratories spent the next hour as its resident janitor. He saved the wall covered in mango for last. Something about it bothered him. Not the mess. Not even the force at which the mangoes must have been thrown to lodge bits and pieces in the wall. But something about the patterns the mess had formed.

Now that the rest of the area had been put back in order he could give it a proper examination. He went up close, once again marveling at the force with which the mangoes must have been hurled. Luce knew that in order to understand the essence of things sometimes it was just as important to view them from afar as it was to view them up close. He made his way across the section of the greenhouse to see the wall from far away.

Xander had lectured Ollie on how beauty could be a distraction but for the moment he let himself be distracted. And what he saw took his breath away. Now that he had a bit of distance, he could see that the mango bits on the wall were arranged to form an image – a perfect image of a bird. The feathers, the motion, the bird's energy were all depicted beautifully in bright orange bits of fruit.

The mango pits lodged in the wall formed the bird's bottomless black eye.

❧ 12 ❧

THE ALMOST-FINISHED
PORTRAIT

Ollie's mother insisted that he keep his room tidy. She liked to use that word, "tidy". It wasn't that Ollie was particularly messy, but he never felt like his room was truly his private space. What did his mother care if a book was out of place or a t-shirt lay on the floor? But she did.

She couldn't tell him what to draw though. That world was his alone. He had wanted his mother to come visit that world, but she hadn't shown a lot of excitement

133

in that regard. But the upside of her lack of interest in his hobby was that his drawings were his alone.

Today though, today was different, Ollie thought as he lay on his bed. Today, maybe, he was more glad than disappointed she had never wanted to visit his little universe of drawings. Because today, he had discovered something, something exhilarating. Not so much about his drawings as about his drawing.

Ollie knew most people would be scared, but he wasn't. Ollie had been waiting for this for as long as he could remember. He'd gone over it in the car in his mind maybe a dozen times already. His mother was lecturing him on the way home and he had nodded compliantly, but he wasn't really listening. He was replaying the events of the afternoon in the greenhouse over and over again.

When Ollie was five he'd discovered that if he closed his eyes and pressed hard on the eyelids with his fingertips he would start to see beautiful patterns of shining lights and something that one of his art teachers had later called a moiré pattern. Ollie had assumed that the periodic fuzzy electric glimpses he got of living creatures was in the same category as those shining lights he would see when he closed his eyes.

But today he knew, that wasn't the case. *It wasn't the case at all.*

When Ollie looked at the bird. When he *really* looked at it, *looked inside it,* so he could draw it, *draw out of it,* he was seeing something he wasn't supposed to see. Something that maybe no one else could see. That moment when the bird realized that Ollie could see something he wasn't supposed to – that was the moment the bird tried to fly away.

But Ollie *could* see. Ollie could see what the bird really was and Ollie refused to look away, *to let go*. And for a minute, or maybe longer, Ollie wasn't entirely sure, the bird was caught. Ollie had a hold of the bird. He had a hold of something precious that the bird needed.

But Ollie needed it more.

For the first time, if only for a moment, Ollie had the power to stop all the rejection. And it felt good.

"Well I would prefer to talk now if that's okay."

Ollie's mother's voice carried all the way upstairs from her study. She sounded angry. But there was another note in her voice too. One that Ollie wasn't familiar with. Ollie got up to close his door so he could keep thinking.

"I'm just at my wits end with him."

Ollie knew immediately his mother was talking about him. Instead of closing the door, Ollie leaned his head out further to hear better.

"There was an incident."

Ugh, he hated that she was talking about him. But, she'd heard what had happened. He'd been attacked by a crazed bird. And as far as she knew, that was hardly his fault. Even the boss of the company hadn't blamed Ollie. Why was his own mother still insisting it was Ollie's fault?

"I've tried. He gets kicked out. I'm convinced he does it on purpose."

Ollie felt shame rising red in his cheeks. He needed to leave. He wanted that new feeling again. That feeling of control. The one he'd had for a moment with the bird. Now that he understood what was possible, he knew he could do a better job. And more than anything right now he wanted to force the bird to sit still. So he could draw it. All of it.

Ollie grabbed his sketchbook and pencil and made sure to stomp extra loudly as he pounded down the staircase and past his mother's study. He wanted her to know he was leaving. He wanted her to know he could hear her. Most of all he wanted her to just stop talking.

"Where are you going?" His mother held the phone in the crook of her neck with her hand as she leaned her head out the study.

"Out." And then he added. "To draw." As angry as he was, he didn't want her to stop him.

"I'd appreciate if you could do quite a bit less stomping when you come down the stairs. And be home in time for dinner please."

Ollie acknowledged his mother's request with an affirmative mumble that was the least he could say and still escape her gaze without being called back. He flew out the front door, his face set and his expression hard.

§

"Maybe you should give him some room Samantha." He responded half-heartedly. There were not many things Henry Huitre wanted to do less than listen to Samantha Trace complain about the difficulties of raising her son, but here he was doing that very thing and there seemed to be no end in sight.

Samantha called him periodically. Up until the previous summer the calls had been about the Jordan children. At first just questions about his notes from their mother's pregnancies and their subsequent births. But when she had learned that he had moved to Madrona, Trace had started pushing for more *current* information. Henry shuddered at the memories of the previous summer's events.

But the phone calls hadn't stopped. As much as he dreaded her pressured requests for information, her sharing of the details of her life seemed somehow even worse. It made him feel like he was covered in dirt that wouldn't come off no matter how hard he scrubbed.

At first it was just complaints about her job and how she too had been pressured to get information about the Jordan children. And that she felt terrible for asking him. *But really after all she was just asking for what amounted to innocent observations.*

But then she started telling Huitre about her challenges raising her son. And then about how lonely she was. Huitre felt he knew where this was leading and he was sure he didn't want to go there. Not in a billion years. And besides, he needed to get off the phone. It was close to dog-walking time.

"He's ten. Why does he need *room*? What possible cares in the world could he have? I'm the one raising him by myself. Everything is provided for him and he just makes my life harder." Trace continued.

"I am sorry this is so hard. I bet this is normal ten-year-old behavior and will eventually pass. Uh, I am so sorry, but can we pick this up another time? I actually have to run now." Huitre said.

"Oh," was all Samantha Trace said in reply. Then silence.

"Samantha? I really am sorry. I know you're struggling right now. But I am sure you are doing the best that can be done."

"Is it that Jordan woman?" Samantha Trace's voice was soft but the question cut through the phone line like an icy knife.

"Uh, I'm sorry?" *What did she know? And more importantly, how did she know?* Huitre's mind raced. He tried to comfort himself by telling him Samantha Trace was quite crazy, and that she had made an incredibly lucky guess.

"We both know about your *history* with her and she *is* single now."

Huitre's throat felt scratchy and dry. Was Trace watching him? She'd had him watch the Jordan kids, why was it so crazy to think that she had someone watching him now. He was afraid to ask. "I have to walk the dog. He is itching to go out."

"I'm just kidding Henry. Just trying to be funny." Trace backtracked.

"Yes, of course." Huitre said weakly.

"Maybe my stress about Ollie has dulled my sense of humor. And besides, we both know that you can do much better than Julie Jordan." Samantha chuckled.

Huitre laughed faintly. "Okay, Samantha. Thanks for calling."

Huitre heard knocking at the door. *What timing,* he thought to himself. Then it was the doorhandle being turned a couple of times. As he approached the entryway he could hear Julie Jordan admonish her youngest daughter in a muffled voice about opening someone's door before you've been invited in.

"Come in. Come in." Huitre did his best to mask the horrible pit he had in his stomach with an extra-friendly greeting.

"See Mom. I *was* invited in." Cassie said.

Julie was going to explain the problem with acting on the invitation before it had been offered, but her daughter was already otherwise engaged with Rembrandt. And besides, *what was really the point,* Julie thought. Drinking a glass of whatever wine Henry had chosen was a much more pleasant prospect then spending more time arguing in circles with an eight-year-old.

§

"I don't think he likes that." Several days of early evening hangouts in the park hadn't softened Binny's attitude toward Zoe. Or more accurately, it hadn't softened her attitude towards the idea of Zoe and her little brother being part of their secret group. But here they were again, all six of them, seven including Rembrandt, spending time together in the park before dinner.

Zoe ignored Binny's advice and kept nuzzling with Rembrandt and talking to him in some sort of dog talk that she was sure Rembrandt understood. Rembrandt wasn't one to say otherwise.

Binny rolled her eyes.

Penny had started doing some eye-rolling of her own over the past few days. One day Penny had made the mistake of saying "Zoe doesn't seem so bad to me." in response to Binny's complaining. The glare she received from Binny in response was all she needed to know. Now Penny just avoided Binny when she was like this.

For the moment, Penny was doing her best to keep Gabe and Cassie as high as possible in the air on the swings she was alternately pushing.

Zach was gently stroking Rembrandt's fur while Zoe occupied the animal's primary attention. Zach preferred to be the dog's secondary focus. But each day he got a little braver in terms of how close he got and how much time he spent with the dog. Zach was determined to prove to Zoe that he could be as comfortable around animals as she was, even if that day seemed very far off in the future.

When she didn't get any traction with Zoe, Binny wandered over to the swings. "You're swinging too high."

"Stop telling me what to do." The sound of Cassie's voice changed depending on the height of the swing.

"I will tell you what to do if you're doing something I think is dangerous." Binny said.

Cassie slowed herself. "It's not dangerous." She pointed a finger in Binny's face when the swing came to a stop.

Binny made a face at Penny who registered sheepish support for her friend.

Cassie walked over to where Zoe and Zach were sitting with the dog. "I'm going to take a walk." Cassie announced. "Alone."

"Uh, I don't know." Binny was quick to say.

"I said, don't tell me what to do!" Cassie wasn't quite yelling but she was close.

Binny was about to put her foot down when Zach put his hand on her shoulder. "Maybe it's okay, if it's just around the perimeter of the park. We can see her almost the entire time."

Binny shot her brother a look. Something about his sudden maturity and reasonableness really rubbed her the wrong way. Binny was sure it was all an act for Zoe's benefit.

"I'll be very responsible. I will stay on the path. I won't cross any streets. And I will come right back here when I've gone all the way around." Cassie pleaded her case.

Zach smiled at his baby sister. "OK. We trust you."

Binny crossed her arms and looked away.

§

Cassie could hear them talking and laughing behind her but she didn't care. She was happy to be on her own, if even for a moment. Just because she was the youngest, didn't mean she was *little*.

Cassie took her time, picking little flowers along the way. Squatting to inspect ants she had spied. Searching for blackberries that hadn't really started to grow in earnest. And in general conducting her own little tour of the park. She imagined that a retinue of photographers was trailing her, snapping pictures as she inspected various points of interest. She imagined how happy her fans would be to get a glimpse of how Cassie Jordan spent her private *alone* time.

Just as Cassie had completed a twirl for the benefit of one of the members of the press, she stopped dead in her tracks. She had reached the far point of the park where there was a cluster of large bushes and a couple of picnic tables. At one of the tables sat a boy with very light fine blonde hair. But unlike Cassie's curls the boy's hair was absolutely straight. He couldn't have been more than a couple of years older than Cassie.

Cassie stayed silent. It wasn't the boy's presence that caught her attention as much as it was what he was doing. He was drawing. He had a pencil and was leisurely drawing stroke after stroke capturing the image of the bird sitting in front of him.

From her angle, Cassie could see the drawing and it was very good. Amazing even. It just looked so realistic even though it was all drawn with just a pencil. But somehow the boy had gotten the bird to sit still for him. And not just still, but close. Cassie had never seen a bird sit so still for so long so close to a human being. It was like the bird was frozen in time. Cassie stared.

"It's okay." The boy said without looking away from his target or his sketchpad. "You can come closer."

"It won't disturb him?"

"Nah, he's posing for me."

Cassie tentatively covered the ground between her and the boy to get an even better look at the lifelike illustration. The boy continued to draw.

"My name is Ollie."

"I'm Cassie."

"Nice to meet you."

"Nice to meet you too."

Cassie watched for a bit. "You're a really good drawer."

Ollie smiled. "I'm not sure that's the right word."

Something about the way Ollie said it didn't make Cassie defensive. "No I guess it's not. Artist maybe? Oh, I know, *illustrator*."

"Ooh. That's a good word." Ollie said.

"My Dad is an illustrator." Cassie said proudly.

"Oh."

Cassie watched as Ollie drew. The bird stayed put. But somehow the drawing was starting to look more lifelike than the bird itself even though it wasn't quite done. Ollie still had to finish filling in the details on the closest wing.

It was strange as the drawing was in black and white, and the actual bird was sitting there right there in the full color of the real world. The bird in the drawing looked like it could fly off at any moment, but more and more the bird posing looked like it had been stuffed and set down on the table in front of them.

"Casseeeeeeeeeeeee." Cassie heard her name being called by her brother followed by an "I told you she's irresponsible" that sounded distinctly like her sister.

"Uh oh. I gotta go." Cassie said.

"I knew there was something good about not having any brothers or sisters." Ollie smiled.

Cassie laughed.

"See ya later Cassie."

"See ya Ollie."

§

"Mom and Dad would not be okay with you letting her do this." Binny grumbled.

"I'm sure she's right behind the bushes." Zach was exasperated. Staying calm in the face of Binny's constant criticism was exhausting.

As they turned the corner, the blonde boy came into view.

"Ugh. It's him." Zoe said.

"Who?" Penny said.

"We've seen him in the park before. He got Gabe to climb higher than he should have on the jungle gym and scared him to death."

But Rembrandt wasn't looking at the boy. Rembrandt spotted the bird. Just sitting there. Not moving. Penny was holding Rembrandt's leash but she wasn't prepared when Rembrandt bolted in the direction of the bird.

Rembrandt moved faster than any of the kids had ever seen him move. He barked as he raced towards the picnic table.

The barking snapped the boy out of his reverie. He turned to greet the group of interlopers with a look of deep disappointment.

Rembrandt ignored the boy and leapt for the bird, but it was too late, the bird was already flapping and Rembrandt's jaws missed a wing by mere inches.

"I wasn't done drawing!" The blonde boy screamed at the group.

Stunned, they watched as the bird flew away, but something wasn't right. It was struggling to fly and travelling in odd loops as if its sense of direction was broken. At times it looked like it couldn't even tell up from down.

"I wasn't done." The boy said in a quieter but deeply angry voice.

"What did you do to that bird?" Zoe accused.

This seemed to catch the boy off guard for just a moment. But he recovered quickly. "Nothing. And I don't need to tell *you* anything."

"You shouldn't be here. This is our park." Zoe took a step toward the boy. She was three years older than him and could be pretty scary when she was angry.

Rembrandt barked at the boy, echoing Zoe's sentiment.

The boy glared at the dog and at Zoe in succession. "It's not your park, but I don't feel like being here anyway." He grabbed his drawing materials and stormed away from the altercation.

"Where the heck is Cassie?" Zach asked.

"I'm right here." Cassie stood behind them holding a handful of tiny purple wild flowers she had gathered.

Binny and the other kids whipped their heads around to the sound of Cassie's voice. "Where were you? You disappeared!"

Cassie stuck out her chest, "I was right there picking flowers. I stayed on the path just like I promised."

Binny didn't look satisfied.

Zach approached Cassie. "Did the boy who was sitting at the bench drawing the bird say anything to you?"

Cassie's eyes went large and her eyebrows raised innocently as she replied, "What boy?"

Zach and Binny exchanged a glance – neither responded to Cassie's claim of ignorance.

§

The image was a little bit grainy as it was shot from a distance, but unlike the video from the security cameras, this was coming to the computer screen live. He watched as the group of children approached the boy on the bench. The boy had been focusing on something but he couldn't tell what.

There appeared to be some sort of discussion or perhaps an argument and then the boy ran off. Only then did the little girl reappear from behind the bushes reuniting with her friends.

Xander Luce thought for a long time about what he'd just seen.

§

"I know it's him. I just know it. He hurt that cat and he was hurting that bird. Did you see how it was flying? Maybe he drugged it." Zoe was pacing back and forth, moving her arms about as she spoke.

"We need to take Rembrandt home right now. If that boy is hurting animals then I don't want him anywhere near this dog." Binny said.

"I agree." Zoe said in a rare moment of solidarity with Binny.

Scared of dogs or not, Zach didn't like the idea of anything happening to Rembrandt either. But he wasn't oblivious to the momentary alliance between Zoe and his sister.

"How do you know he's hurting the animals?" Cassie asked.

"I thought you didn't see the boy." Penny said.

"I didn't. I just wondered what *you* actually saw." Cassie raised her eyebrows as she inquired.

Zach watched Cassie carefully as she spoke, but kept his thoughts to himself.

"I saw enough." Zoe snapped. "And I'm going to make sure he never does it again."

"Cassie, you don't want anything to happen to Rembrandt, do you?" Binny asked her sister.

"No." Cassie's expression turned gloomy.

Zoe was still pacing angrily as Binny and Penny gathered Cassie and Rembrandt and started the walk down the hillside to Dr. Huitre's house.

After the others were out of earshot, Zach asked Zoe, "Did you mean what you said?"

"What did I say? I've been saying a lot of things." Zoe responded without a hint of humor in her voice.

Zach smiled for a moment, but then resumed his serious demeanor. "About finding out what really happened to the cat and now the bird?"

"I know what happened. I said I was going to make sure it never happened again."

"Yeah, that." Zach said.

"Why? Do you have some kind of brilliant idea on how to do that?"

Zach seemed to come to a decision. "I have something to show you."

✦ 13 ✦

THE HOLE IN THE WALL

"But you didn't really see him hurt the bird. You said so."

"I really don't understand why you keep defending someone you say you didn't even meet." Binny responded to her younger sister's interrogation.

Penny watched the interaction between the two siblings closely. Something remained unsaid, but she wasn't sure what.

"Well, it doesn't matter now. Rembrandt is fine and Mom doesn't need to worry about this." Binny concluded.

Cassie shrugged as if to say *fine with me*, and then reached for the handle to Henry Huitre's front door.

"Cassie! Remember what Mom said about knocking?" Binny admonished, but it was too late. The door was open.

Binny felt the air rush from out of her stomach. Standing in the living room was her mom and Henry Huitre... well... it looked like they were... dancing. They were definitely touching, and there was music. The music sounded old-timey.

A female voice sang over strings in French. The only words Binny could make out were 'la mer'. Binny wasn't sure what that meant. All the other words were getting jumbled. Her mother and Dr. Huitre weren't just dancing, they were slow dancing. Her mother's eyes were closed. It was so unbelievably *inappropriate*. And gross.

Years later, Binny would regret this invasion of privacy. Adult Binny would tell herself that looking inside her mother's thoughts wasn't a rational decision. It was an emotional one triggered by the sight of her mother's closed eyes. Binny would never forget that image. Binny would also tell herself that she had hardly needed to look into her mother's mind to know what she was thinking.

Binny looked into her own mind and upward to a sort of screen or projection. Her mother's thoughts were on display. It looked like something that hadn't happened yet. Or maybe something her mother was hoping would happen?

Binny saw stars glowing softly above her mother and Dr. Huitre. They leaned their elbows on the wall surrounding a rooftop patio. They alternated between taking sips of dark red wine and letting their shoulders touch as they looked out over the city below. Binny followed their gaze and recognized the Eiffel tower. But more than anything about the scene in her mother's head Binny remembered the color.

"Are you... dancing with each other?" Cassie wrinkled her nose when she said 'dancing' and punctuated her question with a giggle.

Julie and Henry had been too focused on the music to notice the door open.

"Oh, hello children." Dr. Huitre said.

Binny watched Huitre and her mother hastily disentangle. Huitre strode over to the stereo removing the needle from the record player with a dissonant scratch.

"It's a record player! My mom has one of those." Penny said.

"How was the walk kids?" Julie patted Rembrandt on the head.

Binny's shot lasers at her mother from her eyes.

"Yes. I like the sound of the vinyl." Huitre answered Penny.

"Fine Mom. Can we go now?" Cassie made an impatient face.

§

"Just trust me. This is something you need to see." Zach assured Zoe.

"OK. But I need to go home soon. If I'm too late bringing Gabe home, I'll get in trouble."

Gabe was just happy to be along for the adventure. They wound their way through the Madrona hillside heading east from the park through tree-lined streets and mostly on overgrown switchbacking pedestrian paths. After a long flight of stairs they found themselves at an entrance to the Madrona Woods.

"It's getting dark." Gabe said.

"No it's not. It's just the trees blocking out the light." Zoe answered. And then to Zach, "It's in here? What you want to show me?"

"Yeah. Just a couple more minutes."

Zach was about to take a step, and then turned to Zoe and Gabe, his eyes serious, "Before I show you, I need you to promise me to keep it a secret."

Gabe nodded solemnly.

"How can I promise to keep something secret that I haven't even seen?" Zoe complained.

"Just promise please." Zach implored.

Zoe nodded, but inside remained non-comittal.

The woods felt extra quiet at this hour. Everyone had gone home for dinner. Zach had a pit in his stomach about what he was about to do. But it was the right thing, wasn't it? *Though Binny wouldn't think so.*

Zoe was convinced that the white-haired boy was doing something to the animals. When they'd seen the hurt cat Zach had his doubts about any connection to the white-haired boy. But when he saw the bird sitting next to the boy, and more importantly when he'd seen how the bird had flown away on that awkward and painful looking flight path, Zach knew that something was off, and that boy had something to do with it.

Zoe's instincts had been right all along. And Zach's instincts told him that Zoe was going to confront this boy one way or another. And she shouldn't do that on her own.

Zach knew that Binny would be angry. Probably very angry. But Caleb had said that they needed to be a team. And Zach agreed. That was why he was about to do this. No matter what Binny thought Zach's reasons were, Zach was just following Caleb's advice. That was all.

§

"Are you coming honey?"

Binny remained on Huitre's porch with her arms folded.

"Binny?" Julie implored her daughter.

A deep saturated pink. That was the color Binny had seen.

"Binny, it's time to go home." Julie repeated.

"Home? Which home is that?"

"Binny please. Let's go to our home."

Binny knew what pink meant. "*Our* home? I don't know where that is. I know where *your* home is. And I know where *my* home is. But I don't know where *our* home is. And you know why that is?"

"Binny please." Julie sounded tired.

Binny had seen the pink in Zach's thoughts after he'd first met that Zoe girl. Zach had been positively pink for days. "There is no *our* home anymore. And that's because you left."

Penny shifted on her feet not sure where to look.

"Honey, I didn't leave."

"Well I'm still there. Cassie and Zach are still there. Dad is still there. But you're not. So I'm pretty sure you were the one that left."

"That's not what happened." Julie's voice only slightly more than a strained whisper.

If Binny could ban one color from the spectrum it would be pink. She never wanted to see that shade again. "And now you're drinking wine and dancing with Dr. Huitre dreaming of flying off to Paris with him while Daddy sits at home alone. This is *all your fault.*" Binny said the last three words as if they were underlined.

Julie Jordan looked like she'd been punched in the stomach.

Tears streamed down Binny's cheeks. "I'll come home to *my* home when I'm good and ready. And I'm

155

glad you don't live there anymore because I don't want to see you." Binny turned and ran towards the woods.

Julie tried to hide her own tears as she turned to Penny. "Could you please go after her and make sure she's safe. Just stick with her until she's ready to come home?"

"Of course." Penny said.

"Me too!" Cassie piped up.

All Julie could say was "OK."

§

"Where? I don't see anything." Zoe asked.

"Right... here." Zach pulled some of the ivy aside from the metal door.

"Oh wow. I didn't even see it." Zoe said.

"Cool." Gabe added.

Zach opened the metal door and flipped on the lights that lined the long hallway into the abandoned bomb shelter that sat under the Madrona woods.

They walked until they ended up in what was now the makeshift Madrona Heroes headquarters. Not much had really changed since they first came upon it the previous summer. The dust still lay thick on most things.

Zoe said in a low voice, "What is this place?"

Gabe looked around the room wide-eyed coming upon Penny and Cassie's now faint dust drawing from the previous summer, "The Madrona Heroes? What's that?"

"That's why I brought you both here." Zach's gaze moved from Gabe back to Zoe. He couldn't tell what she was thinking. He usually couldn't. It was disconcerting. But he'd come this far, and even if he wanted to turn back, he wasn't sure that in Zoe's presence he could come up with a plausible excuse for why he'd brought them down here other than the truth.

Zach pushed away the knot in his stomach that was woven out of thick strands of his sister's disapproval and dove in. "I know you don't want to talk about what happened at the playground the first time we met, so I won't."

Zoe's eyebrows inched upward, but she stayed silent.

"I, well we, well, I, well..." Zach knew what he shouldn't say, but what he should say was another matter.

Gabe was listening earnestly with an innocent look on his face.

Zach found it easier to concentrate if he looked more at Gabe than at Zoe. Sometimes, wondering what she was thinking made it impossible for him to form a complete sentence.

Zach tried again. "I have a superpower."

"Wha – " Zoe's lips made the shape of an 'O'. A beautiful O.

"Well, maybe it's not super, but it's a power nonetheless. Or if we're being accurate. I have a certain skill or talent that appears to be unique among humans."

Zach snuck a look back at Zoe's face. He decided he'd better hurry. "I have a really good memory."

Zoe's shoulders slumped. "Oh please. that Pi thing? I could do that given time."

Zach felt her trust slipping away.

"That's awesome." Gabe said.

"It's not just really good. It's exceptional." Zach explained.

"Thanks for showing us the cool hideout, but I better get Gabe home in time for dinner." Zoe motioned to her brother to leave.

Zach took a breath, "0582097494459230781640628".

Zoe stopped moving.

Zach continued, "6208998628034825342117067".

"What are those numbers?" Gabe asked.

"Ask your sister." Zach replied.

Gabe looked up at Zoe.

She replied, "They're the next fifty digits of Pi."

"Want me to keep going?" Zach allowed himself a small smile.

"I suppose there's no point in me checking your accuracy?" Zoe asked.

"Nope." Zach's smile got a little bigger.

"How many can you do?"

Zach could tell the wheels in Zoe's mind were turning. "I memorized about the first 500 before I got bored. But give me a few minutes to read beyond that and I'm sure I could do more."

"OK. I admit it. That and the clubhouse are very cool. In fact, really really cool. I'm impressed." Zoe paused. It looked like she was searching for just the right words. "I'm just not sure how all *this* is connected to me."

"It's not just me. Penny, Binny, Cassie, all have powers too. Nobody else knows. This is our secret hideout. And I believe two things. First, if we use our powers together we can figure out what happened to the animals that got injured, and second," Zach took a deep breath, "I think you're one of us."

§

Binny thought to herself that if she never ever saw that shade of dark pink again she'd be quite happy. *What was her mother thinking? Dancing. So unbelievably gross.*

Binny's legs carried her through the woods on automatic. Her brain dedicated the absolute minimum amount of power to navigation while the rest was on absolute fire with rage and sadness. But what Binny felt most of all was betrayal.

Binny was so lost that she didn't notice that the lights were already on as she entered the long concrete tunnel.

§

"What do you mean, I'm one of you?" Zoe asked Zach.

"What is *she* doing here?!?"

Zach, Zoe, and Gabe jumped a little, they were so surprised by Binny's sudden appearance in the bunker.

"I can explain." Zach took a tentative step forward.

"You're the same. You're just like her. You're both the same." Binny was wailing now. "Neither of you care. You just do what you want. No matter how it affects everyone else."

Zoe looked like she was about to respond, but a look from Zach quieted her. He whispered, "She's not talking about you."

Binny didn't hear over her tears. She just kept repeating herself. "The same. You're both the same."

"I'm so sorry Binny." Zach knelt down next to his sister. "What happened?"

"What do *you* care? You weren't there. You're too busy with *her*." Binny motioned towards Zoe.

"I care."

"There you are." Penny and Cassie burst into the room huffing and panting.

Penny knelt down next to Binny as well. "Your mom was worried when you ran off."

Cassie too patted her crying sister on the back, but after a moment, noticed the new visitors to their secret underground lair. Cassie stood up, walked over to Gabe and Zoe spreading her hands wide, a big smile on her face, and said, "Welcome. Welcome to Madrona Heroes headquarters."

§

Binny had retreated to a seat in the corner by the shelving. Penny sat by her side trying to be comforting, but couldn't really think of much to do other than wait it out. She wasn't sure she'd ever seen Binny this hurt and angry.

Zoe stood on the other side of the room, arms crossed, and also looking relatively unhappy. Periodically Zach would shuttle between Binny and Zoe. None of what he said to either seemed to make the situation any better.

"Are you okay Binny?" Cassie tried to comfort her sister.

"Leave me alone."

"Fine. Sorry I tried to help." Cassie marched off and offered Gabe a tour of their lair.

"I didn't ask to come here." Zoe said to Zach in a low voice on one of his trips to try and fix things.

"I know. It's my fault." Zach acknowledged.

"Of course it's your fault." Zoe's words jumped on the end of Zach's statement.

"She shouldn't be here. Neither of them should be. We discussed this." Binny had gotten up from her chair and was now pointing at Zoe.

"Bet you can't catch me." Cassie said to Gabe.

"Don't point at me. It's rude." Zoe took a step towards Binny.

"I bet I can." Gabe responded.

Gabe started running in circles around the large room with Cassie in tow.

"What's *rude* is being somewhere you weren't invited." Binny pointed again for emphasis.

"I *was* invited." Zoe took another step towards the center of the room. Zoe and Binny were six feet apart. The closer they got to each other, the louder each got.

"Not by me you weren't. Not by me. One person doesn't get to make decisions that affect everyone else."

Penny kept putting her hand on Binny's shoulder as much to comfort her as to stop her from advancing any further.

"Binny, just listen for a second. Zoe belongs here." Zach said.

Cassie and Gabe chased each other through the room with increasing speed and volume.

"Can you two please stop running around." Binny yelled.

"We can't hear ourselves talk." Zoe added.

Cassie and Gabe showed no sign that they'd heard either of their siblings.

Binny turned back to her brother, "No she does not."

"This place is for kids with powers." Zach said.

"You told her? You told her about our powers? What happened to not telling anyone?" The incredulous hurt expression looked like it might become a permanent resident on Binny's face.

"I told you. She's one of us." Zach insisted.

"You told her what happened at the playground?" Now it was Zoe's turn to look incredulous.

"I, I, –" Zach stuttered.

The noise from Cassie and Gabe's horseplay was reverberating throughout the concrete room.

Binny and Zoe turned to their younger siblings and yelled at the exact same moment, "Can you two please STOP!"

Nobody knew whether it was their booming voices that distracted Cassie, made her more determined to run faster, or had nothing at all to do with what happened. One thing was clear, regardless of the reason, Cassie was going to hit the ground.

As Zoe and Binny yelled, Cassie's leg got a little too far out from under her on a turn and she found herself sliding towards the wall on her side. In moments her leg was on fire where the momentum dragged it across the concrete floor.

Gabe was so focused on catching Cassie that he didn't realize until too late that Cassie's slide was not an effort to escape his clutches. Gabe wanted to catch Cassie but he didn't want to trample her. In the split-second he had to decide, the only option he saw available that didn't involve him crushing Cassie's skull or ribcage was to jump over her.

The kids hadn't inspected the walls much other than to draw in the dust that covered them. The walls of the shelter were mostly poured concrete. But one section of wall was covered in a big piece of plywood turned streaky gray with age. It was that precise part of the wall with which Gabe Flowers made contact in his desperate attempt to avoid Cassie's now limp body on the ground.

Instinctively protecting his face, Gabe turned as he jumped so by the time he made impact with the wall he was mostly turned around with his back and his side taking the brunt of the impact.

The last thing everyone saw was Gabe flying through the wall, his arms and legs trailing after him like streamers from a kite. Gabe's scream, which lasted much longer than seemed logical, ended with a distant thump. And just like that, Gabe was gone.

All that remained now was a gaping dark hole where there used to be wall.

⇢ 14 ⇠

THE AWFUL SMELL

"**O**h no." Zoe's voice quavered as she ran to the hole in the wall.

Binny and Zach scrambled over to Cassie who was trying to sit up.

"My leg hurts." Cassie was upright now and rolling up her leggings to inspect the damage.

"Ooh. It's just a scrape. You're gonna be okay." Binny made an effort to sound cheerful.

"Uuuuuuucccccchhhhh." Zoe put her hands up to her face as she backed away from the hole reeling. "It smells awful."

The smell hit the other kids soon thereafter. Penny looked like she was going to retch.

"He's in there. What if he's..." Zoe left the question unfinished, suspended. As the realization of what had happened sank in, she shuddered and started sobbing. "What am I going to do?"

Zach felt his heart hurt when he heard Zoe's wail over her brother. He looked at Binny, eyes pleading.

Binny left Zach to nurse Cassie's leg and strode over to where Zoe was alternating between sobbing and gasping at the terrible smell coming from the hole in the wall.

Zoe and the other children's eyes were glued to Binny as she slowly put her right fist in her left palm and closed her eyes.

Binny stood there for a moment, concentrating intensely, and then suddenly opened her eyes and turned to Zoe, "He's alive."

Relief and surprise washed over Zoe's face. "What? How do you know? What do you mean?" Zoe looked like she was praying that this wasn't some sort of a trick Binny was playing.

"Zach didn't tell you?"

"Didn't tell me what?" Zoe asked, her voice tense.

"I can read people's minds."

"You what?" Zoe didn't know whether Binny was joking or not.

Binny repeated herself more slowly stopping just shy of condescension. "If he were dead, I wouldn't be able to read his mind. I think he's asleep, but he's not dreaming."

Seeing the look of doubt on Zoe's face, Zach added "It's true. Trust me."

"I can tell when someone's dreaming because the picture of their thoughts looks all foggy. Right now with Gabe all I *see* is fog."

"Dreamless sleep." Penny added quietly.

"But something's not quite right." Binny seemed to be analyzing something she was seeing.

"What do you mean?" Zoe asked.

"He's fine." Binny looked back at Zoe reassuring her. "He's just not where he should be. He looks farther away somehow."

Seeing Zoe's confusion Zach added, "She can get kind of a map of where everyone is located in a space by seeing all their feelings. She calls it 'zooming out'."

"Yeah, it's like he's somehow below us."

Zoe felt her heart start to beat faster again. "We need to get him out of there. I'm worried he won't be able to breathe."

"I'll do it!" Cassie was now standing upright quickly forgetting about her injury in a way only young children can.

Zoe smiled at Cassie.

"We'll do it together." Zach said.

§

"Careful with her Zach, she's going to get scraped." Binny lectured her brother. Zoe couldn't quite get through the hole herself, so Zach, Binny, and Penny helped lift her over what remained of the wall and through the space that Gabe had made with his body.

Zoe turned her head back towards Binny offering a small smile of acknowledgement.

"Be careful Zoe. It's crazy dark in there." Zach said hoping his voice contained an appropriate amount of concern for someone who was just a friend.

A look passed between Penny and Binny.

"At least the smell is fading a bit." Zoe said as she tentatively explored the other side of the wall.

"What do you see?" Penny asked.

"I know this sounds weird, but it's almost like a ticket booth." Zoe felt along the wall for a light switch. "I can't find a way to turn on the lights either."

Remembering her mission, Zoe, looked past the dirty glass of the booth and in the direction that her little brother had travelled. "It's crazy dark." Zoe heard the word 'dark' echo. "And I think it's big."

"My turn." Cassie pushed a stool up next to the hole and was scrambling through the opening.

"Cassie, wait, it's not safe." Binny put a hand on her shoulder.

"You're not the only who can help you know." Cassie said.

"It's okay, we're all going to go through and help." Zach reassured.

"There's an edge." Zoe said with more fear in her voice than she intended.

"What do you mean *an edge*?" Binny asked.

"I was feeling along the wall and then it ends. The floor too. It's like I'm on the edge of a pool. A huge pool. I'm not sure how deep it is."

"Wait for us." Zach said as they helped Cassie through the hole and followed in suit.

Zach and Penny were on their knees trying to peer into the abyss of the dark room with no luck. Very little of the light from the room they had been in extended into the extremely short hallway in which they found themselves.

"He's down there." Zoe's heart was beating even faster.

Binny could see Gabe's thoughts in her mind. Binny put a hand on Zoe's shoulder. "He's fine. I think his dreams are even starting to come back too. Something candy related?" Now Binny looked puzzled.

Zoe smiled despite herself. "That's him alright." Zoe sidled up as close to the edge as she dared. "Gabe? Gabe?

Are you okay?" Her voice bounced around in the dark echoing and unanswered.

"I want to look." Cassie said.

"There's not enough room Cassie. It's really tight in here." Zach tried to placate his sister.

"Everyone's had a turn but me." Cassie complained.

"There's nothing to see." Penny added trying to be helpful. "It's pitch black."

Cassie's arms were crossed, her face an angry scrunch. "You keep saying we're going to do this together, but you keep ignoring me. I can help too!"

"I'm sure turning invisible will be a big help." Binny said.

"She can turn invisible?" Zoe asked incredulously, momentarily distracted by the endless supply of amazing news.

"It's not *that* impressive. She can't do it on purpose." Zach chuckled.

"Aaaaaaaaaaaaaaaaaaaah!" Cassie growled in frustration.

A lone gleaming silvery tendril of light sprouted out of Cassie's clenched right fist. It was quickly followed by another from her left ankle. The tendrils snaked up their respective limbs sprouting small offshoots like ivy.

"She always gets this shiny stuff before she disappears." Zach explained.

170

"I've never seen this." Penny said with awe. "It's beautiful."

In moments Cassie's entire body was covered in glowing swarming electric ivy.

"And buh-bye." Binny said.

But Cassie didn't disappear. She just stood there shining brightly.

"You didn't disappear." Binny wasn't sure whether she was making a statement or asking a question.

Even Cassie was surprised at her new luminescence. She waggled her fingers in front of her face watching the trails of light emanating from the ivy wrapped around them.

It took Zach a few seconds to snap out of his reverie, wondering why Cassie hadn't disappeared. But Gabe's welfare was the bigger concern for the moment.

By this point, the light emanating from Cassie was bright enough to make the newly discovered space relatively visible to everyone else.

"Oh wow. It's huge." It wasn't a swimming pool at all. It was a cavernous room. It was the size of a small airplane hangar. Zach could see the entire space like a blueprint from their vantage point. It was subdivided into a couple of dozen rooms of varying sizes. The space had been dug deep into the hillside with the ceiling suspended two stories above the concrete floor.

Zach looked down, "There's Gabe!"

Gabe lay on his side a full story below the others. He wasn't moving.

"He looks hurt." Zoe looked scared as she peered over the edge.

Zach pointed below the precipice on which they were standing. "There's a ladder." Zach lowered himself onto the metal ladder that had been bolted to the sheer concrete wall.

Zoe was next. Gritting her teeth she followed Zach's example.

Binny followed but not before she noticed how tightly Zoe was gripping the ladder. "Take your time. He's fine. We'll get him out of here."

At the bottom Zach noticed old looking signs with arrows. One said "LIVING QUARTERS". Another pointing in the opposite direction said "COMMAND CENTER".

Zoe rushed to Gabe's side when she made it all the way down. After Binny and Penny had descended, Zach caught a still glowing Cassie jumping from the last rung to the ground.

"See. I told you I could help!" Cassie's arms were on her hips as she waited for acknowledgement from the group.

"You were right." Zach smiled at his sister's excitement. Zach thought privately about the fact that his sister could now do two things. Not quite on purpose, but still two. He, Binny, Penny, and Zoe for all he knew, could only do one. Zach's thoughts were interrupted by a voice from behind.

On the ground next to his concerned sister a woozy Gabe raised himself on one elbow and said, "Who farted?"

§

Zach hadn't known Zoe and Gabe very long but he'd never seen her so protective of him. She was fussing over him, inspecting his extremities and making him bend every joint he had.

Zach understood Zoe's concerns as Gabe had fallen quite a distance. Zach imagined that Gabe had landed in the small hallway that they had first entered, and then momentum had carried Gabe over the edge and into the huge room below. Even though the space was lined with concrete Zach couldn't help but think of it as some sort of cave.

"I told you, I'm not hurt." Gabe was more interested in Cassie's brilliant tendrils than he was in his sister's ministrations. "That's awesome!"

"Thank you." Cassie couldn't keep the wide grin off her face. "What can *you* do?"

Gabe's face changed as he contemplated the question. "Well, my sister can make these huge holes in the ground."

Zoe interjected quickly, "Well, that's not exactly true."

"You're groundbreaking!" Penny smiled.

Zach looked at Zoe, his eyebrows raised and his lips pursed. He didn't say anything.

"Okay, I guess that's exactly true." Zoe paused. "But it just happens. I never know when it's going to happen until it's already done."

"That's like me." Cassie was euphoric at having another person who couldn't make their power come on command. "It's always a surprise. But now I can do two things. I can turn invisible and I can shine." Cassie's smile got even toothier.

Binny noticed Gabe's face getting longer as Cassie spoke. She bent down in front of him. "What's wrong?"

"I don't have a power."

Binny adjusted herself so she was sitting cross-legged in front of Gabe and looking up at him as she spoke. "Last summer, I found out that Zach had this amazing memory, my sister could turn invisible, and my best friend could make objects fall apart with just a touch."

Zoe mouthed the word 'cool' to Penny who tapped her finger on an imaginary object in response.

"I couldn't do anything out of the ordinary. No special powers at all. I felt pretty bad."

"Really?" Gabe asked.

"Really." Binny reassured.

"So you're like me? You don't have powers?" Gabe hoped out loud.

"Actually... no. I can read minds now."

Gabe looked deflated.

"But that's not the point. The point is that I didn't need special powers to be part of the group. Zach, Penny, and Cassie accepted me no matter what. And at the moment when I needed a power the most, it came to me." Binny nodded gently to Gabe as she spoke.

"So you think I'll get a power when I most need it?"

Binny hesitated, catching Zach and Zoe's eyes before she answered. "Honestly Gabe, I don't really know. Maybe crashing through walls without getting hurt is your power." Binny smiled, and even Gabe laughed a little. "But I know this. Whatever powers you do or don't have, you're one of us."

§

"Uh oh." Penny was still transfixed by Cassie's glowing tendrils when she noticed that one of them had started to flicker. "I think it's gonna get dark soon."

"Oh no. What time is it?" Zoe and Gabe said almost at the same moment.

"No, I mean in here. I think Cassie is starting to turn off."

"There's no reception down here. And we're late for dinner. Dad is gonna kill me." Zach started moving everyone towards the ladder.

"Come on Gabe, I'm in the same trouble. We've gotta move." Zoe said.

By the time they'd all made it out of the hole Gabe had made on his famous flight, Cassie was almost entirely faded back to her normal self.

"And you couldn't keep it going?" Penny asked.

"I didn't even know I could do it at all." Cassie responded.

"Well, even if you can't control it, it's still very cool. Being able to make something, even just light, is so much cooler than just breaking stuff."

"We're all going to get broken if we don't hurry home." The stress was clear in Zach's voice.

"Before we go, one important thing." Binny turned to Zoe and Gabe, paying special attention to Gabe as she spoke. "No matter what, we never tell anyone about our powers, or about our hideout. OK?"

"Yeah yeah. Zoe already told me." Gabe rolled his eyes.

§

As they closed the large metal door behind them, Zach said, "So, tomorrow morning? We all meet here to explore the cave?"

Nods and smiles all around.

"And we bring flashlights." Zoe said, and then looking at Cassie, "Just in case you're not in the mood to light our way."

Cassie nodded approvingly.

"And air freshener." Penny added.

Zach's cell phone started beeping insistently. Zach braced himself as he pulled it out of his pocket. He tapped on the face of his phone responding to his father's sixth text in the last twenty minutes.

Zach put the phone back in his pocket and said to the group with a resigned look on his face. "See you in the morning. Or in a year depending on how long I get grounded for."

❖ 15 ❖

THE HUNGRY HERO

"Did you see what she did?" Binny whispered to her brother as they made the trek up the hill towards the Jordan house. Zoe and Gabe had already split off heading to theirs. Penny and Cassie were skipping ahead of the older Jordan siblings.

"Uh huh." Zach answered without taking his focus off the hill in front of him.

"She can do two things."

"Kind of."

"What do you mean?" Binny asked.

"She always lights up just before she disappears. Maybe this is the same power but she's just stopping short before she disappears?"

Binny thought about Zach's suggestion for a moment before replying. "Maybe. But even so, there are two different effects so it's *like* she can do two things."

"She still can't do it on demand. And honestly, I'm not sure if that's good or bad. Cassie being able to disappear or light up or anything when she wants may be more trouble than it's worth."

Binny laughed. "Do you think that's true for all of us?"

"That our powers could be a good or bad thing?" Zach's eyebrows were raised in surprise.

"Ha. No. Do you think we might get more powers?"

A look swept across Zach's face that Binny didn't recognize. "Uh, me? No. I hadn't thought about that. I mean, who knows?"

"Do you ever hope you get another one?" Binny asked.

Zach stared straight ahead. "Never." But when Binny wasn't looking, he squinted over in her direction wondering if she'd been reading his thoughts.

§

"Honestly, I don't know where you could be that your cell phone doesn't get signal. Is it really so difficult to text that you're going to be late? You had us very worried."

Zach looked anywhere but directly at his father as he listened to the speech. It was only half an hour. Zach thought his father was overreacting.

The entire Jordan family was standing in the entry way to the house. Penny had gone home to her house for dinner.

"Binny was the one that ran away." Cassie offered from the sidelines.

Zach's head whipped around to look at Binny while Binny's whipped around to glare at her sister.

"She did not run away. She needed some alone time. It's fine." Julie offered by way of explanation. "Let's eat dinner before it gets cold."

Binny shot an angry look in her mother's direction briefly before crossing her arms and resuming her glare at Cassie.

"I guess." Jay said as he moved towards the kitchen. "But Zach, I want you to seriously think about what I'm saying. If there's a place where there's no phone reception, I'm afraid that's a place you can no longer go when you're out and about."

§

"Cassie, you are voracious." Julie Jordan said as she put a third helping of dinner on her plate.

"Whuts four eitches?" Cassie responded through a mouth full of tuna melt.

"I'd appreciate it if you waited until you finished chewing before you asked." Julie gave her daughter a knowing look for emphasis. "And it's not Four H's, It's vor-ay-shuss." She sounded out the word. "It means – "

"Wanting or devouring great quantities of food." Zach interjected.

Julie turned to her son, "Well, yes. Thanks Zach. I was going to say "monsterish eating" but your definition sounds more official.

"It is official. I read it."

"Well nice memorization then." Julie said.

Binny narrowed her eyes at her brother. She didn't approve of anything that could lead her parents to discovering what she and her siblings could do.

"Zach's not the only who can do things you know." Cassie piped up taking a momentary break from finishing her sandwich.

Binny raised her eyebrows at her brother as if to say *see what you did now*?

"Oh really?" Jay smiled at his youngest.

"Really."

"Like what?" Jay asked.

"Owwwwwwwww." Binny yelled. "I knocked my shin into the table leg."

Now it was Cassie's turn to shoot her sister an angry look for trying to change the subject with her fake injury.

"Are you okay sweetie?" Julie asked her daughter.

Binny ignored her mother and just repeated "ow ow ow" over and over again.

Jay shook his head in confusion at Binny's sudden injury and turned back to Cassie. "You were telling us what *you* can do? Hopefully it doesn't involve any dinner-related injuries."

"Well, I used to only be able to turn invisible. But now I can light up too."

Binny's jaw dropped. Zach's eyes went wide.

"Awesome!" Jay said.

"That's lovely honey. We're very proud of you." Julie said.

"I hope you'll use your powers for good." Jay added as an afterthought. "Always for good."

Cassie nodded as she chewed another bite.

§

KNOCK KNOCK.

Binny was sitting on her bed, her face sticking out of her blanket cave, huddled over her computer watching skateboarding videos on the internet.

"Binny?" Zach said.

"What."

"Can we talk for a second?" Zach said more insistently.

Binny closed her laptop and turned toward her brother unsure of what to expect.

"I just came to... to apologize."

"For what?"

"For bringing Zoe and Gabe to the shelter. And also for saying... what I said yesterday. About Mom and Dad. I'm sorry."

"Thanks. But you were right."

"About Zoe and Gabe?" Zach asked.

"About them, and about Mom and Dad."

"I'm sorry." Zach wasn't sure what else to say.

"No, don't be. You were right. That's been made very clear." Binny said.

"What do you mean?" Zach wondered why his sister had suddenly changed her tune.

"Never mind. I'm sick of thinking about it."

"Well, you were really nice to Gabe and to Zoe today. I really appreciate it. Together I think we can figure out what happened to those animals."

Binny paused while she searched for the most diplomatic words she could think of. "I know that Zoe is very sure that someone hurt those animals, but I'm not so sure. Animals get hurt in nature all the time with no help from people."

183

"You saw that bird. Did it look natural to you?"

"Well, no." Binny conceded.

Zach tried a different avenue. "Look, maybe that boy didn't hurt them. But I think we'll have an easier time figuring out what happened if we work together rather than apart. And isn't that the point of getting these powers in the first place? Using them to help others?"

"You mean I'm not supposed to use them to win bets and get good gossip?" Binny smiled.

Zach's shoulders relaxed as he laughed.

But Binny still had a perplexed look on her face.

"What is it?" Zach asked his sister.

"I'm just thinking. I know that Luce Labs didn't give us our powers, and Penny is the proof of that. But..." Binny looked like she wasn't sure how to proceed. "I know this is weird but I just thought, that maybe it was something about our little hillside. Maybe that's why we were the only ones with powers. But now Zoe has a power, how could she have gotten it?"

"She does live in the neighborhood."

"True. But not as close as Penny. And she just moved here recently. And Gabe doesn't have a power. I just..." Binny looked down at her hands as she spoke. "I know you saw *something*. But are you sure that Zoe really has a power? Could it have been a coincidence maybe? Quicksand?"

"Quicksand? In Madrona Park?" Zach smiled mischievously.

"I don't know. I'm just asking if you're sure." Binny threw up her hands.

"Yeah. I'm sure. There's something special about her."

Binny smiled at her brother. "Maybe you should tell *her* that."

Zach flushed a deep saturated pink.

❖ 16 ❖

THE NEW HEADQUARTERS

"Don't drop them." Zach yelled down to Penny as he lowered the hoodie they had wrapped around the bundle of flashlights. They had been snuck out of their respective homes that morning to aid in the exploration of the newly discovered part of the bomb shelter.

"We don't know what's down here, so we need to stick together." Binny instructed.

"I'm with you." Gabe wrapped his arm around Binny's torso.

Binny smiled awkwardly not sure quite what to do with her new adoring fan.

"How about we all go together until we know this place is safe?" Zach offered.

The small group spent the next hour exploring the space methodically. Periodically Cassie and Gabe would run ahead only to be reined in by the older children.

Zach estimated the entire space was roughly 120 feet long by 100 feet wide, and about 25 feet deep. The different rooms they found all had ceilings, and the hallways between the rooms were open air, so it gave the impression of them being in a sort of concrete village as the ceiling of the cavernous space was a full story higher than the ceilings of the various rooms.

When they had completed exploring the entire space, Zach had formed a mental map of sorts. A row of dormitories separated by gender and age – "ADULT MALES", "FEMALE CHILDREN", etc. ran along the leftmost wall. Mattressless bunkbeds enough for thirty people in each room filled seven rooms in all.

Across from the rooms with the bunk beds were a row of bathrooms with separate toilets and showers. The porcelain fixtures looked unused and were covered by a thick layer of dust.

Additional areas including a small infirmary, a kitchen, a library, a laundry, and two large empty rooms marked "ADULT SOCIAL ROOM" and "CHILDRENS SOCIAL ROOM" respectively. For the most part the rooms were empty of everything but large pieces of furniture and heavy equipment.

When the children finished their tour they found themselves in a large open space at one end of the shelter. On one side were long folding tables with attached stools. It reminded Zach of a cafeteria lunch room. The remaining open space had of all things, wood flooring.

"Can you please stop squeaking?" Binny said.

"It's fun." Cassie and Gabe were rubbing the soles of their sneakers on the hardwood making loud echoing squeaking sounds.

"Please?" Zach implored.

"OK. OK."

"Well, it seems like we were never actually *in* the bomb shelter. That room upstairs was just the entryway." Zach concluded.

"Well, this is one pretty fancy bomb shelter if you ask me. Who needs a dance floor when they're hiding from nuclear war?" Penny looked at the floor as she spoke.

"It's not a dance floor." Zoe was pointing above their heads. Above their heads seven flashlights illuminated a basketball hoop and backboard suspended from the wall. There was no net, but the rest looked fine.

"Oooh. Can we play?" Gabe asked.

"Not unless you saw a decaying basketball somewhere in this mess." Zoe said.

"Can we bring one?" Cassie asked.

Zach didn't answer her question directly. "I think we're going to need to bring a lot of things."

§

Cassie and Gabe were playing some form of flashlight tag running around the complex, while the older children had found one last undiscovered room. There had been signs pointing to a "COMMAND CENTER" but they hadn't found such a place until they discovered a staircase hiding behind the folded dining tables.

The staircase was the preferred real estate for the shelter's spider population so there was a fair amount of cobweb removal to do. With that obstacle removed the older children found themselves in a long room positioned on the second story of the shelter. Other than dust, the room's only inhabitants were long metal tables and a few chairs.

Dust-covered glass let the inhabitants of the room look out over the entire space. There was a smaller room at the end with more bunk beds, and then another staircase that led back up to the small hallway that Gabe had "discovered" with his ad-hoc cannonball.

"This would have been a much easier way to come down than that ladder." Zoe didn't hide her distaste for the metal ladder she'd had to climb.

"We didn't notice it yesterday." Zach added, rocking back and forth in one of the chairs with his hand on his chin.

"Can I be the first one to say, this place is *awesome!*" Penny offered.

"This place is dark and dirty." Binny responded. After getting a look from the other three she hastily added, "and awesome."

§

Binny closed her eyes for a moment and pronounced, "Seventeen!"

"Amazing. You were right again." Gabe was giggling. "Okay. You won't get this one."

"That's not a number." Binny waggled her finger at Gabe.

"Sure it is." Gabe insisted.

"Numbers can't have the letters Q and F in them."

The kids had congregated in the large open area that they'd already started calling 'The Gym'. Penny was also demonstrating her powers for everyone's entertainment. Two of the ten tables lay in tons of little pieces as a result of Penny's demonstration. A third would have been destroyed at Cassie and Gabe's urging but Zach intervened saying, "Let's stop breaking stuff. We may want to use some of the things down here."

Gabe had excitedly urged Cassie to glow again or turn invisible.

"She can't do it on purpose." Binny explained.

Cassie looked like she was about to get angry and Binny added, "She can't do it on purpose *yet*."

That seemed to placate Cassie but only for a moment. "I can too. I just don't feel like it right now."

Gabe kept insisting, but Binny let the subject drop by suggesting the guessing game. Penny and the two younger children sat in a circle trying to come up with increasingly complex thoughts for Binny to read.

Zach and Zoe had retreated to the side of the court where they sat on the floor, backs up against the wall.

"Don't you want to do some showing off too?" Zoe joked with Zach.

"Nah." Zach smiled.

"Can I ask you a question?"

"Sure."

"This is cool and all. Really. But how is this forgotten shelter going to help stop that kid from hurting any more animals?"

"Honestly?" Zach asked.

"Yeah." Zoe responded.

Zach took a moment to think before he looked Zoe in the eyes. "I don't really know. Not yet anyway. But I think that working together on making something – on making this place into a real hideout, will help us work together to figure out what's going on with the animals."

Zoe nodded in silence.

"Can I ask you a question?"

"Yes." Zoe said.

"Do you think this is ridiculous?" Zach paused to gather his words for a moment. "I mean, super powers, and secret hideouts, and going on animal rescue mission."

"Honestly?" Zoe asked.

"Yeah." Zach smiled.

"Kinda."

Zach laughed.

Zoe added, "But I'm having fun."

§

"So then why do the lights upstairs work?" Binny asked. They had found light switches at various points on the walls but none of them had any effect.

"We think the space down here is meant to be completely self-sufficient. Off-the-grid." Penny answered.

"So where is this space's power supposed to come from?" Zoe asked.

Zach and Penny had been leading Binny and Zoe around the shelter looking for something. "I think the answer to your question is right here." Zach pointed his flashlight at the side of a small machine. A small sign read "DELCO-REMY". There was an identical machine right next to it. "They're generators."

"Hmmm... I don't think they finished assembling these before they sealed this place off." Binny picked up some of the loose pieces spread on the floor next to the generators.

"Why don't we just run an extension cord from upstairs? That's what Dad always does." Binny offered.

Zach was about to scoff at the suggestion, but stopped himself and said instead, "That's actually a great point. Why aren't we doing that?"

Everyone thought for a moment.

Finally Zoe spoke up. "Wouldn't we have to bring our own lights then? If we want the lights down here to work, wouldn't we need to do more than run an extension cord. I don't think they just plug-in. They're connected directly to the electricity source. At least that's how the overhead lights work at my house."

"Good point." Zach nodded.

Binny frowned, but no one noticed in the dark. "Well how are we going to put this thing back together?"

"Zach's gonna read this." On the wall near the generators Penny grabbed a book labeled "DELCO-REMY Electrical Equipment – Operation and Maintenance Handbook." The booklet apparently cost $1.50 in whatever ancient time it was first published, and printed in a circle around an image of cars, planes, and an oil rig was the company's motto: "Wherever wheels turn or propellers spin."

"What? Why me?" Zach protested.

"Because you have a mind for details." Penny said.

"Fine." Zach took the manual. "There's something you guys can do too."

"What's that?" Zoe asked?

"If somehow we get this to work we're going to need gas to put in it. In fact, we're going to need all kinds of things down here. They didn't exactly leave things fully stocked, and even if they did, I'm not sure I'd like to feast on emergency rations from fifty years ago."

"I think my grandfather has a gas can in the shed he uses for the lawnmower." Zoe said.

"That would be a nice start, but I doubt it would last very long."

"What do you expect us to do about that?" Binny asked.

"Well it's not so much the stuff that we need as much as it is the stuff we need to buy." Zach responded.

"Huh?" Penny said.

"We need money."

§

It had been hours since the kids had started exploring. Zach checked his cell phone for messages. He had ducked out of the shelter periodically to check. It made sure he didn't get in trouble again, but it was a huge pain. Zach thought to himself that a better solution was absolutely necessary. He just wasn't sure what it was.

"So, tomorrow?" Zach asked the group.

"Gas." Zoe said.

"More batteries." Penny said.

"And food. I'm starving!" Cassie added.

§

"I'm hoooooooooome." Penny yelled as she entered the house.

Penny's mother Serena was in her study, staring at her computer screen, her chin in her hands. Jangly guitar rock played over the computer's speakers. "Oh hi sweetie. I've been locked in here all day, writing much less than I should have."

Serena He looked at her watch, "Oh wow. It's late. I better get dinner going." On her way to the kitchen she stopped in front of Penny. "I almost forgot. Your dad and... I mean your dad is getting back into town late tonight and will be here tomorrow morning to pick you up. You guys are gonna spend the day together tomorrow."

Penny smiled ear to ear.

§

"We're going to take Rembrandt down to the water this time. I don't want to meet any weirdos." Binny said to Cassie just as their mother entered the room.

"You guys ready?" Julie started moving towards the door to accompany her daughters on their nightly ritual.

"We can go ourselves. We know the way." Binny said curtly to her mother as she and Cassie prepared to leave.

"Oh. Of course." Julie responded.

Julie stood there for a full minute watching her daughters walk down the walk without her.

"Aren't you going with them?" Jay had popped into the living room from the kitchen where he was preparing the evening meal.

"Binny asked me not to."

"Are you okay?" Jay had known his ex-wife very well for a very long time and could sense that she was sad about something.

"I'm fine." Julie said quietly.

"What's wrong? Come in the kitchen and talk to me while I make dinner. I'm a mediocre cook and a mediocre listener, but when I try to do both at once, then I'm truly lousy."

Julie laughed despite herself. "Well, I've been meaning to talk to you about this."

"Sounds serious."

"I am super grateful for how we've reconfigured things. That you're so easy with me being here. It's not just good for the kids. It's good for me."

"Of course. For me too." Jay smiled.

"Last night, I didn't tell you because I was embarrassed. And I was worried about how you would feel. I, well, when the girls got back from walking the dog, they saw me and Henry dancing."

"Oh." Jay looked surprised.

"Are you okay?" Julie asked.

Jay paused to think for a moment. "I knew this day would come. And it's a good thing. Really, this is a good thing. You're supposed to do this. But I admit, there's a pang."

"I'm sorry."

"Don't be. Really the thing that is the most difficult for me to handle is that he's French."

"Oh stop." Julie chided her ex-husband.

"I'm just kidding." Jay smiled. "It's okay. It's *pangy* but I'll live. And besides, since you went first, now you don't get to complain about the line of women around the block interested in me."

"I was just outside, I didn't see a line." Julie teased.

"Now *you* stop."

"Seriously though," Julie's tone changed, "Binny was really angry."

"Regular angry?" Jay smiled.

"Angrier."

Jay sat down in the chair opposite his ex-wife. "Listen, I'm sure she's got pangs of her own. We've talked about this. Happy parents mean... well... *eventually* mean happy kids. She's going to learn to adapt. Maybe she'll start eating escargot!" Jay looked proud of his joke.

Julie rolled her eyes.

"At the very least I get to tease." Jay insisted.

"Yes Jay. You get to tease." Julie forced a smile, but her eyes still looked worried.

§

"Why *were* you late though?" Zoe's mother asked once again as the plates were cleared. "It's like you disappeared in a black hole. We didn't get you a cell phone this summer so you could ignore it when we call."

"Are you done PopPop?" Zoe asked her grandfather before she cleared his plate.

Zoe didn't wait for his grumble to clear his plate. It looked empty enough to her.

"I went through a black hole." Gabe offered his mother.

"When's Daddy coming home?" Zoe asked her mother.

"I told you already, we found a section of rotting wall that needs to be removed and completely redone. Your father's dealing with that. Don't try and change the subject Miss. You still haven't answered my question."

"It smelled awful." Gabe continued.

Zoe tried to get her brother's attention unsuccessfully.

"What *are* you talking about?" Melissa Flowers asked her son.

"It's okay. They rescued me. They're super heroes."

"Who rescued you? What are you talking about?" Melissa took the dishes that Zoe handed to her and turned her back for a moment to put them in the sink.

Zoe took advantage of her mother's turned back to pinch her brother.

"Ow! Zoe!" Gabe complained.

Zoe's stared into her brother's eyes and raised her eyebrows as far as they could go. For the moment she wished her brother had picked up a little of Binny's mind reading abilities so he could hear her silently screaming at him to *shut his mouth*!

Melissa sighed and her shoulders sagged before she turned around to discipline her children. "What did you do?"

"It was an accident." Zoe whipped her head around to smile at her mother.

Gabe rubbed his arm where his sister had pinched him, looked back at his mother, and answered slowly, "It was an accident."

Melissa put her hands on her hips in exasperation. "OK. What was this about a hole, and you getting rescued?"

"We made some friends in the neighborhood. We've been playing with them. We've been playing superheroes. We pretended that Gabe was sucked into a black hole and everyone had to rescue him."

Gabe nodded unenthusiastically at his sister's explanation.

"Oh. OK." Gabe and Zoe's mother filed away this explanation and returned to the pile of dishes in the sink.

In the living room, PopPop had retired to his favorite chair. And while his head wasn't visible from behind the newspaper he was holding, he wasn't reading a word.

§

"I don't understand why we had to come here instead of the park. There aren't any swings down here." Cassie complained. "You think that someone is hurting animals like Zoe thinks?"

"No. I don't." Binny said.

"Well then why?" Cassie asked.

"I don't know whether that boy hurt that bird, but I do know that I'd prefer not to run into him again."

Rembrandt pulled at his leash, eager to run ahead.

"It's not my fault." Cassie laughed. "See, he's pulling me."

"Don't get too far ahead please." Binny said to her sister.

"I won't." Cassie's voice trailed behind her as she and Rembrandt took off at a brisk pace.

I don't know which of you is a worse listener. Binny thought to herself comparing her sister to their charge. Binny kept her eyes on Cassie and Rembrandt as they made their way forward on the large grassy strip between the sidewalk and the edge of the lake.

A dirty yellow station wagon made a sudden stop. A skinny man with longish hair sat behind the wheel looking nervous. A large woman got out with a metal object. Binny couldn't tell what it was. Cassie and Rembrandt had already covered quite a distance and they were much closer to the woman with the object than they were to Binny.

Binny looked back at the man, and looked inside his mind. All Binny heard was "...get her." The words were enough to snap her out of her reverie. Binny broke into a run.

The woman had left her door open. The cars blinkers were on. Cassie and Rembrandt were almost at the car now. Binny yelled, but neither of them turned around. They were too far away.

The woman raised the metal object, it was a staple gun. An industrial size one. Binny's heart sank. These two must be from Luce Labs.

And then, in a moment of confusion, Cassie and Rembrandt almost ran into the woman. She was twisting around trying not to get caught on the leash that precipitously connected the little girl and the dog.

"Sorrrrrrreeeeeee." Cassie yelled as they kept their forward progress. The woman shook her head and walked over to the nearby telephone pole with her staple gun. From her other side she produced a yellow piece of paper that she proceeded to staple to the pole.

By the time Binny arrived at the car, the woman was already getting back into the car. Her tear-streaked face now visible to Binny up close. All Binny heard before the car door closed and the man drove off was him saying, "We're gonna get her back. I promise."

Cassie and Rembrandt had stopped their forward progress for a visit to the lake. A couple of ducks had grabbed Rembrandt's interest. Binny walked over to the telephone pole and examined what the woman had posted.

The headline read: "MISSING CAT – 'Joni'". Below the headline was a photocopied picture of a black and brown long-haired cat with a white and tan mouth and chest. The cat draped over the shoulders of the woman who'd gotten out of the car. Binny looked at the details. The cat had been missing since the previous night. The address and phone number were on the flyer as well.

Binny folded the flyer carefully into her pocket and went to rejoin Cassie and Rembrandt.

§

"Come here little bird." Zoe motioned towards her cat.

"Why do you call Tango a bird?" Gabe watched his sister from the doorway to her room. "She's a cat."

"I know. It's just my nickname for her."

"I think it confuses her. I think it makes her think she can fly." Gabe motioned towards the half-opened window, "She's going to try and fly away.

"Don't say that!" Zoe said with more emotion than she'd intended. "She knows it's a nickname. She's not as dumb as you." Zoe turned back to her calico cat, nuzzled its nose with hers, and said, "Isn't that right little bird. You know you're a cat. Don't you. You would never fly away and leave me. You'll stay here in the house, safe with me always."

§

"Zach, you still up?" Jay knocked on his son's door. It was late and a warm light shone through the narrow area where Zach's door didn't quite touch the floor.

"Yeah."

Jay cracked the door open.

Zach was sitting at his desk his face bathed in light from the computer screen he was staring at.

Jay sat on the bed by the desk. "Zach-attack, how are you doing?"

"Fine." Zach responded curtly.

"I mean with all the change we've had."

"Fine."

"I realize things have been more complicated, but I think you're old enough to take on the extra responsibility. I really depend on you."

"I know."

"So I can count on you to really help me out? With your sisters? With chores? With all that?"

"Yeah." Zach tried his best to sound sincere.

"You don't sound super enthusiastic." Jay observed.

"I'm just tired." Zach said.

"Well maybe you shouldn't be staying up all night staring at a screen."

"I'll go to bed soon."

When Zach saw the door click shut, he swiveled back to his computer screen and brought up the window he had hidden when his father had first knocked. At the top of the screen were the words: "Geological Survey Research 1962. Department of the Interior." Under that in smaller letters it said: "Mapping the Geology of the Greater Seattle Area via Tunnel Infrastructure (current and abandoned): Infiltration, Peat Bogs, and Volcanic Ash."

Zach was focused intently on the map underneath the words.

✤ 17 ✤

THE UNEXPECTED VISITOR

Serena smiled as her daughter could barely sit still during her breakfast. "You didn't let me finish cutting the cherries into your bowl."

"Oh, sorry Mom." Penny fidgeted. "Do you know where we're going?"

"You'll have to ask your father that." Serena smiled as she reached for a napkin, wiping some errant yogurt from her daughter's upper lip.

BING BONG, the doorbell hadn't stopped chiming before Penny was already out of her seat and running to the front door.

"Hi baby!" Quincy Yang picked up his daughter to give her a big bear hug.

Only when Penny unburied her head from her father's shoulder did she notice, there was a strange man standing behind him. "Who are you?"

§

"I wish *we* had Christmas lights." Cassie complained.

"This was a smart idea." Zach said to Zoe.

"We don't celebrate Christmas." Binny reminded her sister.

"Thanks. Getting the lights out of the basement was easy. Nobody's gonna need them until November. Stopping Gabe from telling my Mom what we're up to is going to be more of a challenge."

"I know." Cassie said to Binny.

"You can't tell your parents about this stuff." Binny addressed herself to Gabe.

"I know." Gabe sounded disappointed.

"No, really. They wouldn't understand. And they wouldn't let us come here anymore. You wouldn't want that would you?"

Gabe shook his head, his expression earnest.

Zach had run an extension cord from a socket in the upper ante-room that had been the sole extent of their hideout for the past year until they'd discovered the entirety of the shelter. The white 'icicle' lights had been strung from wall to wall in the bigger room covering as much of the space as possible. It wasn't enough light to read by, but at least you could walk without the fear of bumping into anything or anyone.

"Where's Penny?" Zoe asked.

Zach finished applying clear tape to the backs of the nine pages he'd printed from his computer. He turned over the poster-sized creation and spread it flat on the lunch table at which they were now sitting.

"She's spending the day with her Dad." Binny responded. "What's this?"

"This," Zach motioned to the large sheet in front of him, "is a map of Madrona courtesy of our friendly internet." Zach took out a red pen and put 'X's next to each other in the rectangle labeled 'Madrona Park'. "This X is where we saw the injured cat. And this one is where we saw the bird.

"You need to draw one more X."

Zoe and Zach looked up from the map to see Binny unfolding a yellow sheet of paper from her pocket.

§

"Penny!" Quincy Yang admonished his daughter. "Don't be rude."

"I'm sorry." Penny shrugged. "But who is that?"

The well-dressed man standing behind Penny's father stuck out his hand. "Hi Penny. My name's

Jonathan. Your Dad has said about a million nice things about you. It's really nice to meet you." He smiled at Penny.

Penny tentatively returned the handshake. "Nice to meet you."

Penny's father added haltingly, "Jonathan is my friend. We've been travelling together. He's going to spend the day with us."

"What?" Penny asked, her eyes wide with disappointed surprise. "I thought *we* were spending the day together."

"Hi Jonathan." Serena had walked into the entryway of the home following her daughter's sprint to the door.

"Hi Serena." Jonthan said.

"I thought it might be nice for the three of us to spend time together." Penny's father said to her.

"Well *I* thought that it was just you and me spending the day together."

"Q, I totally understand. Why don't you guys go out and I'll hang out at the hotel." Jonathan said quietly to Quincy.

"I don't understand who *he* is." Penny said, her mind working overtime to understand the situation.

"Penny, you're being rude. Jonathan is your father's good friend." Penny's mother put her hand on Penny's shoulders.

"You're friends? How did you meet? Why are you travelling together?" Penny peppered her father with questions.

"Penny, let's go sit down for a moment and talk in your mom's study." Quincy tugged at his daughter's hand and closed the French doors behind them.

"Well, at least this isn't awkward." Jonathan joked with Serena.

Serena laughed. "It will all be okay. Penny doesn't have much of a filter. Combine that with her curiosity and this is what you get."

"Q has been so stressed about this." Jonathan fretted.

"I know." Serena said.

A few minutes passed, the French doors to the study blew open. Penny ran past her mother and Jonathan out the door, tears streaming down her face.

Quincy followed soon after, his own face relatively tear-streaked.

"What happened?" Serena asked sympathetically.

"Oh Q..." Jonathan added.

Quincy sniffled, and tried to hold back more tears. "Well, our daughter has a bright future as an investigative reporter or a lawyer perhaps."

"I'm hoping for reporter if that's okay." Serena joked.

"She just came out and asked me." Quincy replied.

"And what did you say?" Jonathan asked.

"I told her the truth." Quincy said.

"And that upset her?" Serena asked?

"She wasn't upset that Jonathan is my boyfriend."

Jonathan put a hand on Quincy's shoulder. "What was she upset about?"

"She was upset that I took so long to tell her." Quincy started crying again.

§

"I'm just saying that maybe we should give him a taste of his own medicine." Zoe insisted.

"And I'm saying that I don't want to see him ever again. A better idea is to split up and do patrols to protect the animals in the neighborhood." Binny responded.

Binny and Zoe had been arguing for what felt like hours to Zach. In reality it had only been twenty minutes since he'd drawn a third red 'X' on the map. Technically it was a fourth since he'd drawn it in the wrong spot the first time and then had to cross it out and redraw it. Zach thought to himself that pen and paper were not really the best tools for this problem.

From out of nowhere, Penny was suddenly sitting at the table.

"You're here." Binny exclaimed. "I thought you were spending the day with your Dad?"

"I'm not. What's with the map?" Penny changed the subject.

"It's roughly where we need to go confront that weird kid who's been hurting the animals." Zoe said.

"Whether we know it was him or not? If we're wrong, then while we're confronting him, some other animals could get hurt." Binny countered.

"We know it's him." Zoe's tone didn't sound like it welcomed disagreement.

Binny shook her head.

"I agree. That kid is creepy. We should find him." Penny said.

Binny's face registered a look of shock and hurt. "Are you serious?"

"Yes. We know it's him so we should warn him to stop." Penny replied without looking at Binny. "If you know something, you should just act on it, instead of keeping the information to yourself forever, and pretending that it's not true."

Zoe, Zach, and Binny exchanged confused looks. Penny didn't notice.

§

"Well that went really well." Quincy joked.

Quincy, Serena, and Jonathan were sitting around the dining room table drinking tea.

"It could have gone worse." Jonathan said softly.

"Could it?"

"Yeah, she could have been my Dad and pretended she hadn't heard you." Jonathan said. "Two years he spent pretending he hadn't heard me."

Now it was Serena's turn to laugh. "Jonathan, you know I think the world of you," Serena turned her head to address the rest of her comment to her ex-husband, "but maybe introducing Penny to Jonathan before you came out wasn't the best approach."

"I think we've clearly established I'm not skilled at this thing you keep calling 'the best approach'." Quincy grimaced as he held up his fingers making air quotes.

Jonathan gave Quincy a sympathetic look.

"Why did you think this made sense?" Serena asked.

"I thought if she could meet Jonathan first and see what an amazing person he is, then it would soften the blow of telling her."

"Our daughter is a thoughtful and savvy human being who loves you more than anything. Why did you think finding out her father is gay would be a blow?"

Shaking his head, Quincy said, "I don't know."

§

"What are you doing?" Binny sat in a chair in the shelter entryway, writing in the new register that she had begun a few days earlier.

"I'm measuring." Zach disappeared back down the hallway.

"What are you measuring?" Binny asked.

Zach didn't hear as he was already far down the hallway counting footsteps.

When Zach's face reappeared Binny repeated her question.

"I'm measuring what it's going to take to make sure I don't get in trouble while we're down here."

"Huh?"

"We need a bunch of stuff down here, but first and foremost is a way to get our cell phones to work down there." Zach pointed towards the hallway that led to the broader subterranean area in the shelter. He and Zoe had cleared away most of the remaining wall that had blocked off the hallway. It had been tougher than it looked. While it was covered in plywood, there was drywall behind the plywood.

"You're going to get the cell phone company to make your phone work down here?" Binny asked.

"Nope. *We're* going to make it work down here." Zach said.

§

"My suggestion is that you two come back for dinner. She'll have had some time to cool down, and we can just take things one step at a time." Serena smiled at Jonathan and Quincy as they headed towards the door.

"Thanks Serena." Jonathan gave her a hug.

"Oh... Jay. You're here." Serena saw Jay Jordan approaching the door through the glass.

"Oh, I'm sorry. I can come back later." Jay apologized after seeing the small crowd in the entryway.

"Hi. It's okay. We were just heading out." Quincy said.

Serena didn't notice the relief on Jay's face when Quincy introduced Jonathan as his boyfriend.

Before the door closed, Jonathan said to Jay, "We're gonna stick around for a few days, so hopefully we'll get to see you again."

A few minutes later, after Jonathan and Quincy had driven off, Serena and Jay were sitting on the porch together looking out on the lake.

Serena finished recounting the morning's events, "Penny was really rough on him. But for the right reasons."

"Binny's been taking a similar approach with her mother." Jay shared what was happening between his eldest daughter and his ex.

"I can't imagine having three of them to contend with." Serena mused.

"The other two are no slouches. I can't tell if I'm being unreasonable in expecting Zach to step up a bit as the oldest and take some responsibility for his sisters. And Cassie, well, I'm pretty sure at this point has convinced herself she has super powers."

"Seriously?"

"Yeah. She's told us a couple of times. I can't tell if it's healthy make-believe or delusions of grandeur."

"Could it be her trying to relate to her superhero-obsessed father?" Serena smiled gently. "Maybe you should embrace it. So your daughter's a superhero. There are worse things she could be."

The two of them laughed.

❧ 18 ❧

THE LUNCH DATE

KNOCK KNOCK. Huitre took one last look around the kitchen. She was early, and he had butterflies. He hadn't felt like this in a longer time than he cared to admit. Normally, Huitre would think that being early was rude. But in the case of Julie Jordan he was prepared to make an exception.

Huitre opened the door and his mouth fell open.

Samantha Trace stood in Huitre's doorway. Uninvited and unannounced. "I'm sorry. Is this a bad time? I was in the neighborhood and thought I would say hello on the off chance you were home. And lucky me. Here you are."

§

"It's peanut butter Nutella banana. I had to get up extra early to make these without my Dad noticing. I'm still not sure what to tell him tonight as at some point today he will no doubt notice that all the bread is gone. And all the nutella. And all the bananas." Binny said as she passed out sandwiches to the other kids.

"And all the peanut butter?" Cassie said with a mouthful of sandwiches, the beginning of a chocolate mustache forming on her upper lip.

"Nope, there's still peanut butter." Binny replied.

"Dad never lets that run out." Zach added.

Zach was first to finish his sandwich and spread out the map they'd been looking at earlier in the day. Zach took out his pen and drew a rectangle in the middle of the Madrona woods. "This is the cave." Zach stabbed a finger at the drawing.

"Why do you call it that? It's a shelter." Binny corrected.

Zach ignored her. "I did some reading last night. If the metal door up above was sealed, then air would not be able to get out, and people staying in here for more than a little while would overheat."

"Let's not close that door then." Zoe said.

"But they had to plan for the door to be closed, which means, they had another way for air to get in from outside. Probably with a filtration system, though from the smell when we got here, I'm guessing the ventilation duct has been closed for some time."

"I agree. Let's not close the door." Penny added.

"Listen, the door isn't the point. We need to make our cell phones work down here. And that means we need a way to get a wire from a little box up above, to another little box down here in the cave."

"Shelter." Binny corrected.

"Why not just run the wire down the hallway?" Penny asked?

"We could do that. But if anyone found the signal receiving box up above, they could just follow the wire right into this place. Making it easy for people to find us seems to go against the whole 'hideout' theme we're creating here."

"But if you can find where the air comes from, we could run the wire from there." Zoe said.

"Exactly. But so far I haven't found where the ventilation is down here. We need to scour the walls, every corner, and the ceiling for a clue as to how air comes down here."

Cassie and Gabe had taken to playing various pretend games in some of the rooms. Mainly the kitchen, and the command center. Sometimes they pretended to cook for all the residents of the hideout. Sometimes they pretended to supervise everyone.

While Cassie and Gabe were busy playing, the four older kids spread out. For fifteen minutes, Zach scoured every inch of the bedrooms with his flashlight. He knew it must be here somewhere. He hoped that the others were applying the same attention to detail as he was to the search. The vent wouldn't have to be super large necessarily, and there could be more than one.

"I found something." Binny's voice echoed off the walls of the shelter.

Binny had taken the north wall of the shelter. They'd explored it on their first day in the space. The wall was lined with heavy doors revealing a series of empty storerooms ready for supplies that were either removed or never delivered.

When Penny and Zach arrived Binny focused her flashlight on a space under one of the dusty shelves. A foot tall rectangular metal panel was mounted on the wall. Zach got down in his back under the shelf, slid a small lever on the panel, and yelled "Helloooooooo" into its face only to hear his voice echo up what sounded like a very long metal shaft.

"Zoe, come, Binny found it." Penny yelled out.

Zoe appeared at the entry to the storeroom. "Actually, you should come with me, I found something too."

§

"You don't seem happy to see me." Samantha Trace said to Dr. Huitre as she entered the home.

"It is not that at all. I am just home briefly before I have to head back to the hospital. Can I get you a drink of water?"

"I didn't come to drink your water."

Huitre's shoulder's sagged. "I am sorry. What can I do for you?"

Samantha spoke as she walked around the living room examining books on the shelves and other items on display. "I've been thinking about our conversation from the other night. I felt bad about how it ended and wanted to apologize."

"Oh, that's very kind of you. No apology necessary. But I appreciate you coming by."

"That's not all. I've been thinking about you. About you and I specifically. I know we've primarily had a professional relationship, but I think that sometimes colleagues can evolve into something more. I think that you and I are more compatible than you may realize."

"Samantha, I –"

"Hear me out Henry. We both have a scientific background. We're both intellectually curious. We've both been on our own for some time. I really think that we should give things a try. We could start today, right now, have lunch together or something. Let's be spontaneous."

Henry Huitre looked at his watch before he looked back at Samantha Trace. Her eyes were wide and hopeful. He had dismissed her as callous and single-minded in the past. He didn't suddenly *like* her. But he could see that somewhere in her stilted overly-formal style was an actual human being.

"I am flattered Samantha. Truly. But I have to tell you that I recently started seeing someone."

Samantha Trace looked mortified. Henry imagined that it was incredibly rare for her to put herself out on an emotional limb like she had with him. And to be rejected on her one and only attempt must have felt like quite a blow.

When she saw the sympathy in his face, Samantha Trace's composure cracked and she started to cry. Not knowing what else to do Henry put his arms around her to comfort her.

§

OK. There was no denying it. *Now it feels like sneaking around*, Julie Jordan thought to herself. She'd taken a circuitous route to Huitre's house so she wouldn't drive by her old house. She didn't want the kids to see her driving by and wonder why she was in the neighborhood in the middle of a work day.

Pulling up in front of the modern style house, Julie scouted the area one more time, craning her neck to make sure none of her children were wandering by as they tended to do on their way to whatever it was they did in the woods.

Julie approached Huitre's front door. The door was framed on either side by glass panes. Julie cocked her head so she could catch her reflection in the panes and examine her appearance one last time before she went inside. But her eyes didn't settle on her own image; instead they saw past her own monochromatic image into the full color living room. Julie felt an instant and unyielding acidic emptiness in her stomach.

Julie quietly turned on her heel, walked to her car, and drove away.

§

"Maybe it's a safe." Binny suggested.

In the very last storeroom, right next to the hardwood floors, a large circular steel door sat mounted in the concrete. Zoe stood by it, proudly showing off her find.

"Oooh. Maybe there's lots of money inside." Cassie rubbed her hands together.

"Why would they need a safe in a bomb shelter?" Binny said to her sister.

"How did we not see this before?" Zach asked.

"We thought all these rooms were empty." Penny said.

"And it was dark?" Binny added.

"Well, we found it now." Zoe said.

"Should we open it?" Penny asked?

Gabe and Cassie immediately registered their approval of this suggestion. Binny was about to register a concern, but not before Zoe said, "Already tried. It won't budge."

"Let me try." Zach put down his flashlight, and started adjusting his shirt, preparing for the physical exertion.

Binny, Zoe, and Penny started giggling.

"What? What? I'm just trying to get in the right frame of mind." Zach grabbed a hold of the wheel at the center of the metal door and tugged *hard*. It didn't budge.

"Sorry Superman." Zoe teased Zach.

"I bet I could open it." Gabe offered.

"No way. You'd hurt yourself trying." Zoe said.

"Watch me. I have powers too." Gabe whined.

"Maybe you should save your energy for when you really need it. We wouldn't want you to be too tired when we need you to do something really heroic." Binny said to Gabe.

That seemed to mollify Gabe for the moment.

Binny turned to Penny. "What do you think?"

Penny eyed the door.

"I'm worried it will fall on her." Zach said.

"It doesn't have to be the whole door. Just the mechanism that opens it." Binny explained.

"What makes you think that breaking the mechanism will open the door. Maybe it will make it even harder to open." Zach reasoned.

"Well right now it's impossible to open, so I don't think it can get harder to open than that." Zoe said.

"I think I can limit it to just the handle and the mechanism." Penny was staring intently at the door handle.

"How?"

"I've noticed that if I do it slowly, I can almost see into the thing I'm breaking. It's like I'm shrinking myself down and flying through the machine itself, popping things loose, and disconnecting things. I can just stop myself before I go too far."

"Cool." Zach and Zoe said in unison.

Binny and Zoe pulled the smaller kids back to a safe distance. Penny put her hands on the handle and closed her eyes. Everyone held their breath.

First there was a creaking sound. Then a pop, and a whoosh. The wheel-shaped handle dropped to the ground and Penny screamed.

§

"Samantha, I am so sorry about this. You have nothing to be embarrassed about."

"Really? Nothing? Come on, admit it, this is just a little bit humiliating. No?" Samantha made a small smile as she took the proffered tissue from Huitre.

"Not at all. Being honest is never something to be embarrassed by." Huitre pronounced as he looked at his watch again. "I am so sorry to say this, but I actually need to be moving along now. Normally I would be happy to talk more."

"Of course, of course, I'm the one who dropped by unannounced." Samantha made towards the door. Before she opened it to leave she said, "One question, this person you're seeing, who is it?"

Huitre knew that he should lie to her. He knew of her animosity towards Julie Jordan. But he thought that maybe this news would make sure Samantha was permanently disinterested in him, which seemed like a good thing. Having her show up unannounced at his house was definitely not something he wanted to ever happen again.

Samantha's eyes burned. "Julie Jordan?"

"Well, it's early yet, but yes."

"Are you serious?" Trace's eyes narrowed. "You're actually interested in her? Truly?"

Since his previous answer had backfired so spectacularly, Huitre was quite sure he had no idea what to say now. Instead he just stood there in silence.

"Oh my god. You know Henry, it's this obsession of yours that got you into trouble in the first place."

"I am sorry?" Huitre's palms were open to the air as he thought frantically of what he could say to calm Trace down.

Trace took several steps back into the living room. "Let me ask you a question *Doctor* Huitre." Trace enunciated his title mockingly. "Do you think that the ethics board at your hospital would approve or disapprove of you being romantically interested in one of your patients?"

"Samantha, she hasn't been my patient in a very long time." Henry tried to smile reassuringly. It only added fuel to the fire.

"Well, do you think that your patient – Ms. Jordan - would feel good about the fact that the only reason she was your patient in the first place is because of your romantic interest in her? Do you think she would feel that your recommendation that she participate in our fertility study all those years ago was free of any conflict of interest? How do you think it would affect your budding romance?"

"Samantha." Huitre lowered his voice. "I never asked you to –"

"Are you playing dumb Henry? You remember exactly what happened. I saw how you mooned over Julie all those years ago. Julie's doctor, your partner, didn't just up and leave for the other side of the country randomly. You knew it wasn't luck or fate or the cosmos that suddenly made Julie Jordan your patient. You knew exactly how she became your patient. And you repaid us – you repaid Luce Laboratories – by making sure she participated in our study."

Huitre looked ashen.

Trace took a breath, and applied a forced smile to her lips. "I'm just saying that being honest is never something to be embarrassed by. And if you're uncomfortable being honest with her, I am happy to do it on your behalf."

§

"Are you okay?" Binny rushed to Penny's side.

"Ow ow ow ow ow ow ow." Penny was leaning on the large steel door with one hand, standing on one foot, while massaging her other foot with her spare hand.

"I'm so sorry." Zach said.

"It'll be okay. It just caught the tip of my toe when it dropped. I doubt anything's broken."

"If your foot had been an inch closer it might have been." Zoe observed.

"We need to be more careful." Zach said.

Before Zoe could stop him, Gabe marched towards the door, grabbed the edge and pulled hard. Groaning creaking sounds of metal that hadn't moved in decades filled the room, but the door swung wide open. "See? I told you I had powers."

"Very impressive." Penny smiled at the others as she patted Gabe on his skinny arm as he made a show of his muscles.

Zoe rolled her eyes at her little brother.

Zach carefully poked his head through the doorway. A tunnel lined with stone and brick stretched to both his right and left as far as the eye could see. Zach's nostrils filled with the smell of moist wet earth.

⋆ 19 ⋆

THE 1911 EAST CHERRY
SEWER TUNNEL

"Awesome." Cassie and Gabe uttered the word in unison stretching it out over several seconds.

Zoe had to put a hand on Gabe's shoulder before he walked through the open metal door and headed down the dark tunnel on his own.

"Before you get super excited, it's a sewer." Zach laughed.

"Ewww. Gross." Binny said.

Zoe wrinkled her nose.

"Don't worry, it hasn't been in use for sixty or seventy years." Zach smiled. "I'm pretty sure we just found the 1911 East Cherry Sewer Tunnel."

"So the poop is really really old?" Penny added.

Gabe and Cassie laughed, hard.

"How did you know what it was called?" Zoe asked Zach.

"I was trying to figure out where the shelter came from and I found all sorts of information about all the various tunnels under the city. Nothing about the shelter though. It got me wondering, what other spaces are under the city that aren't on the official maps."

"So coooool." Cassie was inching forward trying to get a good look at what was through the door.

"We have to explore it." Penny said.

"What?" Binny exclaimed.

"We have to. It's a secret tunnel." Penny responded.

"It's a sewer." Binny said. Finding no sympathetic faces in her audience, she added, "It's not safe."

"I agree we need to be careful. Normally they don't dig tunnels within fifty feet of each other, but it looks like they placed this shelter near the tunnel on purpose. It's kind of a secret escape hatch. I'm guessing they wouldn't have done that if they didn't think it could handle people using it."

"Isn't this distracting us from our main mission?" Binny tried another tack.

"I think, depending on where this leads it could help us with our main mission. What if it gave us our own secret way to get around the neighborhood without getting noticed?"

Binny pursed her lips as she considered Zach's answer. It didn't seem completely crazy.

"Where do you think it goes?" Zoe asked.

"Let's find out." Penny said rubbing her hands together.

§

It took another hour for them to complete all the precautions Binny insisted on before she would agree to venture into the tunnel. Cell phones were checked for text messages, more food and water was snuck surreptitiously, batteries were restocked, and a makeshift first aid kit was assembled from purloined items from the medicine cabinets in the kids' houses.

Zach thought that there were only two real dangers – getting lost and cave-ins. He discounted the first one because he would memorize the way with incredible precision. He kept the second worry to himself. He was pretty sure a first-aid kit wouldn't help much with either possibility but its presence made Binny feel better so he agreed.

The walls of the tunnel bowed in the middle and tapered at the top and bottom. The sewage would have run along the floor of the tunnel which was now dry. A t-shaped platform rose above the floor providing a walkway for the children. The tunnel was lined with stone. At regular intervals, brick arches would brace and support the ceiling above their heads.

"I think this is the right way to go." Zach said after heading to the left through the shelter's escape hatch as they'd all started calling it. "I'm pretty sure either direction is a dead end, but this way there should be a right turn that heads west. I want to see where that one goes. The map wasn't very clear."

"When I look at a map online, I must have missed the option where you get to see all the underground tunnels." Zoe joked.

"There isn't one." Zach replied in a serious tone. I was looking at survey map from 1962.

"1962?" Binny stopped in her tracks. "Are you serious? Who knows what's happened since then."

"Earthquakes. Two of them. Two major ones anyway." Penny said. She didn't notice at first that everyone was staring at her. "I did a report on earthquakes for school. I wanted to get to know the area."

"We're not going to die." Zach reassured Binny.

"Tell that to the people who made your map." Binny said. And then sarcastically she added, "Oh wait, you can't. They're all already dead."

"How can you eat? We're literally in a sewer." Binny asked.

Penny munched on one some chips as they walked. "I'm hongree." Penny said through a mouthful of chips.

Binny rolled her eyes.

Zach, who was leading their single file group, came to a stop. "This is the turn." Zach pointed right, "The Cherry line continues this way." Zach kept walking.

"How deep do you think we are?" Gabe asked, trying to put a brave face on his nervousness.

"I can't sense anyone but us." Binny offered. "But I don't really know how far I can 'see'."

"Are you looking inside me right now?" Zoe's voice had an edge.

"No." Binny explained. "I can kinda zoom out so I'm not looking at anything specific. I just see dots where everyone is." Binny kept to herself that all the dots she saw in her mind's eye had a cracked texture that signified nervousness. All but Cassie's anyway.

But after awhile even Cassie's excitement was starting to wear thin. "How much longer? This is boring."

Even Zach had to admit that the 1911 East Cherry Sewer Line had little to offer in the way of variety. By counting his steps Zach estimated they'd walked about a mile. They hadn't gone particularly fast, and Zach was conscious of the fact that they'd have to retrace their steps just to get home. "Just a little longer."

Zach told himself that he would absolutely definitely turn them around after two more minutes of walking. After all, they could always come back and explore further another day. And then, all of a sudden, the floor under them expanded to fill the width of the tunnel and straight ahead there was nothing but brick.

"Well that was anti-climactic." Penny pronounced.

"At least we're alive." Binny mumbled.

"What's anti-kly-maxic?" Gabe asked.

"It means, that we didn't find anything exciting." Zoe explained to her little brother.

"I'm pretty okay with that actually." Binny said. Binny insisted everyone take a break for a moment, sitting on the stone walkway, drinking some water, and resting before they resumed their journey back to the shelter.

"This is the worst seat ever!" Cassie was sitting up above the walkway, against the curved wall, but hunched over. "Why would they put this metal here?" Cassie complained.

"What metal?" Zoe asked.

In the darkness, nobody's flashlight had happened upon the series of metal rungs sticking out of the stone wall right before the dead end. All at once, the light from several flashlights coalesced on the ladder and followed its path upward.

"We're not done yet." Zach smiled.

Zach offered to go first, while Zoe insisted on bringing up the rear. She said it was to make sure everyone got up the ladder safely. Zach put his flashlight in his pocket as he climbed. When he emerged at the top of the ladder, he could see, dimly, but still, there was light coming from somewhere.

Zach walked around the small room he'd climbed into and touched the smooth tiled walls as each of the other children made it to the top of the ladder behind him. The room was small, but there was a door that wasn't completely closed. That's where the light was coming from. Zach opened the door.

Zach had ridden the subway before on a Jordan family trip to New York City. But Zach had never heard of a Seattle subway. The sign across the tracks, spelled out "Cherry Street (Garfield)" very clearly in large letters made of small mosaic tiles. On either side was smaller lettering, also made of inlaid colorful tile: "Sick's Stadium" accompanied by an arrow to the left, and "Washington (University)" with an arrow to the right.

Lonely lightbulbs had been strung up haphazardly in random locations round the station giving everything even more of a yellowish quality than the space already had on its own.

"This is not supposed to be here." Zach said to the others in a low voice.

"*You're* not supposed to be here." A man said from a bench five feet behind the assembled children.

✦ 20 ✦

THE TUNNEL PEOPLE

Dr. Samantha Trace had spent the last hour at her desk. The more she tried to work, the less work she was able to do. Huitre was infuriating. What did *she* even see in him. And more importantly, what did *he* see in that mediocre Jordan woman? Huitre wasn't even giving her information on the Jordan children anymore.

Luce was not going to be happy. Really, what was she supposed to do? Huitre was useless. Grater was more than useless. And now Luce was spending all this time with Ollie. At least Ollie appeared to behave around Luce. But that made her angry as well. What was it she felt? Irritation? Jealousy?

Ollie listens to Luce but not to me. No wonder Luce thinks I can't get this job done. He thinks I can't even parent my own child. Samantha Trace sat at her desk, her shaking hands balled into fists.

"But why?" Ollie whined to his mother.

Trace had marched from her office straight to the greenhouse where she found Ollie engaged in deep thought over how best to prune a shrub. The label read "Myrciaria Dubia."

"Because I've decided we're going to have a nice mother-son afternoon together."

"But I'm supposed to finish this whole row before the end of the day."

"Go with your mother, son. Everybody needs a break once-in-awhile, and it's a beautiful day out." Xander Luce appeared, seemingly out of nowhere.

Ollie's shoulders slumped.

Samantha's did too, humiliated that she needed her boss to get her son to want to spend time with her.

"Can we see animals, at the zoo maybe?" Ollie asked?

"I was thinking we'd go to the Burke instead." Samantha replied.

"Ah, the natural history museum. That's a fine choice." Luce chimed in.

Samantha grimaced.

Ollie sighed. "All the animals there are already dead."

§

Binny screamed.

"Zoe?" Gabe's voice faltered.

Binny collected herself and motioned to the others to come close. "Everyone get back."

The man was sitting up from where he had apparently been sleeping. Stacks of paperback books were stuffed under the bench. Radiating out from the bench on either side was an assortment of two liter plastic bottles missing their labels. Most were empty. Some contained a liquid that nobody wanted to guess at.

The man wore a military jacket with an American flag patch on the sleeve and a black backwards baseball cap. His hair was pulled back in a ponytail. Rubber bands made several mini-ponytails out of the long hair that covered most of his face. The remaining exposed skin was all deep crisscrossing lines.

"The library is closed for the day." The man said.

Unsure of what to say, no one responded.

"Did the security guard let you in? Or was he not at his post. I'm going to report him." The man wagged his finger as he spoke. "Breaking and entering is what it is. Just because the guard abandoned his post, doesn't mean that you didn't commit a crime breaking into the library. Don't the posted hours mean *anything* to you?" The man was screaming.

Cassie started crying.

Zach yelled, "Run!"

The old man had stepped between the children and the door through which they'd entered the station. Going back the way they came wasn't possible. Zach chose the tunnel heading left as it was slightly better lit. The other kids followed.

Cassie and Gabe couldn't run as fast as the older children who slowed down to match their pace while encouraging them not to let up. The station platform ended with stairs that led to the tracks and the tunnel.

"You want us to run on the tracks?" Binny yelled at her brother, now on the verge of tears herself.

"There are no trains. It's okay." Zach tried to sound reassuring.

Zach looked around nervously for the first time noticing more men and women tentatively coming out of the shadows and looking to see what the commotion was about. In the distance the old man was still yelling that the library was closed and that rules were meant to be followed.

"You didn't know there was a subway station up until two minutes ago. How do you know there are no trains?"

Penny noticed the gathering crowd and grabbed Binny's arm.

"Ow." Binny yelped.

"We have to go, now!" Penny's eyes were wide as she showed Binny the crowd gathering in the distance.

"I vote tracks." Zoe said and sailed down the stairs with Gabe in tow.

Everyone followed. After a couple of minutes, the younger kids were out of breath and needed to take a break. As best as Zach could tell, there didn't seem to be any people in the tunnel itself, so they all stopped to catch their breath.

Zach shined his flashlight on the faces of his companions to see how they were doing and tried hard to ignore the fragments of advice from his father, *being responsible* and *making good choices* that were ringing repeatedly in his head.

"We're going to be fine." Zach said with more confidence than he felt.

"What was wrong with that man?" Cassie asked.

Zach paused for a moment, looking at the other older children for guidance that wasn't forthcoming. Taking Cassie's hand he said, "I'm not really sure. I don't think he was a bad person. But I think he might be sick."

"What do you suggest we do now? We just ran away from the only way out of here. We're trapped. I told you this was a bad idea." Binny was shaking.

"I'm sorry. I'm sorry. We're all still fine. We'll figure this out." Zach turned to Zoe, "I'm sorry I got you into this. I promise, I'll get us out."

A look of anger flashed across Zoe's face. "*You* got me into this? *You* did? *You're* gonna get me out? I thought we were a team. You don't make decisions for me. I make my own choices. You're not responsible for me."

Zach's face fell. Zoe glared at him until he had no choice but to look away.

"There's another way out." Penny said calmly.

"What do you mean?" Binny said.

"Did you see any tunnel people passing us in our hideout?" Penny cracked a small smile.

"No."

"Well they must have come from somewhere." Penny raised her eyebrows to emphasize her point.

"Subway stations usually have exits to the street." Zach rejoined the conversation tentatively.

"Not abandoned subway stations that aren't open to the public." Zoe responded.

Zach tried to look anywhere but at Zoe.

"So we keep going in this direction until we find an exit?" Zoe directed her question at Penny and Binny.

"It said this way to Sick's Stadium on the sign." Zach offered meekly.

"So?" Zoe snapped.

"So, remember last summer, that plaque by home plate?" Penny looked at Zoe, "Oh, you wouldn't remember, cause you guys weren't there. But there's a drug company where there used to be a baseball stadium. We'll tell you all about it on the way. We can definitely get home from there."

They gathered Gabe and Cassie and started walking down the tunnel. As they saw the next station approaching, they doused their flashlights.

"I'm gonna run ahead and scout out the station. Wait here. I'll be right back." Zoe turned and ran in a crouch toward the dim lights of the next station.

It took a minute for her eyes to adjust but when they did she could see human shapes on both sides of the tracks. Some looked like they were sleeping. Some looked to be in conversation in small groups. The large tiled letters on the walls read "Jackson Street". Zoe snuck back to the group.

"This station is filled with tunnel people and it's not our station anyway. I say we walk right down the tracks. If we stay low and quiet, nobody will notice us." Zoe reported.

"What do we do if there are tunnel people in *our* station?" Binny asked in a considerably more conciliatory voice than she had reserved for her brother.

"Let's worry about one thing at a time." Penny said.

With Zoe in the front, and Zach at the back of the line, the kids made it through Jackson Street station unscathed. Binny worried that Cassie might be too loud, or fidgety to follow Zoe's plan, but the old man who had yelled at them had apparently given Cassie plenty of reason to follow instructions.

"Did you see any exits in the last station?" Penny asked.

Zach took another tentative step back into the discussion. "There were stairs on each side of the tracks in both of the previous stations."

"So all we have to do is figure out how to get up the stairs in the Sick's station without attracting any attention." Penny concluded.

The six children walked in silence for several minutes as they contemplated the challenge ahead.

As they approached the now familiar hazy yellow light of the ad-hoc light bulbs the tunnel people had strung up in each station, everyone turned off their flashlights.

"I'll run ahead and scout again." Zoe volunteered.

But before she could leave, Binny grabbed her arm, and put her finger to her lips. Binny made sure everyone saw her signal, and then motioned everyone to crouch.

In the distance, from the center of the upcoming station, a hazy outline of a human being was moving in their direction.

Bunched up against the side of the trench where the trains would have run, the kids tried to make themselves as inconspicuous as possible. Each watched the shape as it moved slowly towards them.

Binny had ventured briefly into the minds of the tunnel people as they'd passed the last station. Their minds were like nothing she'd ever seen. She felt bad for having looked. For many of them, something was clearly wrong. Their thoughts were a jumble as if she was looking through a greasy crystal. Images were distorted and misshapen. For the few who had clearer images, they were coated in a dingy brown and grey. Everything Binny saw was either sad or scary.

Binny focused on the shape coming towards them, first with her eyes, and then with her inner eye. The figure was small – under five feet for sure. Binny guessed it was a woman though she wasn't entirely sure why other than her size. The woman was wrapped in maybe half a dozen blankets. Wisps of long white hair escaped her makeshift hood in various places. Binny looked upward in her mind.

The woman's thoughts came into Binny's mind. Like with many of the tunnel people there were several pictures coming at once, projected as if on the facet of a gem. But unlike the blurry, misshapen images she'd seen from the others, these were crystal clear, and tinged a confident red.

Six facets showed six separate images. Each facet contained an image of one of the six kids in their small group. Zach, Cassie, Zoe, Gabe, Penny, and even Binny herself were all there. Not images of them now, crouched by the side of the tracks, faces all sooty and scared, but images of each of them at home, outside, in the woods, their faces bathed in bright sunlight. Images that this woman couldn't have possibly seen. Binny froze.

"You guys run, I'll keep her busy." Zach suggested.

Zoe looked at Zach but her face didn't betray her feelings.

"No. I looked. It's okay." Binny said, and then added *I think* in her mind's voice.

Binny stood up from her crouching position with the others and took a step forward.

The woman, it was clearly a woman, and an ancient woman at that, made no effort to move any faster. The old woman's face was a mountain range of crags and crevasses. Her small pug nose stuck out like Everest above the other mountains in the range. Despite the lack of light, the woman's eyes were clear and a color Binny had never seen, not brown or hazel exactly, but almost orange – a bright orange.

The woman stopped only feet from where Binny was standing and doing her best not to shake.

"I've been waiting for you for tho long. Come thith way." The woman's voice was sweet and almost comforting, but her attempt to smile was anything but comforting as her mouth was completely without teeth.

Cassie let out a small yelp.

Binny turned to her sister to try and stop her from offending the old woman, but the woman had already turned on her heel assuming Binny and the others would follow.

The old woman walked with the same deliberate pace back in the direction from which she had come. Binny shrugged her shoulders and motioned for the others to follow.

As they approached the mouth of the tunnel that would open up into the station, the woman turned to the right. A staircase had been cut into the concrete. The woman went up the stairs. The kids followed.

After what seemed like an interminably slow ascent up multiple flights of stairs, the woman stopped on a landing and turned to the children.

Penny's flashlight was on and gave the kids a much better view of the weathering the old woman's face had sustained.

Gabe dug his nails into Zoe's wrist until she gave him a look that could not be misinterpreted.

"It'th tho nice to thee you after all thith time." The woman smiled again, and this time it succeeded in putting the kids more at ease. It was really only the missing teeth that made it seem creepy. If one imagined the teeth still being there, the expression seemed caring and genuine.

"You've seen us before?" Binny asked in as polite a voice as she could muster.

"You are all *tho* beautiful." The woman closed her eyes as she said the last word as if she was remembering something.

"How did you see us?"

The old woman ignored Binny's question. She scanned the faces of the children only to stop and lean her head forward when she spotted Cassie half hiding behind Zach.

"You dear. You. You are a little thparkler aren't you." The old woman was pointing unmistakably at Cassie now – the tip of her finger tracing small circles in the air. "I thee you shining dear. I thee you shining. *Everyone* will thee you shine."

Cassie's eyes grew wide. Zach put his hand on Cassie's shoulder, holding her tight.

"OK. Off you go now children." The old woman stepped to the side revealing another ladder – this one wooden and propped up against the wall. It rose up through the ceiling of the room in which they were standing. There was no other exit other than the way they'd come in.

Each kid scaled the ladder as the old woman made encouraging sounds until only Binny was left. Binny motioned for the woman to go first.

"Oh no dear. I can't go up there. I'm not allowed." The woman smiled again mercifully keeping her lips closed.

"Oh." Binny said unsure of how to proceed.

The woman reached out to touch Binny's hand, bringing Binny's index finger up to her own head. "Did you get what you needed? In there?" The woman repeatedly tapped Binny's finger on her own temple never taking her bright orange eyes off of Binny.

"Yes." Binny said tentatively. Not knowing what else to say, Binny added, "Thank you." and turned to scale the ladder.

When she reached the top of the ladder Binny found herself in a small roofed concrete space. She could tell it was above ground because bright sunlight streamed through a narrow gap in the concrete hitting Binny right in the eyes. She tried to look back down to see the old woman one more time but all she saw was darkness. She wasn't sure if the woman was gone, or if the sunlight had just made her impossible to make out.

Zach was the only one left in the concrete space. Everyone else had already exited through one of the gaps. Zach helped Binny through one of the holes and onto the surrounding grass and then shimmied through himself.

The six of them found themselves sitting on the manicured grass on the edge of the Luce Laboratories campus. The greenhouse in which they'd hidden last summer was only feet away.

⁑ 21 ⁂

THE PAPAYA BREAK

"You okay?" Binny walked over to her brother who was sitting on the grass at a distance from the others. Everyone but Zach was finding ways to shake off the stress of the trip through the tunnels. For Cassie and Gabe that meant trying to poke Penny and Zoe when their backs were turned.

"Yeah." Zach responded.

Binny took a seat next to Zach on the ground. "I know you were just trying to be helpful and responsible."

"I'm not sure everyone knows that." Zach stole a glance at Zoe who was horsing around with the others.

"You could tell her yourself." Binny suggested cautiously.

"Yeah. You keep saying that. But it's not just her. It's everyone."

"Everyone?"

"Well, Dad. Somehow I'm supposed to be like a parent all of a sudden. What if I don't want to be? Why is it my problem that they're divorced?"

Binny was surprised by how red Zach's eyes got as he spoke. Binny bit her lip. She hadn't realized how her parents' breakup was affecting her brother. The two siblings sat in silence for a few minutes.

"I'm hungry." Cassie appeared in front of her brother and sister, her eyes sparkling and flashing a toothy grin.

"Wanna see if we can get some mangoes?" Now it was Binny's turn to smile.

§

"And who are your new friends?" The old man said with a big smile.

Binny and Penny had explained to Zoe and Gabe some of the adventures of the previous summer including the part where the greenhouse caretaker had a bunch of fresh mango growing for snacking purposes. This time however they had knocked on the door to the greenhouse before entering.

"I'm Zoe." Zoe offered.

"I'm Gabe." Gabe stuck out a hand to the old man.

The man kneeled to look Gabe in the eye and shake his hand. "So nice to meet you Zoe and Gabe. You can call me Xander." Xander turned to the rest of the group, "I'm so glad you *all* came back for a visit."

"I really liked that mango you gave us last summer." Penny said with a sheepish grin.

"Ah yes, mango. It is a hot day, and that would be the perfect thing. Alas, I am a little low on mangoes today."

Gabe's face gave away his disappointment.

"But," Xander looked at Gabe as he spoke, "could I interest you in some papapya? Man cannot live on mango alone you know."

"Papaya?" Gabe's face brightened.

"I've never had papaya." Cassie added.

"It's delicious." Gabe reassured her.

"You can even use the greenhouse sink to wash up. You kids look like you've been traipsing around in a coal mine."

§

It had been almost two hours since Julie was supposed to stop by for lunch. Not only had she never showed up, but she hadn't responded to any of his texts or calls. Huitre was bewildered. And he was starting to get a little bit worried as well.

Samantha Trace's visit was unsettling to say the least. He had known she might harbor romantic feelings towards him, though Huitre had tucked that observation into the dark recesses of his brain. But that option was no longer available as Trace had forced the issue into the light.

Trace seemed quite unstable to Huitre. *Would she tell Julie what had happened?* For years, Huitre had told himself all too often that he had acted responsibly. That he had acted professionally. But had he? What if he had crossed a line? Was he burying his own guilt in the same place he'd buried his knowledge of Trace's feelings?

For the first time in years, Henry Huitre actually saw a possibility of finding someone to share something with. What kind of bad luck did he have that before he and Julie even were able to have their first, now aborted, lunch date, their relationship was already fraught with challenges?

Henry Huitre made up his mind. Samantha Trace would not decide what happened between him and Julie. He would tell Julie himself what he had done, and as the Americans say, *let the chips fall where they may.*

§

After hands and faces had been washed, fruit had been picked, sliced, and mostly eaten, Xander asked, "So, what's this summer's mission? More science experiments?"

"Uh..." Binny just now remembered how he'd come to their rescue the year before.

Zach stepped forward, "Actually, we *are* on sort of a mission."

"How can I help?" Xander cocked his head to one side to listen.

"Well, we started noticing a few days ago that our neighborhood – we live in Madrona – had several injured or missing animals."

"Oh." Xander's face remained placid and attentive. To Zach it even looked sympathetic.

"We think there's something strange going on." Zach said.

Zoe stepped forward. "What he *means* to say is that we think this kid we saw in the neighborhood is hurting them."

"Oh, that's serious indeed." Luce nodded. "You've seen him or her do this?"

"It's a him. He's very pale, with white hair. Scary looking." Zoe affirmed.

Xander put his hand to his chin and rubbed it side to side. "Ah. I see." After a moment of thought, he crossed his arms and addressed the children. "Well, that's not okay at all. Something should definitely be done about this. I'm so glad you kids are on the job."

§

"I tell ya, this chick was gorgeous, and she was *so* into me."

Victor Barrios listened to his boss' story politely as he always did. His calm face belied his annoyance. He'd heard stories of Grater's magnetic charm, from Grater himself of course, maybe five hundred times at this point. Not one of the stories had sounded believable. But as Grater was his boss, Barrios kept nodding politely.

Grater interrupted himself, "Is that?"

Barrios and Grater were on their daily appointed rounds of the campus passing between the greenhouse and the records room.

"It's those kids." Grater announced and marched towards the entrance to the greenhouse without seeing if Barrios was following.

The door swung open. "Everything okay here sir?" Grater asked Xander Luce.

"Why of course Gore. Why wouldn't it be?"

Grater couldn't think of why the very children he'd been instructed to observe each evening were now sitting here in the middle of his workplace.

"Uh. Right. Yes." Grater stuttered. "We'll continue our patrol."

"Absolutely." Xander winked to the children.

Barrios gave the children a sheepish nod before he trailed Grater back outside.

"As I was saying children, if there's ever anything I can do to help you with the mystery of the missing and

injured animals, please don't hesitate to let me know."
Xander smiled broadly. "And you can always stop by for
fruit of course."

§

The moment the greenhouse door closed, Gore
Grater had put his cell phone to his ear.

Barrios listened to Grater's one-sided conversation
without saying a word.

"Yes ma'am."

"I know, I'm sorry to interrupt."

"Those children,"

"Yes, the same ones."

"They're here."

"*Here* here. At the campus. In the greenhouse talking
to Luce."

"Yes ma'am."

§

"But we just got here." Ollie complained.

"We've been at the museum for awhile already."
Samantha Trace said. "And besides, you didn't even
want to come."

"But I wanted to see the dinosaur bones." Ollie had
preferred the zoo, but the natural history museum was

more interesting than he had wanted to admit. But now just as it was getting good, his mother was insisting they go back to work.

"I thought you had more pruning and cataloguing to do today at the greenhouse. We had a nice little visit to the museum, and now I'll take you back to finish the day's tasks." Trace tried engage her son.

"I don't feel like it." Ollie said.

"I promise, we'll go to the zoo another day."

"Can we just go home please?" Ollie sulked the entire car-ride back to the Luce Laboratories campus.

The route from the museum back to Luce Labs took Samantha Trace through the Central District, on the outskirts of the Madrona neighborhood where they lived.

"But I have to go back to work for a bit." Samantha found herself surprisingly pleased that her son wasn't excited to spend the rest of the day working in Luce's greenhouse.

"I could walk from here. I know the way."

Samantha thought for a moment. "It'll only be a couple of hours. You think you'll be alright on your own?"

Ollie brightened at the prospect of finally getting his way.

Samantha continued, "You'll go straight home? No stops? No sidetrips?"

Ollie reassured his mother with as much earnestness as he could muster.

Samantha Trace pulled over, let her son out on the sidewalk, and sped away towards Luce Labs.

§

"This was easier last year when we had our bikes." Penny complained good-naturedly.

"Those tunnels stretch pretty far." Zach said.

"I don't ever want to go back in those tunnels." Binny asserted.

"I do." Cassie grinned.

"You were scared out of your mind." Binny responded.

"I liked them too." Gabe added.

Zoe shook her head in disbelief.

"I think the people down there are mostly harmless." Zach said.

"I liked that old lady. She said I was a *thparkler*." Cassie did her best impression of the old woman's lisp.

"That old woman," Binny looked at the others, "the old woman who helped us, said something weird to me after you guys had gone up the ladder."

The children stopped in their tracks to listen to Binny.

"She asked me if I'd gotten what I needed from inside her head."

"She said 'from inside her head' just like that?" Zach asked in disbelief.

"Not exactly. She said 'from in there' and tapped on her skull as she said it."

"Maybe she was referring to *your* head." Zach responded.

"Maybe she was cray-cray." Zoe added.

"That first guy we met, he was clearly having some kind of issue." Penny added.

Binny made a sound signifying that she'd heard everyone's opinion, but that she had yet to be convinced.

Trying to close the issue for the moment, Penny said, "Well, I think the tunnels were cool."

Zoe looked at Binny for a moment before adding, "Yeah, they were pretty cool."

"Can we get ice cream?" Gabe asked. The walk had gone quicker than they'd thought, and the group now found themselves outside Madrona Dry Goods across from the park.

"You don't need ice cream." Zoe said. "And besides, I don't have any money with me."

"I have *some* money." Zach offered to buy everyone's ice cream after counting out that he had enough.

"That was nice of you." Binny told her brother. They had crossed the street to the park to eat the treats Zach had paid for.

"Oh nooooooo!" Zoe's words burst out of her in a wail.

They all ran to her side where she was crouching next to a bush. At first they couldn't see what she was looking at, but then they saw what she saw.

A black paw was sticking out from under the bush. Crouching a little further down they could see it was attached to a cat. The cat wasn't moving. This cat looked very much like the injured cat they'd seen the other day in the park.

Zoe and Cassie looked stricken. Zach and the others stood around feeling awful and not quite sure what to do.

After a minute, Binny said in a quiet voice that left no room for argument, "It's time to tell an adult."

§

As Zoe and Gabe's parents weren't home, and Penny did not under any circumstances want to go back to her house, the group decided to go to the Jordan house and tell Jay what they'd found.

"Guys, calm down. You're all talking over each other."

After introducing Zoe and Gabe to her father, Binny started to explain what happened. But soon, most of the others were adding their observations as well.

"Can I explain?" Binny said.

Binny took Jay through the events of the previous several days, including the injured cat in the park, the bird, the missing cat sign by the beach, and now the dead cat that at least according to Zoe was the very same cat they'd seen injured earlier in the week.

"And we're sure that boy had something to do with it." Zoe added when Binny had finished the retelling.

"We think it's possible he may be involved." Zach added.

Zoe shot Zach a look before turning back to Jay.

Jay took a moment to process everything he'd just heard, and invited everyone to sit in the family room. "First of all, I just want to say, thank you, to each of you. I think it's admirable that you care so much, and want to do something about it. Great job."

The younger children beamed at the compliment.

"I'm going to call animal control and make sure they remove the cat from the park." Jay got up to make the call.

"Wait, that's it?" Zoe said.

"And of course I'll also let them know about the missing cat poster, and the bird." Jay looked at Zoe. "And about the white-haired boy."

"Dad, we're superheroes. We're going to rescue the animals ourselves." Cassie said.

Jay smiled at his youngest, "Of course you are sweetie."

Cassie's eyes went large and she nodded her head up and down as she said, "No, really. We have a hideout and everything."

Jay took his daughter's hands in his own. "Sweetie. I know. And you're *my* superhero forever. But make-believe is one thing. And this isn't make-believe. I don't want you touching any dead animals you find around the neighborhood, and I don't want you chasing after people. You stick to pretending."

"You think I'm pretending?" Cassie asked, clearly wounded.

"No, I think you're *awesome* at pretending."

§

Huitre had considered calling the police, but realized that adults don't call the police when they've been stood up for a last minute lunch-date. Had Samantha already somehow contacted Julie and warned her away from him? Huitre told himself that was a crazy thought.

Huitre considered sending one final text to make sure that Julie was okay when his phone buzzed. He picked it up in a heartbeat and saw the message sent in response to the three concerned texts he'd sent. The response was only five words.

"Got stuck at work. Sorry."

❖ 22 ❖

THE GIFT

"You're not supposed to use that word." Gabe said to his older sister.

"Well it's true. That was terrible. He didn't take us seriously." Zoe said, hands on her hips.

"She's right. It sucked. My Dad didn't take us seriously." Zach added.

Zoe had been teary the whole walk from the Jordan house back to the shelter. The kids sat glumly at one of the lunch tables on the basketball court.

"What's wrong Cass?" Binny asked her sister.

Cassie had her arms crossed and hadn't spoken a word since her father had made it clear he hadn't believed a word she'd said about her powers.

"He didn't believe me." Cassie said in a low growl.

"He didn't believe any of us." Zoe said.

"And we agreed we wouldn't tell him about our powers or about the hideout." Binny gently chided her sister.

Zach took a moment to examine the long faces around him. "Look, I know we are kids. And kids depend on adults for all kinds of things. But we are not normal kids. We have powers."

"I don't." Gabe said.

Zach looked right at Gabe. "Not yet you don't. But I believe you will. And in many ways, kids with powers are stronger than adults." Zach saw the faces start to nod.

"We need to stop thinking first about how to convince the adults to help us, we need to think about how we can do things on our own."

"It's easy for you to say Zach. You do something useful, and you're in control of it. Cassie and I aren't in control of what we can do." Zoe said.

"I kind of agree," Penny added. "It's great and all that I can do it on command, but I'm only good for breaking things."

Binny noticed an extra note of sadness in Penny's voice.

"Do I need to remind you that you were the one that got us into the tunnels?" Zach asked Penny.

"Hey, I did that!" Gabe said.

"Yes. You did it too." Zach smiled at Gabe. "Look, I really feel that we're just scratching the surface of what we can really do. I think that if we work together, we'll find ways to do things we never dreamed were possible." Zach saw five wide-eyed faces hanging on his every word. "These powers, I don't know where they came from, but I do know that they've made us special.

"I know where they came from."

Six heads turned around to see Caleb Adams, baseball cap on his head, looking around the shelter.

Caleb whistled. "You sure did find yourselves quite a hideout, children."

"You know where they came from." Zach said. It was a statement – not a question.

"Who are you?" Gabe asked.

Caleb walked over to Gabe. "Nice to meet you Mr. Flowers. My name is Caleb." And then turning to Zoe. "You too Miss Flowers. I had the pleasure of meeting you both when your mother came in with you to buy flowers in my old shop up the hill." Caleb pointed in the direction of the Madrona commercial district.

Zach thought Caleb should've been pointing more *up* since they were so far underground.

"Nice to meet you." Gabe replied.

"Will you tell us?" Binny asked in a quiet voice.

263

"Tell you what Miss Jordan?" Caleb replied.

"Tell us where our powers came from?"

"Why they came from me, of course."

§

It took a few seconds for the kids to do anything more than stare at Caleb in stunned silence. And then it took a few minutes for them to stop shouting questions over each other. Caleb had to put his hands up to shush them so he could try and focus on one at a time.

"Before we get to all that, let me try and tell you what I know. I think if you let me wax poetic for a bit, then all your questions will be answered."

"You're gonna wax something?" Cassie asked?

"I'm gonna talk for a bit." Caleb reassured her.

The kids made room for Caleb at their table so he could take a seat.

"I don't know how long I've had the gift. Definitely since I was a child as young as some of you. Maybe since I was a baby. Maybe since even before then in my Momma's belly. But I too can *do* something special."

"What can you do?" Cassie asked, wide-eyed.

Caleb smiled. "Well, the most important thing I've been able to do is give the gift to others. And that's how each of you have come by it."

"Me too?" Gabe asked hopefully.

"I'm sure of it." Caleb answered.

Turning back to the others, Caleb continued. "This gift that you have, these powers that I gave you, they aren't without hardships. At first you'll think that they'll give you an advantage, that they'll make your lives real easy. And in some ways, they do. But in other ways, they invite problems and challenges too."

"I have been watching you – all of you. You are fine children. Each of you strong, and honest, and true of heart. That is one of my powers too you know." Caleb added conspiratorially. "I can tell what people's hearts are made of. And I can tell that you are the right children to bear this burden."

"Why did you give them to kids instead of adults? Wouldn't that have made more sense?" Penny asked.

"What burden?" Zoe asked.

"Let me take one at a time." Caleb laughed. "The powers can't be given to adults." Caleb's trademark gentle smile disappeared off his face momentarily. "It doesn't work on adults. The gift needs to be given to children, who are still growing, and are still learning who they are and what they're capable of. The more you grow, the more your powers will grow with you. But you have to start before you're fully grown."

"As for the burden, that's why I'm here. Mr. Jordan," Caleb gestured to Zach, "Kindly told me about what's been going on with some of the smaller creatures in the neighborhood." Caleb looked momentarily at Cassie, "I'm talking about ones even smaller than you."

Cassie giggled.

Caleb scanned his audience as he spoke. "Who's going to look out for those animals? I think it should be you all."

"We found an injured cat the other day, and today, we found it dead." Zoe was shaking as she spoke.

"I'm so sorry to hear that Miss Flowers."

Zoe's body seemed to relax at Caleb's words, her fists unballed.

"Mr. Jordan told me that you believe that there is a young man involved in these horrible incidents. And I agree that he most certainly is involved. Children who hurt animals grow up into adults that hurt people. I think you need to think of this as your first real challenge as a team."

Binny saw Cassie wince as Caleb made his prediction about the white-haired boy.

"Having these gifts is a burden because when there are opportunities to use them, to decline would be disrespectful. This, is such an opportunity, and there is nobody but you who can stop that troubled young man."

"What about you? You've got powers." Penny asked.

"Excellent question Miss Yang. That's why I'm here. To be part of the team. But if you don't mind, I'm a touch older than you. And my powers have not excused me from the drawbacks of getting old."

"If you're sure I'm getting powers, then how come I don't have them yet? Can you give them to me now?" Gabe asked.

"Gabe. Don't be rude!" Zoe admonished her brother.

"It's okay. It's a good question. Now you must understand children, there are many things about this that I simply don't understand, so I'll do my best to answer each question, but there are many holes in my knowledge." Turning to Gabe, Caleb said, "Just because the gift is given doesn't mean that the powers come immediately. For example, most children are born with the gift of speech, but that doesn't mean they don't still need to be taught language in order to use that gift."

"Can you teach me?"

Caleb looked at Gabe with empathy. "I wish I could. But, in my experience with these powers, circumstances are the best teacher."

"I have a question." Zach said. "Why did you tell us now? We've asked you before. *I've* asked you before. And you lied."

"I never lied to you."

"You let us go to Luce Labs and look for the cause of our powers even though you knew Luce Labs wasn't the source of them." Zach was getting heated. "That's called a lie of omission."

"I should know better than to debate with someone with perfect recall." Caleb smiled gently. "You're right, I'm sorry. That was not a nice thing to do. I'm sorry to each of you for not telling you sooner. I'll confess to you that I'm not entirely sure of the right way to go about this. As I said, this gift can be a burden."

Extra creases appeared on Caleb's forehead as he thought for a second before he continued. "When you first get the gift, there's no telling how long it will take for your powers to develop. And even once they do, it's not clear how each person will respond. In baseball, sometimes it's important to let the game develop before you make any rash decisions."

"I have zero idea what that means." Gabe said matter-of-factly.

Everyone laughed.

"It means, I'm doing my best and I'm sorry for not telling you sooner." Caleb said.

"Binny said we shouldn't tell any adults, but you're an adult." Cassie observed.

"Your sister is correct, but you are not Miss Jordan." Caleb raised his eyebrows. "You shouldn't tell any adults. But *I* am not an adult. *I* am an old person. Adults love bossing around children and elderly folks like myself. That's why we need to stick together." Caleb let one corner of his mouth rise in satisfaction.

"My dad didn't believe me when I told him." Cassie said, contemplating Caleb's instructions.

"My mom didn't believe me either." Gabe added.

Caleb looked at the two youngest members of the group. "Children, I understand your desire to tell your parents about what you can do. And normally I am a strong believer that honesty is the best policy. Especially between kids and parents. But I believe this is the exception that proves the rule."

"What's that?" Gabe asked.

"That means that the fact that this is the one time you shouldn't tell your parents something, proves that the rest of the time you should be completely honest with them."

"But why can't we tell them this too?" Cassie said.

"As you know from last summer's adventures, adults react in strange ways to things they don't understand. Maybe your parents would be fine, but the more people you tell, the more likely someone will be curious about what gives you your powers and want to poke and prod you to find out more." Caleb raised his eyebrows to underscore what he meant by "poke and prod".

Caleb continued, "And even worse, they may be afraid of you. Adults do that. A lot. And when they're afraid, they do hurtful things." Caleb saw the scared looks on the youngest children's faces. "But there's a more important reason to keep your powers a secret."

"There is?" Cassie looked hopeful.

"You are in a secret club now. Only a very few people on this earth have powers that are genuinely super human. This gift will bind the six of you together for the rest of your lives. You need to protect each other, and that starts with protecting your secrets from others."

Gabe and Cassie nodded along with everything Caleb was saying. Penny, Zoe, and Zach looked like they were in agreement as well.

Binny had been listening quietly to Caleb's answers but a slight look of worry had crept across her face. There was a momentary pause in the conversation and Binny made a decision. "Caleb, are we the only ones you've given powers to?"

Caleb paused, his trademark smile vanished momentarily as he collected his thoughts.

"Miss Jordan, no one else has the gift that each of you have been given."

To the others it looked like Binny was watching Caleb as he spoke. But Binny was watching the mental television in her head that let her see into the minds of the people around her. Binny watched the images in Caleb's mind as he spoke.

Caleb looked younger somehow. Afternoon sunlight streamed into Madrona Bouquets, Caleb's now retired neighborhood flower shop. Binny watched as her father entered the shop. He looked younger too. Next to her father was a happy toddler with curls. It was Cassie.

Jay was picking up flowers. Flowers for Binny's mother. Binny felt a hand clench around her heart as she watched the scene unfold. Younger Caleb walked around the counter with a single flower in a tiny pot. It was a pink cyclamen. Younger Caleb crouched down to toddler Cassie and was presumably giving her instructions on how to care for her gift.

Toddler Cassie's face lit up when she realized the flower was for her. Her arms shot out and she gave younger Caleb a big hug. Caleb hugged her back lifting her up into the air. Toddler Cassie giggled at the airlift. Younger Jay smiled.

Binny had done her best to respect Caleb's privacy. She truly had. But all this news, it was a lot. A lot of new information. And information that Caleb could have given them a lot sooner. Binny just wanted to take a quick peek into Caleb's mind. Binny wasn't entirely sure what she was looking for, just that she needed to see the truth.

Binny had learned over the past year that the substance of the things she saw in other people's minds were only part of the story. There were textures and colors that meant different things. Binny didn't have a handle on all of them quite yet – though she'd had quite enough of the deep pink for a lifetime – but the hues on the scene in Caleb's mind were familiar.

During the year Binny and Zach had devised a method using playing cards for Binny to hone her skills as a lie detector. Zach would look at each card and tell Binny what he saw. But sometimes Zach would lie and picture a different card than he was looking at. After some trial and error Binny could consistently predict when Zach was lying. Truth came in red. Lies in yellow.

The scene in Caleb's mind was awash in red. That felt good. But just before Binny looked away she noticed that a thin edge surrounding the entire scene was glowing a bright yellow. It was like truth wrapped in a lie.

Binny responded to Caleb, "OK. I believe you." and walked away.

§

It was past time to head home for dinner at everyone's respective houses. The kids and Caleb had walked from the hidden entrance through the woods and were now at the point in the neighborhood where they had to split up to head home.

"So what do we do next?" Zoe asked the group.

"I have an idea of what to do. But we're going to need some help." Zach looked at Caleb. "Caleb, we need to outfit the shelter with some equipment. A dark hole in the ground with no electricity is not really the best place to make our plans."

"And how can I be of assistance with that Mr. Jordan?" Caleb bowed his head towards Zach.

"For now, the main thing I need you to do is let me have some packages sent to your house. If they were to show up at my house, I think my father would ask too many questions."

"Nothing explosive of course Mr. Jordan. Correct?" Caleb looked like he was only half joking.

Zach smiled. "I promise. No explosions."

⤜ 23 ⤛

THE BOOKS ON RESERVE

Jay had hoped that with the kids out of school, he'd be able to sleep in more often during the summer. And even though he didn't have to get up early to shuttle them off to school, he still found himself getting up earlier than he'd hoped.

Jay normally tried to muster the early morning energy to get properly cleaned up and dressed before he would wander down to his study. But today wasn't one of those days. Jay sat in the shorts and t-shirt in which he'd slept staring at his drafting table wondering what to draw in his groggy state.

Jay's eyes wandered to the windows in his office. From his vantage point he could see across the street to Penny and Serena's house. Serena's words were still echoing in Jay's mind since their last conversation.

Jay knew he was lucky that he and Julie had remained friends. It was lucky for the kids, but it was lucky for him too. But Julie's frequent presence aside, Jay was still often a single parent. And despite that, he thought he was doing a decent job.

Jay wondered if he was being insecure, but he was extra vigilant to signs from his children that they were unhappy. Binny's anger seemed to be currently directed at her mother so Jay was letting Julie handle that. Zach was getting more and more distant and maybe even a touch surly. *Was that standard operating procedure for newly minted teenagers or was something else going on?*

And Cassie. That's who Jay was thinking about this morning as he alternated between staring at his blank sketchpad and the reflection of the rising sun on the windows of Serena's house.

Cassie had always lived in her own world of pretend. Jay had encouraged it. He thought it was creative. It made him feel a connection with his youngest child. But was her pretending going in an unhealthy direction? *Was she having trouble separating fiction from reality?*

Cassie seemed so hurt when he'd told her that he was pretending to believe that she had super powers. *Could it be that she was trying to relate to her superhero-obsessed father?* Was he crushing her dreams and imagination when he told her he didn't believe her?

Jay started to sketch. Jay always started with the villain. He already had a rough idea of what the hero would be doing, so he needed a formidable challenger that Cassie could vanquish. Jay drew a thin woman with mousey brown hair sprinkled with gray and pulled back tight in a bun. She had a cape. Despite their impracticality, Jay drew all his superheroes and villains with capes. Incredibles be damned!

On her chest Jay drew a huge index finger covering a pair of lips, an action she was mimicking in the scene. Out of the librarian's mouth Jay drew the sound "SHHHHHHHH" in big gradient filled letters.

Jay's evil librarian hated noise of all kind. He didn't have a name for her yet. The Shusher? The Quiet Storm? Evilbrarian? They were all lousy, but it didn't matter. This wasn't her comic. Jay drew his youngest daughter in generously bedazzled pink spandex. Cassie's entire body glowed brightly, and she was singing loudly. Her voice was her weapon and it was aimed directly at The Shusher/The Quiet Storm/Evilbrarian who's eyes were wide in shock at whatever effect it was having on her.

Above the battle, Jay drew a logo. In large letters the name Sparkle Girl hung over the scene in 3D. The name jumped off the page. Off to the left he carefully wrote "#1". *A collector's item,* Jay thought.

Julie might object to the "girl" in the name, but figured that when Sparkle Girl got older she'd rename herself Sparkle Woman. Or maybe just Sparkle. *Oooh, that was cool.* Sparkle Girl's cape was see-through and prismatic making the gems underneath that much brighter in the comic book sun.

Time passed quickly as Jay colored in his outlines, fleshing out the scene. Before long he was looking at a fully rendered comic book cover sitting in front of him. Jay couldn't help but smile as he thought about how excited Cassie would be to see she was the star of her very own comic book cover.

§

Xander Luce couldn't remember the last time he'd slept past five in the morning. For years it was a point of pride for him that he'd trained his body to need less sleep than most. But as his body had inevitably slowed down, Xander found he couldn't sleep longer if he'd wanted to.

But on this morning, it wasn't discipline or age that was interfering with his ability to sleep, it was a feeling. Something was bothering him, and his brain was going to be jumpy until he figured out what it was.

Artfully manicured trees, shrubs, and other greenery made the Luce Labs campus park-like above ground. But Xander hadn't wanted to waste an inch of the prime real estate and had made sure that the buildings, named after greek demigods, had almost as much space underground as above.

Xander's beloved greenhouse was named Triptolemos after the agricultural demigod. And while employees used the demigod names for most of the structures on campus, Xander had finally acquiesced to standard practice and also just referred to it as "the greenhouse".

But unknown to most employees was that, much like all the other structures, the greenhouse *too* had an underground component. Xander had named it Rhadamanthys. It had private lab space for Xander himself, as well as a small but comfortable apartment. Xander had always felt the press of time on his ambitions, and commuting to work seemed unnecessary and inefficient if he could live and work in the same spot.

Xander carried his teacup and a saucer containing a single biscuit as he walked from the small kitchen to the elevator that would carry him up to his office in the greenhouse. Sitting at his desk Xander took a bite of the biscuit and washed it down with a sip of the tea. Leaning back in his chair he closed his eyes and tried to get in touch with that feeling of uneasiness.

Could it be my standard fear? Xander's fear of dying before he completed his work was like a scratchy sweater that was impossible to remove. It was warm and familiar, but sometimes it poked at him and made him uncomfortable.

Xander was in fine physical shape given his age, but he'd already spent decades pursuing his scientific aims, and had little real progress to show for them. He knew that the children who'd visited him the day before were his best chance at a breakthrough in a long time. Xander savored the moment he'd first known that they actually had powers – a year ago sitting nearby in front of the video monitors that lined one of his walls.

Xander worried the Jordan children were his last best chance to get what he needed. Or maybe he already knew they were his last chance. Either way, despite his age, Xander Luce had responded with caution – especially after Dr. Trace's bungled efforts of the previous summer. Xander had decided that his clearest path was to observe them from afar and find ways to get them to work with him. And now they had fallen into his lap again – showing up at the greenhouse yesterday. But that wasn't what was bothering him. The pea underneath the mattress was his other cross-generational relationship – the one with Trace's son Ollie.

Luce liked Ollie. Genuinely. Xander respected Trace's abilities and loyalty but he couldn't say that he'd ever genuinely liked her. She always seemed so uncomfortable in her own skin. But her son, he *was* likeable. He just craved affection and attention.

But now his worlds were colliding. The Jordan children had decided that his young assistant was responsible for hurting neighborhood animals. *Could that be?* The boy had seemed unlikely to want to hurt much of anything in Xander's estimation.

But that wasn't quite right. *Was it.* Xander took another sip of tea and let his mind wander. And then as usually happened when Xander Luce let his mind wander, it took him to where he needed to be.

Xander replayed the scene from a few days earlier when the bird in the greenhouse had attacked Ollie and Ollie had fought back with the mangoes nearby. Xander remembered seeing some of the mangoes stuck into the wall and wondering how much force had been required to achieve that effect. Certainly more than he thought a ten year old boy could muster.

Xander wheeled over to the wall of computer screens and started typing on the console's keyboard. Scanning through the calendar he found the video from the day of the bird attack. Xander Luce clicked on the video file recorded by the camera in the relevant portion of the greenhouse and replayed the scene.

Luce replayed the video over and over in slow motion. His mind churned through the evidence before him. Ollie hadn't thrown the mangoes at the bird. They had thrown themselves – streaking through the air with increasing velocity as Ollie had thrashed under the bird. With no evidence that someone with the power of invisibility was whipping fruit at the bird, only one option remained – young Mr. Trace was telekinetically firing mangoes at his attacker. Xander Luce's new assistant had a super power of his own.

§

Zach was tempted to stay for the eggs his father was cooking, but grabbed a granola bar instead as he rushed out the door. Cassie and Binny weren't awake quite yet, but Zach had things to do before they all met at the shelter.

Zach headed to the Madrona branch of the Seattle public library. It was located in a small former firehouse around the corner from Madrona Dry Goods and named for the woman who'd fought for its creation. In more recent years, budget cuts had reduced the small library's hours, but this was one of the few days it opened early.

"Hi." Zach said to the woman behind the desk. She had deep brown eyes and wore a colorful headwrap. The placard on the desk said "Ms. Tawfeek."

She looked up, surprised to see someone in the library so early. "Oh, hello. How can I help you?"

"Hi. I ordered some books. My name is Zach Jordan."

Ms. Tawfeek motioned for patience as she disappeared behind a divider for a couple of minutes. When she reappeared she said, "I'm sorry, I didn't see anything under that name."

"Are you sure? I reserved them online. They should be here." Zach was gently insistent.

"I searched the *stacks* for them." Ms. Tawfeek responded.

"The stacks?" Zach looked puzzled.

"Oh. That's just what we call them. Big libraries, have back rooms or basements where they put all the books that aren't on the main shelves. All we have is the old firehouse basement."

"Neat. Could I see?" Zach's interest was piqued.

Ms. Tawfeek paused and made a face that Zach couldn't quite interpret. Then she stood on her tippy-toes surveying the small library. "I suppose it won't hurt. But don't tell anyone. Only librarians are allowed down there." She motioned to Zach to follow her down the stairs.

"This is cool." Zach surveyed the small room. It was carpeted, painted a bright color, and lit with overhead fluorescent lights. Cubbies filled with books on reserve, and in need of filing or repair lined most of the walls. "What's in there?" Zach pointed to heavy metal door sitting closed on the far wall.

"Even librarians are not allowed in *there*." Ms. Tawfeek had a glint in her eye as she let her words hang in the air for a moment. "I'm just teasing. I mean, we aren't allowed in there, but it's nothing particularly exciting. Periodically the city traipses through our library mucking up our carpeting to inspect some of the equipment in there. I think it's the utility pipes for this building and for the school across the street."

Madrona's elementary school sat across the street from the little firehouse library.

"It connects?" Zach had the tunnels under Madrona on his mind lately. This was one more piece of the puzzle.

"I think so. But as I said, librarians are not allowed, so I've never explored." Ms. Tawfeek winked. "Now about that book." Ms. Tawfeek did a methodical search of the cubbies behind her. "I don't see anything under your name." She was about to give up when she noticed sitting atop the cubbies a large stack of heavy books that wouldn't fit in one of the regular slots. "Oh wait."

"Are you going to be able to carry all these home?" Ms. Tawfeek pointed at the stack of books Zach had reserved.

Zach smiled. "I think so."

After carrying them all back up to the desk, Ms. Tawfeek spent a couple of minutes checking each one out in Zach's name on her computer. "We're the smallest branch in the system. Smart of you to order these. We never would have had these here in Madrona."

"Would you mind my asking you a question?" Ms. Tawfeek said to her only patron. "How old are you? I'm sorry if that's none of my business. You're obviously a curious boy, but these books, they're just, so *grown up*."

"Modern Multivariate Statistical Techniques" sat on top of "The Theory of Probability" which itself rested on "Statistics, 9th Edition." The last one was a college text book. There were several more books of equal density.

"I'm thirteen."

"Are you," Ms. Tawfeek paused for a moment, "taking a college course?"

"Nope. I just like math."

"And secret underground rooms." Ms. Tawfeek smiled.

§

"It's polenta." Melissa Flowers said to Gabe.

"It's grits." Gabriel Walker shook his head from behind his newspaper.

"But it's all mushy." Gabe complained.

"That's the way we have it for breakfast."

Gabe poked at the contents of his bowl with his spoon.

Zoe was already halfway through hers. "I'll eat yours if you don't want it."

"Look, it's got bacon and egg too." Melissa reassured her son. A thick cut slice of bacon and a poached egg sat atop the grits.

"What's the green stuff?" Gabe was still squeamish.

"Salsa verde. Just like you put on your tacos."

PopPop rolled his eyes.

"Seriously, I'll eat it." Zoe repeated.

"Zoe, you will not eat it. Dad, stop rolling your eyes. And Gabe, you *will* eat it. You've had all these things separately before. Now they're just together. Eat." Melissa Flowers stared at her son who reluctantly transferred a few molecules of grits from his to his mouth. Now it was Melissa's turn to roll her eyes.

"Hmmm. This isn't bad." Gabe took a bigger spoonful this time.

Satisfied with Gabe's progress, Melissa set about finishing cleaning the kitchen after breakfast. "Your father's already at the restaurant, and I have to go soon. What do you two have planned for the day? More superheroing with your new friends?"

"No. Definitely not. We're definitely not superheroes. And we definitely don't have superpowers." Gabe said between enthusiastic mouthfuls.

Zoe stared down at her bowl.

PopPop, brow furrowed, briefly glanced over his newspaper to examine his grandson.

Melissa raised her eyebrows at Gabe's response. "OK. Well are you going to hang out with your new friends and not be superheroes?"

"Zoe's friend is named Zach." Gabe blurted out.

Zoe stared even harder at her now empty bowl.

"Oh. A boy." Melissa paused for effect. And then she said, "How nice. Well, I would like to meet these children, and perhaps their parents at some point. You know I like to know what you're up to and who you're up to it with."

"Can I have more?" Gabe held up his empty bowl to his mother. It had been licked clean.

§

"I've been thinking," Ollie sat at the kitchen table eating a bowl of cereal as his mother drank her coffee standing. "I would like to walk home every day from your work. Maybe even leave a little early?"

Samantha Trace put her coffee down on the counter and crossed her arms. "Oh really."

"Yeah. I walked the other day after we went to the museum and I got home safely."

"It's a pretty long walk. Longer than from where I dropped you off."

"I know." Ollie said.

Samantha Trace looked over her son as he ate. She had not spent time fantasizing about being a mother as a young girl but she had taken to parenthood in her own way. Ollie was not always easy, and she didn't always understand him, but he was a bright boy, and more importantly, he was hers.

Samantha was torn. Ollie was getting a lot of attention from her boss. At first Samantha had worried that Ollie would be a bother. But Luce and Ollie genuinely seemed to like each other. She didn't mind not having to worry about getting angry calls from camp directors. But something about her son's relationship with Luce bothered her.

"You want to leave a little early? Are you not enjoying your time in the greenhouse?"

"Nah. It's good. I just want some extra time for the walk home. Maybe stop at the park and draw birds before I get home." Ollie spoke through a mouthful of cereal.

Samantha frowned. "Isn't that ice cream shop across the street from the park? And finish chewing your food before you answer please."

Before Ollie had a chance to swallow, Samantha continued. "Okay, fine. We'll try it. But hurry up. You're gonna make me late."

§

"How are your eggs-in-a-nest?" Jay asked his daughters.

285

Binny was almost done. Cassie was still working on hers. Both indicated their approval as they ate.

"Cassie, I've been thinking. I owe you an apology."

Binny's ears perked up. Cassie kept eating.

"I'm sorry I doubted you were a superhero. I got up early this morning and designed you your own costume on your very own comic book cover." Jay pulled out his drawing from earlier that morning, now complete, and displayed it proudly to his daughter.

Binny froze.

Cassie stopped eating.

Jay continued, "See, you're glowing and fighting the evil Shusher – she's a rogue librarian and going around trying to force everyone to stay quiet. You're singing voice has powers. Oh, and also, you glow and sparkle when you use your power."

"No I don't." Cassie responded quietly.

"On the cover I mean. When you're out being a superhero. See?" Jay pointed at his drawing.

"I don't glow. I don't have any powers. I'm not a superhero."

Binny held her breath.

Jay sighed gently. "I know sweetie. I just wanted to do something nice for you. I'm sorry I doubted you before."

"It's okay. I'm sick of superheroes. Can we talk about something else?" Cassie said.

Jay looked dejected. "Okay honey. I'm sorry. I'll hold on to this for you if you want it."

§

Penny ate her yogurt in silence.

"Do you want more raspberries in your yogurt?" Serena asked her daughter.

"I can get them." Quincy started making to get up from the table and head to the kitchen.

"No thanks." Penny said between spoonfuls.

Her father and mother sat at the table watching their daughter nurse her yogurt and her hurt. Penny knew they loved her, but right now she was still angry. Mostly at her father, but at her mother too. At least her Dad's friend – *boyfriend?* – wasn't there. He didn't belong. Penny's father hadn't told her the truth, but the more she thought about it, the more she realized that neither had her mother. They both lied to her. And Penny wasn't feeling very forgiving.

The doorbell rang. Binny and Cassie let themselves in without waiting for an invitation. "Are you ready to go?" The two Jordan girls stood expectantly, big grins on their faces.

"Would you ladies like some breakfast?" Serena asked?

"Are you Penny's Dad?" Cassie asked.

"Why yes I am." Quincy smiled.

"I'm Binny, this is Cassie." Binny said.

"Nice to meet you both." Quincy said.

"Let's go." Penny got up to take her dish to the sink.

"No breakfast for you two?" Serena asked a second time.

"My dad already made me an egg-in-a nest. He's a good cook." Cassie boasted.

Binny put her hand on Cassie's shoulder and gave Penny's parents a look of embarrassment.

"Oh is he?" Serena asked. "I'll have to try his cooking."

"Come on. Let's go." Penny headed to the door with Binny and Cassie in tow.

As they watched the three girls walk down the hill, Serena put her hand on her ex-husband's shoulder and said, "Give it time. It's going to get better. I promise."

"I'm not going anywhere until it does." Quincy promised back.

⇥ 24 ⇤

THE BROKEN GENERATOR

"You're late." Binny said matter-of-factly.

"Uh, it took me a little longer than usual." Zach motioned to the pile of books he had just set down on the long lunch table.

"What are all these?" Zoe asked.

"I'm hoping they're solutions to a couple of our problems." Zach said.

"You don't expect us to read these do you?" Binny asked.

"Nope. I'm gonna read them." Zach said.

"And how will *Modern Multivariate Statistical Techniques* help us?" Zoe asked sarcastically.

"I'm going to apply these techniques to some information." Zach said smugly.

"What information is that?" Zoe asked.

"That's where you guys come in." Zach smiled.

Zach explained to the rest of the group that if animals really were disappearing from around the neighborhood, there would be more signs like the one that Binny had found by the water.

There were at least nine different public gathering areas in Madrona ranging in size from a duck pond with a gazebo, to the lakefront beach, all the way to the woods under which they were now located. Additionally there were a dozen stores in the tiny Madrona commercial district. Between the parks and the stores, there were several bulletin boards where neighborhood residents might post notices of a missing animal.

"While I'm busy reading these and trying to get the generator running, I need you guys to find out just how many animals are missing, and what the phone numbers and addresses are of their owners, if possible."

"I'm not going." Penny announced. She had been sitting against the wall, off to the side of the group. Something about her tone ensured that nobody challenged her.

"Well, we better get going then." Zoe announced.

Zoe and Binny gathered their younger siblings and headed out towards the shelter's exit to find out just how big the animal problem really was.

As they walked out, Zach could hear Cassie and Gabe talking excitedly.

"I think we're really on a superhero team now."

"Definitely."

§

"Good morning son." Xander Luce was waiting for Ollie as he entered the greenhouse.

"Good morning." Ollie would have thought he was in trouble had Xander not been smiling so broadly.

"Did you have a good afternoon with your mother?"

A cloud momentarily crossed Ollie's face. "Yeah. It was fine."

Luce looked like he was trying to think of how to broach a delicate subject, but just hadn't decided on the right approach. Ollie had his own difficult subjects that he too hadn't yet figured out quite how to talk about.

Ollie broke the silence. "Xander?"

"Yes Ollie."

"Can I ask you a question?"

"Of course."

"You mentioned that sometimes Luce Labs experiments on animals, and even human beings."

Luce sat down on a stool and motioned Ollie to do the same. Luce looked unexpectedly pleased with the direction the conversation had taken. "That's true."

"I know you told me this before, but can you tell me again when it's okay to do that?"

Xander smiled a broad grandfatherly smile. "This is an excellent topic, and one I have wrestled with all my life."

"All your life?"

"Yes." Xander's smile faded into a more serious expression. Ollie felt Xander's icy blue eyes pierce his own.

Luce continued. "I have spent my life on a quest. A quest to help humanity. Now Ollie, you must understand, I am not trying to claim that I am a humanitarian or a martyr. This is also selfish quest, as I am human too. But I am on a quest to help all of us reach our true potential."

"There are so many things in life that can stop each of us from reaching our potential. We could be born into a country with a corrupt government. We could be born into a family with neglectful parents. We could be injured or killed in an accident. We could suffer from disease."

Ollie's eyes got wider as Luce spoke.

"I don't tell you these things to scare you. I tell you these things because I believe in truth. I have had some challenges in my life. Some have had more, and some have had fewer. And while I've had some luck too, ultimately, everything I've accomplished, I've accomplished on my own."

"I've built this business. I've contributed to the community. I've created jobs for my neighbors and for your family." Luce winked. "And most importantly, this company that I created has created medicines and techniques that have helped others reach their potential. Drugs Luce Laboratories has invented have literally saved people's lives."

"Now I am not patting myself on the back. I am simply stating facts. And while I consider myself a very lucky man, these things I have done were not without sacrifice."

Ollie wondered what sacrifices Luce was talking about.

Luce continued as if he'd heard Ollie's question. "Not the least of those sacrifices Ollie is that I never had time for a family. Now I am not telling you this looking for sympathy. I am still, just stating facts. Everyone has challenges, everyone tries to reach their potential, and everyone makes sacrifices on that journey."

"And do you know why I chose to make those sacrifices?"

Ollie shook his head slightly.

"Because I believe that we humans have barely scratched the surface of our capabilities. I believe that in the future, humans will unlock more and more of their potential and do things that will amaze you and I both." Luce winked again.

"The things we see today Ollie, computers, surgeries, medicines, machines – when I was your age – these things would have looked like miracles. And sometimes to me they still do. I have seen things Ollie. I have seen amazing things. And I have a feeling that you have too."

Ollie felt butterflies in his stomach.

"So the answer to your question is this Ollie: We are all in this together. Humans, animals, even the plants. Everything on our planet. We all face challenges, and we must all make sacrifices. So when you ask me, is it ok to experiment on living creatures, what do you think I'll say?"

The question hung in the air for several seconds. Ollie was too nervous to answer.

Luce lowered his voice to just above a whisper. "If you are one of the few people who are trying to help humanity reach their potential, then yes son, it's not only okay to experiment, it is your sacred obligation."

The last forty-eight hours had been a whirlwind for Ollie. He supposed he had always known there was something going on inside him. But since the bird had attacked him in the greenhouse, those vague suspicions had come more and more into focus.

At the park, he'd come even closer, controlling that bird. The girl with the curls, Cassie, she'd seen him do it. At least until that gang of kids, Cassie's siblings and their friends had interrupted him. And since the park he'd tried again and come even closer. And though Ollie couldn't bring himself to say it out loud, or even admit it to himself, he liked it.

Ollie liked exercising his power. Ollie liked feeling strong. Ollie really liked being unique. And the fact that he liked it so much made him feel bad – because there was cost. There was sacrifice. The animals he'd been drawing, the animals who's energy he'd been soaking in, well, they were the price for Ollie learning about his power.

Ollie liked hanging out with Xander in the greenhouse, but he was getting less and less enthusiastic about drawing plants. Drawing animals was just so much more... *fulfilling*.

"Xander?"

"Yes?"

"Would it be okay if I left early sometimes in the afternoons? My mom already said I could leave a bit early and walk home on my own."

Luce wondered what his young charge would be doing on those afternoons but thought better of asking. "Of course Ollie. I'm just glad to have your help as often as you enjoy coming by."

§

"Oh. Hi. What a pleasant surprise. Come in. Come in." Since the kids had left after breakfast, Jay had been avoiding work, and allowing himself to wallow in a touch of self-pity at Cassie's lack of excitement over the drawing he'd made for her.

"I'm sorry if it's a bad time. I don't mean to be a bother." Serena said.

"Oh no, I'm just procrastinating, and I'd rather not do it alone anyway. Come in, come in." Jay motioned to Serena to come in.

Walking by Jay's office Serena lingered at the wall of Jay's drawings. "I hope you don't mind, I really like them."

"Mind? No, I could spend all day watching people admire my drawings. But it would be tacky to say that out loud. So pretend I didn't say that. Instead, let's pretend I said something self-effacing like – Oh, those? They're not very good. Feel free to look but don't judge me too harshly." Jay smiled broadly.

Serena smiled too.

Jay and Serena spent the next while going through his various drawings. Jay explained his regular job and how he usually spent way too much time procrastinating from that and drawing the things he loved instead of the things his clients were asking for. It made deadlines more pressured, but it seemed to be the only way he could cope.

Serena instantly understood. She explained to Jay that her work patterns as a writer were eerily similar. "But instead of writing things I love, I come by and bug my neighbors to get out of doing the things I'm supposed to do."

"Oh, you've bugged others?" Jay remarked with a raised eyebrow.

Serena smiled sheepishly, "Well, I guess I should have said 'bug the neighbor' as you're the only one I've bugged."

Jay sensed that there was something else on Serena's mind, but he didn't want to press. "Can I offer you some coffee or tea?"

"That would be nice."

§

"This is where I saw the sign." Binny said to Zoe, Gabe, and Cassie.

They had walked on one of the many rough hewn paths zigzagging down the hill through the Madrona woods until they'd reached the shore of the large lake on which the neighborhood was situated.

"It's still there. But now there's another one." Zoe looked at the telephone poll solemnly. Next to where the yellow sign looking for "Joni" had been was another one in green with a photocopied picture of a small gray tabby called "Sprinkle".

Binny tore a phone number off of the new poster and put it in her pocket. "Let's keep going."

The four kept walking, faces grim.

§

Penny had clearly been in no mood to talk, so Zach tried to steer clear of her. That's why he was surprised when she came ambling over to him.

"Whatcha doin'?"

Zach was sitting cross-legged in front of one of the generators. The light from the Christmas lights and the flashlight he'd propped up wasn't quite enough to stop him from squinting as he read the generator's manual.

"I think it's safe to say that I have no idea at all what I'm doing."

Penny laughed a little despite herself, but quickly choked it off.

Zach continued, "I've got the gas in the right place. I've replaced the spark plugs with new ones."

"Where did you get those?" Penny asked.

"I spent the last of the contents of Cassie's piggy bank on them this morning on my way here."

"Oh."

"It's okay. I'm not complaining. We'll get more money."

Penny wasn't sure how they were going to get more money, but she let Zach's statement pass without a question.

Zach continued ticking off a mental checklist. "I've checked the fuel line. And I've even turned the crank. But nothing is happening."

"Well, I'd help, but as you know, fixing things is not quite my specialty." Penny's sarcasm had a note of anger in it.

Zach forced a smile towards Penny. He knew she was upset but he didn't know why.

§

"Is everything okay?"

Jay and Serena were on their second cups of coffee. The conversation had stalled for a moment as they'd exchanged stories about the trials of single-parenting. Jay hadn't wanted to ask, but the look on Serena's face told Jay that she had something on her mind she wasn't sharing.

Jay continued, "I don't mean to pry. It's none of my business."

"No. You're being very kind. Thank you." Serena took another sip of her coffee and looked like she was steeling herself for a needle at the doctor. "Things have been a bit of a challenge lately for Penny. I mean, I know everything's going to be okay. But she's going through a bit of a rough patch with her dad and there's not much I can do to help it pass any faster."

Serena continued relaying the story of how when she and Quincy had decided to split up, he had stayed in the Bay area and she had moved north with Penny. They'd been planning to do it for awhile for her work, but when the separation happened, Quincy had decided to stay behind to embrace the new chapter in his life. Serena thought he was running from their daughter's disappointment as much as he was running *toward* his future, but she also understood how hard it was for him.

"And now it's all coming out – as it were." Serena looked up from her coffee cup and offered Jay a shy smile. "I've been prattling on for awhile. I'm sorry about that."

"No, I appreciate you sharing. I see Penny often so it's helpful for me to understand what's going on in her life. Thank you." Jay smiled.

Looking suddenly eager to change the subject Serena noticed the piece of paper sitting on the kitchen table with Jay's drawing from earlier in the day. "What's this?"

Jay shifted in his chair and took a breath. "Well, you encouraged me to embrace Cassie's superhero fantasies."

"*Cassie's* superhero fantasies?" Serena raised her eyebrow and one corner of her mouth in Jay's direction.

"Fair point." Jay conceded. "*Anyway*, she had come to me yesterday with all sorts of superpower talk and I discounted it and told her it was pretend. But then your voice was ringing in my head –"

"My voice? I'm honored." Serena teased Jay gently.

"Yes yes." Jay dismissed her joke with a smile. "And I asked myself why I was crushing my eight-year-old's creative spirit. So I got up early this morning and drew her as the hero of her own comic book."

"I see that. Honestly, spirit-crushing aside, it looks really pro. I could imagine this on the newsstand. Have you done these for real?"

"Real comic books? Oh no. I usually just do my little vignettes. But I decided to do a full cover for her to, you know, make up for the soul-crushing. This is my first one. Needless to say, she was unimpressed."

"Well I'm impressed."

"Thanks." Jay looked a little embarrassed.

"So what are you waiting for?"

"What am I waiting for?"

"Yes." Serena raised her eyebrows looking expectant.

"I'm not sure what you –" Jay said, slightly confused.

"Jay Jordan, you've been telling me how much you love drawing your kids as superheroes, and how little you like drawing medical equipment, and illustrations for boring magazine articles. Why aren't you making Sparkle Girl into a real comic book?"

"Into a real..."

Serena nodded excitedly. "Yes. Into a real comic book. Or maybe all of them, not just Cassie. Like that drawing you did with Penny in it."

"Oh my god. They'd be so mortified."

"We don't get paid for being parents. Embarrassing our children is one of the perks of the job." Serena smiled widely.

Jay's mind was racing with the possibility. Could he really draw an entire comic book? And what about the story? Who would write it? "So, let's say I did follow your advice, and put together a comic book starring the kids as superheroes. It's not that I don't appreciate your encouragement but there's one thing you haven't considered in your little scenario."

"Oh really? What's that?" Serena cocked her head.

"The story. I can draw the panels, but someone needs to write the story and dialogue."

Serena was caught speechless for the moment.

Jay looked smug. "Know any good writers?"

§

Zach had been rereading and rechecking the manual for over an hour. Penny had watched his meticulous work in silence, lost in her own thoughts.

"I'm gonna give this one more shot today, and then I'm gonna do something else. I've kind of had enough of this thing for the day."

Zach stood up, wiping the dust from his pants with his hands and took a firm hold of the crank. One turn. Two turns. Three turns. Zach was sweating. The crank was difficult for adults to turn. Zach was thirteen.

Penny watched, the expression on her face inscrutable.

"Ugh. Enough." Zach threw his hands up in the air in frustration. Zach reached for the crank to remove it and set it back in its place beside the generator but it wouldn't come out. It was stuck.

Zach turned to Penny, "Would you mind giving me a hand pulling this out? I want to put all this away so Cassie and Gabe don't get into it."

"You're sure you're not worried about me breaking it? Everything I touch seems to fall apart." Penny said in a quiet bitter voice.

"Actually, I'm kind of counting on that. It's stuck. I'm hoping a little Penny power will pry it loose." Zach smiled.

Penny rolled her eyes but got up to help. They both pulled and nothing happened. Penny concentrated harder. Nothing.

Penny directed Zach. "Maybe if you turn the crank while I touch the generator."

"OK." Zach set himself firmly and started to turn the large crank.

Penny placed her hands on the generator and closed her eyes. The familiar feeling swirled around her head and her hands. The feeling that told her something was about to snap.

The small but loud explosion surprised Penny into opening her eyes. *Oh no, I did too much.* She looked down expecting to see the generator in pieces. But a second small explosion cleared her mind. The generator was growling, and then it was humming. And then the fluorescent bulbs that hung from the ceiling in the bomb shelter which hadn't been turned on in decades sparked into life.

Zoe, Binny, Cassie, and Gabe had just returned to the shelter from their reconnaissance mission and had wandered over to the generator to see what Penny and Zach were doing. Now they all stood there along with Zach, mouths open, alternating their intense stares between Penny and the lights above. Everything was illuminated.

Penny was confused. "Did I break it?"

Zach spoke. "Penny, you didn't just not break it. You fixed it. I think you can fix things too."

⇥ 25 ⇤

THE FIXER

"I'm starving." Penny said to nobody in particular as they all walked the long hallway out of the shelter towards the woods and back home for lunch.

"Special delivery." Caleb announced as the kids poured out the big metal door buried behind decades of overgrowth in the heart of the Madrona woods.

"Caleb!" Cassie exclaimed.

"It's addressed to you Mr. Jordan." Caleb handed the package to Zach.

"What is it?" Zoe asked.

"If it's what I ordered, it's gonna keep us from getting in trouble with our parents while we're down in the cave." Zach smiled at Zoe.

Binny rolled her eyes.

As if on command, Zach's phone buzzed. Zach looked at the screen and shook his head. "He wants me to pick up some groceries this afternoon on the way home." Zach muttered as he responded affirmatively via text.

Zach looked up from his phone. "You guys go ahead. I'm gonna stay and get this set up."

Cassie turned to Gabe and Zoe, "Want to come to our house for lunch? I bet my Dad will make peanut butter and banana sandwiches. Sometimes he lets me dip the sandwich in Nutella between bites."

"Can we go? Can we go?" Gabe turned to Zoe.

Zoe thought for a moment. "Do you guys promise to come right back here?" Turning to Binny? "Would you mind if I stayed and helped Zach? I'm not that hungry."

Binny glanced back and forth at Zoe and Zach. "Yeah, okay. No problem."

§

"I'm hooooome." Penny yelled as the front door clattered behind her. "What's for lunch?"

Serena raised her eyebrows at Quincy at their daughter's noisy return. "Hi Pen." They said as they peered through the kitchen door to welcome her.

"We're making salad and salmon." Serena added.

"Where's Jonathan?" Penny asked.

"He ran out to the bookstore." Quincy said.

"Oh. Well, I'd like to talk to the both of you actually." Penny said.

The seriousness of Penny's tone got her parents' attention. Serena and Quincy sat down at the kitchen table and gave her their full attention.

"Here we are." Quincy said in a soft voice.

Penny sat down opposite her parents, seemingly bursting with energy, and took stock of her parents before she started talking quickly.

"Thanks for sitting with me. I know that our family has been broken for a long time now. Dad, with you living far away, and me and Mom living up here. And I also know that this isn't your fault."

Penny's parents exchanged glances.

"Mom, I know that over this past year I've broken a lot of things. And I'm really really sorry about that." Penny looked to her father briefly, "I've been really clumsy." And then readdressing both of them, "But that's over now. Well, maybe not quite over. I still might break things. But I can fix things too. I can fix things!"

Penny leaned back with her arms crossed as if she'd made her case.

"Of course you can honey. Everybody breaks things. And of course you can fix things." Serena said, somewhat confused at the direction the conversation had taken.

Quincy raised his finger, his mouth open, a worried look on his face, but said nothing.

"No Mom. Don't you see. I can *fix* things. I broke this, and I can fix it." Penny responded to her mother.

"Oh Penny." Quincy said, his voice filled with sadness.

"Fix what honey?" Serena asked, suddenly nervous at the response.

"Us. Our family. I broke us, and now I can fix us."

Serena burst into tears. Penny's father's eyes were red-rimmed.

"Why are you crying? It's okay now. I will fix everything." Penny smiled at her parents.

"Penny," Quincy took his daughter's hand. "You didn't break us. None of this is your fault."

"OK. Fine. But I can still fix things. I can fix things now." A note of uncertainty crept into Penny's voice. Penny spoke more quickly, "Dad can move back in. And we can be a family again."

Now the tears were streaming freely down Quincy's face.

"Honey. Look at me." Serena held up her tear-streaked face to her daughter. "I know things have been hard. I know things have felt broken. And I know you want Daddy to live here with us. But the changes we've been going through, they're not your fault, and they're not reversible."

"Things can go back to how they used to be. We were happy before, and we can be happy again." Penny was rapidly losing the courage of her convictions, but she raced through her words as if getting to the end of her sentences would make them come true. "I can fix things."

"No sweetie. We can't go back to the way things were. None of us have the power to make that happen." Serena told her daughter.

Penny had been so sure. The hum of the generator. The lights coming on in the shelter illuminated the idea in her mind. She could fix things, fix every thing. But no. Even *that* wasn't good enough. Her family would be broken forever. Penny shattered.

§

"Helloooo. Helloooo. Helloooo." Zoe was lying on the floor of the shelter in one of the storerooms repeating herself into a metal grate. Zach had explained that it was a ventilation shaft to let air in and out of the shelter. Zach was above in the woods trying to find the other end.

"Helloooo. Helloooo. Helloooo." Zoe knew that Gabe was her responsibility, but Binny clearly had experience dealing with little siblings. And besides, Zach needed help. But of course that's not why she had stayed behind. The real reason was that she simply wasn't that hungry.

"Helloooo. Helloooo. Helloooo." Zoe pictured Zach up above hunting among the trees and growth for a small vent. Maybe metal, or concrete. Zach hadn't been specific. Zach was sure all this effort would be helpful in finding who was hurting the animals. It was really very nice of him to take on her cause. He really seemed to want to help.

"Helloooo baaaack." Zoe heard Zach's voice coming through the vent. Tinny and a little bit far away, but still, it was him. He'd found the other end of the shaft. "I'll be down in a minute."

Zach arrived in the storeroom with a screwdriver, a cardboard box, and a big smile on his face. He immediately got down on his side and started unscrewing the metal vent panel.

With the panel removed, Zoe saw a small cable dangling from the shaft above. Zoe watched Zach take an electronic device from the box Caleb had delivered, plug the dangling cable into it, and plug the box into the nearby wall socket that was now live courtesy of Penny's amazing new power. Zoe hoped nobody saw the look on her face when they all realized that Penny could now fix things as well as break them.

Zoe's eyes wandered down to Zach. He looked so serious and determined. "Now, will you tell me what you're up to?"

Zach got up from the floor with a big grin on his face. "Nope. But I'll show you."

Zach pulled out his cell phone and dialed some numbers. In a moment Zoe's ringtone was echoing off the walls of the shelter. Zoe had to pull her phone out of her pocket and look at the screen before she realized what Zach had done. Zach just stood there grinning like an idiot.

"Wait, how did you do that?" Zoe asked.

"How many bars do you have?" Zach responded.

"Five."

"Me too." Zach was triumphant.

Zach must have seen the look on Zoe's face shift a bit as he quickly changed his tone. "What's wrong?"

"That was really smart." Zoe conceded.

"But?" Zach asked.

"But nothing."

"Your face is disagreeing with your words."

Zoe laughed despite herself. "Fine. Fine. It's just, that was really smart. And you weren't even using your power. Penny's got this amazing new thing she can do. What Binny can do is just ridiculously cool. And I know this is totally selfish sounding, but I'm just feeling pretty lame."

"I saw what you did. It was pretty amazing too."

"A hole in the ground? You think making a hole in the ground is amazing? The Grand Canyon is an amazing hole in the ground. What I did was distinctly not amazing. I mean, really does it even technically count as a power?" Zoe was getting worked up.

"I can't do it." Zach said.

"Neither can I. At least not on command. It just happens when I get really upset."

"Well, even without a power, it's great to have you here." Zach was being conciliatory.

"Oh yeah, why?" Zoe asked. "What about me is so great to have around?"

Zach flushed.

"You don't have an answer do you." Zoe demanded.

"I... I..." Zach tried to get the words out.

"I don't need your pity you know."

"I know. It's not pity." Zach fumbled.

Zoe waited for Zach to say something else. But he didn't. "Whatever." Zoe walked away.

§

Quincy came back into the kitchen. He'd stepped into the hallway to text Jonathan to take his time at the bookstore.

"Sweetie, let me ask you a question. When you grew out of your shoes last year, were you broken?" Serena asked her daughter as she rubbed her back.

"No. Of course not." Penny's eyes were red-rimmed and puffy.

Quincy sat back down opposite Penny and Serena.

"But your shoes didn't fit anymore. They didn't really work the way they had." Serena said.

"I don't always wear shoes anyway."

"That's not the point."

"What is the point?" Penny was getting frustrated.

"The point is that people grow. And it's not just their feet. People grow in different directions, and sometimes things don't fit the way they used to."

"You're talking about you and Daddy."

"Yes." Serena responded to her daughter.

"So are we going to throw Daddy out like we did my shoes?" Penny asked.

"I'm not sure I like where this analogy is going." Quincy smiled.

Penny shot her father a look making it clear she didn't think he was being funny.

Serena continued, "Well, some people when they get divorced, they do kind of throw each other away. But even though your father and I don't fit the way we used to, it's not because something broke, it's because we both grew."

"You mean Daddy likes boys now."

Serena looked at her ex-husband, her eyes forming a question.

Quincy girded himself to answer his daughter. "Yes. That's true. But it's not just that. Your mother is the most amazing woman I've ever met. She's my best friend. And she's given me the single best thing in my life – you. But we've both grown and are trying to figure out how to best rearrange our family."

Penny's anger was fading a bit, replaced slowly by a determined look.

Serena interjected, "We know it feels bad. We know it feels like things are broken. And we're so so sorry. But I promise, we're growing. And these feelings are growing pains. We're going to get through this growth spurt, and find that we're taller, and stronger, and even happier."

"When?" Penny asked.

"When what honey." Quincy answered.

"When will the growth spurt be over?"

"Soon. I hope soon." Quincy Yang said to his daughter and to himself.

§

"Come in." Zach said closing his laptop quickly.

Jay Jordan came into his son's room and sat on the bed. It was late, and the girls were already asleep. His face looked serious. "We need to talk."

"OK."

"You forgot to pick up the things I needed for dinner tonight." Jay began.

"Oh. Shoot. I'm so sorry."

Jay cut off his son before he could say anything else. "Look, I know you work hard during the year, and that's why your mom and I haven't scheduled you for all kinds of activities during the summer. But I need a minimum of help from you around the house, and to be honest you're not even doing that."

"I like that you're out and about most days. The fresh air is good for you. But your head seems to be in some far away place. It worries me. I'm expecting you to be responsible for your sisters while you're all out. But if you're so distracted that you can't remember to pick up some things at the market, I worry that you'll be too distracted to look out for your siblings. What is going on with you?"

For the second time that day, Zach felt tongue-tied. Zach was distracted. With super powers, and missing animals, and setting up their headquarters, and Zoe of course. But there were exactly zero of those things he was going to tell his father about.

And besides, Zach was annoyed that his father was questioning whether he was being responsible for his sisters. That's most of what Zach spent his time doing – being responsible. For his sisters, for the missing animals, for their friends.

Zach had even spent a bunch of time today making sure that his cell phone wouldn't be out of reach when they were in the shelter. He'd done that so his father could always get in touch. *Wasn't that more important than some stupid groceries?*

Zach's mind raced with a hundred retorts to his father's patronizing concern. But all he said, was, "Sorry."

"I love you Zach. I really need you to step up a bit."

Jay kissed Zach on his forehead and left to go to bed.

Zach didn't have time to dwell on his frustration with his father or with his life in general. The moment the door clicked closed, Zach raced to reopen his laptop.

Damn! Zach thought. Jay's little father-son chat had cost him $350.

⇒ 26 ⇐

THE PICTURE FRAMES

Zach noticed a routine to the days that followed. They would gather in the mornings and plan out their day. Most mornings Caleb was also in attendance, nodding sagely at the plans that were being made.

Zach would focus on getting the shelter organized while the rest of the kids would do their standard circuit of the neighborhood searching for more mentions of missing animals. Sometimes the kids would return to their own houses for lunch, and sometimes they would all gather at one house.

Zach and the others didn't know that Ollie was doing his own circuit of the neighborhood in the afternoons when he would leave the greenhouse early and have a few hours to himself before his mother got home from work.

In the evenings before dinner, Zach would usually go to pick up groceries while his sisters went to walk Rembrandt. Often Penny would go too. Even Zoe and Gabe had taken to joining the regular evening walks with Rembrandt periodically. And even though she was often there for the Jordan evening meal, Julie Jordan had stopped accompanying her daughters to Dr. Huitre's. Binny noticed but said nothing.

Each day ended like the previous with Zach, alone in his room, staring at his computer late into the night.

§

After a few of these days Zach was in a particularly good mood on his way to the shelter. Binny, Penny, and Cassie were trailing along when they ran into Caleb, wearing his overalls, his baseball hat, and carrying his milk crate full of gardening tools.

"Caleb? What are you doing here?" Zach said.

Caleb paused, looked around, and said, "Should I not be here?"

"You're supposed to be at home waiting for the packages. Today's the day." Zach sounded slightly frustrated, though it was hard to get really worked up with Caleb as he always remained so calm.

"Oh." Caleb raised his eyebrows in what might have been mock surprise. Zach wasn't sure. "I'm sorry. My mind isn't what it used to be."

"What's going on?" Zoe and Gabe had just arrived on the little summit happening in the middle of the woods.

"The packages are arriving this morning at Caleb's house. We need to bring them down to the shelter." Zach responded.

"You haven't told us what's in them." Only a hint of frustration was discernible in Zoe's voice.

"I want to surprise you guys." Zach smiled.

"If there are a lot of packages, I'd probably need help bringing them down to your secret lair anyway." Caleb turned to the assembled kids and said, "How about a bunch of you strapping youngsters head over to my house, and bring everything down here once it's been delivered."

"I'm strong!" Gabe stepped forward and made a muscle.

Zach saw Binny smile at Gabe's bravado. The contrast between his attitude and his relatively small size always made her smile.

"I'll go with you Hercules." Binny put her hand on Gabe's shoulder. Zoe, Penny, and Cassie volunteered too, and the fivesome started trudging back up the path towards Caleb's house overlooking the Madrona park.

Caleb called after the kids before they were out of earshot, "Oh children, the door isn't locked, and help yourself to some lemonade in the fridge while you wait."

§

Samantha Trace was uncomfortable. She was a senior research scientist at a highly successful pharmaceutical company. She was the head of her own division. She had dozens of patents to her name. She was spectacularly successful in her own profession by any conventional standard.

But, something ate at her. Xander Luce, her boss, the namesake for and founder of the company, had put her on a special project fifteen years earlier. And what did she have to show for it?

She had always looked up to Luce, respected his vision, and desperately craved his approval. Maybe that's why she'd been so willing to believe his incredible theories about super human powers developing in children. He had a dozen theories that he'd had her test over the years, but he'd never wavered that what they were searching for was real.

Early on, Trace had pressed him, gently, for why he was so certain. Luce had never felt it necessary to go into a detailed explanation of just how he knew that powers only ever seen in comic books and movies were real phenomena. But he'd also never wavered in his absolute certainty that they were real.

And while many of their research efforts were confined to the lab, one family had been integral to two or three of Luce's exploratory directions – Julie Jordan and her three poorly raised brats. Samantha had spent years viewing the woman from afar, and with the advent of the Internet had gathered even more detail on her life.

But no amount of gathered information could tell Samantha what Luce – or anyone for that matter - thought was so incredibly special about Julie Jordan. It wasn't how she looked certainly. It's not that Samantha thought Julie was unattractive, Samantha just thought she looked relatively plain – and over the years, more and more tired.

Samantha had spent a fair amount of time reviewing Julie's public persona through the content of Julie's company's website. Julie's job was in a technical field but was a senior management role. Managers were usually the people that couldn't actually do whatever it was the company needed, so they would get promoted to *supervise* the people doing the actual work. In her research, Samantha had discovered Julie's Masters Degree in European history. She snorted imagining how little the engineers at Julie's tech company appreciated *that* expertise.

But at least Julie had a job. That now ex-husband of hers, Jay, appeared to sit around the house all day drawing, of all things. What an incredible waste of time. And if Julie looked plain, Jay was really nothing special – a man-child spending his time doodling instead of working for a living. How Jay's parents had let him grow up with no actual marketable skill Samantha had no idea. Julie could do better than Jay and obviously had finally realized that. But what had made her stay with him as long as she did?

Dr. Samantha Trace had been toiling on a seemingly impossible project for almost fifteen years for her boss, but thinking about the disappointment that was Julie Jordan seemed to temporarily take her mind off her own frustrations.

For the moment, in fact, Samantha felt energized. She was determined to earn Luce's approval. She'd worked her entire career at this one company. She'd helped build it into what it was. It was too late to jump ship now. She was determined to prove to Xander Luce that she was worthy of the trust he had put in her.

When he'd first told her, it wasn't quite as spectacular sounding as it was now when she repeated their mission. Back then Luce had expounded on the human brain's untapped potential. He'd shown her anecdotal though incontrovertible scientific evidence of humans doing amazing things – super strength, tolerance for extreme temperatures, incredible memorization skills, unheard of flexibility, and more. Samantha remembered that as Xander spoke, there was no question of whether these feats were possible. He acted like he'd seen them with his own eyes.

When they spoke of the project, Xander would always be bursting with the benefits that would occur when they succeeded. Samantha would always nod in agreement. Yes, the successful completion of their mission could save lives from terrible diseases. Yes it would even be likely to stop wars. And although Xander never mentioned this, completing their mission would definitely make Xander Luce obscenely and stratospherically wealthy instead of just plain very very rich.

But now, after all this time, Samantha Trace thought she understood the true nature of their mission as well as Xander Luce himself. It had never been more clear in her mind. Xander Luce had enlisted Samantha Trace to help him discover, replicate, and nurture the mechanism for creating 'super powers' in human beings.

§

"Isn't it weird that he leaves his door unlocked?" Binny asked no one in particular.

"It's weird." Zoe said conspiratorially as she passed Binny following Gabe and Cassie into the kitchen where they made a beeline for the refrigerator.

"Remember, Caleb let us in his home to wait for the packages, not to have a party." Binny said.

"He said we could have lemonade." Cassie said, clearly considering the argument closed.

"Just be neat." Binny added.

"I'm gonna lift all the packages by myself." Gabe pronounced after a long swig of lemonade.

"You think we're all here to watch you and your amazing feats of strength?" Penny teased Gabe.

"Won't you let us help you a little bit? Just to make us feel useful." Binny asked with no hint of sarcasm in her voice.

"I'll think about it."

Cassie had wandered into the living room. A broad window looked out onto the porch. Cassie put her lemonade down on the end table next to a collection of old photographs in standing frames. Cassie examined the closest one. Soon the others had joined her to wait.

"Who are these people?" Cassie asked as she stared intently at a black and white photo set in an oval. A young couple stared back, hopeful smiles on their faces.

"Let me see." Zoe examined the photo. "It looks like she's wearing a nurse's uniform. And he seems to be wearing a uniform too. He looks like he works at a hotel maybe with that hat. Zoe turned the frame over. "1936" was scrawled on the back. "It's old for sure." Zoe did some math in her head for a moment. "I bet its Caleb's parents."

"They kinda look alike. Caleb and the man. And the lady's eyes are like Caleb's." Cassie mused.

Cassie grabbed a much smaller frame that had been hidden behind the first picture. In it a young man, perhaps in his early twenties sat smiling with a young woman on his lap. The young woman's complexion was alabaster in contrast with the young man's dark skin. The picture was very small and torn at the top like it had been ripped from a strip of images. "Maybe Caleb is in this picture."

The others looked away from the first frame to the smaller one in Cassie's hands.

"That's Caleb for sure." Penny added.

"Who's she?" Cassie asked.

"They look happy." Binny said.

"She kinda looks like you, Binny." Cassie mused.

"Oh yeah... the same smile I think." Zoe said.

Binny grabbed the frame. "What are you talking about?" Binny examined the image closely. "I don't see it."

Before Binny could protest further, the doorbell rang. The packages had arrived.

§

"Are you busy?"

"Never too busy for you Sam." Xander Luce replied with a smile. "Ollie's down the other end of the greenhouse right now."

"Uh, yes. Thanks. But I'm here to talk to you actually." Trace smiled briefly before continuing. "I just wanted to give you an update on my progress."

"Actually I'm glad you came by. I wanted to talk to you about that as well." Luce said.

"You did?" Samantha was caught off guard.

"You know I've always had the utmost respect for your scientific acumen, your work ethic, and your loyalty."

Samantha was waiting for the 'but' to come.

Luce continued, "And I've been especially grateful for your commitment and discretion when it comes to our special project. But it occurs to me that I've had you spending so much time on that over the last few years especially, that there may be other directions, directions of your own, that you'd like to pursue here at the lab." Xander leaned in closer as he spoke. "You know the world is your oyster here and I will support and fund any project you'd like to pursue."

"But sir, –" Samantha was getting nervous.

"Sam, it's Xander, please." Luce smiled.

"But Xander, I'm as committed as you are to seeing this through. I have Grater monitoring the Jordan children every night, and I believe we'll have incontrovertible evidence of the powers manifesting themselves in no time. Then we can proceed to up-close clinical observations."

"Yes. Yes of course. What about our man, Dr. Huitre. Doesn't he owe us?" Luce asked.

"I'm afraid he's served his purpose. He's not particularly talented either as a Doctor or as an asset to our efforts. I wouldn't expect much there."

Luce looked surprised at Trace's assessment. "Oh? I had thought he was particularly helpful last summer at getting the youngest Jordan child into the lab. Wasn't he? Did something happen?"

Samantha briefly panicked that her boss could read her guilty thoughts. "No, nothing happened." Samantha shook her head. "Huitre helped to the degree that he was able. Unfortunately, some people can only improve up to a point before they reach their limitations and are simply not that useful anymore. I'm afraid, our man Dr. Huitre has reached that point. It's not meant to be an insult. It's just a fact of life."

"I understand." Luce nodded in agreement.

§

Dr. Samantha Trace had Gore Grater, the head of Luce Labs security head straight to her office so by the time she had walked back from the greenhouse, Grater was already there fidgeting.

"Stop fidgeting." Samantha spoke to him as if he was her son.

Grater stiffened.

"I want you to assign one of your men to take over your daytime responsibilities for a while."

"Did I do something wrong?"

Trace looked confused for a moment before she shook her head. "No. We need to move faster on your other responsibilities. I want you to start watching the Jordan children during the day. We're not spending enough time monitoring them to capture what we need."

"Oh. Of course. Whatever you need." Grater paused for a moment before continuing, "Dr. Trace? Can I ask you a question?" Even though Gore Grater had never served in the military, he carried himself as if he was an army officer in a war – or at least the way army officers conducted themselves in movies. Though despite his bravado, for some reason, Dr. Trace intimidated him.

"What?" Trace responded curtly. The 't' at the end of her question was articulated with particular care and emphasis.

"I've worked here for years. Nothing is more important to me than carrying out my responsibilities for the Lab. I'm not trying to stick my nose where it doesn't belong, but it might help me do a better job *capturing what you need* if I knew what it was you were looking for."

Samantha thought for a moment, weighing the risks. She had never told a soul of the true nature of the mission she was on for Luce. She'd always told half-truths and misdirections when she'd had other Luce Labs employees help her with various efforts she couldn't carry out alone. But this morning, Luce had told her that maybe she should do something else. He had said it nicely, but she knew what it meant. Xander Luce felt that she was no longer an asset on his most important project. And that was something she could not abide.

More extreme measures were called for. And while Gore Grater wasn't the brightest bulb, he was loyal. Like a big brutish dog who bites only who you tell him to. Trace made a decision.

"You are about to be one of only three people who know the true nature of our project. Do I need to explain to you how critical it is that you keep this to yourself?"

"No ma'am."

"We have reason to believe those children may have developed extranormal abilities. What they refer to in comic books as *super powers*." Trace made a face as she said it. "It is your job to do what it takes to observe and document them using those *powers* so we can bring them in for further clinical study."

Grater sputtered, "Powers? Are you serious?"

"Mr. Grater, do I look like I'm joking?"

"I'm just... I'm just..." Complete sentences were coming hard for Grater. "When were you gonna tell me?"

"I'm telling you now."

Samantha Trace's normally pinched face looked extra tight anchored by her piercing black eyes staring holes through Gore. And then it hit him. Gore Grater was transported back to almost exactly a year ago when he and his team of security professionals couldn't capture a ten-year-old girl.

"I'm sorry. That girl. The middle kid. She has powers. That's why she was able to escape me last year. I knew it!" Grater sounded triumphant.

Trace didn't have any patience for Grater being incredulous or for him trying to reason away his own failings. "That is our hypothesis."

Grater heard the ice in his boss' voice and got his emotions under control. "Yes ma'am. I'm on it."

§

Grater replayed the news in his head as he walked from the security office to his parked vehicle. He'd just discussed his new assignment with Victor Barrios who he'd assigned to take over his daily supervisory role at the Luce Labs campus on an interim basis. But even as he spoke to Barrios, his mind was awash with the implications of positively mind-bending news – *super powers were real.* And he was one of only three people who knew this information.

Gore Grater had always known that his non-scientific role limited his ability to rise in the Luce Labs organization. But this changed everything. Running security for a company that would be conducting experiments on humans with powers would need to be done with utmost care, secrecy, and precautions.

There was a small and virulent part of Gore's mind that was jealous. But by the time those feelings made it to the part of his brain with which he was in touch, they had turned to fear and loathing. Humans with super powers would have an unnatural advantage over everyone else. They couldn't be trusted, and they would need to be controlled. Gore Grater was thrilled that this mission had fallen to Luce Labs, and to him. He knew he was ready for the increased responsibility.

"Gore?"

"Oh, yes, Dr. Luce." Gore whipped around at the sound of Xander Luce's voice.

"Please, just Xander."

"Yes sir." Gore had stopped walking as the company's founder approached.

Luce shook his head smiling but continued, "I assume Dr. Trace has asked you to ramp up your observation efforts."

"Yes sir. I mean, yes Xander."

"Excellent. Thank you for being a critical part of the team."

Gore Grater was beaming. It wasn't often he got positive feedback. But now he was more motivated than ever to show Dr. Trace, and Xander Luce, just how valuable he could be.

✤ 27 ✤

THE PACKAGES

There were so many packages that Gabe didn't even bother pretending that he could carry them all by himself. Between the five of them they managed to find a way to get them all balanced. Nobody wanted to make a second trip. Walking with them however proved to be slightly more difficult than they had anticipated.

"Ugh, I'm tired." Cassie complained.

"You're carrying the fewest packages." Binny snapped.

"Not true. Zoe is."

"She's got one of the biggest!" Binny was getting frustrated.

"I don't care. I'm still tired."

"Let's take a quick break. But then we need to keep moving." Zoe intervened.

They continued in this stop-and-go fashion for awhile. It felt to Binny like each 'go' effort was getting shorter and shorter.

§

Morning felt like a month ago to Gore Grater as he drove the short distance from the Luce Laboraties campus to the Madrona neighborhood nearby. The revelation about super powers possibly being real was confusing and amazing to be sure. But what really had him energized was the confidence they'd shown in him. Not just Dr. Trace including him trusting him with the confidential information, but Luce giving him his signoff as well. Gore Grater's usual beefy scowl had turned into an awkward smile.

Grater drove his black sedan slowly through the tree-lined Madrona streets. He'd started at the Jordan house and when he'd seen no evidence of the children, he'd driven in ever-widening circles around the neighborhood in hopes of finding them.

After a few minutes of this Grater found himself cruising along the main Madrona thoroughfare. He'd been so excited about his new responsibilities he'd forgotten to get lunch. He would run into the convenience store quickly and then continue his search. But just as he started to look for a parking space he spotted a gaggle of children out of the corner of his eye.

It was the Jordan children for sure with their friends – the girl who'd been at Luce Labs the previous summer, and the two new kids. The boy wasn't there but Gore Grater had found his quarry. Lunch would have to wait. Grater slowed his car to a stop by the side of the road, took out his phone, and waited.

§

"I don't think we're even halfway there." Binny said, glaring at her younger sister.

"It's not my fault." Cassie whined.

"It gets easier from here as it's all downhill." Zoe intervened between the squabbling sisters.

The group gathered up their packages and started on the next leg of their journey. Penny was bringing up the rear to make sure no packages were dropped and accidentally left. For some reason she couldn't quite put her finger on, Penny decided to look not just at the ground in front of her, but stole a quick glance over her shoulder.

"Hey Binny, come help me keep an eye out for drops back here?" Penny said.

When Binny was close, Penny whispered, "Don't say anything, and don't stop walking, but I think someone is following us. There's a man in a black car back there that keeps creeping up in the direction we're going."

Binny stiffened but followed Penny's instructions. "Can I look back?"

"Yeah."

"Do you think you could do your mind invasion trick and see what's goin on?"

"Already ahead of you." Binny would have winked if she wasn't so scared at the prospect that someone was following them. Binny reached out to see what the person in the car was thinking.

"What's the matter? What did you see?" Penny said.

Binny looked queasy. "Remember the guy from Luce Labs last summer who drove us in the van? The security guard guy? We saw him again at the greenhouse a few days ago. Remember?"

Binny remembered him in detail. She had only just come into her power that day a year earlier and one of her first experiences with it had been seeing Gore Grater's vicious and violent thoughts up close. She had never forgotten his anger. His mind today was no different. Angry, aggressive, but now somehow smug as well. And once again, Binny herself was the object of his ire.

"Yeah." Penny said in a low voice.

"It's him. And he's angry."

"I need a break." Cassie announced and sat down unceremoniously on the pavement.

"We need to keep moving." Binny said trying to keep her voice calm.

"What's wrong?" Zoe asked, immediately sensing something in Binny's voice.

Binny raised her eyebrows at Zoe and whispered the situation in her ear.

"You know what Cassie, I bet we can take a couple of your packages and make it easier. Zach's counting on us to get this stuff down to the shelter. We should hurry." Zoe said.

Cassie grumbled but acquiesced. The three older girls communicated with their eyes and with statements that wouldn't alarm the two younger children. All three of them stole glances over their shoulders watching the man in the black car. It seemed to Binny that he wasn't just keeping pace, he was getting closer.

Penny suggested they turn down one of the numerous alleyways that dotted Madrona. "I'm pretty sure this alley is a shortcut to the woods."

Zoe and Binny quickly agreed.

"Why are we going so fast?" Gabe complained. "I mean, I could go much faster if I wanted to. But still."

"Why do you keep looking over your shoulder?" Cassie asked.

At Cassie's question, the group stopped to look backwards. The black car had just turned into the alley.

"We need to go. Now." Binny said. She was no longer making an attempt to hide the fear in her voice.

The only way now was straight to the woods. The kids walked as fast as they could while still carrying the huge number of deliveries. The car continued to creep closer as they walked.

Binny was doing her absolute best to focus on moving the group quickly, and not drop anything. It helped keep her mind busy so she could resist the temptation to look inside Grater's mind and reacquaint herself with his malevolence.

It was impossible at this point to conceal what was really happening from Gabe and Cassie. But like the older children, they soldiered on, moving as quickly as they could down the alley.

"We're almost there. I can see the woods." Binny tried to sound encouraging.

"Is that a fence?" Zoe exclaimed. "Why is there a fence?"

"It's okay, there's a door. We just have get past the fence and then we can disappear into the shelter. The road ends and the car can't follow us into the woods." Binny responded.

What if he gets out of his car? Penny thought but dared not say out loud. The car was a hundred feet behind them now. Penny could see the driver. She recognized him from the previous summer. The security guard who had chased Binny. He looked worse somehow. Like he was sick. He was holding something as he drove. It looked like a phone.

"The door. The door. There's a padlock. It's locked! He's coming!" Zoe was panicking. There was no hiding the nervousness in her voice anymore.

"Zoe? Are we gonna be okay?" Gabe was on the verge of tears.

Before the tears could start in earnest, Penny dropped her packages as gently as she could and moved through the small throng of kids towards the door and placed her hands on the lock. A second later three distinct pieces hit the ground – steel pieces thudding gently on asphalt.

"Move. Move. Move." Binny shoveled everyone through the now open door in the fence. "Don't stop. Keep moving." Binny wasn't yelling, but her commands were unmistakable. "What are you doing?" Binny said to Penny who had gone through the door but was putting her packages on the ground on the other side. "He's coming!"

"Your turn." Penny pulled Binny through and then bent down to pick up the pieces of the lock. "I have one more thing to do."

Binny was about to protest but Penny's confident actions left no room for argument. Penny reassembled the pieces of the heavy steel lock through the same eyehole. The black car was no more than fifty feet away. There was now a puzzled look on the man's jowly face.

Penny closed her hands around the broken pieces of the lock and seemed to mouth some words of encouragement under her breath. Binny wasn't sure whether Penny was giving herself a pep talk, or telling the lock what to do. Either way, it didn't matter, as when Penny took her hands away the lock remained. Just as it had when they'd been on the other side. Penny gave it an extra hard twist and tug to make sure it wasn't going anywhere.

"Let's go." Penny said. She was almost giggling with excitement as she gathered up her packages.

"You're amazing." Binny told her friend.

Penny was smiling broadly now.

Binny took a brief moment to look behind them. The car had stopped abruptly a mere thirty feet away. The man behind the wheel stared, slackjawed at Binny and Penny. *Apparently this was his first time witnessing superpowers in action.* Binny knew she was playing with fire, but she couldn't help give Grater the same smug grin she'd given him when she'd escaped his clutches the previous summer.

Grin delivered, Binny turned and followed Penny and the others, disappearing into the heart of the forest.

§

The piles of packages sat on the long lunch table deep under the Madrona forest. Zach wasn't sure exactly where to start.

"We were followed." Binny said.

"Penny saved us!" Zoe was still bursting with nervous excitement.

"Penny is awesome." Gabe added.

Penny blushed.

"What happened?" Zach forgot momentarily about diving into the loot.

Binny recounted the story of their trip from Caleb's house to the hideout, and Grater's unwelcome intrusion.

"You're sure it was him?"

"Yeah. I'm sure." Binny said.

Zach understood immediately that Binny had done more than recognize him from his face. "And you're sure he didn't follow you here?" Zach tried to keep his tone even.

"Penny made sure he couldn't." Binny said, a big smile spread across her face.

Penny turned an even deeper shade of red.

"I'm glad you're okay." Zach said.

"You guys weren't kidding about how scary things were last summer." Zoe added.

"We're going to have to be a lot more careful going forward." Zach said.

"Why was he following us?" Cassie said in her smallest voice, trying to sound braver than she felt.

Nobody had a good answer for her.

§

The older children set to busying themselves unwrapping packages and then opening the boxes contained within. One large box remained unopened. When asked, Zach had said that he wasn't sure what to do with that one yet.

Gabe and Cassie helped for awhile, but got bored relatively quickly. The pile of boxes and wrapping grew quite sizable. For awhile the boxes themselves kept Gabe and Cassie busy, but eventually they tired of that too and wandered off while the others carried, plugged, and configured all the stuff.

Inside one of the larger boxes which was now empty and on its side, Gabe and Cassie sat in their clubhouse-within-a-clubhouse.

"How does it feel?" Gabe asked.

"What?" Cassie responded.

"You know. Doing the thing you do. Lighting up."

"I can turn invisible too." Cassie remembered too late that Gabe had no powers. "But, it's really no big deal."

"Come on. It's awesome." Gabe didn't notice Cassie's attempt to soften the blow.

"OK. Yeah, it's awesome."

"But how does it feel?"

"It feels like, it feels like," Cassie searched for the right words. "It feels like I'm wrapped in a warm blanket. A warm invisible blanket. And I can see everything through it, but it's a little blurry, you know?"

"Yeah." And then after a moment Gabe continued, "Actually, no. I don't know. But it sounds really neat."

"It is."

The silence resumed for a little while and then Gabe tentatively added, "I wish I could do something like you."

"You can do lots of things." Cassie reassured.

"No. You know what I mean. Something amazing."

"Oh." Cassie thought for awhile. "Your sister can do something. There was awhile where me and my brother had powers and my sister didn't. And then suddenly she did. Her powers came last even though I'm the youngest."

"I hate being the youngest."

"Me too."

"People think I'm even younger than I am. It's really annoying. They think I'm this little kid. Adults call me stupid names like 'pint-size' or 'short-stuff'. They think they're being funny. But they're not. They're just being mean."

Cassie didn't spend an enormous amount of time thinking about people other than herself, but Gabe had really pressed on her heart. "Which one do you think you'll get?"

"Which *what* do I think I'll get?"

"Which power? Dummy." Cassie teased.

"You think I'll get a power?" Gabe asked hopefully.

"Of course. The only question is which one."

Cassie's confidence seemed to lift Gabe's spirits or at least distract him from his fears.

"Promise you won't laugh?"

"I promise."

"I want to grow." Gabe looked at Cassie intently to make sure he didn't spy any laughter. When all he saw was earnest listening, he continued. "I want to grow big. Like the size of a building. But only when I feel like it. When I'm done fighting, or saving the city, I can shrink back down to my regular size and go home and fit in my bed."

Cassie giggled.

"You think it's funny?" Gabe started to get defensive.

"No. No. I think it will be awesome. I was just wondering, when you grow so big..."

"Yeah?" Gabe was still suspicious.

"Well, what will happen to your clothes? What if they don't grow too?" Cassie burst out in laughter.

Gabe laughed despite himself.

Cassie and Gabe sat for a bit, the change in mood palpable. But then it was Cassie's turn to be contemplative.

"Can I ask *you* a question now?" Cassie said.

"As long as it's not about what happens to my clothes when I get giant-sized. Cause I haven't thought it through yet."

"I promise." Cassie forced a small smile and took a breath. "That boy, at the park. The blonde boy. Do you think he's the one hurting the animals? I mean really, I know some mean kids, but even they wouldn't do that."

"I don't think he's mean."

"You don't?" Cassie sounded surprised.

"No. I think he's an angry person. I saw him once before you know. The first time me and Zoe met your brother. He was drawing in the park, and he said he would draw me as a superhero if I went higher on the jungle gym."

Gabe looked at Cassie with a serious expression on his face. "I'm not scared to go high up anymore you know. That was awhile ago. I was much younger then."

Cassie nodded seriously.

"Anyway, when I got scared, he got mad. Not in a really mean way, but like I was doing it on purpose. I think he was mad at me for letting him down."

§

"OK. I think we're ready to go." Zach sounded excited.

Cassie and Gabe had wandered over seeing that most of the heavy lifting had been done by the others.

"You guys stay here. When I give you the signal, each of you press one of these buttons." Zach pointed to the surface of three identical devices raised up on empty

344

boxes that were sitting on the lunch table. They were plugged in via a long snaking extension card that went to one of the nearby walls.

Zach raced off, headed up the stairs, to the command center where they'd set up a good chunk of the equipment that had been delivered. The group waited a minute until Zach called from above. "Okay, press the buttons."

Zoe, Penny, and Cassie – Cassie had insisted on pressing the button instead of Binny – pressed their respective buttons and the three projectors stirred into life. It took a few seconds for each to warm up, but once they did, they projected enormous images onto the concrete wall that made up one end of their underground shelter.

Zach was running multiple laptops up in the command center. Those screens were now what was being projected on the wall. The first showed a color image of the Madrona woods.

"That's right outside our door." Gabe said.

"Exactly. I hid a camera in the branches of one of the trees. This way we can see if anyone's coming."

The second image was a rotating slide show of all the posters the kids had collected from the neighborhood. There were seven of them. It was more than they'd remembered. Seven small animals. Pets reported missing by their owners.

As each poster faded into view, a pin would drop on a map on the third large projection. The map was of

Madrona. The pins signified the locations of each animal's home. Once the slide show had completed its first loop, all seven pins remained on the map. It was a constellation of sadness, spread over their neighborhood.

Zach pressed a key on one of the keyboards and the view above the map changed as if the camera viewing the neighborhood was mounted to a bird which then flew lazy circles above giving the kids a tour of all the homes that had reported a missing animal. When the camera was done flying around, it resumed its perch directly above the neighborhood. Each pin pulsed an urgent red.

❧ 28 ❧

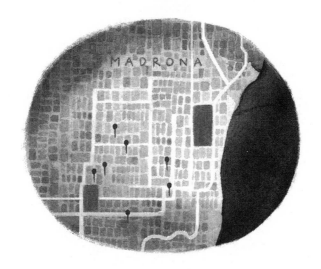

THE LAST WALK

66"**W**ow." Gabe uttered.

Zoe's mouth was in the shape of an 'O' and the other kids were also clearly impressed.

Zach skipped down the stairs to the basketball court. There wasn't much he could do to conceal his grin at their reaction. "Good huh?"

Binny grabbed Zach's arm and said in a low voice, "How did you pay for all this?"

"Trust me. I got it all covered." Zach whispered back.

347

"You didn't do anything illegal did you?"

To Binny it looked like Zach was doing some mental calculations before he finally answered. "No. I mean, I'm pretty sure."

Binny considered looking in Zach's mind to find out for herself, but decided she wasn't ready to know the source of their income.

"How did you do all that?" Gabe interrupted Zach and Binny's side conversation.

"I didn't do much. You guys did it by collecting all the missing animal information. I just entered the data into the software. But there's more. Come with me."

Once Zach had everyone gathered around the laptops up in the command center, he continued his explanation. "I've been thinking that if we can find a pattern in the locations of where the pets went missing, it might lead us to where the person taking them actually lives."

The kids looked at each other, excited and speechless. Zoe looked only at Zach, hanging on his every word.

Zach continued, focused intently on the screens in front of him. "If we assume the perpetrator is a kid, and kids don't have cars, then we've got to assume that they live in the neighborhood. My next assumption is that it is unlikely that they would want to grab a pet that's too close to their own house for fear of getting found out."

"Oh I remember the last time you did this. It was on your computer in your room. Remember?" Cassie was excited to find a way to participate in the explanation. "It was a couple of weeks ago."

"Uh..." Zach looked flustered.

"Why were you doing this a couple of weeks ago? That was before all the animals went missing?" Zoe asked.

"I'm kind of a map nerd. I just like playing with them." Zach's statement sounded almost like a question.

Zach continued without waiting for more discussion on what he'd done a couple of weeks earlier. "Anyway, see how the pins form kind of a circle?"

"There's an empty spot right in the middle of all of them." Binny had been watching the screen intently.

"Exactly! We need to look where there are no pins. That's where the person we're looking for lives." Zach pressed a button on his keyboard and a green pin dropped dead center on the map. "Right there."

"How did you figure all this out?" Zoe asked.

Zach glanced over at the nearby pile of library books and smiled sheepishly. "I've been doing a bunch of reading."

"Let's go. Let's go stop him now." Penny said.

"What?" Binny sounded scared.

"We know where he lives. Let's go there and end all this." Penny was excited.

Zoe perked up at the suggestion. "I agree. Let's go."

"Hold on a second." Zach interrupted.

"Why?" Penny asked.

"We can't just march on over there. We need a plan. There are some things we need to do." Zach explained.

"Like what?" Zoe said.

Zach looked nervous at her inquiry, but continued. "Well, for one, this is just a prediction. The computer doesn't *know* that this is where the petnapper lives, it's just making an educated guess. So the first thing we need to do is confirm who lives there."

"Can't we just look that up on the Internet?" Zoe asked.

"I already tried. The information for that house is unlisted." Zach replied. "Secondly, it could be one of the houses nearby. There's not a ton of data on the missing pets, so it's not super exact."

Zoe and Penny looked like they were going to protest more, but Zach continued before they could start. "But even once we find the right house, I think..." Zach took a deep breath before he finished his sentence. "I think once we identify the house, and confirm that the kid lives there, we should call the police and let them confront him."

Even Binny looked surprised at Zach's last sentence.

"What happened to doing things ourselves and not depending on adults?" Zoe asked, hands on her hips.

"I still believe in that. I definitely do. But if we can confirm that the same kid we saw in the park lives where the computer predicts, then I think we'll have all the proof we need to let the police do their job. What are we going to do, arrest him?"

The kids all nodded their heads slowly in reluctant agreement. Even Zoe, who looked skeptical, but accepted Zach's logic. Everyone except Cassie, who had a look of grim determination and sadness on her face. Nobody noticed that though.

§

"I miss Rembrandt!" Cassie said.

The kids had all gone to their respective homes for the night agreeing that it was too late to start their surveillance effort until the next day.

"Do we have time to walk Rembrandt before dinner?" Binny asked her parents.

Julie Jordan gave her ex-husband a glance as he was busy making dinner.

Jay checked the time. "Yeah, okay. But not crazy long. Dinner's going to be ready soon. So a quick walk, okay?"

"Uh-huh." Cassie was nodding vigorously even as she was walking towards the front door. "I'll see if Penny wants to go too."

"Are you coming Mom?" Binny asked. Her mother hadn't been accompanying them on their dog-walking outings lately.

"Uh, no thanks honey. I'll stay and help your father with dinner." Julie gave her daughter a strained smile.

Binny wasn't sure why her mother suddenly seemed less interested in Dr. Huitre. But Binny was thankful either way as she was still uncomfortable with any connection between the two. Binny headed out of the house to find Cassie and Penny waiting on the sidewalk.

"Your Mom's not coming?" Penny asked.

The trio had started the short trek down the hill to Huitre's house.

"Nope." Binny responded.

Penny thought better of digging any further.

"I could do this alone you know." Cassie interrupted the silence.

"Do what?" Binny asked.

"This. Go to Dr. Huitre's house. Walk Rembrandt. The whole thing."

Binny rolled her eyes.

"I'm getting older you know. I know the way. I can cross the street."

"Whatever." Binny dismissed her sister.

Cassie, annoyed with her sister's reaction, sped up her pace and walked a ways ahead of the other two, muttering under her breath, "See. I can do it."

"You alright?" Penny asked her brooding friend. "I can't read *your* mind you know."

Binny laughed. "Yeah. I guess. It's just every time we head over there, I get stressed. I don't like the thought of..." Binny's voice trailed off.

"I get it. Believe me, I get it." Penny said wistfully.

"Oh, yeah. Is your Dad still around?"

"Yeah. He's around. I guess it's just confusing."

Binny wasn't entirely sure what was confusing Penny but Penny didn't seem to want to elaborate so Binny left it alone. Clearly though, Penny had been wrestling with something. Binny's thoughts immediately returned to her own predicament and the thing she was most afraid of.

"We're here!" Cassie announced as Huitre opened his front door. "Were you worried that we weren't coming Rembie?" Cassie rubbed the dog's head and brought her face close getting slobbery kisses in the bargain.

Penny laughed.

Binny rolled her eyes.

"Is your mom busy at work I guess?" Huitre tried to sound casual.

"No. She's at home helping my Dad make dinner." Binny responded.

"Oh."

Binny's stomach clenched. Why was he even asking about where her mother was? The whole thought of Huitre's interest in her mother just made Binny feel so weird. Binny followed Cassie and Penny for the next twenty minutes, not really listening to Cassie's pronouncements of how she could walk the dog on her own, and just what a dog-walking expert she now was.

Binny was still lost in her own thoughts when they returned Rembrandt to Huitre's. And then an idea occurred to her. "You guys go ahead. I'll be right there." Binny bent down as if to tie her shoe, but her shoelaces were already in order.

Binny let her mind float a bit until she found Huitre, just twenty feet away in his living room. But she wasn't looking at him, she was looking at his thoughts. Huitre was looking at Rembrandt. He was remembering him as a puppy. It was hard for Binny to imagine that the enormous animal was ever that small.

There was pink, but it was a light pink. Thinking of Rembrandt as a puppy made Huitre happy. Binny felt sad for Huitre for a moment, because she knew he must be thinking of Rembrandt's age. He had said that Rembrandt was already much older than the age at which most dogs of his breed died.

But then a face appeared in Huitre's mind. It took Binny a moment to adjust, as the face was familiar but not. And then it hit her, the smiling woman Huitre was thinking of looked just like Binny's mother – but much much younger. Her hair was longer too. The color of the imagery in Huitre's mind had taken on a dull brown tinge. The color looked like sadness.

While Binny hadn't wanted to admit it to herself, somewhere in her own mind she knew that some sort of connection was brewing between her mother and Dr. Huitre. And even though she hadn't seen evidence of it for a few days, she knew it was still there. She'd seen it with her eyes and even with her mind.

Binny had assumed that this was a relatively new development. But here was Huitre feeling all dull brown about Julie's mother from years ago? How many could it be? Ten? Fifteen? Twenty? Certainly from before Zach was born.

The wheels in Binny's mind were turning furiously trying to understand this new information. And then it struck her, like a bolt through her heart. Huitre had been in love with her mother since before Binny and her siblings were born.

Getting Binny's mom into the Luce Labs study had been Huitre's idea. Probably some part of his plan to get her to fall in love with him. And he'd probably been plotting all these years to break up her parents. And it had finally worked. Binny's thoughts were coming into sharp focus. Who was it who had come into their lives, skulking around the neighborhood, right at the same time her parents had announced they were splitting up? Henry Huitre.

Binny stood up and started walking fast to catch up with Penny and Cassie. She wasn't sure exactly how, but she was going to make sure her mother never talked to Henry Huitre again.

§

"Mom, before you go, can we talk?"

Binny had been near silent throughout dinner and the post-dinner cleanup. Zach was in his room, Binny's father was reading a book to Cassie upstairs, and Binny's mother was getting ready to head back to her apartment for the night.

"Of course honey. You've been so quiet tonight. What's up?"

"I have something to tell you." Binny said.

"OK. I'm here." Julie took her eldest daughter's hand in her own.

"I know you like Dr. Huitre."

Julie was taken aback. "I..."

"It's okay Mom. I understand." Binny had thought long and hard on the walk back and through dinner on exactly how to approach her mother on this topic. "I just think there's something you should know about him."

"We're just friends honey." Julie said the words, knowing that they weren't true but hoping Binny couldn't tell the difference.

"I know, but I don't think a friend would get you involved with that Luce Labs study."

"Honey, we weren't friends back then. He was my doctor. Your father and I wanted children very badly, but it wasn't easy for us. And besides, you said yourself I was in the control group, so whatever it was they were dispensing I didn't even get."

Binny thought back to the previous summer, and why she'd kept the truth from her mother. Julie had looked so scared that her participation had endangered her children that Binny would have done anything to make her feel better. Including lie.

So why was she willing to tell the truth now? Just to make sure that her mother didn't fall in love with Dr. Huitre? Wasn't that selfish? Wasn't Binny hoping against hope that her mother would fall in love with her father again?

No! Binny told herself. It's not that. Binny told herself that Huitre was clearly not trustworthy. Not as a doctor, not as a friend, not as whatever it was she was scared he would turn into with her mother. It was never selfish to protect someone you love from someone untrustworthy.

"I lied a little bit then." Binny admitted to her mother.

"You what?"

"You were feeling so bad about Cassie, I didn't want you to feel like you'd done anything wrong by participating in that study."

Julie Jordan gasped, since when had her eleven-year-old daughter acquired such incredible empathy, as well as what appeared to be mind-reading skills. "Honey, it's not your job to protect me. It's my job to protect you."

"I know Mom. And you do a great job of that. It's just that now that you know that nothing bad happened as a result of that study, I don't think you were there by accident."

"Of course I wasn't there by accident honey. Your father and I agreed to it."

"Yeah. I know. But the thing you didn't agree to was being the only participant in the study."

"What?!" Julie gasped.

"There was no control group. I didn't want you to worry. But I knew that the Luce Labs lady wouldn't want anyone to know that you were the only participant and that she would let us go rather than have you find that out."

"You're kidding with me right?" Julie's mind was reeling.

"No. I'm not kidding. I just think that Dr. Huitre must have known you were the only participant. I mean, he convinced you to participate. He must have known at the very least that you were his only patient to participate."

Julie stared ahead trying to process all the information. Everything started to fit together. It wasn't just that Huitre had betrayed her romantically with that woman from Luce Labs. From what Julie could now tell, Huitre's interest in her had been feigned. Just something to get close to her and get her involved in the study, and now get her involved in who knows what else. Henry Huitre had been playing her for over a decade. Julie's chest was filling up with hurt and anger.

But despite the new wounds, Julie's analytical mind couldn't help but divine conclusions from Binny's news. If she had been the only participant in the study, there clearly was no control group. And that meant, that she had participated in the study. Aside from the scare the previous summer, the kids seemed healthy. She seemed healthy. But now she had something new to worry about.

Binny saw the worry lines forming on her mother's face. "I'm sorry Mom."

Julie collected herself and turned back to her daughter. "It's okay honey. It's okay. Just promise me you won't do that again."

"What?"

"Lie to me to protect me. It's my job to keep you and your brother and sister safe – not the other way around."

Binny let out a muffled "OK." from inside the vise-like hug her mother was now giving her.

✵ 29 ✵

THE SEATTLE
POLICE DEPARTMENT

"How much longer do we have to wait?" Cassie asked for what seemed like the hundredth time.

Zach would have been more annoyed at the question if he didn't know that Cassie was only voicing what everyone else was feeling. The day had been long, and aside from a patrol of the neighborhood eliciting one more missing cat poster, everyone was going a little stir crazy in the shelter.

Zach took a deep breath. "As I said, we'll go in the hour before dinner because the odds are better that a parent will be there.

"But we're bored." Cassie whined.

Binny shook her head at her sister but then appealed to her brother. "She's not exactly wrong. Can't we help with what you're doing at least?"

"What exactly are you doing?" Zoe poked her head into the conversation. When the new missing animal turned out to be another cat, Zoe had gotten even more agitated than she already was.

Zach lit up a little when the others seemed interested in what he was up to. "OK. So you remember yesterday how we had the computer show where all the animals were missing from, and it guessed as to where the person doing the kidnapping lives?"

The others nodded in rapt attention.

"The computer can do other kinds of predictions too."

"Like what?" Penny asked.

"Every time you guys collect a new piece of information about where an animal has gone missing, the computer notes the way the perpetrator moves from one point to the next. The software then tries to figure out the similarities between every choice made."

"Huh?" Gabe looked puzzled.

"The computer is trying to think like the person who is taking the animals." Binny explained.

"Exactly!" Zach smiled broadly.

"Why would the computer want to think like that horrible kid?" Zoe asked, a look of disgust on her face.

"So it can tell us where he'll strike next." Zach replied with a serious look on his face.

"Oh. Can you show us?" Zoe's tone changed dramatically.

"Sorta. First of all, this prediction is not quite as accurate as the first prediction it made. Secondly, this one is gonna take some time. I've never done this before, so I'm doing my best to make it work. And even once I get it working, the computer's gonna take some time to think the problem through."

Zoe looked deflated.

"Don't worry, we're not gonna need this anyway. We're gonna end this tonight. I'm sure of it." Zach said.

Zoe tried to smile, but was only capable of a grimace.

§

"We're gonna miss walking Rembrandt." Cassie suddenly remembered.

"Whisper!" Binny mouthed to her younger sister, her eyes filled with condescension.

The six kids had planted themselves behind some shrubs that lined a passthrough located just two houses down from the home the computer had identified. They had a good view of that house plus several others in the immediate vicinity.

Cassie continued in a quieter voice but still insistent. "I think I should go walk Rembrandt."

The memories from the previous night came flooding back to Binny. She alternated between anger at Huitre for his nefarious involvement in her family's life, and how sad she was to tell her mother the truth. Well, some of the truth anyway. The whole truth would not have been super helpful. Binny could just imagine how 'productive' the conversation would be if she told her mother she had the ability to read minds.

Binny tried her best to sound normal. There was no point in involving Cassie in the details of what was going on. "I'm sure Dr. Huitre hasn't forgotten how to walk the dog on his own."

"I can do it on my own you know." Cassie insisted.

"Guys, shhhh. I think I see something." Zach interrupted.

All eyes followed Zach's to see a boy walking down the street. His skin looked red in places, like he'd gotten some color from being outside. But his hair was still a striking blonde, almost white, in the late afternoon sun.

"It's him." Zoe stood up. "Let's go."

Before Zoe could take a step, Binny put a hand on her shoulder. "Wait. Remember, the plan."

Zach looked expectantly at Zoe as well.

Zoe balled her fist, but resumed her crouch.

The boy was on the same side as the house the computer had identified. The children held their breath as he got closer and closer. But when it came time to turn onto the walk, the boy didn't stop, he kept walking.

"Uh oh. He's gonna see us." Binny said, the stress evident in her low voice.

"If he sees us, he's gonna run, and then we'll never find him. We should just get him now." Zoe looked ready to pounce.

Zach spread out his palm lowering it towards the ground letting everyone know to stay put and said one word. "Wait."

They waited. The boy was about to cross in front of the next house, but then approached a tree that stood on the property line. The boy was looking upwards, staring. They couldn't see what he was looking at.

A few seconds passed, when a pine cone hit the boy squarely on the forehead. The boy raised his arms to his face and looked away. As he did so, a bird shot out of the tree flying far far away. The boy picked up the pine cone and threw it as hard as he could in the direction of the bird, but it was too late. The bird was long gone.

Zoe clutched her heart with her hand. She hadn't realized she'd been holding her breath until she was sure the bird was okay.

Binny was squeezing Cassie's arm to make sure she stayed quiet.

After looking around to see if there had been any witnesses, the boy started crossing the lawn back to the exact house the computer had predicted. After bounding up the steps, the boy disappeared through the front door.

Zach did his best to restrain his excitement. "I knew it!" He sounded as excited as someone trying to be quiet could sound. "I'm calling them now."

Zach pulled his phone from his pocket and dialed the non-emergency number for the Seattle Police Department. Zach knew that while he and the others felt that this was an emergency, adults might not agree that missing pets were worthy of a call to 911. Zach was sure this maturity on his part would impress the police.

"Seattle Police, this call is being recorded." Zach heard on the other end of his phone.

"Yes. Hello. I'd like to report someone who is hurting animals."

"What is your name please." The voice said.

Zach hadn't realized that he would need to identify himself, but pushed forward anyway. "Zach Jordan."

"You say you're witnessing someone hurting an animal sir?"

"No. Not exactly. It's a kid. He's been hurting animals. I can tell you where he lives. We're outside his house. He just went inside."

"So you saw him hurting animals?" The voice said.

This wasn't going quite how Zach had expected. "Well, not exactly. We haven't seen him do it with his hands exactly. But there was this bird. And it was clearly in pain. And then a missing cat. And all these animals in the neighborhood –"

"Zach? How old are you?"

Zach let the question hang in the air for a moment. Why did it matter how old he was? He'd gotten the computer to predict exactly where their target lived. And sure enough, the very kid they suspected lived in the house the computer had identified. And on top of that, Zach had a super power, and was in a secret club of other kids with super powers.

And yet, the voice on the other end of the line only seemed to care about his age. Zach felt a familiar sense of frustration welling up in his chest. A desire to yell out the truth. To question authority. To say how he really felt. No holding back. No pulling punches. Just the raw truth of what he actually thought.

Instead, Zach just said, "Thirteen."

The others could only hear Zach's side of the conversation, but from the frustration in his voice and his red-rimmed eyes, it was clear to everyone that the police weren't reacting as they had hoped.

"Zach. Do your parents know that you've made this call?"

"Listen, we know the kid has been hurting animals. We didn't see him do it yet. But he's definitely going to do it again. We just saw it. He was about to hurt a bird. Here. Here's the address of where he lives." Zach told the voice the address.

"Zach. Listen to me closely. Calling this number is not to be done lightly. You could get in huge trouble for tying up the line while important calls need to get through. But you sound like a good kid. So I'm going to do you a favor. I'm going to hang up the phone. And when I do, you need to go home. If you've seen something that we need to deal with, tell your parents, and they can decide the right course of action, including calling us if necessary."

"But –"

"Goodbye Zach." The line went dead.

Ashen-faced, Zach looked at the others. "They hung up on me."

§

"What now?" Zoe asked, frustrated by the group's paralysis. "I say we go knock on his door."

"I agree. Let's just go tell him to cut it out." Penny said.

"And then what?" Zach asked in a quiet voice.

"What do you mean 'and then what?'" Zoe sounded angry.

Zach's voice got even quieter. "I mean, what happens then?"

"He'll stop." Zoe sounded very sure of herself.

"What if he says no?" Zach asked.

"We could tell his parents." Binny suggested.

367

The group ambled over to the house the computer had predicted and the boy had entered. Cassie stood at the very back of the group as they huddled on the steps to the boy's house. After a moment of hesitation where nobody seemed to want to ring the doorbell, Zoe pushed her way to the front of the group and pressed.

It was probably only ten seconds until the door opened, but it seemed like forever to Zach. The sting of the police operator's reaction was still fresh in his mind. He'd made an exception by calling the police despite his certainty that adults were not to be depended on for these kinds of things. That had blown up in his face spectacularly.

What must Zoe think of his plan now? He'd felt so good about the map prediction software. It had been right after all. But the police were not quite as impressed. Zach imagined Zoe was even less so. And now they were depending on adults again – the blonde boy's parents.

The door opened. A thin woman with blonde hair, tied up in a tight bun stood in the entrance, her mouth pinched in what seemed like permanent disapproval. "Isn't it way too early for Girl Scout cookies?"

Zoe looked over her shoulder wondering if a pack of Girl Scouts had lined up behind them to make a sale. The other kids were gathered behind Zoe looking down at their feet. After a moment Zoe realized the woman's confusion. "We're not girl scouts. We're here to talk to you about your son."

"Excuse me?" The woman looked confused.

"That blonde boy. About ten years old. He's your son, isn't he?"

"What do you want?" The woman's voice took on a steely tone.

The other kids had barely looked up since the confrontation had begun, afraid of how uncomfortable things were going to be. But something about the woman's voice made them look up. Especially Binny.

Zoe continued, "I'm sorry to be the one to tell you, but your son has been hurting animals around the neighborhood."

Ollie Trace wandered into the frame of the open door next to his mother. "Who's there Mom?"

Despite the strange context, the reality of the situation suddenly clicked for Binny, and for Zach and Penny a moment later. The blonde boy's mother was the woman who'd tried to get Cassie to reveal her powers at Luce Laboratories the previous summer. And the white-haired boy was her son.

"Oh no." Binny uttered.

Samantha Trace finally took her focus off of Zoe for a moment and sized up the entire group realizing that this was the group of children, now slightly expanded, that she had been tracking, and had caused her so much heartache.

Rage welled up in Samantha Trace's stomach, and although she wasn't technically yelling, the anger, and frustration in her voice were unmistakable. "You." The word came out like it had multiple syllables. "All of you! GET! OUT!"

§

Dorothy Lawson had been a police officer for twelve years. She'd helped children cross the street, walked a beat, done stints at schools and homeless shelters, been on several task forces including ones focused on drugs, gangs, and car theft. Her husband had fed their two sons dinner on his own many times before, and tonight would be no exception.

Advanced degrees in criminal justice and police management had helped. But an African-American woman climbing the ranks of the Seattle Police Department, even in this day and age, had to be perfect.

Dorothy had handled many more challenging and frankly dangerous situations than this. But whether it was a gang shooting, a cat in a tree, or her sons fighting in the back seat on a road trip, Dorothy took it seriously. Perfect meant zero exceptions.

Dorothy had pulled up next to the address given to her by the dispatcher hoping it would amount to nothing. Apparently, the boy had called the precinct desk with some animal abuse accusations. Worried that the boy might try and take actions into his own hands, the dispatcher had asked Dorothy to drive by the address to make sure there was no disturbance. But a disturbance was exactly what Officer Lawson found.

"That's him. He's been hurting animals. Cats. Dogs. Birds. We saw him hurt a bird." Zoe was yelling now.

Ollie looked stricken for a moment, but his mind quickly surrendered to his own rising anger. "I did not!"

"I said get out. Now!" Samantha repeated her order.

"I was drawing them. I never touched them." Ollie explained. His voice high-pitched and drawn.

"There. He said he never touched them." Ollie's denial lowered Samantha's anxiousness if not her malice. She took stock of the group. "Listen you little bastards. I don't know what kind of scam you're trying to pull here, but trust me, it will not work. If you ever accuse my son of anything ever again, or even come near him, I will personally make sure you regret it."

Cassie and Gabe were cowering at the bottom of the steps, ready to bolt. Even Zoe, who had been so confident at first was losing her nerve quickly. None of them had ever been spoken to like this by an adult.

But before anyone could run, Zach stepped forward. "Dr. Trace. A bunch of animals – family pets – have gone missing in this neighborhood recently. The disappearances spread out evenly on a map from this exact point." Zach pointed at the porch beneath his feet.

The red was rising in Samantha's otherwise pale cheeks. Ollie fidgeted progressively faster as Zach spoke.

Zach continued, "On two occasions we've personally witnessed your son interacting with two birds that looked hurt. No. He didn't touch them. I know that makes no sense. I know you don't believe us. I don't quite believe us sometimes either. But however he's doing it, he's hurting those animals."

"Good evening everybody. Is everything okay?" Dorothy Lawson stood behind the kids on the walk. Nobody had seen her approach the porch.

Ollie looked stricken by the police officer's presence.

Seizing the opportunity, Samantha Trace pasted on a pained smile at the police woman's approach. "Ah. Thank you for coming officer. Everything is distinctly *not* okay."

"Is there a Zach Jordan here?" Officer Lawson said.

Zach identified himself meekly but without hesitation.

"Son, you can't, just go to people's houses and make accusations. This is really something you should let grownups handle. Was this your idea?"

All the kids but Zach seemed to take two or three steps backwards trying to melt into the background. Ollie breathed a sigh of relief. Samantha flashed a smug smile that only the children could see before she reconfigured her face to one of pained sympathy.

"Yes. It was my idea. Nobody else's." Zach responded.

"I'm sure the children's hearts are in the right places. But they're telling some fantastical story about animals getting hurt without even being touched." Samantha put her hand on Ollie's shoulder. "They've really upset my son. He's very sensitive."

Ollie winced.

"Shouldn't you kids be home for dinner soon?" Officer Lawson said to the assembled children who murmured their assent. "Well, why don't we just chalk this up to a misunderstanding and promise that you won't come here and bother this nice family again."

"Thank you Officer." Samantha extended her hand in thanks.

"No problem ma'am." Dorothy responded, turning her head to look after the six kids who had already started down the walk. "Uh, Zach?"

Everyone froze.

"Yeah?" Zach said.

"Why don't I take you home myself. I think that would make the most sense." And then officer Lawson added, "You kids all live close?"

Every sound was pounding in Zach's head. The click of the lock being turned after the door to the Trace home had closed behind him sounded like the crack of a bat. Zach heard the muffled discussion of the other five kids as they walked quickly down the street, heading home no doubt.

The last sound he heard before the tears began was the heavy *thunk* of the back door of the police cruiser closing him inside. Zach put on his seat belt and Officer Lawson started the short drive to the Jordan house.

✢ 30 ✢

THE ISLE OF MAN

"I really hardly even know what to say to you Zach." Jay Jordan shook his head as he looked at his son across the kitchen table.

Zach stared ahead silently. He'd already apologized profusely and simply wasn't sure what else he could say.

"Have you not been listening at all when I talked about using good judgment? Setting an example for your sisters? What exactly did you think was going to happen?"

"I called the police first, and reported it like you said." Zach replied weakly.

"I didn't tell *you* to call the police. I told you tell me and I would call the police if it made sense. Which as you can see, it most certainly did not." Jay was on a roll now. Lecturing. Not really listening to his son.

Briefly pausing to take a breath, Jay heard the front door close and two pairs of feet walk into the house.

"Girls? Come here please." No child in the world speaking any language would be confused at what Jay's tone of voice meant.

Binny and Cassie presented themselves in the kitchen, stealing quick glances at their brother's dry but puffy face.

Jay faced his daughters. "And what were you two thinking? Just because your brother is making terrible choices, doesn't mean you get to go off the deep end with him."

Zach spoke before either of his sisters could respond. "I told you Dad, they tried to convince me not to do it. It was my idea. They tried to stop me."

Binny and Cassie looked at their feet and remained silent.

"I'm honestly not quite sure what to do with you guys. Thankfully that Officer Lawson was nice about it and decided to look the other way. Zach, if it weren't for her, you could be in serious trouble." Jay paused for a moment. "Or rather, you could be in *more* serious trouble than you already are."

§

"We were thinking of all watching a movie together." Serena said as she motioned to Penny with her eyes where to place the dinner dishes.

"Thank you so much for dinner Serena." Jonathan said as he put some of the food away.

"Oh you don't have to do that." Serena said.

"Which movie?" Penny asked.

"Why don't you pick one?" Quincy said.

"To go with whatever movie you pick, I have three words of advice for you." Everyone looked in Jonathan's direction. "Parmesan truffle popcorn."

"Ooh." Serena raised her eyebrows at the prospect of the snack. "How?"

"We got truffle oil at the market today. Drizzle it on the popcorn and then shave parmesan on top." Jonathan instructed. "The only downside is that it will be gone long before the bad guy gets caught." Jonathan smiled.

"You're not staying for the movie?" Penny interrupted her internal movie musing and faced Jonathan.

"I was going to let you guys have some family time." Jonathan said. "I know there are some bookstores I haven't depleted, I mean *explored* yet. I'm really coming to love this city."

Serena and Quincy froze watching the interaction between Jonathan and Penny.

"You can't just suggest the movie snack and then not stay and eat it with us. You should watch the movie with us. And besides, this way, you can make the popcorn and make sure it comes out right." Penny said as if the decision had been made.

Jonathan looked wide-eyed at Quincy and Serena before responding. "Okay, Penny. It would be my absolute pleasure. Thank you for the invitation."

After the dishes had been put away, the extended Yang family sat on the couch eating truffle popcorn and watching the movie Penny had picked. For the first time this summer, sitting between her father and Jonathan on the couch, Penny Yang felt like her family wasn't quite in pieces. It didn't look like she thought it would, but it still felt pretty good. And the second batch of truffle parmesan popcorn was just as delicious as the first.

§

"It wasn't too bad." Zach lay back in his bed, his face lit by the phone he had up to his ear.

"Did you get punished?" Zoe's voice crackled on the other end of the conversation.

"Grounded."

"Oh. I'm so sorry."

"It's only for tomorrow. My Dad said that even though I was completely irresponsible that my heart was in the right place.

"I don't see how it's *completely irresponsible* for you to try and stop that Ollie kid from hurting any more animals.

"My Dad didn't share your perspective." Zach laughed wryly.

"Well, I'm really sorry you got in trouble." Zoe said.

"It's okay."

"And, I'm sorry I didn't say thank you sooner."

"You're thanking me?" Zach asked.

Zoe paused before she answered. "Yeah. I saw what you did. We all did. Telling the cop that it was all your idea. If I'd been taken home in a police cruiser I'm pretty sure that would be the end of them buying me a camera after the summer. Not to mention, they'd probably ground me so long, I'd have gray hair the next time you'd see me."

Zach laughed. "Oh. No biggie. There was no point in everyone getting in trouble."

"I guess I'm just not used to people doing stuff for me." Zoe sounded wistful.

Zach stayed quiet as it sounded like Zoe had more to say.

"Sometimes people act like they're your friend, and then do horrible things. That's when you realize, they were never really your friend in the first place."

"Oh. That sounds lousy." Zach wasn't exactly sure what Zoe was referring to so he just tried to sound supportive.

Zoe took a breath, calculating what she was willing to share with Zach. Something about talking on the phone and not having to look him in the face made things a little easier.

Zoe thought back to three summers earlier when she'd found a group of girls her age in the neighborhood. The leader of the group, Brittany Branch, took an immediate shine to Zoe telling her that they had so much in common and should be best friends. Brittany had been especially excited to play with Zoe's cat. Zoe's *first* cat – Sneeze.

Zoe loved Sneeze. Sneeze was fat and had rings of gray and black and was more dog than cat really. He had showed up at Zoe's old house one day as if he belonged there and had never left. After Zoe's parents made sure Sneeze had his shots, he and Zoe were inseparable. Sneeze slept in Zoe's bed every night.

Brittany decided one day that they should take Sneeze on a walk. Zoe pointed out that cats didn't take walks, but Brittany insisted. But when they walked to the park, Sneeze wouldn't follow instructions. Before Zoe knew what was happening, Brittany was grabbing Sneeze by his scruff and trying to drag him along but Sneeze was having no part of it.

Zoe tried to intervene, but things had progressed beyond her control. The more Brittany pulled, the more Sneeze fought, until Sneeze did something Zoe had never seen him do – he scratched. Brittany ended up with an elongated deep gash on her arm. It did the trick. She let Sneeze go and he bolted.

Zoe finished her story for Zach. "He ran straight into the street and right into a truck." Zoe's voice was quavering as she spoke. "My parents told me that the right thing to do was to let him go, and that there was nothing we could do for him." Zoe took a deep breath and her story seemed over.

The silence on the phone hung thick. "I am so so sorry about that. That's horrible." Zach said.

Zoe seemed to collect herself a little. "Oh, I almost forgot. After she got scratched Brittany yelled at me for having a horrible cat, marched off, and never came over again."

"She sounds like a horrible person."

"I don't know. I never saw her again. But now, when people act like they like me, I know the truth." Zoe said with finality.

After Zoe's story, Zach wanted to make sure more than anything that Zoe didn't think he liked her. Zach said the only thing he could think to say. "Oh yeah. Of course.

Zach continued trying to sound casual, "And as far as taking the blame, I knew I had to make sure nobody else got in trouble. If we all got in trouble, who would be there tomorrow to figure out what to do next?"

"Right. Of course. That's why." Zoe said.

Zach thought he had narrowly avoided disaster with Zoe by making sure she didn't think he cared about her. But for some reason all he heard in her voice was disappointment.

§

A mile away another phone conversation was in progress.

"Where the hell were you?" Samantha Trace demanded.

"I've been canvassing the neighborhood trying to find out where they hang out." Gore Grater was on the defensive.

"Well I think we know where they've been hanging out. My house!" Samantha thought Ollie was already asleep, but she didn't want to chance anything and kept her voice low. Despite the volume, there was no mistaking her tone.

"I'm sorry Dr. Trace. I really am. Can I ask what they wanted from you?"

Samantha Trace was caught off guard for a moment. "Oh, who knows *what* they wanted. They could have been selling girl scout cookies for all I know. Suffice to say they were harassing me. Acting like hoodlums."

Grater tried to sound contrite. "I'm sorry ma'am. Did they – use their powers?"

Grateful for the change in topic, Samantha tried to sound more conciliatory. "No. Not that I saw. But who knows what they're capable of. Bottom line, I just wanted you to be aware that they were coming as far as my house. So hopefully that will give you a sense of where they're running around in the neighborhood."

"Thanks Dr. Trace. I appreciate the information and I'm sorry you had to deal with that. I promise, I'll get what we need." Grater said.

"I expect you will." Trace ended the call.

§

Ollie was still going over the events of the previous night in his mind. It probably didn't help that the greenhouse took on a bit of a gloomy quality when the sky was filled with clouds. Ollie imagined, that if it rained, the drops would be loud on the glass panes of the greenhouse.

"You okay kiddo? You seem a little bit down in the dumps." Xander asked his charge.

Ollie had known that those kids didn't like him. Except for the little blonde girl, maybe – Cassie was her name. But really it was that Ollie knew what to expect from pretty much all kids. They all treated him badly. He wasn't even going to camp anymore, and he still had to deal with other kids making him feel miserable.

What did they know anyway? This was the very issue that was scaring Ollie the most. What did they know? More than Ollie had realized. They'd obviously seen him with the animals. But they didn't seem to know what was actually happening. Ollie wasn't quite sure *he* even knew what was actually happening. But he did know that he couldn't risk having them watch him anymore.

"Can I ask you a question?" Ollie looked up at Luce. "If I'm going to be a scientist, like you, and my Mom, don't I need a place to do that? Like you have the greenhouse and she has her office and her lab?"

"Why you can have your very own spot right here my boy." Luce answered enthusiastically.

Ollie smiled a thin smile. That would keep him hidden from the neighborhood kids, but the thought of Luce or his mother seeing the consequences of him paralyzing and hurting animals with his mind was too terrible to contemplate no matter how much Luce might assure him it was okay. "Thank you. I appreciate that. But I wouldn't want to get in the way. I was thinking I could find somewhere that was really my own. Maybe somewhere between here and home."

The sliver of disappointment that Xander Luce felt that Ollie wanted to conduct his experiments in private was still vastly outweighed by how fortunate Xander felt that his patience was finally paying off. Not only was Ollie one of the very specimens he'd spent his life looking for, but Ollie was young and impressionable, and looking to Luce for guidance.

Xander Luce had exhibited incredible patience to get to this point. Just a little more wouldn't hurt. He didn't want to lose the game in the ninth inning.

"Of course. Of course." Xander tapped his finger on his nose as he thought and continued conspiratorially, "If you can keep a secret, I think I know just the place."

Ollie's attitude seemed to pick up measurably at Luce's suggestion.

"And I *know* you will be careful. It is most definitely supposed to be off-limits. *Especially* to children." Xander warned.

Xander was smiling to himself when he noticed Gore Grater standing by the door to the greenhouse.

Luce left Ollie contemplating and approached Grater. "Thanks so much for coming by Gore." Luce kept an eye on Ollie's facial expressions sitting out of earshot at one of the greenhouse workbenches.

"Of course sir – I mean Xander. As you know Dr. Trace has me engaged in *off-campus* activities during the day. Is everything okay? If it's about last night..." Grater kept his voice low as it was clear Luce wanted to keep their conversation private.

"Last night?" Xander raised an eyebrow.

Grater fumbled for a moment realizing that the old man might not know what had happened the previous evening. "Dr. Trace is just eager for me to make progress. And though it's not a huge neighborhood, I'm just one pair of eyes."

Luce knew that Grater wasn't being entirely forthcoming but he had his own agenda to cover. "Ah yes. Of course. You couldn't possibly be expected to keep an eye on every nook and cranny in that neighborhood all by yourself." Xander said with his typical gentle politeness. "But I have an idea that might help."

"You do?" Grater responded eagerly. Grater resembled a dog waiting for its master to throw a ball.

"Before I give you the specifics of my suggestion, I have two things I need. First, could you please demonstrate for me the technology you've been using to capture those videos? And second, if you don't mind, let's

385

keep this just between you and I. Dr. Trace has my complete trust of course, but she's so busy. I'm sure she would have suggested this on her own if I hadn't already loaded her up with so much to do."

§

"Can I sit with you?" Penny asked.

Binny looked up from her spot up against the cool concrete wall of the shelter. The kids had all gathered earlier that morning minus Zach. "Yeah. Of course."

"It's not our fault you know. We all decided to confront Ollie. We couldn't have known what would happen."

"Zach didn't want to go to the house but he was the one who got into trouble." Binny responded.

"Yeah. That was really nice of him to cover for everyone."

"Yeah. He'll be okay. They only grounded him for a day." Binny looked far away.

"That's not what's bothering you?" Penny asked.

"I guess not. After the police brought Zach home, my Mom came over to discuss things with my Dad. What to do about Zach you know?"

Penny nodded.

"My Mom was just so bummed out."

"Probably because her son was brought home by the police." Penny's gentle sarcasm didn't make Binny laugh.

"It was more than that though. She's just really sad I think."

"What else could she be sad about?" Penny asked earnestly.

"Me. Well, Huitre. Well, some things I told her about Huitre."

"What did you tell her?"

"I just don't trust him. And when I looked in his mind the other day, I found out that he's been in love with my mom for a long time. Since even before we were born. I told my Mom that she was the only one in the Luce Labs study, and that I thought Huitre knew that when he signed her up for it."

"Why did you tell her that? I thought you didn't want to make her feel bad."

"I didn't. But I also don't want her to fall in love with him. I can tell that she likes him. And if she ends up with him, that will just be the end of our..."

Binny didn't need to finish the sentence for Penny to understand what she meant.

Binny and Penny sat for a while in a silence interrupted only by the echoes of the other kids playing in another part of the shelter.

Penny finally broke the silence. "Remember when were in your room, and I was upset about my dad and you said that maybe I was right, and the pieces do stay broken?"

"Yeah."

"I think you were right. They do. But I also think that when something is in pieces, it can be rebuilt. Maybe not better than it was before, maybe not worse, just a little different."

§

The building had been built only a year earlier. They'd needed a new expanded headquarters long before that, but the company had been growing so quickly, the physical space simply couldn't keep pace with the needs of the growing enterprise.

Kiera Knox had only been working at the company for less than a year herself, and she still hadn't quite adapted to the remoteness of the location. This was not exactly the job she'd expected to take after an advanced degree in computer science from Cambridge University.

"Whaddya think?" Kiera's pudgy companion asked as he wiped the orange powder from his fingers onto the sides of his ill-fitting black t-shirt.

"Well Borg, I think Julie Jordan is very very good at Texas Hold 'Em."

Engilbert Björgmundsson, all his co-workers called him *Borg*, was wrapping up his shift. And even though Kiera was here to relieve him, and it was already 9:30 at night, a half hour after his shift was over, he hadn't seen fit to go home. Kiera noticed that on days her shift followed his at the security station, he always seemed to stick around much longer than required.

"Yes, of course. She is very good. But how does she play so many games at once. You think maybe *Julie Jordan* is a bot?" Borg ate another crisp.

"Impossible. You know all the precautions we put in place." Kiera responded without taking her eyes off the array of computer screens. Kiera thought of the virtual security measures they'd built as analogous to the physical security of the island itself. Internet casino companies needed to operate from odd locations that would accommodate their *special* legal needs. Sitting in the Irish Sea between the much bigger islands of Great Britain and Ireland, the Isle of Man was just such a place.

"She would have to have a memory like a computer to accomplish this, no?" Borg asked. "She's already made over $50,000 U.S. Dollars."

Kiera didn't respond, perplexed at how the feat was being accomplished.

Borg continued, "I bet Julie Jordan is quite pretty."

"Don't get too excited." Kiera rolled her eyes. "She's probably not even a she. It's probably some kid with nothing better to do sitting in his underwear at a computer screen in the middle of the night on one of his parents' accounts. Maybe a bunch of kids, all playing at once under one name. Nobody could do this alone. I'm afraid she's not very likely to be your poker-playing dream girl."

"Well whoever Julie Jordan is, she is either very very good at online poker or very very lucky."

§

389

While the sun had set on the Isle of Man, it was still high in the sky over Madrona. Grounded, in his room, and with nothing else to do, Zach Jordan sat in his underwear in front of his computer screen managing twenty-two windows at once, and becoming extraordinarily proficient at Texas Hold 'Em.

Less than a mile away, deep underground, Zach's software had finished its calculations. Zach had spent a lot of time carefully transcribing concepts from his statistical textbooks into scripts on his computer that would predict the home address of the next animal to go missing.

Less than twenty-four hours after Zach had started running the program, the computer had spit out an answer. The software had finally dropped a glowing virtual pin. But with Zach grounded, and the group seemingly out of options at combating Ollie, nobody in the shelter had thought to monitor the computers in the command center. Zach's program had placed the glowing pin directly on the home of Dr. Henry Huitre, but nobody was there to see it.

⇜ 31 ⇝

THE LONE WALK

"What's with all the moping, Madrona Heroes?" Caleb Adams asked.

"Oh, Hi Caleb." Cassie said.

The other four kids were sitting around the shelter, bored, and not sure of quite what to do next.

"Where's Zach? Caleb said.

"He got grounded." Binny answered.

"Oh?"

The group proceeded to recount the events of the night before to Caleb. By the end of the retelling, their morale was even lower than it was at the beginning.

"Well, I can't say I'm surprised." Caleb said.

"What?" Zoe said?

"Haven't we discussed the lack of trust adults have in those of us that are very old or very young?" Caleb said.

Binny was getting annoyed at Caleb's lack of empathy for the situation. Normally Binny would have bitten his head off, but Caleb was different somehow. Binny didn't quite understand him. She stayed quiet.

"What should we have done?" Penny asked.

"That is an excellent question Miss Yang. What should you have done?" Caleb responded.

"She just asked *you* that." Gabe giggled.

"Fair enough Mr. Flowers. I know that answering a question with a question can be frustrating to those expecting an answer." Caleb smiled before he continued. "I'm not trying to frustrate you children. I'm trying to teach you."

"Teach us?" Cassie asked.

"If you can't count on adults, then who can you count on?" Caleb asked.

"No one." Zoe said with finality.

Caleb raised his eyebrows and said nothing in response.

"Ourselves?" Penny asked.

"Exactly Miss Yang. Exactly."

"How exactly do you propose we stop Ollie by ourselves?" Hands on her hips, Zoe was channeling some of Binny's annoyance without realizing it.

"I believe you need to catch him in the act." Caleb's words hung in the still air of the shelter.

Binny finally couldn't hold back. "Catch him in the act? How do you expect us to find him? We can't go to his house or his horrible mother will freak out. She'll probably call the police back to arrest all of us."

"Binny's right. We can't go back there." Zoe said.

"Children, whatever this young man is doing to the animals, he needs somewhere safe and out-of-sight to do it. I suspect that is not his house as his mother, however *horrible* she might be, would not condone his behavior." Caleb responded calmly.

"Don't be so sure." Binny muttered.

"OK. So he's hurting the animals somewhere else. Even if we could find him, and catch him in the act – then what?" Zoe asked.

Binny heard Zoe echoing Zach's line from the night before and grinned briefly despite herself. Zach would love to know that Zoe was listening to him so intently.

Caleb sighed. "Children, have you forgotten something?"

Five pairs of eyes stared back at him blankly.

"You have powers." Caleb was getting more animated than usual. "You are not normal children."

"I'm normal." Gabe said sullenly.

Zoe put her hand on his shoulder.

Caleb continued. "You children have a gift. It is in various stages of manifesting itself in each of you, but it is there. Miss Yang here can do things today she wasn't able to do last week. Isn't that true?"

Everyone nodded.

"You were given these powers for a reason. Did you think that they were free?" The volume of Caleb's voice rose as he spoke. "With great power comes –"

"Great responsibility?" Penny smirked.

"I was going to say *a heavy burden*, but you get the idea. You don't get to just stand idly by. You don't get to complain that adults won't listen to you. You need to do something about this boy. You've been given special abilities that every child, no, every human on this planet would kill to have."

The image of Gore Grater bearing down on them in his black sedan flashed in Binny's mind.

Cassie and Gabe were doing their best to stay strong as they listened to Caleb, but fear was visible in their eyes.

Seeing the looks on the faces of the younger kids Caleb tried to moderate his tone. "Children, I am not trying to scare you. But your little superhero headquarters here, your running around the neighborhood, these are not make-believe. Did you think your powers are here for your entertainment, to make your summer more *fun*?"

Caleb's tone approached the edge of mocking, but then got more serious. "Billions of people live on this planet. Many of them in pain. Don't you think they would trade places with you in a heartbeat? These powers, these gifts, they were given to you. What you decide to do with them is up to you. My only question is this: will you be selfish or selfless?"

Everyone sat around stunned. The summer *had* felt like make-believe. Even confronting Ollie had felt unreal. They were never in real danger, despite the outcome for Zach, all the running around had been fun, exciting. It felt like a play they were in. And even though they hadn't said it out loud, at the end of the summer, the play would be over and they could go back to their regular lives.

But if Caleb was right, this wasn't make-believe. This was real life. And for the first time since getting their powers, the children wondered if they really wanted them at all.

Zoe was the first to speak. "You didn't answer my question."

"What question is that Miss Flowers?" Caleb asked.

"So we catch him in the act. What do we do then?"

"You stop him." Caleb said firmly. "For good."

§

Tomorrow will be a better day, Binny thought to herself. *Zach will be ungrounded and we can regroup*. After

Caleb's 'pep' talk everyone had gone home. Each of them carefully considering what Caleb had said. Each of them feeling the burden on their shoulders and wondering what it really meant.

"Honey, do you know where your sister is?" Julie Jordan poked her head in Binny's room rousing her daughter from deep thought. "Your father was eager for her to clean her room. You know, improve things from *health code violation* to *minefield*."

"We came home together. I haven't seen her since." Binny responded.

"I saw her since then, she asked me if she could walk Rembrandt on her own."

"What did you say?" Binny asked, nervous about the response.

Julie paused for a moment, embarrassed. "Well, I just thought it might be best if we took a break from that for awhile. So I told her no."

Binny's face fell. "I know where she is. I'm going to get her."

§

This would show Binny. Rembrandt had been perfectly behaved. Cassie was doing a great job. And she was doing it without anyone's help – exactly as she had said she could. Why Binny didn't believe she could do things on her own, Cassie didn't know. Being the baby of the family didn't mean you were actually a baby.

"Hey Cassie."

Cassie stopped surprised at hearing her name called. She had wound her way to Madrona Park. She whipped her head around to face the owner of the voice. "Oh. Hi." Cassie Jordan said sheepishly.

Ollie trace said, "Nice dog."

"Thanks. His name is Rembrandt." Cassie was still hesitant. "You can pet him. He's super friendly."

Ollie bent down to say hello to the large shaggy animal.

"Um. Listen. I'm really sorry about last night. About my brother and sister and my friends." Cassie shuffled her feet as she spoke.

Ollie looked up briefly. "It's okay."

"It is?" Cassie was surprised at how easy Ollie was being.

"I knew you didn't mean it."

Cassie felt a weight off her shoulders. "Can I ask you a question? I mean I already know the answer, but I was just wondering..."

"Of course not." Ollie replied without looking up.

Cassie felt even more weight lift off her shoulders. Weight she didn't even realize was there. "It's just that everyone's so sure." Cassie said.

"I would never hurt an animal. See?" Ollie looked up again as he scratched Rembrandt on the back of his head. "I like to draw them sometimes though."

"I think he likes you." Cassie smiled. "My brother and sister are not always right. Do you have any brothers or sisters?"

"Nope. It's just me and my mom." Ollie said.

"Where's your dad?" Cassie asked out of curiosity.

"I don't really know. I've never met him."

Cassie nodded. "My parents are divorced."

"Is Rembrandt your dog?" Ollie changed the subject.

"No. He's Dr. Huitre's dog. He lives nearby. But I walk him sometimes." Cassie smiled proudly. "I really love him."

Rembrandt barked as if to underscore Cassie's point.

Ollie jumped a little, but laughed.

"You didn't bring your drawing pad today." Cassie said.

"Yeah. I forgot it. Maybe next time." Ollie thought for a moment. "Maybe one day I could draw *you*."

"Cassssssssieeeeee." The yell came from the other side of the park.

Ollie and Cassie looked up to see Binny racing towards them.

"Get away from her!" Binny was yelling.

Ollie sighed. "I better go."

Cassie had an uncomfortable look on her face at the prospect of a confrontation between her sister and Ollie. "Yeah. I'm really sorry."

"It's okay. Maybe we can hang out, just us, another time." Ollie winked and turned on his heel.

It took another thirty seconds for Binny to catch up to the spot where Cassie was standing with Rembrandt.

"What were you thinking?" Binny yelled.

"He didn't do it you know." Cassie tried to project confidence.

"You don't know what he did and didn't do. And you just put Rembrandt, and yourself, in danger. Mom is *so* angry with you for just leaving. She told you not to walk the dog."

"I can do it on my own. I don't need you, or Zach, or Mom, or anyone. And the proof is that I'm fine, and Rembrandt is fine. All Ollie did was pet him."

"I'm dropping you off at home and then I'm taking Rembrandt back to Dr. Huitre's house. You're in huge trouble."

Cassie's overwhelming frustration and anger acted as kind of a stopper for the tears that were welling up behind her eyes. She wouldn't start crying until she was sent to her room.

⋗ 32 ⋖

THE NEW PATIENT

Binny had gotten some satisfaction from seeing Cassie get in trouble with their parents at the house. But they were only mad at her for walking the dog on her own. They didn't have any idea how reckless Cassie had been by introducing Rembrandt to Ollie, the neighborhood's animal abuser. She would tell Zach about that for sure.

But Ollie hadn't done anything to the dog. Not yet anyway. Maybe because Cassie was there watching. Maybe he liked to do whatever it was he did on his own. How Cassie didn't see there was something wrong with that boy, Binny didn't know.

Not only might Ollie have hurt Rembrandt, he might have hurt Cassie too. Caleb had said that kids who hurt animals grow up to be adults that hurt people. Binny wondered how early the transition came from animals to people. Was ten too early?

Each thought got Binny more scared, more angry, and closer to the one person who seemed to be at the root of all the problems – Dr. Huitre. He was the one who got her mother involved with Luce Labs. He was the one who was connected with Dr. Trace and her weird son. And while she wasn't sure exactly how, he was somehow the cause of Binny's parents' divorce.

"Oh hello Binny. Where is Cassie? Did you do shifts today?" Henry Huitre opened his door to let Rembrandt in. Binny's thinking had carried her all the way to Huitre's house.

Binny stood at the door, fists tightly balled, not sure whether to scream or run.

"Come in Binny, come in. Is everything okay?" Huitre said.

Binny couldn't bear to look at him. Binny watched Rembrandt who was curling up on a couch by the fireplace.

"You know you are not supposed to be there." Huitre admonished his dog. The turning to Binny, he explained, "He's so old, I can't bear to banish him from that spot." Huitre's eyes crinkled accompanying his pained smile.

Binny's eyes traced the features of the room from the couch to the fireplace to the mantle above it where a series of small framed pictures sat. Some looked old in black and white, several were of Rembrandt. But one caught Binny's eye and sent a jolt down her chest.

"What are you doing with this?" Binny pointed at the picture as she marched across the living room. "Why do you have this?" Binny was screaming now, waving the picture around wildly as she spoke.

"Binny, Binny, what is wrong? Please be careful. Why are you so upset?"

Huitre's confusion just made Binny angrier. The picture she'd seen on the mantle was the very picture she'd seen in Huitre's mind when she'd looked two days earlier. It was the picture of her mother from before Binny or even Zach were born.

"Why do you have this picture of my mother here?" Binny demanded.

Huitre slumped a little at Binny's question. "Binny, that's not your mother."

"Of course it is. Look at it." Binny shoved the frame towards Huitre.

"Binny, that is a picture of my wife. My wife Jacqueline." Huitre's hands were out, palms up, as he explained.

"What? Your wife? You don't have a wife!" Binny felt a crack forming in her righteous anger.

"She died Binny. Jacqueline died 15 years ago."

Binny was speechless.

Huitre reached out his hands and gently took the picture frame from Binny. Turning it around he pointed to a corner. "Don't you see who that is in the corner of the picture?"

In the corner of the image were the unmistakable ear, nose, mouth, and front paws of a puppy – a Bernese Mountain Dog puppy. Rembrandt. When Binny had seen the image in her mind, she hadn't noticed the dog in the corner.

Binny's rage started to subside.

Huitre continued, I bought Rembrandt for Jacqueline when I asked her to marry me. She had the same dog growing up. This is the day she met him. It was a long time ago. He's much much older than he should be. That's why I let him stay on the couch sometimes. Huitre leaned over and stroked Rembrandt's fur.

"She looks... she looks like my mother." Binny grasped at the last straws she had.

"Yes. I am afraid she does. And I am afraid, their resemblance is one of the main reasons you and I are sitting here right now."

Binny kept her distance from Huitre, but sat down on the other side of Rembrandt and listened.

"Binny, I know you are not happy with your mother and I becoming friends. And as far as I can tell, she is no longer happy becoming friends as well. I understand why you feel that way and I do not blame you. But I have also not been completely honest with your mother. There are things I need to tell her, and I think I owe you an explanation as well. I understand that neither of you may ever want to be friends after I tell you this, but I still need to tell you the truth. OK?"

Huitre looked up at Binny waiting for an acknowledgement. His face looked sadder than Binny had ever seen. Binny nodded.

"Fourteen years ago, my wife died. Pretty suddenly. Where I am serious, Jacqueline was funny. Where I am heavy, she was light. She balanced me, you know? There was so little time between when we found out she was sick and when she was gone, I didn't get time to adjust, I didn't get time to really say goodbye."

"For me Binny, as a doctor, it was especially hard to know I was helpless to keep Jacqueline. Where she balanced me, I became unbalanced. I got more serious. More heavy. And only two things kept me from completely falling apart. The first was my work, and the second is this big pile of fur that you have been so kind to walk around the neighborhood these last few weeks."

"Your mother was a patient of my partner. You already know that your mother and father were very eager to have children and my partner was helping them. You also know Dr. Trace from Luce Labs last summer. She was working hard to get my partner to include your mother in their new fertility study. But my partner did not like Dr. Trace."

"I had never actually met your mother until one day in the hospital cafeteria. Dr. Trace was complaining to me about my partner's unwillingness to include your mother in the study. But suddenly I couldn't focus on Dr.

Trace's complaints. Your parents stopped in after an appointment to get a drink or something. And that was the first time I saw your mother. For several seconds, I thought Jacqueline had walked into the cafeteria."

Binny did her best to not reveal her thoughts, but Huitre could see her the expression on her face.

"You must understand Binny, I was grieving. I knew your mother was not my late wife. But the resemblance was so uncanny that for a moment I thought your mother was a ghost."

"Binny, I am about to say something that is not very nice. I am not saying this to excuse my behavior. I am just trying to tell you the truth. Like I would to an adult. OK?"

Binny nodded.

"Dr. Trace is not a nice person. I do not know what made her this way, but alas that is how she is. She is worse now, but she was not very nice then. She was and still is manipulative. Dr. Trace noticed my reaction to your mother. Dr. Trace knew my wife had recently died. A plan formed in Dr. Trace's mind to get what she wanted."

"Within days, your mother's physician, my partner had made plans to move across the country. The reason? A spectacular job offer for her husband. The company he went to work for was owned by Luce Laboratories. This was arranged by Dr. Trace."

"How do you know?" Binny asked.

"When my partner left she had to find a new doctor for her patients. Naturally, most of them came to me – including your mother. A few days after your mother became my patient, Dr. Trace came to visit me to talk about including your mother in the study."

"Now, normally, I am not opposed to including patients in studies. And Luce Labs was well known for creating many important drugs. But Dr. Trace bothered me. I was worried about subjecting your mother to her clutches. I also didn't understand why the only one of my patients in which she seemed interested was your mother."

"When I told Dr. Trace that I thought I would not recommend participation, she got very angry with me. She told me that she had seen how I had looked at your mother, and that she had arranged for her to become my patient, and that now I owed her."

"I told her that I had asked for no such thing. I demanded that she leave my office and never come back. She told me that if I didn't have your mother participate in the study, she would tell my superiors at the hospital that she had colluded with me to make your mother my patient. And that I had a romantic interest in your mother."

"Now Binny, I need to tell you at this point, that your mother is an incredible woman, who I have become very fond of. But fifteen years ago, your mother was a married woman, and I was overwhelmed by grief. I wasn't interested in anything but hanging on to the fading memories of Jacqueline. Your mother's chance resemblance to Jacqueline was just a symbol for me. This I promise you."

Huitre looked Binny in the eye to make sure she'd heard him and then continued. "When Trace told me what she would do, I was horrified. I knew her story was a lie. But I also knew that even the accusation would ruin my career. And what I did next is something I have regretted and will regret for the rest of my life."

"What did you do?" Binny asked.

"I convinced myself that maybe the study would be beneficial to your mother's possible infertility. I convinced myself that I shouldn't discount the possibility that the experimental drug might help your mother just because Dr. Trace was someone I didn't like. I accepted Trace's explanation that her interest in your mother was because the study needed a very specific demographic profile for its participants."

"I convinced myself of all these things because I was ashamed of how I'd reacted to seeing your mother. I was ashamed of how much I'd revealed about my pain to Dr. Trace. I convinced myself because I was afraid of losing one of the only two things that were keeping me from losing my mind. I convinced myself because I was selfish. And for the last fifteen years, Samantha Trace has held this over me."

"That's why you tried to get us to Luce Labs last year."

"I am afraid so. I convinced myself then too. I convinced myself that they would find a way to get to you with or without me, and at least if I was there I could try and protect you. I've been trying to atone for my selfishness for fifteen years. But all I have to show for it is lies and endless shame."

"Why are you telling me now? Why are you telling me the truth?" Binny was leaning forward, elbows on knees. Her anger had evaporated, but her sadness still weighed heavily on her heart.

Huitre closed his eyes briefly before he finished his confession. "Remember Binny, I told you that I had only two things after Jacqueline died? My work, and Rembrandt?"

Binny nodded in rapt attention.

"I compromised my work the day I put your mother in that study. As for Rembrandt, he is much older than he has a right to be. Most dogs of his breed live until eight or ten at most. He is fifteen years old. And I can see him finally slowing down. Once he's gone, I'll have nothing left."

"Your mother deserves better than I have given her. And while I can't resurrect everything I have lost, I can tell the truth. I became your mother's doctor to help her and your father have children. And they did – three beautiful children. I don't know if it was despite or because of the Luce drug trial. But here you are. And you deserve better from me too. I'm sorry it has taken so long to be... better."

"Dr. Huitre?"

"Yes."

"Are you in love with my mother?"

Huitre smiled and rubbed his eyes. "Your mother is an amazing woman. I've really enjoyed getting to know her and I like her very much. And I will tell you honestly – you are quite wise for an eleven-year-old – that I would very much like to get to know her better. But as best I can tell, she is no longer interested in getting to know me."

"Do you like my mom just because she looks like Jacqueline?"

"Ha. You know all the hard questions to ask, do you not?" Huitre smiled and continued without waiting for an answer. "No. Your mother and Jacqueline don't really look at all alike to me. I was in a haze of mourning back then. Now that I've gotten to know your mother as a friend instead of a patient, she is very different than Jacqueline, on the outside *and* on the inside. And I quite like her for who she is."

"Dr. Trace is awful." Binny said, the wheels in her mind turning as she processed all the new information.

Huitre nodded in agreement as he laughed a little. "I cannot argue with you on that front."

Binny's eyes got wide as the pieces in her mind fell into place. "She tried to get you to get us to Luce Labs last summer. And now she has her security guy following us around."

"What?" Huitre's mouth was open in shock? "Following you? You must tell your parents immediately."

"My dad is already mad at us for getting into some trouble this summer."

"Binny, then you should tell your mother." Huitre took on a sterner tone.

"I don't think you're the one to lecture me on being honest with my mother." Binny responded sharply.

"OK. But Binny, no matter how angry you or your mother are at me, I will always be here to give you and your family anything you need. I mean this Binny. If you need me, I will always be there."

Binny looked hard at Huitre trying to decide if she could trust him. His thoughts were awash in pure red. Binny made her decision. "What I need is a way to get Trace to stop coming after us."

"Well, I suppose you could do something that I never had the courage to do." Huitre suggested.

"What's that?"

"Inform her management at Luce Laboratories of what she's up to."

❧ 33 ❧

THE HARVESTING

"That's it. Cut it right there. No lower though." Xander Luce watched closely over Ollie's shoulder as Ollie cut the stalks of the plant.

When Ollie had shown up in the greenhouse that morning, Xander had announced that it was a harvest day. A dozen or so of the hundreds of plants in the greenhouse were ready to be culled for the lab.

"What's going to happen to this stuff?" Ollie asked as he used the sharp scissors the way he'd been instructed.

"Extraction!" A smile flashed across Luce's face.

"Extraction?"

"There are different techniques depending on the plant, and depending on the compound we're trying to isolate, but at a high level, we put the plant material in a solvent, and apply heat. That process draws out the plant's constituents – the pieces that we're looking to isolate.

"Why don't we just pull the whole plant out of the dirt? Wouldn't that be faster?"

"Well, sometimes we do that when the elements of the plant we're trying to isolate are in the roots. But for many plants that's not necessary." Luce explained.

"Yes. But wouldn't it be faster?" Ollie asked again.

"I suppose, but then the plant would die."

"Cutting it doesn't kill the plant?" Ollie sounded puzzled.

"Oh no. In some cases it can make the plant stronger." Xander was excited to enlighten Ollie on this topic.

Ollie thought for a moment. "Does this work with animals too?"

Xander's eyes showed that the question had caught him off guard. It took a few seconds for him to think about his response. "Well, I wouldn't apply sharp scissors to an animal the way we are to this plant." Xander laughed briefly. "But, in principle, yes. When done properly of course, it is possible to experiment on animals without killing them. And, in my mind, preferred."

"And they'll grow stronger afterwards? Like the plants?"

"I suppose. Yes. That's certainly possible." Xander stopped what he was doing to spin Ollie around to face him. "But Ollie, that requires the scientist to have a deep understanding of the subject of his or her experiment. They must know the plant or animal inside and out. In other words, it must be done with utmost thought and care."

Ollie nodded and went back to his harvesting. In the relative silence, Ollie's mind kept going over what Xander had said.

§

"Are you sure he's the owner of the company?" Penny asked again.

"I told you, when Huitre suggested we go to Dr. Trace's boss, I had no idea who he was talking about. But I just couldn't imagine two people in the same company with the name Xander." Binny trailed off.

Binny had messaged everyone to meet in the Madrona Park that morning with their bikes, instead of gathering at their usual spot in their underground headquarters.

"Why is the guy who started the company working in the greenhouse? He didn't look like the big boss to me." Zoe asked.

"That's what I asked Dr. Huitre when he told me Xander was in charge." Binny said.

"I guess the boss gets to do whatever they like – including, work in the greenhouse." Zach added.

"Well, let's see how bossy he gets when he finds out that Dr. Trace has been having us followed." Binny said.

Zach wondered why Binny was so sure that Xander Luce didn't know what Dr. Trace and the security guard were up to, but he kept that to himself.

§

"Xander? I was wondering if I might head home early today. I have an experiment of my own I'd like to work on. I already finished all the cutting I was supposed to do." Ollie held out the shiny scissors, returning them to Xander.

"You don't need the scissors for your experiment?" Xander asked.

Ollie was taken aback by the directness of the question. "Uh, no. No. I don't."

Xander smiled. "Of course Ollie. Thanks for your hard work this morning."

"And Xander? Would you mind not telling my mom I left this early." Ollie asked.

"You want me to lie to your mother?" Xander replied with a note of incredulity on his face.

"Well. Not exactly. I mean, she never said how early I could leave. And I promise I'll be careful and I'll get home on time."

Luce could feel Ollie's excitement to get started on whatever experiment he had in mind. "Okay Ollie. I will keep your confidence." Luce raised his eyebrows implying there were unspoken details of their agreement, but said nothing more.

"Thank you." Ollie said, and raced out of the greenhouse.

§

"Xander?" Binny's voice didn't go far in the greenhouse, absorbed by all the foliage.

"Oh, hello children." The old man looked flustered for a moment at the unexpected visit but quickly recovered his poise. "To what do I owe the pleasure of your company?"

"Why didn't you tell us?" Binny's hands were on her hips.

"Tell you what Binny." Xander looked bemused.

"Tell us that you are Xander *Luce* – the founder of this entire company." Binny responded.

"You never asked." Xander replied.

"But we thought..." Binny's voice trailed off.

Xander picked up the thread. "You thought that the old man in the greenhouse couldn't possibly be the founder of this sprawling concern?" Xander spread his hand to gesture at the buildings beyond the greenhouse.

"Well..." Binny shuffled in place.

The other children were shuffling as well.

"And now that you know my secret identity, what will you do with this information?" Xander chuckled a little.

Binny looked at the others for reassurance quickly regaining her composure. "Why is one of your security people following us around our neighborhood in his car?"

"Oh my. Are you sure?"

Binny was so focused on confronting Luce that she hadn't thought to peek into his mind to see if he was telling the truth. "You didn't know?" Penny added her voice to the conversation.

"Aren't you in charge?" Zoe piled on.

Luce rubbed his temples, and let out an exasperated sigh. "I am so sorry children. I thought I had put an end to this."

"Put an end to what?" Binny eyed him suspiciously.

"Mind if I sit children? I'm not as sturdy as I used to be." Luce grabbed a nearby stool not waiting for an answer. "I thought I had put an end to this last summer. I'm afraid I wasn't as effective as I thought."

"I try to let my employees pursue their own initiatives here at Luce Laboratories. After all, I'm pursuing the things *I* love best." Luce motioned around the greenhouse. "I suppose that sometimes I can be too *permissive*?"

"Last summer, one of my top scientists, Dr. Samantha Trace, got carried away with one of our studies. I found out what happened and put told her to end that effort. But I found out and ended it only after you four children," he nodded at Penny and the Jordans "had to experience that unpleasantness."

"Now children, I must tell you, Dr. Trace is an excellent scientist. She just gets carried away sometimes. So please, on behalf of Luce Labs, I give you my deepest apologies." Luce bowed his head slightly.

"But it wasn't Dr. Trace who was following us. It was your chief of security." Binny countered.

"Ah yes. Mr. Grater. He is a good man. But he was no doubt taking orders from Dr. Trace. I am so sorry about that."

Zach had been considering Luce's explanations for some time when he finally piped up. "If Grater is doing what Dr. Trace wants, then why is Dr. Trace so interested in us?"

Luce nodded at Zach, "That is an insightful and excellent question Zach. Very impressive. You have a keen analytical mind. You'd make an excellent scientist yourself someday. Asking the right questions is so important." Luce smiled, and then shook his head as if remembering something. "But I haven't answered your question."

"I'm afraid there's no delicate way to say this children, so I'll be direct. Dr. Trace has been obsessed with you children because she believes you have extranormal powers. Super powers if you will."

Binny felt as if the air was sucked out of the greenhouse. Trace suspected the truth. That's why she tried to get them to the greenhouse. That's why she was having them followed. And Binny was the only one that knew that Trace had been targeting the Jordans even before any of the kids were born.

Binny croaked out a half-hearted question. "Uh, super powers?" Binny tried to sound casual. "That's ridiculous."

Luce leaned towards the children, lowering his voice. "Ridiculous? Oh I don't think there's *anything* ridiculous about being able to turn invisible. Right Cassie?" Luce directed his question at Cassie alone.

Cassie said nothing, her mouth making a perfect 'O'.

"You knew." Zach said.

"Of course I knew. We have cameras in the exam rooms. I saw Cassie flickering in and out of existence on the video. And I have kept your secret ever since." Luce's eyes went wide and he nodded to reinforce his point.

"Your own employee thought Cassie had super powers, and she was right. But you didn't tell her? Why didn't you say anything?" Binny asked, incredulous.

Luce sighed again. "Children, this is a bit of a complicated answer, so I apologize in advance. But try and bear with me. OK?"

Binny silently reprimanded herself for not testing the veracity of Luce's claims to this point with a little look inside his mind as he spoke. *Was Luce another adult they couldn't trust?* Binny started reading Luce's mind as he spoke. *Better late than never,* she thought to herself.

Six heads nodded up and down.

"As a scientist, I am thrilled and fascinated at the thought of humans with actual super powers. I can only start to imagine the possibilities of what we could do with super powers to improve our planet, cure diseases, stop wars, and that's just the start." Luce was getting animated.

"And while I have no children of my own, I can only imagine how I'd feel if it were one of my children – or grandchildren – " Luce winked, "that had super powers. I don't think they'd necessarily want anyone to know about them or be poked and prodded by scientists in a lab."

"Does Dr. Trace want to poke and prod me?" Cassie said in a small voice.

Xander said through a pained smile, "I'm sure she would never want to hurt you. But at the end of the day, no matter how important science is, it's not up to Dr. Trace. It's up to you, if you want to learn more about your powers, how they work, and how we can leverage them to make the world a better place. And that goes for any of you who have found yourselves with any *special* abilities."

Binny had been watching Luce's thoughts for even a hint of a lie, but everything was pure red. Binny was so surprised by Luce's last sentence that she stopped looking inside his mind and just listened to what he had to say. Binny was satisfied that Luce was telling the truth and someone they could trust.

The children shuffled their feet, looking uncomfortable, and silently debating how much information to reveal to Xander.

Zach seemed to decide the matter by moving on to another topic. "Dr. Trace is not the only one doing things they shouldn't be doing."

"Oh?" Xander raised his eyebrows expectantly.

"Her son is hurting animals from our neighborhood. We're not sure exactly where." Zach sounded more and more forceful as he spoke.

"We tried going to his house. But Dr. Trace wouldn't listen to us." Zoe added, balling her hands into fists emphatically.

Luce nodded sympathetically as he spoke. "Yes. You mentioned this the last time you visited. And you're sure now that it's Dr. Trace's son?"

Zoe and Zach nodded.

Luce continued, "That sounds terrible children. I've met the young man before. I never expected him to do something like this. What can I do to help?"

"Aside from telling Dr. Trace and your security guy to stop following us around?" Binny added sarcastically.

Xander looked at Binny earnestly, "Of course."

"And maybe when you talk to Dr. Trace, if you can get any ideas about where her son is conducting his experiments you could let us know?" Zach asked, holding up his cell phone.

"I'll do my best, of course."

Zach wrote down his phone number for Luce. The kids said their goodbyes, and gathered themselves to leave.

"Oh and children?" Luce added before they exited the greenhouse. "I am impressed with your powers of poise, maturity, and knowing right from wrong. These are super powers that are more rare than you might think. Especially in ones as young as you."

"I know you will use *all* your powers for good to solve this animal 'situation'. And as I promised, I'll see if there's anything I can do to help in your quest. But once you've solved that puzzle, if you are ever interested in finding out just what's possible with Miss Cassie's powers," Luce ruffled Cassie's hair as he spoke, "or anything else you're interested in sharing with me, my door is always open, and my mouth will always remain shut."

§

"I still can't believe he knew." Zach said.

The kids had ridden back to Madrona after their visit to Luce Labs. The trip back was upbeat. They hadn't stopped Ollie, but they'd gotten to the bottom of their Luce Labs problems, and had a new adult that believed in them and would keep their secret. They were still recounting and analyzing their discussion with Luce when they arrived in the shelter.

"I can't believe he didn't tell Dr. Trace about Cassie." Binny said.

"I still can't believe he's the boss." Zoe smirked.

"Do you think he knows about the rest of us?" Penny asked.

"I think he suspects." Zach said. "I'm not so sure about him."

"I think we can trust him. I did a little checking while spoke." Binny tapped her temple for emphasis.

Binny's assurances seemed to close the subject for the moment.

"What about Caleb?" Zoe asked.

"Yeah. What about Caleb." Binny responded rolling her eyes.

As everyone pondered the question of Caleb's intentions, Zach headed up the stairs to the command center. "Be right back. I just want to check on something."

§

The children raced through the woods at top speed. It was only when they reached the edge of the woods that they even understood why they were running. Zach had been clearly agitated when he'd come flying down the

422

stairs from the command center, but in the hurry to mobilize everyone, he'd only shared fragments of what was happening.

Zach repeated himself, breathing hard from the running, "The program predicts where Ollie will strike next. The pin was pointing directly at Dr. Huitre's house."

Cassie was stricken with fear. The others were not doing much better.

"You don't think..." Binny's voice trailed off.

"We're almost there." Zach said as he raced the last few yards to Dr. Huitre's door and rang the bell repeatedly.

Dr. Huitre opened the door, smiling at the unexpectedly large group at his door. "Oh wow. What a gathering today. But why so early?"

"We're here to walk Rembrandt." Binny announced. "Is he here?"

"Of course he is here. Where else would he be?" Huitre laughed, a gently puzzled look on his face. "It's lucky that I am off today to let you in. Rembrandt has not yet mastered doorknobs."

Cassie pushed through the group and past Huitre into the house. "Rembrandt. Rembrandt." There was no sign of him in the house. Cassie turned back to Huitre, "Where is he?"

"My my. Everyone is so eager. I'm sure Rembrandt will be excited for an unexpected lunchtime walk."

Huitre smiled. "He's in the backyard. Sometimes he prefers the grass for his naps."

The children raced past Huitre towards the sliding back doors and piled into the backyard. But after a minute of repeatedly calling his name and exploring every possible hiding spot in the fenced-in space, it was undeniable – Rembrandt was gone.

❖ 34 ❖

THE POSTERS

"I got home as soon as I could." Julie said as she walked into the Jordan home.

Six long faces decorated the family room.

"Mommmeeee." Cassie ran to her mother, her face streaky with tears. "Rembrandt is gone."

"Oh honey." Julie hugged her daughter. "Don't worry, I'm sure he just went for a little solo walk."

"I don't think so Mom." Zach said.

Jay cleared his throat before speaking. "Zach still believes that the boy they saw is somehow responsible for Rembrandt's disappearance."

"Not just Rembrandt." Binny added. "Lots of animals in the neighborhood.

A look passed between Jay and Julie before Jay continued, "Zach has agreed not to call the police again on his own or go to the boy's house. But regardless of how it happened, the dog is missing, and all the kids are very upset."

"Well I'm sure Dr. Huitre is out looking and will find Rembrandt soon." Julie said.

"Mom, we need to help him. He can't do it on his own." Binny said.

Julie Jordan looked at her daughter, the daughter that had made it clear in no uncertain terms that Dr. Huitre was not to be trusted. And yet, here she was eager to help the very same man. Julie told herself that Binny's efforts were motivated by her love of Rembrandt, and not by some newfound trust in Huitre. And if her eleven-year-old daughter could make that separation, then she should probably rise to the occasion as well.

"Okay Binny. I understand. We'll help." Julie put her hand on Binny's shoulder.

"My parents are on their way too." Penny piped in. "I asked them to help."

Moments later, Serena, Quincy, and Jonathan were all at the Jordan's front door. Introductions were made, and everyone was brought up to speed both on

Rembrandt's disappearance as well as the kids' theories of how he had disappeared.

"Why don't you kids stay here and eat some lunch. The adults will go out and look."

"I'm sorry Mr. Jordan, but no." Zoe stood up and spoke for the first time. "We're going to help look."

Jay had a surprised smile on his face. "Zoe, you and you brother of course can do what you like. But I'm not sure I want my kids traipsing around the neighborhood searching for Rembrandt when you're all this this upset. Let the adults handle things."

All at once five young voices started complaining, crying, and arguing.

Jay put up his hands, unprepared for the onslaught.

Zach's voice cut through the cacophony. "Shhh... everyone, hold on."

Everyone in the Jordan family room stopped mid-sentence and waited to hear what Zach had to say.

"Dad, you're right to be concerned. We *are* upset. One of the reasons we're upset is because we've been telling you about animals disappearing in the neighborhood for weeks now. And every time we say anything, you've not really taken us seriously."

Zach continued, "But just because we're upset, doesn't mean we're dumb. We know the neighborhood better than the adults. We're smaller than the adults, so we can see things you might not. And including us means there are just more pairs of eyes looking for Rembrandt."

Jay's voice took on a new tone of respect for Zach's well-reasoned arguments. "Well said. But not even for a moment do I think any of you are dumb. I just worry about your emotional state resulting in you making a bad decision. And it's our job to keep you safe from your own bad decisions."

Zach took a deep breath, he somehow looked even taller than he had a minute ago. "Dad, protecting us from ourselves is not your job. Your job is to give us the opportunity to learn from our decisions – both good and bad."

Jay's jaw dropped.

"Smart kid." Serena said.

"I'm impressed." Quincy added.

"Can I take credit for that?" Julie joked.

"Well I certainly can't." Jay laughed at himself, slightly pink from embarrassment.

"Look," Zach continued, "this is about trust. You can trust us to make the best decisions we know how, look out for each other, and ask for help when we need it."

The other kids were all looking at Zach, marveling at his conviction. The adults were doing much the same.

"I haven't been doing that much lately, have I. That *trust* thing?" Jay said.

"It's not too late to start now." Zach smiled at his father.

"I suppose it isn't. Thanks for the coaching kiddo." Jay Jordan hugged his son, his cheeks flush, but a big smile on his face.

§

Henry Huitre had known that Rembrandt wouldn't be around much longer, but he didn't expect the end to happen so suddenly. Of course, that was defeatist thinking. Rembrandt had likely just found a way to wriggle through the fence and had gone exploring. Knowing Rembrandt he'd be home as soon as he got hungry, which could be in mere minutes given Rembrandt's usual appetite.

Henry kept getting up to start heading out the door to search for his dog, but each time he would think better of it wondering if walking around the neighborhood would mean he wasn't there for Rembrandt's return.

Finally, the feeling of helplessness tipped the scales in the direction of doing something. *Anything.* Henry stood up and headed to the front door, intending to hop in his car and go searching for his best friend of fifteen years.

But when he opened the door, a small crowd had gathered on his porch, about to knock. The gaggle of children that had first discovered Rembrandt's disappearance and a bunch of their parents were at his door.

"Hi Henry. We're here to help find Rembrandt." Jay looked around at the group of ten adults and kids behind him and then back at Huitre. "All of us."

§

Jay and Serena had sat down to draw signs. Jay illustrated images of Rembrandt using the same markers Cassie had used a year earlier. Serena was writing text onto the posters. Quincy and Jonathan were cutting little tabs into the row of phone numbers at the bottom of each poster.

In this moment of potentially devastating loss and loneliness, Henry Huitre was surrounded by helping hands.

Henry approached Julie, who was standing in the corner of the kitchen on her own. "Julie, I just wanted to thank you for bringing everyone to help look for Rembrandt."

"Don't thank me. Thank my children. They're the ones who raised the alarm." Julie replied coolly.

"Of course. I will thank them as well. And Julie..." Henry started to say.

Julie looked expectantly waiting for the words to come, but they never did. Finally Henry just nodded in thanks and walked back to the group making signs.

Binny approached her mother. She could sense the distance between Huitre and her mother from across the room. "Mom, thanks for coming home from work."

"It's fine honey. I'm happy to help." Julie said to her daughter.

"Mom, listen, what I said the other day about Dr. Huitre, I'm not sure it was really the whole picture."

"Were you not telling me the truth?" Julie raised an eyebrow as she asked the question.

"No. I mean yes. I mean it was the truth. I'm just not sure I understood the whole story of what happened back then." Binny said.

"I'm sure you didn't understand the whole story. But the truth is that you probably still don't darling." Julie consoled her daughter.

Binny could still sense the distance in her mother's voice. "Mom. Maybe I was wrong about Dr. Huitre?"

Julie looked in Binny's eyes as she stroked her hair. "Sweetie. It's okay. You didn't do anything wrong. Let's not worry about that right now. Let's just focus on finding Rembrandt. OK?"

Binny nodded in agreement, but as for whether she had done anything wrong, she wasn't entirely sure.

Zach had been busy tapping away on his phone since they'd arrived at Dr. Huitre's house. In quick succession, all the adults cell phones started beeping.

"I've texted everyone a map of the neighborhood. On the map I've made several notations. 'S's are where the signs should be hung up. 'W's are different paths the girls usually take Rembrandt on walks. 'K's are areas where the kids should look for Rembrandt. 'A's are areas where the adults should look.

431

"We're splitting up?" Jay asked?

"We can cover more of the neighborhood more quickly if we're not all in one big group." Zach responded without looking up from his phone.

"Can we mix the adults and the kids at least?" Jay pleaded.

The looks from the other adults in the room told Jay all he needed to know. He'd been outvoted and he was surprisingly happy about it.

§

"We need to take a left here." Julie said glancing at her phone.

Jay and Julie Jordan started walking up the Madrona hillside from Dr. Huitre. They had half the signs that Jay and Serena had made and a stapler.

"Are you sure?" Jay asked.

"Your son has made our instructions very clear." Julie pointed at the map Zach had sent to her phone.

"Indeed he has." Jay smiled. "He's been making a bunch of things clear as of late."

"Indeed he has." Now it was Julie's turn to smile.

Jay and Julie walked up the hill towards the Madrona park stopping every block or two to post one of the signs.

"These signs are really great. I can't believe how fast you made them." Julie said.

"I had help." Jay said.

"I noticed. You and Serena made a good team back there." Julie winked.

"What?" Jay sputtered. "What do you mean?"

"Just what I said. You seemed like a good team." Julie was smiling broadly now, enjoying how uncomfortable she was making Jay.

"Are you..." Jay hesitated. "Are you upset?"

"Upset?" Julie's eyes looked up as she made a show of searching her feelings. "No. Definitely not. I'm happy for you. I get pangs sometimes. But they're just pangs. I know we made the right decision. Things keep getting better, and this is just part of the process."

"It's nothing you know. We're just being neighborly." Jay tried to sound casual.

"If you say so." Julie winked.

"Well, we did talk about maybe her helping me with a creative project." Jay conceded. Eager to change the subject, Jay continued, "What about your new *friendship*? You haven't been going over to 'walk the dog' lately." Jay put his fingers up, making air quotes.

Now it was Julie's turn to be reticent. "That's nothing."

"Are you sure?" Jay asked gently.

"Yeah. I'm sure." Julie thought for a moment and then added. "Well, I think I'm sure."

The subject seemed closed as they arrived at the top of the rise. Only two more blocks to the park where there was a big bulletin board where Madrona residents would post notices.

"Can I ask you a question?" Jay stared straight ahead as he spoke. "Do you think I've been treating Zach unfairly?"

"Oh Jay. Don't beat yourself up. This stuff is hard." Julie consoled.

"It's just that he's growing up so quickly. I have to keep readjusting my expectations of him. I'm not growing. He gets to treat me the same, but I have to keep giving him more room." Jay tried to joke, but there was an undercurrent of worry in his statement.

"Listen, this is part of the process. Kids are resilient. They'll get through it, and so will we." Julie did her best to reassure.

"He's been trying to get me to listen about this whole missing animal thing lately, but I haven't really taken him seriously. I guess, now that Rembrandt is missing, I'm feeling kind of bad." Jay confessed.

Julie rolled her eyes. "You've got to stop being so hard on yourself. Don't you think if there was an epidemic of missing animals in the neighborhood we would have heard about it by now?"

As Julie asked her question, the pair reached the bulletin board in Madrona park. Jay went to put up a sign but there was no room on the board. It was filled completely with homemade posters of missing Madrona pets. The posters flapped in the gentle breeze as Jay and Julie stood stunned.

§

"Who's got the stapler?" Serena asked as she peeled another poster from the pile.

"Here you go." Jonathan said.

While Jay and Julie had headed to the top half of the neighborhood, Serena, Jonathan, and Quincy, were covering the lower half that hugged the lake.

"These drawings are quite good that Jay did." Jonathan said.

"Yeah. He's talented." Serena agreed as she stapled the poster to the pole. It took her a moment as there were at least a half a dozen other missing pet posters vying for space.

"Lot of missing pets in this neighborhood?" Jonathan asked, observing the crowded pole.

"So it appears." Serena said as they kept walking.

"So what's the scoop with them?" Quincy asked.

"The missing pets?" Serena said.

"Uh, no. The neighbors. Binny and Cassie's parents." Quincy answered.

"They're divorced. She lives real close though and is over all the time. They're making the best of it I think." Serena said.

"Oh." Quincy thought about what Serena had said. "Is there a lot of this kind of thing?" Quincy directed his question at his ex-wife.

"*This* kind of thing?" Serena looked momentarily confused.

"Lots of dealing with last minute kid-related emergencies on your own?"

"This is how it goes." Serena said gently. "Penny spends a lot of time with Binny so it's not too bad."

"I guess you *and* Jay are both doing quite a bit of single parenting." Quincy seemed to be trying to work something out as he spoke.

"Well, that's true." Serena took a moment to think through just how she wanted to continue her statement. "Jay's got three to deal with, so that's harder. But he's also got Julie nearby, so that makes it easier."

Serena looked at Quincy as she spoke. Quincy could tell from her expression that she was not speaking out of anger.

"Quincy, it's gorgeous here." Jonathan interjected. The summer sun was out in full force and had just passed over the lake making everything glint and sparkle.

"Yeah, it's pretty." Quincy responded absent-mindedly still chewing on something.

"Really pretty." Jonathan emphasized.

A look passed between Jonathan and Serena and Serena smiled a quiet smile to herself.

✦ 35 ✦

THE ICE CREAM BREAK

Ever since Gore Grater had seen the children escape into the forest, he'd been focusing his efforts on the woods and the streets immediately surrounding the Madrona woods. In the time he'd been searching without success, his philosophy had also changed. If Dr. Trace wanted to see the kids use their powers, why wait for them to use them on their own.

Gore wasn't entirely sure what he'd seen at the fence, but it didn't look like the little girl unlocked the padlock with a key. It looked like she'd broken it into pieces and then somehow reassembled it. *Was that one of them using their powers?*

Gore suspected it was. And it didn't *just happen*. It happened because Gore himself had pushed them into a corner. Gore intended to find those kids and as many corners as it took to get them to reveal what they could really do.

Gore didn't enjoy traipsing around in the woods. Despite the shade, he would get sweaty quickly as the paths in the woods crisscrossed the hillside and invariably had him hiking uphill for some amount of time. He'd seen one particular tree no fewer than three times. He knew because its bark was peeling profusely.

"Are you enjoying our woods?"

Gore stopped in his tracks, almost tripping over the old man crouched by the side of the path. "What are you doing in the path? I almost tripped."

"I'm repairing the path so you *don't* trip." Caleb Adams responded. "So you can enjoy the woods." Caleb smiled.

"Hmm." Grater grimaced. He was breathing heavily from all the walking. "Have you seen a bunch of kids running around here?"

"Can't say that I have." Caleb had resumed attending to the rocks that had been dislodged from the side of the path. "May I ask why you're looking for them?"

Grater had to stop for a moment, realizing that he hadn't prepared for a question like this.

Caleb continued in Grater's silence. "Maybe, Mr. Grater, if I see them I could tell them you're looking for them."

Grater's hand involuntarily went up to his name embroidered on his pocket, and then went back down as it was too late. The old man knew his name. "I, I, well, it's official business. Nothing bad of course. Just need to find them."

Caleb stopped what he was doing, and stood up. Even though his height had started to diminish over the past decade or two, he was still taller than Grater by a couple of inches. Caleb smiled, but his eyes were steel. "Of course. Official business. I understand. But I think you shouldn't look in these woods anymore. Do you understand? These woods, they scare you. Badly. And besides, there are never any kids in these woods, so you can do your job without ever coming in here." Caleb paused for a moment and then added, "You should probably go now."

As the old man spoke, Grater's eyes darted from branch to branch. His head swiveled suddenly at every tiny animal sound. Beads of sweat formed on Gore Grater's forehead and started their slow descent down his thick face.

"You're sure there aren't any kids here?" Grater asked, his voice filled with dread. "I saw some run into the woods the other day."

"Oh, I'm quite sure. They might hang out around the edges, but they would never go beyond that. They get too scared in here. Don't worry, you'll still be doing a good job even if you never come into these woods again."

Gore Grater turned on his heel and ran down the path towards the edge of the woods without another word.

§

"We've covered the neighborhood twice already. There's no sign of him." Zoe said in frustration.

"Rembrandt or Ollie?" Binny asked.

"Both." Zoe harumphed.

"I'm hungry." Gabe complained quietly.

As frustrated as she was, even Zoe had to admit they hadn't eaten in hours.

"I'm hungry too." Cassie added.

Binny spoke up. "I know it feels awful while Rembrandt is still missing, but we're not going to have any energy to find him if we don't eat something."

"You read my mind." Zoe said.

"I promise I didn't." Binny said.

Despite how serious and sad they all felt, everyone laughed.

"Can we get ice cream?" Gabe sensed the tide turning in his direction.

"It is really hot." Cassie added.

"Ice cream isn't lunch." Zoe said.

Zach raised his eyebrows at Zoe. "I can pay." Zach let the words hang in the air.

"Alright, alright. Ice cream for lunch. But today only. And no telling Mom and Dad." Zoe acquiesced.

They were only two blocks from the Madrona commercial district and a few minutes later they found themselves in line at Soul Repair looking over the menu.

"Children, children, welcome." Kay Athanasios, the proprietor of Madrona's handcrafted ice cream shrine stood behind the counter as the kids funneled into the shop. Afternoon sunlight snuck into the shop making the pale aquamarine crystals in Kay's long curly black hair sparkle. Despite the heat of the day, the shop was relatively empty in the early afternoon.

"Hi Kay." Binny said.

"Hi Binny, Zach, Cassie, Penny. Who are your new friends?" Kay asked.

"This is Zoe and Gabe." Binny responded.

Zoe and Gabe waved.

Kay leaned in to examine Gabe. "Gabe, you look very familiar to me. Your last name isn't Walker, is it?"

"No. It's Flowers." Gabe explained.

"Walker is our grandfather." Zoe explained.

"Well that would explain it." Kay smiled that her hunch had been correct. "You know, when kids come into my shop on a hot day, they're usually smiling ear-to-ear. Not you six. What's wrong?"

Zach stepped forward. "A dog we really like has gone missing. We've been trying to find him, but we've had no luck so far."

"Oh my. Another one?" Kay pointed at the bulletin board in Soul Repair that was covered in missing pet notices.

"We're gonna find him." Zoe said determinedly.

"Of course you are Zoe. Of course you are." Kay reassured. "But you all look pretty wiped. I think a quick ice cream break might be ok in this case. Just so you can recharge for a bit. Sound good?"

Six heads nodded in agreement.

"But I have a favor to ask." Kay pursed her lips. "I want to experiment on you today."

"You too?" Cassie blurted out.

A puzzled look crossed Kay's face.

Binny put her arm on Cassie's shoulder. "She's just kidding."

Kay continued, "Do you guys like playing baseball on a hot summer day?"

"Not as much as ice cream." Gabe said, suspicious of where Kay was heading.

"Fair enough Gabe. And points for honesty!" Kay laughed heartily. "And to be quite honest myself, I kind of agree. I know you all have your favorites, but I have some new items I've been experimenting with. Would you be willing to be my guinea pigs?"

From the freezer below, Kay pulled out several trays of frozen confections. One tray was filled with what looked like watermelon slices. In reality they were entirely made of ice cream, with little white and dark chocolate 'seeds'. Summer seemed to be the theme as another tray had little cups filled with what looked like local blackberries but each turned out to be made from Kay's renowned blackberry sorbet set into blackberry-shaped molds.

The final tray was the oddest of all as it was filled with what looked just like baseballs.

"That's ice cream?" Penny asked.

Kay's eyes went large as she nodded, smiling. "Yep."

"They look just like baseballs." Gabe said in admiration.

The kids all huddled closer to marvel at Kay's creations.

"They look so real." Penny marveled.

"They come in a bunch of flavors. Each one is draped in white chocolate. And I can't even begin to tell you how long it took me to get the stitching to look so realistic. I was worried by the time I figured it out, baseball season would be over."

As Kay distributed the last of the ice cream, she added, "And remember, these are for eating, not for playing with. They would just melt all over your gloves and make a big mess."

Most of the ice cream baseballs were well on their way to being eaten. Cassie was going the slowest as usual. She had taken a watermelon slice and was claiming she wanted it to last cause it was "so watermelonly delicious". By this time the kids were the only customers in Soul Repair.

"Everyone feeling replenished I hope?" Kay sat down at the table with the kids. "OK. Let's talk about where you're going to look next for your furry friend."

"We've been everywhere." Zoe sounded hopeless.

"Well, you haven't been everywhere." Kay said confidently. "Or you would have found him already."

"We've looked in all the parks, the alleys, the woods, everywhere he likes to walk." Penny said.

"So you've looked in all the places you think he should be. Now it's time for you to look in places he shouldn't be." Kay nodded seriously.

"If he's not where we think he is, then he must be where we think he isn't?" Zach asked.

"Exactly." Kay smiled.

§

Gore Grater felt lucky that he'd met that old man in the baseball cap. He was even feeling kind of happy. The emotion surprised him. The old guy had been absolutely sure no kids *ever* came into the woods. And that made sense to Gore as the woods made his skin crawl. Gore wasn't afraid of much, but that place was positively frightening. But thanks to the old man's assurances that the kids were just as scared of the woods, Gore could avoid them as part of his surveillance.

Gore fished around on his front seat for the ever-present bag of chips, but to his disappointment, it was already empty. It had been so hot out, that chips weren't what he really wanted anyway. He was still sweaty from his adventure in the woods, and really wanted to cool down.

Gore had driven by Soul Repair, the neighborhood ice cream shop several times already, but had never had the time to stop in. He knew Dr. Trace was eager for him to make progress, but he was human after all and deserved a break. A quick stop into the ice cream shop wouldn't hurt anyone. Gore eased his black sedan into a parking spot across the street.

As he raised his considerable bulk out of the front seat, he glanced over to the ice cream shop and saw a mass of curly hair sticking out the front door. Several children behind her. That was the girl who had cried over the cat a couple of weeks earlier. Once again Gore Grater had found his quarry when he least expected it. Gore started moving faster.

§

"What are you doing?" Gabe whined as Zoe shoved him back into the shop.

"It's him!" Zoe said, almost gasping for air.

"Who?" Binny peeked out of the window. "Oh no." She answered the question herself.

"Everything okay?" Kay appeared by the door.

"There's a man following us. He's coming straight here. We need to get away." Binny said the words as fast as she could.

Cassie and Gabe were trembling. The older kids weren't doing much better.

If they'd expected Kay to not take them seriously, they were wrong. She didn't question. She didn't doubt. She pointed in the direction of the back of the shop and said two words, "This way."

Kay glided across Soul Repair's smooth wood floors to the back wall. Centered in the wall with a chimney rising to Soul Repair's second floor loft area, was a fireplace. When Madrona was icy, the fireplace would be called into action, and Soul Repair would get extra toasty and everyone would want to come in for hot chocolate.

Kay pushed hard on a brick on the right side of the chimney and the entire inner chamber of the fireplace moved to the left a few inches. Kay then grabbed the now exposed edge and pulled the bricks all the way to the left revealing a passage beyond.

"No dallying please. Let's go. One by one." Kay ushered each of the six children through the makeshift brick gateway. When the last of them were through, Kay put her index finger to her lips and then pulled the inner portion of the fireplace back into place.

§

Zach found the light switch just in time before the secret sliding fireplace closed them in total darkness. A small table lamp lit the room. Little pale yellow 'shingles' made of glass, and outlined in lead covered the surface of the shade. At the bottom of the shade brown, green, and red panes of different shapes seemed to make a ring of owls, silently watching the children.

The lamp sat on a small but tall table. Like what you would see at the entrance to a restaurant. Behind the table was a floor to ceiling curtain in deep burgundy crushed velvet. The space the children were in was small and cramped but none of them dared say a word. Through the recently repositioned fireplace they could hear yelling.

"I know what I saw." Gore Grater boomed.

"You look like you've been working hard. Maybe your eyes are a little tired?" Kay Athanasios responded calmly.

Grater returned from poking his head out the back door off the small kitchen in Kay's store. He'd seen no signs of anything other than a lone garbage dumpster in either direction down the long alley behind the row of shops. *They must be inside.*

"We have some new flavors." Kay said, keeping her voice light.

The children heard Grater's considerable bulk pounding up the stairs.

"They must have gone *somewhere*." Grater sounded deeply frustrated to the children.

"Why don't we set you up with some ice cream." Kay's voice carried gently from behind the wall.

"That sounds great actually, because guess what? I'm not leaving until those kids come out of whatever hole you've stuffed them in."

The next sound they heard was one of Grater plopping down in the big easy chair right in front of the fireplace.

⇥ 36 ⇤

THE SPEAKEASY

"We're trapped!" Zoe whispered. She felt Gabe's grip tighten around her arm and gave him a reassuring glance.

"What about this way?" Penny poked her head behind the velvet curtain at the back of the little hallway. "There's a staircase."

The small group tried to wend their way down the ornate wrought iron circular staircase in as quiet a fashion as possible. But Gabe and Cassie's nervous whispering, and the shushing from the others made that an impossibility. It didn't help that the further they descended, the darker it got.

Zach felt around on the wall and found a switch. A dozen light fixtures hanging at regular intervals from the vaulted ceiling buzzed into action.

"What is this place?" Penny asked to no one in particular.

"I think it might be a bar." Binny said as she ran her hand on the heavy and ornate wooden surface that ran the length of the left wall. Covered with shelves, a very long mirror ran behind the bar. Every few feet the mirror and shelves were interrupted by decorative columns.

"It's a concert hall!" Cassie had already covered the relatively large space and was on a raised platform at the other end of the room. An old upright piano was collecting dust on the stage.

"Don't play that." Binny interceded before Cassie was about to plunk out a few notes. "He'll hear us."

"Don't break that." Zoe instructed her brother who was tapping on the keys of a fancy old cash register at the other end of the bar.

Gabe stuck his tongue out at his sister but was more gentle going forward.

"Why is there a bar underneath Soul Repair?" Penny asked.

"It's not just under Soul Repair. I think it stretches underneath a bunch of the stores." Zoe said.

"And I think I know why it's here." Zach had been absorbed in reading signs and articles framed and posted on the right hand wall above several banquettes.

The headlines read: "Prohibition A Shock To Seattle", "U.S. is Voted Dry", and "Prohibition Officials Search Puget Sound for Rum-Running U-Boat". And there were official looking signs as well. "Closed for Violation of National Prohibition Act" and "Keep and Enforce Prohibition" among them.

"It's a speakeasy." Zach rendered his judgment.

"What's that?" Penny said.

"It's a secret bar." Zoe added. "The government banned alcohol in this country like a million years ago, and so adults had secret clubs where they could drink."

"Even though it was against the law?" Binny asked.

"Especially *because* it was against the law." Zoe said.

"It's weird. Madrona has so much secret stuff underground that nobody knows about." Penny mused.

"Seattle has a lot of that. Not just Madrona." Zach added.

"I love a good secret underground discovery as much as the next person, but right now we're trapped. I thought Xander was the boss at Luce Labs and was going to stop that guy" Zoe pointed back up the circular staircase "from following us around."

"Maybe he didn't get a chance yet." Binny added. "We were just there this morning."

"Well, that doesn't help us now, does it?" Zoe snapped. "Every minute that we're trapped down here is a minute that we're not finding Rembrandt." Zoe was getting more and more agitated.

"I'm sure he won't be up there too long." Zach tried to sound reassuring, but Zoe looked unconvinced.

Zach ran upstairs and was back down quickly after listening from behind the secret fireplace entrance, a look of dejection on his face. "He's ordering seconds."

"I knew it. We're trapped!" Zoe looked as if she might cry.

"Maybe there's another way out." A small voice said from across the room. Situated between the bar and the edge of the small stage, Gabe had found a door behind a curtain. It was marked "PRIVATE".

While the main space was underground it had been appointed quite beautifully. But this new room was relatively spare in terms of decoration.

Two large copper tanks sat in the center of the room. The entire right wall was lined with three rows of deep unfinished wooden shelves housing a couple of dozen wooden barrels. A ladder was propped up against the barrels.

On the opposite side of the room, most of the length of the brick wall was lined by a long workbench filled with various combinations of empty glass bottles as well as crates piled high to the ceiling containing more bottles. But there was one stretch of wall that was all brick. But the bricks' pattern was somehow different.

The way the bricks were laid out made it look like there had once been a doorway there which had been sealed up.

Zach wondered what was beyond the wall that was so important that someone had decided it should be sealed off. Or perhaps, they were already standing in the space that needed to remain hidden. And then it struck Zach, "This must be where they made the illegal alcohol. It's a distillery!"

"Wow." Cassie and Penny both said at the same time.

Zoe's frustration stayed on simmer when Gabe had found the additional door. She had thought it might lead them out of this place and back to the mission at hand. But now that seemed a false hope. Zoe darted back and forth in the space looking for another exit. But at the far end of the room was only a solid brick wall. Standing with her hands on her hips the stress in Zoe's voice was apparent to everyone. "There's no way out. I told you."

"We'll find a way out." Zach tried to calm her down.

"He's still there." Binny said quietly. Her pinched face made it clear to everyone that she'd just had a look inside Grater's mind.

At the news that Grater hadn't moved, Zoe's frustration started to pick up steam. "I can't wait anymore. I don't want ice cream. I don't want to tour Madrona's secret underground. I don't want to make illegal alcohol. I want to get out of her and find Ollie before, before..." Zoe's voice trailed off for a moment before she boomed, "We need to leave *now*!" As Zoe sounded out the last word she shook her fist and stamped her foot for emphasis.

Cassie was the only one who was looking directly at Zoe's feet. Maybe because she was lower to the ground than most of the others. Later she would recall that she'd seen waves emanate from Zoe's ankles in what seemed at the time like slow motion.

Zoe's stomp was followed by loud horrible sounds of cracking brick, grinding stone, and moving dirt. A circular area of floor and whatever lay below it started falling, and Zoe with it.

Zach expected Zoe to stop sinking into the disappearing floor when the surrounding area reached her waist – roughly what had happened in the park. But faster than anyone could react, her body off kilter, Zoe descended into the dark... to whatever lay below.

Five children stared at where she had stood seconds ago, but Zoe Flowers was simply gone.

§

"I know. I know." Jay said remorsefully.

Dr. Huitre and the rest of adults had all gathered in the Madrona park and were marveling at the sheer number of lost animal signs pegged to the community message board.

"It's not *your* fault." Serena said.

"But they said something, and I didn't listen. Zach tried to tell me." Jay shook his head.

454

"I don't believe half the things they tell me." Julie reassured Jay with a weak smile.

"We've covered everywhere we were supposed to according to your son's map." Quincy said.

"And put up all the signs. Which were very well made I might add." Jonathan added with a smile.

"Why yes. They were very well drawn and written as well. Very heartfelt." Julie agreed. "Excellent teamwork."

All eyes were on Jay and Serena who looked slightly embarrassed.

Huitre took the moment to address the group. "Thank *all* of you. For helping me look for Rembrandt and for everything you have done. I am afraid I have already imposed too much on your time. You all have lives to get back to. I will continue the search and let you know what happens."

Glad for the interruption Jay responded immediately. "Nonsense. I don't know about you guys, but I'm happy to keep searching." Serena, Jonathan, and Quincy all made sounds of agreement as well. Julie just nodded.

Jay continued, "I think the kids might need some lunch. It's already well past that time. Maybe I'll stop and grab some ice cream down the street and bring it home, so we can give them a little sugar-based energy boost before they continue the search. I'm guessing they've already covered three times as much ground as we have."

"I can't believe we haven't seen them yet. You'd think with all of us blanketing the neighborhood they would be right under our feet." Serena said.

"We'll grab some ice cream, text the kids to meet us, and, then head back out after a quick break. OK?" Jay asked everyone.

Everyone agreed.

§

"Are you okay?" Zach said.

Five pairs of eyes looked down at a dusty but unhurt Zoe who was sitting on a pile of bricks, rocks, dirt, and who knows what else at least fifteen feet below.

"I think so?" Zoe said still not quite sure herself as she was still accounting for all her extremities and making sure they all still functioned as expected.

"*That* was pretty cool." Binny said.

"Me falling on my butt?" Zoe looked annoyed.

"No. Your power. You making that hole. It felt... big. And powerful." Binny said still in awe.

"Oh." Zoe looked contrite.

Penny grabbed the ladder from the barrel wall and lowered it down to Zoe. "Come back up."

"No. Wait." All eyes were on Zach. "Don't you guys see? Zoe found the way out." Zach was smiling.

Zoe was having a hard time looking anything but bewildered and embarrassed after her fall.

"That's the abandoned sewer line isn't it?" Binny looked at her brother.

Zach nodded up and down vigorously, his eyes conveyed his excitement at the discovery.

As they ran through the abandoned sewer tunnel under Madrona, following Zach who seemed to know which way to go, Gabe looked up at his sister and said, "You really do have a superpower."

Zoe knew that more than anything Gabe wanted one too, and how generous it was of him to give her this compliment.

"Thanks Gabe. Yours is coming soon. I'm sure of it." Zoe reassured.

"It's okay. I'm just happy to be part of the group." Gabe said.

Zoe looked at her brother wondering when he'd gotten so grown up.

Zach stopped so suddenly, everyone almost toppled each other coming to a stop. They had arrived at the entrance to the shelter. On the other side of the large round door that divided the shelter from the sewer tunnel stood Caleb Adams, silhouetted by the light from the shelter's overhead fluorescents.

"Welcome home." Caleb said with a smile.

§

"I'm afraid you're going to have to go now." Kay said.

Gore had already finished his third serving of ice cream, and even *he* couldn't eat anymore.

"I just bought three helpings of your mediocre ice cream and now you're kicking me out? Am I taking a seat from another customer?" Gore motioned to the empty store.

Kay Athanasios said nothing. She smiled from behind the counter, took off her apron, and then walked across Soul Repair until she had perched herself on the chair across from Grater where she took a seat.

"I want you to listen to me, and I want you to listen closely. I've been patient, and I've been respectful, but now it is time for you to leave. I can only imagine what the police would think when I tell them that you won't leave and have been raving about a bunch of children that you insist are hiding somewhere in my shop."

Grater was fuming, but knew when he was beaten. As he stood up his napkin fell off his lap and onto the floor. For a moment Grater considered leaving it there, but something about the steel in Kay's eyes made him reconsider. He bent over, picked up the napkin, and dropped it in the trash on his way out.

§

"Isn't that...?" Julie craned her neck as she tried to get a good look at the hulking man shuffling out of Soul Repair just as they arrived.

Julie looked at Huitre as the rest of the group let Kay describe her latest flavors. Julie wasn't listening though. She had kept an eye on the man who exited the shop. She was almost positive it was the security guard from Luce Laboratories from the previous summer. This man just looked somehow, wider. Julie was almost positive it was the same man. And *if it was him, what was he doing here?*

As she wondered, Julie looked out of the corner of her eye to examine Huitre's face closely. He didn't look guilty. He just looked tired. And sad. He didn't look like he had anything on his mind other than his dog. Julie wished she could peer inside and know for sure.

Was it a coincidence that the Luce Labs guard was here in the middle of a work day? Could Huitre have had something to do with that? Was this Rembrandt disappearance more manipulation? When Julie looked at Henry, she didn't get that impression.

"We're getting ice cream for the kids." Jay said to Kay.

"The kids are a couple of steps ahead of you." Kay laughed.

Kay explained that the children had just been there and tried her latest confection. "But I hope that doesn't mean that you won't be getting anything for yourselves. You all look like you could use a boost."

"They must be nearby then. No?" Serena said.

"I suspect they're quite close by." Kay reassured.

Kay packed several pints to go for the assembled group. But before she bid them farewell she came out from behind the counter and took Henry's hand in her own. "I'm sure you'll find that enormous dog of yours. You've got a crack team on the job." Kay gave his hand a reassuring squeeze.

As they walked away from Soul Repair and headed down the hill to their houses, Jay looked down at his phone. "Zach returned my text. They're not hungry. He said they already ate and are going to keep looking." Jay laughed as he looked up. "Of course, he neglected to tell me they gorged themselves on ice cream."

§

At first, Kay was worried. She'd gone through the fireplace and down the spiral staircase and still there was no sign of the children. The hem of Kay's long black dress dragged across the ragged edge of the hole in the floor of the distillation room. Kay peered over the edge. If anyone had been below, they would have seen a broad smile on Kay Athanasios' face.

✦ 37 ✦

THE PLACES YOU
SHOULDN'T BE

Samantha Trace had read the same paragraph three times. The words were like sand through her fingers at the beach. Something was bothering her. She hated to admit it, but those Jordan children had gotten under her skin.

Samantha knew she wasn't a typical mother. The other mothers at Ollie's school weren't exactly warm to her, but she preferred it that way. There wasn't only one way to be a mother. Rather than spend every waking moment driving children on field trips, Samantha Trace had chosen to give her son a model of what it meant to be an adult.

And for Samantha that meant having a purpose. Her career at Luce Laboratories, her purpose, were intertwined and essentially indistinguishable. Showing Ollie her commitment to her work was her way of loving him. Samantha didn't like to admit it, but somewhere in the back of her mind she knew that someday Ollie would leave her for his own life. So why not focus on her showing how to be a purposeful adult by focusing on the thing that wouldn't leave. Her work would *always* be there.

So when the summer had taken an unexpected turn, and Ollie had ended up with a pseudo-internship at her very workplace with her actual boss, it was the ultimate extension of her parenting philosophy. What better way to help Ollie grow up than to show him how she functioned as a grownup – up close.

And the funny thing was, it was going pretty well. Or it had been for a couple of weeks anyway. Until those Jordan children had come by with some new recruits for their little mob, and spat out their accusations.

Hurting animals? What a horrible thing to say. Samantha knew of Ollie's interest in animals. But that was to draw them, not hurt them. The worst way Ollie had ever hurt anyone was by insulting their artwork. And while Samantha would never say this out loud to a soul, she was quite sure the talentless little brats deserved Ollie's blistering critique.

But the accusation hung there. It refused to leave Samantha's mind – like a mangy stray dog that attached itself to you begging for scraps. And now that mangy dog was getting in the way of Samantha doing her job. A fourth reading of the paragraph yielded no better results. Samantha had a few minutes before her next meeting and she decided that maybe seeing her son's face might eradicate the awful words from her mind.

The mid-afternoon sun seemed exceptionally bright, casting everything in sharp contrast as Samantha Trace made the trek across campus to visit her son at the greenhouse. Samantha knocked gently on the door marked 'PRIVATE'.

"Oh, hello Samantha. What brings you to our little neighborhood?" Luce appeared.

"Hi." Samantha forced a smile. "I had a few minutes and wanted to say a quick hi to Ollie. Make sure he was behaving himself." She had meant it as a joke, but the tenor of her voice was tense.

"You needn't worry Sam. He's quite gifted. And has been lovely during his tenure here with me."

"Is he here? I promise I won't distract him too much." Samantha said.

"He must be here somewhere, unless, oh, I had needed him to take some cuttings across campus for me. So it's possible he's running that errand for me. I apologize. Maybe take a look around?"

Samantha surveyed the sprawling greenhouse doing mental calculations on how late she would be for her meeting if she covered it all. "It's fine. Really."

"Are you sure? I can help you look. We can cover it twice as fast if we're both looking." Luce said.

"No no. You have important work to do. Just do me a favor please? I know he's been leaving early as part of his push for *independence*." Samantha raised her eyebrows as she said the last word. "I'm booked till the end of the day today and I'd really like to go home together. Will you please let him know that I'd like him to stay put until I come get him later today?"

"Of course Samantha. Whatever you need." Xander Luce put his hand on his chief scientist's shoulder and gave it a squeeze.

§

"What do *you* think she meant by that?"

Zach was slightly annoyed as Caleb was always answering a question with a question, but he tried not to let it show.

"She said that if Rembrandt wasn't where he should be, then he was probably where he shouldn't be. But if he *should* have been at home, then isn't anywhere that's not Dr. Huitre's house where he *shouldn't* be?" Zach reviewed.

"Yes. I suppose that's true. But maybe we could narrow it a bit by looking at the question a little differently." Caleb said slowly.

Zach and the others still looked bewildered.

Caleb smiled and continued. "You're not just looking for a dog. You're looking for a dog and a boy. Correct? So you need to find somewhere in the neighborhood that neither of them belong. Somewhere that kids and dogs aren't allowed. Most likely some place none of *you* are allowed."

"Madrona is mostly houses. How many off-limits places could there be?" Zach mused.

"I'm not allowed to swim in the lake without supervision." Gabe offered.

"The lake? Really?" Zoe rolled her eyes. "You think he's taking animals into the lake to hurt them?"

"Dogs like to swim." Gabe defended.

"Where else might you go to swim Mr. Flowers?" Caleb lowered his head a little as he looked directly at Gabe.

"Well, I wanted to go to the pool, but their doing something to it, so it's closed till the end of the year." Gabe looked disappointed.

"Wait. Gabe. You're a genius." Penny said.

Everyone turned to Penny. Caleb's eyes twinkled.

Penny continued, "The pool. We should go look in the pool. It's big, it's private, and it's closed right now."

"And the library." Zach added.

After some quizzical looks from the others Zach continued, "There's a basement that the city uses for pipes and utilities. It extends from under the library to the basement of the school. The librarian that let me sneak a peek said that even she's not allowed in there."

"Sounds like you've got two good candidates." Caleb said.

"Which one should we do first?" Binny asked.

Zach clapped his hands together. "Both. Let's split up."

§

"I'm still not sure why Zach couldn't come with us. He's the one who knows how to get to the *stacks*." Binny complained. Binny, Zoe, and Gabe had drawn the task of looking in the basement of the library.

"It's okay. He drew us a little diagram." Zoe waved a folded piece of paper in her hand. "And besides, he was worried that the librarian would recognize him and get suspicious."

"Yeah, I guess." Binny conceded. "Well, I'm glad it's you two doing the part of the plan that involves sneaking around. I think I'd be too scared to do it myself."

"Thanks." Zoe flushed a little. "And we're glad you're doing your part, because well, we can't read minds!"

§

"Are you sure nobody's looking?" Penny said.

"I told you, I'm looking out. Nobody's around." Cassie insisted.

Zach said to Penny, "Doesn't this seem vaguely familiar – the two of us breaking into places we're not supposed to be?"

Penny gave a nervous laugh.

"It's not just the two of you. I'm the lookout." Cassie added.

Zach nodded to Penny to confirm Cassie's assessment that they were on their own. "Go ahead. Do your thing."

A moment later, Zach, Penny, and Cassie had silently slipped into the darkened lobby of the Madrona neighborhood pool.

"Wait. I forgot my bathing suit!" Cassie laughed at her own joke.

It was just the thing Zach and Penny needed to relieve their nervousness. Cassie for some reason seemed free of fear. Zach imagined that was probably because she hadn't had his recent experience being brought home in a police car – an experience Zach hoped to never repeat.

§

"Thanks Ms. Tawfeek. I really appreciate your help. I've never used this before." Binny said as the librarian pulled up a seat next to her at the computer terminal.

"Haven't you searched on the Internet before?" Ms. Tawfeek sounded surprised at Binny's professed technical ignorance.

"My parents don't really allow that." Binny said earnestly.

Zoe and Gabe had been loitering by the magazine rack, just close enough to listen to Binny's conversation, but far enough away for the librarian to not notice them. Once Binny had firmly entangled the librarian in her search for books on skateboarding, Zoe squeezed Gabe's arm and they made a beeline for the stairs behind the librarian's now empty desk.

§

"Before we go in there, remind me what we do if we find him?" Penny said.

"If we find Rembrandt, we take him home. If we find Ollie, we signal Zoe to bring the others here. And they're going to follow the same instructions on their end." Zach answered.

"I'm still nervous." Penny said.

Even Cassie looked a little less confident as they approached the doors to the cavernous room that housed the Olympic size pool.

"Me too." Zach said.

"Are you still thinking the words Binny told you?" Zoe asked her brother after they reached the carpeted basement room Zach had called 'the stacks' in his hand drawn map.

"Not yet. Not yet. Not yet." Gabe said the words mechanically.

"You're not thinking the words yet?" Zoe was nervous about Gabe doing his part.

"No. Those are the words I'm supposed to think over and over again, and now you made me stop." Gabe chastised his sister.

"OK. Sorry. Keep doing what she said. Keep doing it. I won't interrupt." Zoe looked up from her brother who had resumed his mental mantra to see the large metal door that Zach had described. Zoe took a breath, gathered her courage, and walked up to the metal door, put both her hands on the huge pipe-like handle, and pulled.

§

The lights weren't on, but the skylights provided enough light from the late afternoon sun to reveal the contents of the under construction pool.

"Binny would love to skateboard in there." Penny pointed at the huge empty pool. It's curved sides usually not visible when the pool was in service.

"Can I play in there?" Cassie's words echoed in the large empty space.

Zach pursed his lips in frustration. "This place is empty. There's nobody here. I hope the others are having better luck than we are."

§

"Thank you so much for your help. I'm sorry for taking so much of your time, but I was also wondering whether there was fiction starring heroes who skateboard. I've always wanted to read a book where someone's skateboarding skills save the day."

Miss Tawfeek had already tried to end her support session twice, but this girl seemed to have an endless number of questions when it came to finding skateboarding-related books. Miss Tawfeek sat back down, put a new smile on her face, and started walking Binny through the process once again.

§

The room was filled with the quiet thrum of water moving through large pipes. Off in the distance, a turbine was spinning.

Zoe looked over her shoulder and saw Gabe was still standing at the doorway repeating the mantra Binny had given him in his head. Zoe didn't know how much longer Binny could distract the librarian.

The room was long and Zoe explored it at a jog. At the opposite end, Zoe found a twin to the metal door they'd used to enter. But this one was at the top of a concrete staircase. Zoe tried the door. It was locked. The room was completely empty. Zoe hoped that Zach, Penny, and Cassie were having better luck than she and Gabe were.

As Zoe and Gabe slipped past Binny and Miss Tawfeek, still hunched over the library computer, Gabe looked to his sister for confirmation. Zoe nodded that it was time, and Gabe started thinking of a new phrase. *We're done. We're done. We're done.*

§

"What do we do now?" Zoe said. She was feeling emotional but she was too exhausted even to cry.

"I'm hungry." Gabe said.

Everyone was in general agreement with both sentiments. They'd run out of ideas on how to locate Rembrandt, and they were hungry. Again.

Zach's phone buzzed.

"Dad wants us to come home for dinner. He says even superheroes need a break sometimes." Zach managed a faint smile.

The six children said reluctant goodbyes in the park. Gabe and Zoe headed off to their house, while the others headed down the hillside. It was an unusually silent walk for the usually chatty foursome.

As they neared the Jordan house, Binny said quietly to Zach, "I'm worried about Rembrandt."

"Me too." Zach said.

Binny took a breath. "Is he gonna die too?"

They walked for what seemed like forever until Zach found the words to answer her.

"I don't know. I don't know."

§

Henry Huitre sat on the edge of his deck in his back yard staring at the open gate as if he could will Rembrandt to walk through it. He'd walked more of Madrona in the past several hours than he had in the past several weeks of walking his now missing dog.

The familiar emptiness in his chest was no longer content with the spot it had occupied for the last fifteen years. It was growing out of control. It consumed everything in its path leaving only pitch blackness in its wake.

Henry Huitre hugged his knees to his chest and cried.

❧ 38 ❧

THE LINDEN TREE

It was a little after five o'clock in the evening as Dr. Samantha Trace walked the curving paths of the Luce Laboratories campus. The streak of sunny days had come to a halt. The sky was overcast and everything seemed kind of washed out and gray.

She had been anxious about her son all day, but something inside her had flipped. Samantha had a renewed excitement about spending time with her son. Maybe she would surprise him with dinner out that evening. The zoo was open late that night so maybe cheeseburgers and a visit to the giraffes.

Samantha walked into the greenhouse. "Hi. I'm here for Ollie. Is he ready to go?"

Xander Luce turned on his heel. "Samantha, so good to see you. I'm so sorry, but you missed him."

Samantha was caught speechless. She'd asked Luce to tell Ollie to wait for her. Her son was only ten years old. Where could he be?

Seeing the look on Samantha's face, Xander continued, "It's my fault I'm afraid. I forgot to mention your request to him, and then by the time I'd remembered, he'd already left for his usual afternoon constitutional." Xander smiled gently. "I'm sure you'll find him at home by the time you get there. I'm so sorry for screwing up. I feel terrible."

Samantha saw the regret in her boss' eyes and swallowed her anger. "It's okay. You're not a babysitter. And you've already been so generous with your time with him this summer. I think you've been a good influence on him. I'm grateful."

"Of course. Ollie is a talented young man. It's my pleasure." Xander said.

"If it's okay, I'm gonna go find him now."

"Of course. Of course. Let me know if there's anything else I can do to help." Luce smiled.

§

"It's gonna be okay." Julie Jordan told the three sad faces plopped down on the couch.

474

Julie's reassurances went unanswered.

"You guys must be exhausted. I'm gonna make you a great dinner. Zach you don't even need to get any ingredients. I've got everything covered." Jay tried to cheer up the kids.

Still no response.

"How about you guys just sit there and don't say anything. We'll tell you when dinner is ready." Jay smiled but found no takers for his jokiness.

Jay and Julie retired to the kitchen. Zach, Binny, and Cassie sat on the couch. The TV was on but the sound was off. They weren't paying attention anyway. Cassie had fallen asleep curled up in the corner.

Zach's phone buzzed. Zach reached for it, read the message and his face got suddenly animated. He shoved the phone in front of Binny so she could read the message. Binny's eyes grew wide as she read.

Zach walked into the kitchen while Binny tried to wake Cassie. "Dad?"

"Dinner will be ready in a half hour. Just sit tight and we'll get you guys feeling better. It's taco night!"

Zach smiled and worked up his courage. "Would you be okay if we skipped dinner?"

"What?" Julie put a hand on Zach's shoulder.

"No taco night?" Jay made a sad face.

Zach took a breath. "We want to go out and look for Rembrandt some more."

"Honey. You guys are exhausted. Take a break. You've already done everything you can. Cassie's asleep on the couch." Julie counseled.

"I'm awake!" Cassie wandered into the kitchen with Binny behind her.

Jay sat down at the table in front of the children. "Kids, what you guys are doing is admirable. But you've blanketed the neighborhood, what, probably half a dozen times today? There's nothing more you can do."

"We think there is." Zach said.

Jay thought back to the conversation earlier in the day and realized the opportunity that was presenting itself. "You really want to do this?"

"Yes." Zach said.

Binny and Cassie nodded vigorously behind him.

"OK. I admire your perseverance. But home by nine ok?" Jay said.

"What about dinner?" Julie asked, surprised that Jay had acquiesced.

"We'll grab peanut butter sandwiches to go." Zach said.

"Banana in mine please." Cassie added.

"Hope you're hungry. We have way too many tacos for just you and me." Jay joked with Julie.

§

Gabriel Walker's house sat on a quiet street on the edge of Madrona bordering Seattle's Central District. Yellow slats of wood were interrupted periodically by white framed windows. James Flowers had painted the house the previous summer before the family had moved in with his father-in-law.

Zoe sat in the white-framed window of her small room in the old house petting her cat. She'd been nervous about leaving her window open with Tango about. Tango was most definitely an indoor cat. Zoe had insisted on that when they got her. As such, she didn't have a lot of experience outdoors except for the periodic escape out the front door, and the tall tree in front of the house looked like it might be a tempting destination for Zoe's calico-colored friend.

Zoe wasn't sure how to think about the day. Her power, *such as it was*, had finally manifested itself in front of the other kids. Something that had embarrassed and puzzled her for some time was now out in the open. And while it wasn't as impressive as what the other kids could do, it was at least something that made her feel like she belonged.

Though she still couldn't do it on command, it had come at the right moment, letting them escape back to the shelter so they could resume their search. But what had that really bought them anyway? The pool and the library basement had been empty. Rembrandt and Ollie weren't there. As far as she could tell, they had vanished into thin air.

Zoe absent-mindedly scratched under Tango's chin and let her eyes go out of focus as she looked down the street and to the sliver of mountains that were visible from her windowsill. But then, as happens sometimes, something interrupted her moment of reflection. A blurry gray blot was walking up the street.

Zoe took a moment to focus her eyes. The smudge at the bottom of her vision sharpened into focus – four kids walking down the street at a brisk pace. Zach, Binny, Penny, and Cassie were walking towards her house! The surprise woke her out of her reverie and gave her a small ray of hope. *Maybe they've got a clue?* Zoe tried to temper her enthusiasm, but couldn't help shooting down the stairs to greet her guests at the front door.

Zach was about to press the doorbell when the door opened. Zoe stood there, her hair as large as ever, and despite the circumstances, a big smile on her face. She was happy to see them.

"Hey. What are you guys doing here?" Zoe said.

"How did you know to open the door before we rang the bell?" Binny asked.

"Another one of my super powers." Zoe winked.

"You have another super power?" Gabe made an appearance at the door.

"Or I saw you coming from my window." Zoe smiled at Binny. "It's one or the other."

Zach handed Zoe his phone and showed her the message he'd received. "I tried texting you but you didn't answer so we came to get you."

"Zoe, your phone buzzed." Gabe was holding Zoe's phone which she'd left downstairs when she went up to her room.

"Thanks." Zoe said sarcastically to her brother, and then to the others, "OK. Give me a minute to tell my grandfather."

"Tell your grandfather what?" Gabriel Walker, PopPop as he was known to his family, stood over his grandchildren in the doorway examining the kids standing on the front porch.

"Oh, Hi PopPop. Gabe and I were just going to go out and play with our friends." Zoe explained.

PopPop pursed his lips. He looked as if he was literally chewing on something. After a moment his pursed lips turned into a look of disapproval. "You haven't eaten your dinner yet. Your parents left strict instructions."

"We brought you sandwiches." Cassie held up a little bag she'd been carrying. "Peanut butter and banana. My Dad makes the best ones."

"Oh does he?" PopPop scowled at Cassie but it only made her giggle.

"Please PopPop?" Gabe said.

"What exactly are you kids planning on doing running around the neighborhood?"

"We're getting exercise." Zoe said.

"Exercise huh? You sure you're not getting into trouble?" PopPop looked unconvinced.

"You're the one who always complains that *kids these days watch too much TV*." Zoe did her best impression of her grandfather.

Gabe giggled.

PopPop appeared to be making a show of being disagreeable but finally said. "Just make sure and exercise your good judgment. If you're not back before your parents get home, trouble will have found *us*."

"Oh, a kitty." Cassie squealed with delight. Zoe's cat was poking its head between the legs of everyone gathered inside the front door.

Zoe said, "Careful, don't let her out PopPop!" But before the words were out of her mouth, Tango shot out the door and scampered up the closest tree.

PopPop shook his head. "Well that didn't take long. Looks like you've already got some trouble to deal with. Good luck children." Gabriel Walker went back inside the house to take a seat on his favorite chair and get back to reading his newspaper.

§

The house felt unusually quiet. Whatever excitement Samantha Trace had felt about surprising her son with an evening out doing his favorite things had completely disappeared. The unease she had felt in the morning had blossomed into a thick dread.

Ollie wasn't anywhere on the regular path he took from the Luce campus to home. Ollie should have been home by now. But he wasn't. Samantha Trace walked out her front door to search for her son.

§

"You guys should go ahead without me." Zoe said teary-eyed.

"We need to hurry. We don't know how long Rembrandt has." Binny said. Privately she wondered if it was already too late, but she kept that to herself.

The six children were gathered at the base of the Linden tree whose branches reached out to Zoe's windows. It was in those very same branches that Zoe's cat Tango was now concealed.

"We're not going without you." Zach said.

"We split up before." Zoe argued.

"We had two destinations before. Now we only have one. And we need everyone there to look out for each other." Zach insisted.

Zoe's face was getting tighter and tighter as she kept speaking. "I can't leave Tango in the tree. I just can't. I'm sorry." Zoe was starting to tear up.

Everyone's eyes followed Zoe's. Tango was sitting on a branch about thirty feet in the air. As best as any of them could tell, despite Zoe's pleading, Tango had zero interest in coming back down any time in the near future.

"The fire department usually gets cats out of trees." Penny offered.

"I'm not thrilled about the idea of calling the fire department." Zach said.

"It would take too long anyway." Binny said.

"I'll climb up and get her." Gabe volunteered.

"Absolutely not." Zoe forbade her brother. "You'll crack your head open if you fall out of that tree."

"I'll do it." Zach volunteered.

Zoe glared at him. "Why not me? It's *my* cat after all."

"I just thought that you were..." Zach let his words trail off before he finished his sentence. Something about Zoe's face made it clear that he should stop talking.

Finally satisfied that Zach wasn't going to say anything else, Zoe turned back to the tree and approached it with trepidation. The kids stayed silent for the next several minutes as Zoe climbed the old branches.

At one point Zach offered advice telling Zoe not to look down. She did and he resumed his silence. Zoe picked her way carefully up the branches. At times she would pause before a particularly large traversal and close her eyes for a moment before she advanced. In those moments they were all holding their breath.

Zoe made it all the way to the branch Tango was inhabiting. She could see into her own window from here. Zoe marveled at how safe and inviting her bed looked from her current location, but tried to shoo that thought from her mind and focus on her current task.

Tango was staring at her now. The cat seemed to be debating what to do. Zoe cooed and made little cat sounds trying to get Tango to come to her. When that didn't appear to be enough, Zoe started shuffling herself a little closer to Tango every few seconds.

Zoe inched closer and closer to Tango and finally was within arm's reach. When Tango stood her ground, Zoe decided to make a grab for the scruff of her neck. Tango came to a decision at the very same moment.

Just as Zoe lunged, Tango jumped down to the branch below and scrambled down the trunk of the tree. In her effort to grab her cat, Zoe had not considered that the fur she was aiming for wouldn't be there when she grabbed. She lost her balance. For a moment it looked like she might right herself.

Five children looked from below, helpless.

"Oh no." Binny said.

"Zoeeeeee." Gabe wailed.

And then the scales tipped, Zoe slipped from her perch, and she started the swift journey to the ground below.

§

Samantha Trace had not spent any significant time in Madrona Park for years. When she'd been younger, and Ollie was a toddler she would sometimes bring him there to play. She'd had so much to do between her career and single-parenting her new son, that she didn't have time to feel sorry for herself. And besides, she had been doing a good job at both and it made her feel good.

Sometimes she would bring Ollie into the flower shop. It was gone now, replaced by some sort of candleholder boutique. Samantha had no idea why anyone would spend forty dollars for a colored glass candleholder but periodically housewives from all over the city with nothing better to do would form a line around the block when they went on sale.

Even though those days when Ollie was younger were hard, they had their moments. As she searched for her son, those moments held special significance in her mind. The old man who ran the flower shop used to make up unique bouquets for her as if he could tell when she needed a pick-me-up. He would see her pushing Ollie's stroller in the park and motion for her to come in to his shop and show her what he'd made for her.

She had never been particularly into traditional bouquets, but somehow that old man had created combinations that made her feel like he understood her. That wasn't something that Samantha Trace experienced often. She had been alone then, but not really. Now with Ollie missing, Samantha Trace knew what it meant to feel truly alone.

§

The kids were so focused on Zoe losing her balance that they didn't notice as Tango shot straight down the trunk and passed them on the way to the front door of the house.

The only thought Zoe found in her head as it dawned on her that she was actually going to fall from the tree, was how glad she was that she hadn't let Gabe do the climbing and maybe a little part of her also felt vindicated that her fear of heights was not completely baseless.

Zoe's body fell to the ground at with a sickening acceleration. Rather than flail, she pulled her extremities inward into a sort of cannonball. At some point during the descent Zoe decided keeping her eyes close was the best choice.

Zoe suspected that she might experience the fall in slow motion, but this was getting ridiculous. In fact, it didn't feel like she was falling anymore at all. Had she not noticed the impact of the ground when she'd hit it? Had her spine been severed and cut off all communication between her brain and her now mangled body? Was she dead?

Zoe Flowers opened her eyes. She hadn't realized how tightly she had closed them. The first thing she saw was five pairs of legs. She looked up slightly to see the other kids all staring down at her, mouths open. Then Zoe looked down to see the ground she couldn't feel.

It was there, but not. Zoe's fall had stopped a full foot before she'd hit the ground. And now she was floating, no longer moving toward the earth. A foot below her, a breeze that only seemed to exist between her and the ground gently swirled blades of grass, dirt and the periodic weed.

Zoe realized she had been holding her breath and took a big gulp of air. Zoe was now gently swaying in place. As she flexed muscles she couldn't name, still in a reclined position, she rose an inch or two from where she had stopped, and then floated back down, losing the altitude she had gained.

"She's floating." Gabe said.

"No," Zach corrected, "She's flying."

Zoe had been lost in the feeling of hovering above the ground, but Zach's pronouncement brought her out of her dream state. She fell the final foot to the ground with a thud.

"Are you okay?" Binny said, kneeling down to help her.

The front door opened. "Ah, I see you got your cat to come down." PopPop said as Tango scuttled back into the house through his legs. Tango had been scratching at the door to get his attention. "Maybe next you could teach it to use the doorbell instead of mussing up my front door."

Gabriel Walker shook his head in disapproval, closed the front door of the house, and went back to his favorite chair.

✦ 39 ✦

THE HOUSE IN THE WEEDS

"That was the coolest thing I've ever seen." Binny said. She moved her hands, mimicking Zoe's descent from the branch.

The six children were walking towards the center of the neighborhood. The clouds overhead were hastening the darkness that normally wouldn't have fallen over Madrona for another hour or two.

Zoe was giggling as she walked, not entirely sure how to respond.

"Can you do it again?" Gabe asked.

"I think so?" Zoe wasn't entirely sure herself.

As they walked, and after looking up and down the street to make sure they were alone, Zoe started to lift off the ground with each successive step, almost as if she was walking up an invisible staircase. Everyone else stayed firmly on the sidewalk. By the time she got to the third 'step' her balance was a little off and she started to wave her arms.

"Come down. Come down." Binny urged.

Zoe regained her balance with her arms out like she was walking a balance beam and gently floated down to the sidewalk.

"That was much better than before." Zach said smiling.

Zoe blushed.

"Flying is the absolute awesomest." Penny gushed.

"You're next you know." Cassie said to Gabe who was still staring at his sister, amazed by her new ability.

"Who me?" Gabe said, bewildered.

Binny gave Cassie a look indicating that she shouldn't promise things she couldn't deliver.

Cassie responded as if Binny had made her comment aloud. "Oh, I'm sure of it." And then to Gabe, "Yes, you. I'm not sure exactly when but it's coming."

"Maybe it will. Maybe it won't. It's pretty cool to hang out with superpowered kids. Nobody else gets to do that. So I'm already pretty lucky."

Binny and Zoe looked at each other in surprise at Gabe's mature outlook on the situation.

"That's a very grown up attitude little brother." Zoe patted her brother on the shoulder.

"Just promise you'll give me a ride someday." Gabe smiled at his big sister.

Zoe thought that it might be awhile before she could make sure she didn't injure herself much less be responsible for someone else. And besides, she couldn't lift Gabe on the ground. How would she lift him while flying? Zoe kept those thoughts to herself and just said, "Absolutely!"

After consulting the text he'd received earlier one last time, Zach suddenly said, "OK. We're here." The group came to an abrupt halt.

"Where is here?" Zoe said.

"I don't see anything." Gabe was looking at the line of tall shrubs that defined the property line. They were dense and in the spots where one could even see between them, a tall fence lay behind them.

"Let's walk around the block. There's bound to be a way in."

"And you're sure this is the place?" Zoe said.

Zach took out his phone. "The text just gave this address and said. 'I believe you'll find what you're looking for there. Good luck.'"

"Did he mention why his security guard was still after us today?" Binny rolled her eyes.

"He did as a matter of fact." Zach read a follow-on message from Luce that said he'd be meeting with Grater the next morning to make sure he left the kids alone.

"I guess." Binny let the matter drop.

"Why didn't we think of looking here before?" Zoe pointed to the teal roof that was now just visible over the fence and overgrowth.

"When we did our search before, I assumed that Ollie wouldn't be in someone's private home, because who would let him in? So I figured it had to be a public place. It never occurred to me that there would be an abandoned house in the neighborhood. I guess I didn't know there were any abandoned houses around here." Zach said.

"The plants are doing a good job of hiding it." Penny joked.

The home sat directly in back of and across the alley behind the row of shops in Madrona's retail district.

"Hey, we're behind Soul Repair." Binny said.

"Yes. That's their back door." Zach pointed to the door with the darkened inset window featuring the Soul Repair logo.

"It's open." Directly opposite the Soul Repair door, Gabe tugged on a gate that had been set into the fence that bordered the home. It was easily missed as the surrounding overgrown shrubbery had almost concealed it.

"How did you find that?" Binny asked in surprise.

"Some things are easier to see from my height." Gabe was beaming.

"Maybe that's your power, finding things nobody else can find." Cassie added.

"It's not open exactly. More like broken." Zach traced his finger along the chain that hung loose on the fence. "Some of your handiwork?" Zach joked to Penny.

"I had nothing to do with it." Penny smiled.

"It means he's here." Zach said.

The excitement at Zoe's new power seemed to evaporate with Zach's pronouncement. The faint sound of distant thunder echoed and the sky got noticeably darker.

§

"Did you hear that?" Julie Jordan asked.

"You worried about them?" Quincy Yang said.

Julie smiled sheepishly. "Yeah."

"Thanks for coming over to help us eat all this food." Jay said to everyone at the Jordan's kitchen table.

"Thank *you* for inviting us over. Your daughters weren't exaggerating about your cooking." Serena said.

"What did they say?" Jay raised his eyebrows in mock fear.

Everyone laughed.

"I know I'm the only one of you who isn't a parent. But I think it's great that you trust your kids to run around the neighborhood on their own." Jonathan said.

"We do?" Jay joked.

Julie and Serena gave Jay a look.

"I mean, we *do*." Jay retreated.

§

The structure sat in the heart of Madrona like a corpse buried just below the earth. Rotting and invisible. It looked like it had once been a home. Zach thought it had really been more of a mansion really. The dilapidated structure stretched twice as wide as even the biggest homes in the neighborhood. And the grounds could have fit at least three, maybe four other houses on them.

In the fading light, Zach could still tell that the house had once been painted white, but just barely. Paint was peeling. But the teal clay roof tiles still shone bright.

There is a garage of sorts as well. Zach thought it would have been called a carriage house given how old it looked. Zach and the others walked the grounds surveying the property. It was hard to find an entrance given that the house seemed to float in an ocean of overgrown foliage and weeds. A sign hung from the porch ceiling over the front door, but the letters were so faded that Zach couldn't tell what it had once said.

492

"Binny, would you mind checking to see if he's in there before we go in?" Zach asked.

Zach, Zoe, Binny, Penny, Cassie, and Gabe stood at the foot of the steps to what had at once been the front porch.

"I was afraid you were gonna ask me to do that." Binny responded.

"Afraid?" Penny asked, concerned.

"Afraid of what I might see." Binny confided in the group.

"I don't want to risk going in there if we're wrong. It doesn't look exactly safe." Zach said.

Binny took a deep breath and closed her eyes. She took that familiar path in the front of her mind, but somehow above it to the screen that showed what the people around her thought. Her companions were various shades of focused dark green, but with nervous cracks spreading across their emotional landscapes like shattering ice.

Binny zoomed out so she could see beyond her immediate vicinity. Smaller, further away, was another mind. The angle reminded her of when she'd seen Gabe knocked out, lying below them in the shelter. The blob of consciousness sparkled. Well, not quite. The closer Binny zoomed in, the less it was sparkling, and the more it looked like television static. Sometimes she would see tiny angry purple flecks. Binny zoomed closer.

And then the pain began. Binny's head started to ache all at once. Not a dull pain either. Sharp needles forcing their way into her skull. The closer Binny got to the static, the more it hurt. It took Binny a couple of seconds to realize the connection and retreat completely.

"What's wrong?" Everyone saw Binny double over.

Once she'd pulled back in her mind, the pain disappeared, but the shock did not. Binny touched her hand to her skull and then brought it in front of her face expecting to see it covered in blood. Binny started crying, scared by what had happened.

Penny and Zach rushed to put their arms around her to see if she was ok.

"I'm alright." Binny tried to gather herself and stop the tears that were now flowing freely.

"What happened?" Zach said.

"What did you see?" Zoe asked.

"I'm not really sure." Binny wiped her face with her shirt. "Something, well someone, is definitely down there. In the basement. I can tell. But when I got close, I couldn't see what they were thinking. Just a whole bunch of noise. And the closer I got, the more my head started to hurt. Whoever is down there, I don't think I can see what they're thinking."

"It's him." Zoe said.

"How can you be so sure?" Zach asked.

"Who else could it be?" Penny said confidently.

Nobody had an answer for her.

§

Henry Huitre felt his phone buzzing. He pressed the button to answer it without even looking to see who was calling and immediately regretted his choice.

"Henry? I'm sorry to bother you. Really." Samantha Trace said on the other end of the line.

"What is it Sam?" Huitre forced himself to sound as polite as he could.

"Ollie's missing. I've been walking around the neighborhood for over an hour and I can't find him." Trace sounded close to tears.

"Does he not have a phone? It seems like every kid has one these days." Huitre asked.

"No."

"I'm sure you'll find him soon. He probably just got distracted by whatever game he was playing and lost track of time." Henry hesitated a little before continuing. "I'm afraid I'm looking for my dog as well. He seems to have run off."

"Oh, I'm so sorry to hear that." Trace said on the other end of the line.

"I am gonna head out soon and look for Rembrandt some more. I promise, if I see your son, I will call you immediately." Huitre said.

"I'll do the same. And Henry?" Samantha said.

"Yes?"

"Thank you."

§

"Everyone be careful where you step. I don't want anyone to twist their ankle." Zach instructed.

Large sheets of plywood covered all the windows. Penny approached the pair of front doors gingerly hoping the floorboards on the porch wouldn't decide this was the moment to give way.

Penny tried the handle. It was locked.

"It's Pennytime." Zoe spoke in just above a whisper.

Penny blushed a little and then turned her focus back to her task. She placed her hands on the handles and went to her *breaking* place. It took less time than usual. The entire handle and locking mechanism fell to pieces. Some dropped on the porch. The kids could hear the clatter of the pieces that fell inside the house.

Penny pushed the doors but they wouldn't budge. A look of surprise crossed her face. "Uh. I'm not sure what's wrong."

Gabe had pushed to the front of the group and was peering in through one of the small windows that were stacked vertically on either side of the front doors. It looks blocked.

Zach leaned in to inspect as well. "There's furniture piled up in front of the door. We need to find another way in."

"How are we gonna do that?" Zoe asked.

"Ollie got in somehow, so there must be a way in for us too." Zach responded.

"Fine." Zoe seemed stumped for the moment.

Another search of the grounds yielded no obvious answers.

"Tell me again, what you saw when you looked for Ollie with your mind?" Zach asked Binny.

"Please don't make me do that again." Binny looked nervous.

"No. I promise. Just remind me what you saw." Zach said.

"It was like static, like you see on a television when there's no picture." Binny answered.

"Right, but what about *where* he was?" Zach asked.

"Yeah. It looked like he was under the house. In the basement maybe?" Binny said, unsure of exactly what her vision had meant.

After some long seconds of tapping his fingers on his leg as he was thinking, Zach suddenly said, "I have an idea."

❖ 40 ❖

THE LONG WAY AROUND

"That's going to take too long." Zoe said. "And what if he leaves while we're running all the way around?"

"Some of us should stay here and wait." Zach said.

"How do you even know there's a way in?" Zoe said.

"I don't." Zach conceded. "But we're wasting time. If I run the whole way I should be able to make it in ten minutes."

"I still don't understand why you don't go through Soul Repair." Penny said.

498

"We'd have to break in. It's closed now." Binny said.

"That's not a problem." Penny said waggling her fingers and raising her eyebrows.

"We're not breaking into Soul Repair. It would hurt Kay's feelings." Binny said in a way that left no room for disagreement.

"It's fine. I can get back to the distillery room from the shelter." Zach explained.

"Great. Why don't *I* go and *you* can wait here?" Zoe suggested, arms crossed in front of her chest.

Zach's shoulders slumped in exasperation. "I know the way the best."

"*I* can fly." Zoe responded with raised eyebrows.

"And if the way in to the basement was on a cloud, *you'd* be the perfect choice." Zach sniped back.

"You know what Zach Jordan?" Zoe pushed her face forward as she spoke. "You don't trust me. You don't think I can do it. I don't need you to look out for me. You don't tell me what to do!"

Thunder sounded in the distance. This time lightning had been visible across the lake before it sounded.

Zach took a deep breath, exhaling through his nostrils before he stepped forward to within inches of Zoe and said in a low but firm voice, "You know something Zoe? I like you. I like you a lot. I know that you don't like to hear things like that, so I won't say it again. And this probably means you won't be my friend.

But just know this: you are a hurricane of strong and smart and funny, and better than me at most things. I just think this may be one of the very few exceptions because I've already memorized the way."

Binny and Penny looked at each other, mouths open. Even Cassie and Gabe were taken aback by Zach's declaration.

Zoe stood still, her mouth a perfect 'O'. All speech seemed to have been disabled. After a few seconds she managed to squeak out one word. "OK."

"Can I go with Zach?" Gabe said to his sister and then leaning over to Zach, "I run really fast."

"Sure. OK." Zoe said.

"Me too." Cassie chimed in.

Before they turned to leave, Zach said to Zoe, Binny, and Penny, "Just make sure, if he tries to leave that he doesn't get away." And then Zach and the two younger kids were gone.

Zoe plopped down on the ground to wait. Binny and Penny stayed a few feet away as Zoe seemed to be lost in thought.

"Maybe we should walk around the house, you know, to make sure Ollie doesn't try to escape. Just until Zach gets here." Penny suggested.

Binny and Penny looked to Zoe for a reaction. When they got a barely perceptible nod, they started patrolling the perimeter of the house.

"Can we at least bring them some proper clothing for the rain? An umbrella or two maybe?" Julie asked the assemblage of adults. The thunder in the distance wasn't sounding so distant anymore in Julie's mind.

"I agree. No point in letting them get sick." Quincy said.

"I'll text Zach and find out where they are." Jay laughed a little as at least for the moment, he was no longer the most overprotective parent in the group.

§

"Come on." Gabe shouted encouragement at Zach.

"I admit it. You guys are fast." Zach was genuinely surprised at Gabe and Cassie's stamina. Maybe all that time sitting in front of a computer screen wasn't doing him any favors. "Give me one second."

Zach's phone buzzed. He read the message and thought to himself, *if I tell you where we are, you'll never believe* me. Zach told his parents that they would be at the park in the center of Madrona in twenty minutes or so. Time was not on their side. Zach forced himself to start running again.

The trio flew through the Madrona woods, into the shelter, and all the way to the large round circular door that led to the sewer tunnels.

"Ok, now I have to be in the lead you two speed demons." Zach asserted.

"Why?" Cassie said.

"Do you know the way?" Zach asked.

"Yes." Cassie and Gabe said in unison.

"Fine. But could you just let me lead anyway so that I can feel a little bit useful?" Zach begged.

Cassie and Gabe giggled. "OK. OK."

Zach started running, leading Gabe and Cassie down the long, dark sewer tunnel back to almost exactly underneath where Binny, Zoe, and Penny were standing above ground.

§

"Whatcha guys looking at?" Zoe asked.

Binny and Penny were briefly startled as they'd left Zoe to herself in front of the porch and hadn't heard her walk up behind them.

"We've been trying to figure out how Ollie got in." Binny said.

Zoe nodded, glad to be talking about anything other than Zach.

Binny continued, "We keep looking around the first floor. But maybe we should be looking up higher."

"The second floor windows are all boarded up too." Zoe said.

"But that one isn't." Penny pointed to the third floor of the mansion where a small railing surrounded a cupola with a door that had not been boarded up. The mansion had a widow's walk. It was hard to see from immediately around the house except from the spot where the three girls now stood.

"I guess nobody thought anyone could get up that high." Binny said.

"But how would *we* get up that high..." Zoe's voice trailed off as she saw the two girls faces plastered with big grins.

§

"Give her more space." Penny said to Binny.

"Now be careful once you're inside. The whole place is rotting. We don't want you to fall through a floorboard." Binny said to Zoe.

"I'm not even sure I can get up there." Zoe looked nervous.

"Don't look down. That's my advice." Penny said.

"That doesn't fill me with confidence." Zoe tried to joke. Her voice quavered despite her small smile.

Binny and Penny backed up a little bit to give Zoe more room. She looked at them one last time, their faces filled with expectation and excitement and made her decision.

Zoe stood straight, raised her head up to the sky, and raised her arms over her head like she'd seen so many times in the movies. *I think this is how it's done,* Zoe thought to herself.

That familiar feeling that had always preceded Zoe's hole-making ability was returning. It felt like pressure downward, emanating from her feet, really her legs, or maybe even from her whole body. It was like she was a human jet engine. The force started swirling the dirt under her in little whorls, like the beginnings of hurricanes fit for ants. But instead of pushing down on the force, Zoe let it lift her.

Zoe couldn't help herself, she looked down only to see two wide-eyed, open-mouthed faces shaking their heads.

"Don't look down." Penny echoed her earlier warning.

Zoe snapped her gaze back up and saw the third floor of the mansion rapidly approaching. Zoe leaned towards the façade and felt her trajectory adjusting. This wasn't so hard after all. She could really get used to this.

The railing of the widow's walk was now only a few feet away. Zoe reached her hands out was able to grab it firmly. It felt relatively stable in her hands. Zoe pulled on the railing to haul herself in, and hopefully onto more solid footing on the wraparound balcony itself. But her feet had a plan of their own.

Zoe's feet kept going up in the original direction she'd been ascending. Zoe wrapped her arms around the railing hoping against hope that the likely rotten wood wouldn't give way. Zoe's grip on the railing and her power of flight eventually reached a stalemate. Zoe's torso waved gently in the breeze like a helium balloon tied to a fence.

Zoe's mind was cycling furiously trying to figure out how to stop. She'd never had to do that before, not that she'd ever really flown before. As she hung there, mostly upside down, Zoe realized she could see quite a distance. The view of the neighborhood was beautiful from here even with the clouds rolling in over the lake from the east.

Zoe remembered that after she'd fallen out of the tree, something had broken her power of flight and set her on the ground. It occurred to her that she better hold on to the railing even tighter because if her defiance of gravity suddenly gave out, she didn't want to tumble all the way down to where Binny and Penny were standing.

What was it that had snapped her out of it in front of PopPop's house? Usually it was the fall into whatever hole she had created that turned off her power. But after her fall, it had been... Zoe concentrated hard, replaying the scene in her mind. And then she remembered. It was Zach's voice. He'd sounded so impressed with her and his approval had banished all other thoughts from her mind.

And then suddenly Zach's statements about how cool she was, and how much he liked spending time with her, rushed like spilled water into her mind. Without warning, Zoe's body flopped down to the side of the railing, the wrong side.

It creaked and it groaned, but it held fast. Zoe wasn't sure whether she'd gotten the wind knocked out of her by her impact on the railing or if she'd just lost her air gasping in surprise at the sudden loss of power. Either way, she knew she had to move quickly. Zoe clambered over the railing and sat for a minute, catching her breath and feeling the pleasure of being on relatively solid footing.

When she felt ready, she stood up, and peered over the railing. Penny and Binny looked small three floors below. Zoe gave them the thumbs up and opened the unlocked door. The door swung outward, and as Zoe went in, the edge of the door gently tapped the railing that Zoe had depended on just a minute earlier.

Apparently that was the last straw as Zoe heard a crack and saw a the three foot chunk of railing on which she'd been hanging, tear itself from its moorings and fall to the ground. Zoe rushed to the edge, and peered over it to see where it had landed. Luckily it had caught on some decorative elements on the second floor.

"You okay?" Penny yelled from below.

"I'm fine." Zoe yelled down. But seeing how close she had come to falling made her feel anything but fine. Zoe scurried into the third floor of the abandoned mansion.

§

"You two first. I'll hold." Zach said, looking at his two young charges.

Gabe started climbing.

"It's a good thing we left this ladder here or we couldn't get back up there." Cassie observed.

"My sister could." Gabe said.

"Yep. She could. But luckily we don't need to do any more flying tonight." Zach said encouraging Cassie to climb.

Zach surveyed the distillery room. Orienting himself he faced the long brick wall. "This should be the side facing the abandoned house."

A long table covered most of the wall, but Zach had remembered a section on the left where the table didn't extend. In that section the bricks didn't follow the normal pattern. It looked like there had been a doorway there with the bricks making an arch. But what would have been empty space under the arch was now also filled with brick.

If Zach's mental map of the neighborhood was correct, Ollie and Rembrandt would be located directly behind the brick wall at which he was staring. Zach scratched his chin lost deep in thought and wondered how they were going to get through.

§

"Are you okay in there?" Binny yelled through the French doors that graced the entrance to the mansion.

"I'm fine. These things are just heavy." Zoe answered back.

507

After another minute one of the doors finally opened about a foot. Just enough for Binny and Penny to squeeze through. The entry had been barricaded at some point with furniture from the home. Zoe had moved as much as she could lift to let Binny and Penny inside.

"Thanks. Just in time. The rain just started." Binny said.

"What is this place?" Penny said, shaking the droplets off her head and marveling at the ancient décor. It seemed like the home had been left one day to rot and collect dust. Everything the residents had used, furniture, carpets, etc. was still sitting as it had been. Nothing had been removed.

"We don't have time to look around now." Binny warned as she made room for them to pass by pushing the furniture that Zoe had moved back in place against the front door.

"I agree." Zoe said. "We need to find the way to the basement.

The light was rapidly disappearing but there was still just enough to find their way around. Binny couldn't help but notice the framed photographs on the wall. Rows of posed faces looked back. It was too dim to make out much more than that.

The sixth doorknob proved to be the pivotal one. The first five revealed a pantry, a small bathroom, a small study, and two separate coat closets. After turning the sixth, the girls found a set of stairs heading down. They looked at each other for a moment, and descended.

From the top of the stairs the basement looked pitch black, but by the time they'd gotten to the bottom they could see a faint yellow glow coming from a distant corner. The basement itself was a warren of pipes, wooden barriers, shelving, wash basins, and hundreds of boxes containing who knows what. The basement itself was lined with concrete except for one wall on which they could make out the faint outline of brick in the flickering yellow light.

§

Zach had kicked, punched, and hit the bricks with everything he could find, including his own fists and feet. Nothing budged. With each minute that passed he was getting more desperate.

Zoe, Binny, and Cassie were still waiting outside the house and probably getting impatient. He would have sent them a message, but his phone wasn't getting any signal. It was also getting close to the time he'd told his parents they would meet in the park. Time was running out.

Zach had found a metal rod and was now scraping at the edges of a brick that had seemed a little bit loose. At this rate, Zach thought to himself, they would catch Ollie sometime before he left for college.

"Should we go back?" Cassie asked her brother.

Zach responded in frustration. "Maybe. I don't know. Just give me another minute to see if I can come up with a way through here."

§

For weeks now, Zoe Flowers had been certain that Ollie was hurting animals. She had never wavered for even a moment in her conviction. And yet, approaching the source of the yellow light in the basement she was completely unprepared for what she saw.

Ollie Trace stood in rapt concentration. All his attention was focused on Rembrandt. Rembrandt was standing. But his stance didn't look right. He looked almost stuffed. But those were the least strange things about the scene. Superimposed on Zoe's view of Rembrandt was another image, also of Rembrandt. But this one was painted in whorls of yellow light that slithered around Rembrandt like a hundred snakes.

"Oh no!" Binny gasped as the tears started to flow.

Penny grabbed Binny's shoulder as much to comfort her friend as to steady herself.

"What are you doing?" Zoe yelled as she took two steps towards Ollie.

Ollie either ignored her, or didn't hear her.

Zoe took another step towards Ollie. "Let the dog go right now!"

Ollie slowly looked up from Rembrandt. Rembrandt remained motionless. The only word Ollie said was "No", and then returned his gaze to the dog and the wriggling light that echoed every facet of Rembrandt's shaggy body. Ollie no longer needed paper to 'draw' the energy from the animal out.

Zoe had had enough. "If you won't stop, I'll stop you." She marched towards Ollie.

At first it looked like Ollie was going to just stand there, but at the last moment, Ollie turned his head to Zoe, stared at her hard, his eyes following her trajectory as she flew through the air and thudded into a wooden post. When it was done, Zoe was stuck to the post, floating three feet in the air, and completely unable to move.

Without a word, Ollie returned his gaze to Rembrandt.

At first Penny and Binny weren't sure what had happened. They thought that maybe Zoe had flown to that spot in the basement. But after a second it became clear that Zoe's body was perfectly still. She looked frozen much like Rembrandt.

The only thing Zoe could still move was her head. And that's when she started screaming.

⊰ 41 ⊱

THE WAY OUT

Zach was the first to realize what he was hearing. "Come, we've got to go, now." Zach called to Gabe and Cassie to follow him down the ladder. They had been sitting on the other side of the room watching Zach's efforts to find a way through the wall.

"What is going on?" Cassie asked, sounding frightened.

"I don't know, but we've got to hurry." Zach insisted.

Gabe headed to the ladder, but the muffled screams from behind the bricks continued and stopped him in his tracks.

"That's Zoe." Gabe said. "Zoe's in trouble." Gabe started running towards the sound, heading directly to the bricks that Zach had failed to penetrate.

Gabe is going to hurt himself. Zach lunged from his perch at the edge of the hole Zoe had made to grab Gabe before he smashed his slight frame into the brick wall, but missed by inches. Zach landed flat on his stomach.

Cassie watched in horror.

Zach looked up just in time to see Gabe lower his shoulder as he made contact with the bricks. Zach could almost see the bones in Gabe's body crack under the impact of the collision. Gabe would be hurt very badly.

But that's not what happened. It took Zach a moment to process the scene. He'd so expected Gabe to be hurt that at first he thought the dust and broken brick that had exploded in a cloud was the wall falling on top of Gabe. But after a moment, it was clear that Gabe had created an enormous hole in the wall by smashing through it as if it was made of paper. After a few seconds, the dust settled some. Zach and Cassie saw Gabe was standing on the other side of the now destroyed wall. Gabe was completely unscathed and trying to make sense of what he was seeing.

While Zoe's efforts hadn't distracted Ollie from his task, Gabe's entrance did. Ollie staggered back a step. The yellow light evaporated from around Rembrandt, and Rembrandt collapsed in a heap on the table on which he'd been frozen. Zoe slid down the post and crumpled onto the basement floor.

Zach scrambled over the broken bricks with Cassie not far behind. Zach ran to Zoe's side. Cassie remained on top of the bricks, suddenly quiet.

"Are you okay?" Zach lifted Zoe's head with his hand?

Penny and Binny rushed over as well, surrounding Zoe with concerned voices.

"I'm fine. I'll be fine." Zoe reassured them, still groggy from the experience. "Where's Gabe?" Zoe craned her neck to try to find her brother who had suddenly disappeared.

Gabe had already shifted his focus to Ollie. "What did you do to my sister?"

"Nothing." Ollie spat out. "Nothing. Your sister is nothing. You're all nothing."

Binny stepped forward, trying to get between Gabe and Ollie. "Nothing? Nothing? You're worse than nothing. You kill animals."

Zoe was weak on her feet but trying to get close to Rembrandt to tend to him. It was hard to tell his state as his eyes were closed, and everyone was covered in dust from the impromptu door Gabe had created.

"Kill them? Kill them? I'm not trying to kill the animals. I'm trying to... I'm trying to..." Ollie's voice trailed off.

Zoe had made it as far as Rembrandt. "He's not dead, but he's not doing well. You did this!" She pointed at Ollie.

"I can do it without killing him. Don't you see? He's not dead." Ollie protested.

"He's not dead *yet*." Penny corrected Ollie's assertion.

Zach made his way forward amidst the shouting and recrimination. His presence quieted everyone as he walked right up to Ollie and said in a low voice. "Do what without killing him?"

Ollie stared at Zach for a moment, defiant, his chin raised. And then he started to fall to pieces. Amidst the tears, Ollie tried to explain. "Don't you see, I'm trying to see them. To see what's inside. They have something to give me. It's like a present. For me. I don't want to hurt them, I'm just trying to figure out how to see inside without hurting them. You've got to see it. You'll know. It's beautiful." Ollie's words were coming out in fits and starts between his tears and choppy breathing.

"Ollie, you need to stop hurting the animals. You need to stop now." Zach said firmly in the same quiet voice he had used before.

"No. No. No." Ollie's voice was getting louder and higher as he saw all the disappointment, anger, and pity on the faces around him. "You don't understand. I'll show you."

Ollie took a deep breath through his nose, stemmed his tears, and concentrated. Rembrandt started getting up and back into the pose he'd been in when they'd first entered the basement. Little balls of yellow light appeared at various points on Rembrandt's body. Each ball started slowly travelling along Rembrandt's exterior, leaving a slithering trail of light behind them. Soon Rembrandt's body, while still visible, was encased in a web of greasy yellow light – as if Ollie had drawn Rembrandt in three dimensions using electric yellow paint.

"See? See?" Ollie said excitedly. "Don't you see it now?"

Rembrandt's eyes looked blank.

"You're hurting him." Zoe yelled.

"No. I'm. Not!" Ollie screamed.

Zach grabbed Ollie's arm hoping to stop him from whatever he was doing, but Ollie swung the arm outwards and Zach went flying, ending up stuck to a wall. Gabe, Zoe, Binny, and Penny all swarmed Ollie who immobilized them each in similar fashion against posts and various spots on the basement walls.

The tears were flowing freely down Ollie's face now. "You don't understand. Nobody. Ever. Understands."

Cassie remained standing, alone on the pieces of wall that Gabe had turned into a pile of bricks. The light from the dim bulbs in the distillery room and the dust that still filled the air silhouetted Cassie's small frame. The other children, frozen in place by Ollie, all looked at her.

After a moment, when Ollie's exclamations had faded into mumbling, Cassie got his attention. "Ollie?"

Ollie looked up, seeing Cassie as if he hadn't noticed her there before.

Cassie continued, "*I* understand." Cassie gingerly took a step forward off the pile of bricks and towards Ollie.

Binny whispered a shout from her awkward perch, "No. Cassie. Stop."

Cassie paused for a moment.

"Run. Get help." Binny said.

Cassie looked up to her brother who was pinned to the wall.

A rush of memories came into the foreground of Zach's mind. Finding Ollie alone in the park with the bird. Cassie should have been right there, but she wasn't. As if she had disappeared. Then Zach remembered Binny's report of Cassie taking Rembrandt for a walk alone and without permission and ending up talking with Ollie for who knows how long before Binny arrived on the scene to break it up.

Zach looked at Cassie and nodded his head in approval. Cassie took another step forward.

"No! What are you doing?" Binny was no longer whispering.

Zach looked at her and said two words, "It's okay." Zach followed it with a look that made it clear that she should stay quiet.

Binny looked stricken with fear but kept silent.

"You understand? Really?" Ollie said meekly.

Cassie continued her path forward but instead of heading for Ollie walked slowly towards Rembrandt. "Yes. It's beautiful. He's beautiful. You drew this?"

Ollie wiped at his cheeks with his fists. His words came out between his snivels. "Well. Yes. I mean no. I mean, he showed me this and I just wanted to show you."

Cassie nodded her head and smiled gently. "You're showing me what you see?"

"Yes. Yes. Exactly."

"But Ollie, I'm worried about Rembrandt." Cassie put her hands on Rembrandt, one on his back and one on his chest.

"No, don't you see, Rembrandt's gonna be fine. I can do it without him getting hurt." Ollie nodded vigorously.

"I know. I see you." Cassie started hugging Rembrandt. "You can let him go now. I understand."

All at once the snakes of pale yellow light that had surrounded Rembrandt dissipated, fading into nothing more than a sparkly dust like the end of a fireworks display. Cassie hugged Rembrandt tighter, laying him down as gently as she could, given his size.

Ollie released the pinned children, slowly this time. Each approached the ground feet first though somewhat dazed by the experience.

All seven children, and one large dog stayed still for a few moments, not quite sure what to do next.

"Ollie?" A woman's voice pierced the silence from the edge of the basement.

All heads turned. A pair of wide doors that looked like an extension of the ceiling lifted slowly. The rain had started in earnest and water along with the last shreds of evening light streamed in through the widening gap. Soaking wet, and with a desperate look on her face, Samantha Trace entered the basement of the abandoned mansion.

Cellar doors! Zach thought to himself. *They must have been covered by all the overgrowth. That's how Ollie got in.* Zach shook his head, berating himself for missing the entrance and making things more difficult.

"Mom." Ollie uttered.

"Ollie, are you hurt?" Samantha Trace rushed down the cluttered steps to her son landing on her knees in front of him and checking him to see if he was hurt.

"I'm fine." Ollie said.

"He's not fine. He's been hurting animals, just like we told you." Zoe said.

"That's not what I was doing." Ollie said.

"Does that dog look like he's okay?" Penny said.

Samantha Trace stood up and placed herself between the other children and her son. "Listen to me. I don't know what kind of game you've all been playing here, but I want you to leave my son out of it. Stay away from us!" Samantha took Ollie by the arm and headed for the cellar doors.

The children watched them leave in stunned silence.

"Ollie, you scared me half to death." Samantha had regained some of her firmness now that the immediate danger seemed to have passed.

"I'm sorry Mom. Really." Ollie said as they walked home. And then after a moment, "Mom?"

"Yes?"

"I wasn't hurting the animals. Really, I wasn't." Ollie looked at his mother, his eyes brimming with fresh tears.

"I know Ollie. I know." But in her heart, Samantha Trace wasn't sure at all. "Let's get you home and dry and forget about all this."

Ollie sniffled. "How did you know where I was?" Ollie worried over what Xander might have shared with his mother.

Samantha stopped walking for a moment to address her son. "Ollie, you're all I have." Samantha looked at her son in earnest, and then with a tired smile added, "Also, searching the entire neighborhood helped."

Almost as an afterthought, Samantha Trace added, "And I don't want you spending any more time with those children. They are a bad influence."

"OK." Ollie said, silently adding, *except for maybe one of them.*

Gore Grater sat in his car in the rain. He'd made zero progress since almost catching the children at the ice cream shop earlier in the day. He was tired, and he'd had enough.

Gore looked up from his sandwich, a pair of huddled figures catching his eye. He couldn't be sure, but it looked like Dr. Trace and her son heading home. Since the incident where the children had appeared at her house, Gore had included it in his patrols.

For a moment Grater thought of offering them a ride, but looking around at his trash-filled car, he thought better of it. *If she can call it a night, then so can I*, he thought to himself. And besides, the big boss wanted to see him first thing in the morning. Gore figured he better get a good night's sleep so he could be ready for the meeting.

Gore Grater started his car and headed home.

§

Cassie was focused on Rembrandt. The others rushed to her side to see what they could do.

"Is he alive?" Penny asked gingerly.

"Yes. He's alive. He's just tired." Cassie reassured.

"How do you know?" Zoe asked.

"I don't know. I just do. I can feel it." Cassie responded not letting go of her patient.

"Gabe?" Zoe said to her brother.

Gabe looked up, the tone in his sister's voice made him nervous. "Am I in trouble?"

"Are you in trouble? Hmmm... Let's see. No. You saved me. How long have you been able to break through brick walls?" Zoe grabbed her brother in a bear hug.

"I did? Oh yeah. I guess I did." Gabe mused. "Wait, does that mean...?"

Binny smiled at Gabe. "Told you it would come."

"I'm not sure I can do it again just yet." Gabe said in a concerned voice.

"That's okay. Once is enough for tonight." Penny joked.

"And you..." Zach got Cassie's attention. "You knew just what to do. You were absolutely amazing Cassie."

Cassie's blushing cheeks would have been more obvious if there had been more light.

"Zach is right. You saved Rembrandt from that nutjob." Binny said.

Cassie smiled back at her sister's praise. But she kept the pinch she felt in her heart to herself.

"Uh oh." Zach uttered. "We've got to hurry. Mom and Dad are waiting for us in the park."

⊱ **42** ⊰

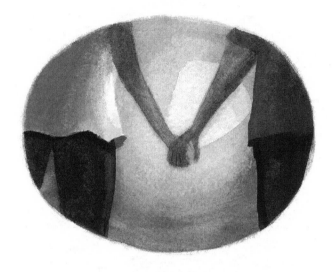

THE SECRETS THAT BIND

"Everything?" Gabe looked disappointed.

"Everything." Zach said.

"Not even my incredible super strength?" Gabe flexed his bicep.

"Especially that." Zoe added. "And don't go doing anything crazy either. You still don't know how to even turn it on."

Gabe made a face but acquiesced.

"Do you think he can make it? Binny stood in the middle of the wild greenery that had so effectively hidden the cellar doors.

"I think so." Penny was breathing hard trying to gently lift Rembrandt in the right direction.

"Come on. You can do it." Cassie said encouragingly as she patted Rembrandt's head.

"Are you talking to him or to me?" Penny asked.

"Both I guess?" Cassie giggled.

Rembrandt looked like he'd been woken up from a nap that he had preferred to continue.

"We can't talk about *any* of this. Not even about Ollie." Zach said.

"What?" Zoe turned on Zach. "Why not?"

"Because, if we explain what Ollie did, then we have to explain to our parents that we went running around an abandoned rotting house. Once they've grounded us for that, they'll make us explain how we got into said house. I don't know about your parents, but with mine, it won't end until they've gotten us to admit that we have powers and have gotten personal tours of our hideout." Zach said. "And also, everyone, wipe as much of the dust off your clothes as you can."

"So he's just gonna get away with it?" Binny joined Zoe in her indignation.

"What would happen to him anyway? I mean really? His mother seems to be able to deflect anything. The only people that would get in trouble are us. And besides, I don't think Ollie will be kidnapping any more animals." Zach asserted.

"And why is that?" Zoe asked.

"Well, while I'm pretty sure Dr. Trace won't let him get into any trouble, that doesn't mean she won't keep a much closer eye on him. I saw how she was looking at him and Rembrandt. She knew something was up." Zach continued, "Second, I think he got what he wanted."

"What does *that* mean?" Binny said.

Zach squeezed Cassie's arm as he spoke. "It means that while we were all going to use our powers to stop him, Cassie used her powers of persuasion. I think he did this to prove something, to himself, or maybe even to Cassie. And I think he did that."

"Caleb said that kids who hurt animals grow up to hurt people." Penny said solemnly.

"I know. I think we have some time on that though. Let's deal with one thing at a time."

"There's something we haven't discussed." Binny said. "Ollie has a power."

"Yeah, that didn't feel good." Zach said.

"No kidding. He did it to me twice." Zoe said.

"Caleb told us he only gave powers to us." Anger crept into Binny's voice. "Where did Ollie get his?"

"I think he's waking up." Cassie said nuzzling Rembrandt as he walked next to them.

"Yeah, he is looking perkier." Binny added. "His nose is wet again."

Zoe smiled at Rembrandt's progress and turned back to Zach. "So what are we gonna tell them?"

"I'll think of something." Zach flashed a smile.

The kids exited the grounds of the abandoned mansion and headed down the alley and around the block to Madrona park and their waiting parents. The dark had finally descended but the rain had moved through the area quickly and was now down to a spatter.

§

"Hmmm... Zach said they'd be here five minutes ago." Jay muttered.

"Patience. He'll be here. Remember, you're in your new trusting mode." Julie said.

"I *trusted* him to be here five minutes ago."

Jay, Julie, Serena, Quincy, and Jonathan were all waiting for the kids in the playground area in the Madrona park.

"Somebody should tell the city, this looks kind of dangerous." Quincy pointed at the wide hole that had been dug out under the jungle gym.

"I wonder how something like that happens." Jonathan mused.

"Ants." Quincy said to Jonathan.

"Ants?" Jonathan asked.

"Yeah, lots of ants driving lots of tiny construction equipment." Quincy replied.

"You are insane." Jonathan joked.

"Henry!" Serena shouted.

Henry Huitre was walking on the other side of the park. He'd been looking for Rembrandt and walked slowly to the other adults.

"Any luck?" Jay asked.

"I am afraid not yet." Huitre replied. "I hope you are all not out here on account of my dog."

"The kids couldn't help it. They've been out searching. We brought them some rain gear, though it looks like we're too late on that front." Serena held her hand up above searching for any remnants of the precipitation.

"Those children are amazing. Really." Huitre said, his voice bittersweet.

Julie noticed the children first as they rounded the corner and came into view. Julie leaned her neck forward trying to get a good look. "I think that might be them."

"It's about time." Jay said looking at his watch.

"Shush." Julie said.

Five of the children had rounded the corner, and a moment before it occurred to Julie to wonder where Cassie was, Cassie rounded the corner, with Rembrandt in tow.

"I can't believe it." Jay said.

"Mon dieu!" Huitre exclaimed.

"Still upset about them being late?" Julie elbowed Jay.

Wide grins broke out on each of the parents' faces.

Huitre's shoulders lowered for the first time since he'd first realized his backyard was empty. He hadn't realized how much weight they'd been carrying. Rembrandt ran into his arms and let out a celebratory bark.

Once the hugging and congratulations had died down a bit, Huitre asked the kids, "I do not understand. How did you find him? Where was he?"

"Well, we have to tell you something." Zach said solemnly.

The group got quiet.

"When I told you we had lunch today, I didn't tell you what we had for lunch." Zach said.

"Oh really?" Jay said, feigning surprise.

"We stopped in at Soul Repair for some ice cream. I know it wasn't the healthiest decision, but were in a hurry, and it was hot out." Zach explained.

"And Kay has the coolest new ice cream. It looks like a real baseball." Cassie nodded vigorously.

"I do not understand. What does that have to do with how you found Rembrandt?"

"Well," Zach looked around, all the kids were staring at him, fascinated to find out what he was going to say.

The adults were hanging on his words as well. "It seems that Rembrandt got the same idea."

"Rembrandt got ice cream?" Huitre laughed for the first time since Rembrandt had disappeared, drying his face with the back of his hand.

"In the alley behind Soul Repair there's a dumpster. I think Rembrandt smelled some food in there, somehow got in, and then couldn't get out." Zach explained.

"We were right there today." Quincy said.

"He doesn't look any worse for the wear." Julie said.

"Maybe I'll try spending the afternoon napping and eating in a dumpster." Jay joked.

"Maybe you should." Julie teased.

"How did you guys even think to look in there?" Serena asked.

Zoe stepped forward. "It was Zach's idea. We'd looked in so many places where Rembrandt was supposed to be, that Kay suggested we look where he wasn't supposed to be. Zach realized the dumpster was the one place where we hadn't looked."

Zach looked embarrassed.

Zoe gave Zach a look letting him know that he wasn't the only one who could weave a good story.

Jay ruffled Zach's hair. "I'm proud of you. I'm proud of all of you."

"Thank you so much. I am so grateful to each one of you." Huitre looked up momentarily from where he was kneeling and petting Rembrandt. It looked like he never planned on letting him go.

"How did you guys stay so dry? It was pouring out. We came to bring you some rain jackets." Serena asked, puzzled.

"We have raindrop dodging super powers." Penny said.

Everyone laughed.

§

The adults were still chatting amongst themselves, but the kids had dispersed to various structures in the playground. Zach and Zoe sat on the same bench they'd sat on together weeks earlier watching Cassie and Gabe take turns pushing each other on the swings.

Zoe confided in Zach that she worried Gabe's superpower might return unexpectedly and he'd send Cassie flying halfway across the neighborhood.

Zach laughed but had a serious expression on his face.

"What's wrong? Not funny?" Zoe asked.

"No." Zach smiled. "It was funny. It's just, these powers, they are so amazing. You, your brother, everyone can do these incredible things. And I know that what I can do is pretty cool as well. But in the end, I don't feel like I really solved anything."

"Penny broke us in everywhere, Xander texted us the address that told us where to go, Binny found where Ollie was, you flew into the house, Gabe broke us into the basement, and Cassie got Ollie to stop. I'm really glad that everything turned out, and I don't need to be the hero, I just wish I could have done something, *anything* to help." Zach confessed.

Zoe cocked her head at an angle, sizing Zach up as she thought about her words. "Zach Jordan, you have been the one leading us to this point from the moment we saw that poor cat. Without you, none of this would have happened."

"But..." Zach tried to interrupt.

Zoe shushed him and continued. "Never mind all the times your clever ideas, and ridiculously cool memory powers saved us or got us closer to catching Ollie, it's become obvious to everyone but you that you have a second super power."

"Oh yeah? What's that?" Zach said doubtfully.

The tone of Zoe's voice got softer as she answered, "You make the people around you better."

Zach was speechless which he thought was probably a good thing because if he tried to speak he would probably cry. Zoe's words were the nicest thing he'd ever heard.

"Zoe. Shouldn't you guys be getting home to your house? I don't want your parents to worry." Jay had walked over, rescuing Zach from certain embarrassment.

"I called my grandfather. He says it's okay if we walk Rembrandt home, but then we have to come home straight after." Zoe answered.

"Well then we better get going." Jay smiled.

§

The caravan proceeded in small clusters. Rembrandt led the way. Not only did Rembrandt's ordeal appear to not have had a lasting negative effect on him, but Rembrandt seemed to be full of energy. Energy that Huitre hadn't seen in some time.

"You know," Serena sidled up to Jay, "this story, of the neighborhood kids rescuing a dog – it's got some potential."

"Yeah?" Jay said.

"Yeah." Serena answered. "You up for doing the illustration."

"I think so?" Jay joked.

"That's the way to be confident." Serena said sarcastically, and then encouraging Jay, "You've already got some good practice drawing Rembrandt."

"True enough." Jay smiled, excited at the prospect.

"What's my power going to be in the story?" Cassie joined Jay and Serena's conversation.

"I want one too." Gabe appeared to be attached to Cassie at the hip.

"Well, that's something I guess we'll have to figure out." Serena said to the kids.

§

"Do you think you could lift me in the air?" Penny said as she walked between her father and Jonathan holding one of each of their hands.

"I'd worry about pulling your arms out of your sockets. I think your parents would be upset if that happened." Jonathan said.

"But I want to fly." Penny responded.

Jonathan smiled at Penny and then glanced up for a moment. The third floor widow's walk of an enormous, and apparently abandoned home was just visible over the overgrown shrubs that lined the edge of the property. "Wow. Some beautiful homes in this neighborhood."

"Yeah?" Quincy said.

"That one alone could keep me employed for a year or two." Jonathan gave Quincy a knowing look.

§

Binny watched Penny as she joked easily with her father and Jonathan. But elsewhere in their small procession, Cassie had taken over Rembrandt duty so Dr. Huitre and her mother were walking on their own.

Binny caught up with Dr. Huitre. "Are you feeling better?"

"My dear, you cannot imagine how much better I feel." Henry responded.

Binny took his hand in her own. Huitre's eyebrows went up in surprise but he said nothing.

"I'm glad." Binny smiled.

Huitre's phone rang and he answered it with his other hand.

Julie was walking a few feet away. Binny reached out her other hand to her mother. Julie obliged.

Huitre spoke into his phone, "Yes? Oh good. I'm glad to hear that. I've got my Rembrandt back as well. Glad to hear it. Yes. Bye."

"Everything okay?" Binny asked Huitre once he'd put his phone back in his pocket.

"Yes. Just some unfinished business." Huitre responded.

"Is it done now?" Julie asked Huitre.

"Yes. Completely." Huitre answered her.

After a minute, Binny left her mother and Huitre making an excuse that she had to discuss something urgently with Penny. But instead of dropping their hands, she joined them before she snuck away saying, "Keep them warm for me please."

The two adults looked at each other and smiled tentatively. They'd been expertly trapped.

§

Zach and Zoe walked behind all the others. They'd slowed down a bit, neither wanting the day to end quite yet. Unlike the others, they were walking in relative silence. They'd both already said so much, they couldn't think of anything to add.

Zoe saw Binny join Huitre and her mother's hands and got an idea.

At first Zach didn't quite understand what was happening, but then it dawned on him. He had a super power. He was friends with five other kids with super powers. They'd just rescued their favorite dog from certain death. His parents were proud of him. And the most amazing girl he'd ever met was holding his hand.

❧ *43* ❧

THE CHANGE IN PLANS

Deep underground in the never used and now forgotten Sick's Stadium train station, a woman sat dressed in rags with her knees huddled up to her chest. Her orange eyes were closed but she was watching six children rescue a large dog from a seventh child.

While it wasn't always recognizable as such because she had exactly zero teeth left in her head, she was smiling.

§

In almost exactly the very same spot, just several stories directly above the old woman, another person was smiling. Much like he'd done almost exactly a year earlier, Xander Luce sat in his private office watching the video over and over. The wireless video system he'd asked Grater to install in the abandoned mansions' basement had performed exactly as he'd hoped.

In fact, just about everything had gone exactly as he'd hoped. There was the question of the small boy breaking through the wall, but Xander would think about that another time. Watching Ollie develop his abilities with that dog was fodder enough, but seeing Ollie's telekinesis manifest itself as well, and with such power and precision, was positively delightful.

He had wrestled with how to win the confidence of the youngest Jordan girl, but it appeared he wouldn't have to worry about that after all. She seemed like a sub-par specimen anyway. It wasn't clear that she could even control her powers. But Ollie, Ollie was another matter entirely.

The boy was discovering his true strength with each passing day and taking to the task like an honors student. Now all that was left was for Xander to finish becoming the teacher who would help Ollie on his journey. But that was a task for tomorrow. For now, it was getting late, and Xander Luce needed to sleep.

§

"Sir, you wanted to see me?" Gore Grater said as he walked into the greenhouse.

It was early in the day after the events at the abandoned Madrona mansion, and Seattle's gorgeous summer weather had reasserted its command over the city.

"Gore? It's Xander, please." Xander Luce gently chided.

"Yes. Of course. Sorry Xander."

"I'm sorry to ask you to come in extra early this morning. I know you've been working many extra hours and I'm grateful."

"And I promise you, I will achieve our goal. I just need some more time. I'm very close." Grater sputtered.

"Oh Gore, you've done more than that. You've accomplished your goal. Because of your hard work, I've gotten everything I need. I think we can now safely return you to work that's more suited to your talents, and not rely on you to go traipsing after children in the neighborhood." Luce said.

"You have everything you need?" Grater was confused.

"Those cameras you installed were very revealing." Luce explained.

"Oh." Gore thought for a moment. "I'd love to see the footage. Understand what we're dealing with here. You know."

"I understand your curiosity, and no doubt there will be a time for that. But for now, if you don't mind, I think we need to compartmentalize the information for security purposes." Luce said firmly.

538

"Oh. Of course. Compartmentalization. I completely understand." Grater stood up a little straighter.

"And Gore, I hope it's okay, but given your accomplishments, I've asked Human Resources to elevate your pay. I realize that money is not what motivates a man like yourself, but I hope you'll allow an old man his quirks. Old habits die hard as they say." Luce smiled.

"Oh. Of course. Thank you sir. I mean Xander. Thank you." Gore was grinning.

"Thank *you* Gore. We're glad to have you back on campus full time." Xander said.

Gore took Xander's remark as a dismissal and started for the greenhouse exit.

"Oh Gore, one more thing?" Xander called after Gore almost absentmindedly.

"Yes?"

"This aspect of your work, the cameras in the basement, and the footage, we'll need to continue to keep that from Dr. Trace if you don't mind. Compartmentalization you know." Luce said.

"Of course. Protocols are there for a reason."

"Thank you Gore. I knew I could count on you."

§

"So we're in sync Ollie?" Samantha Trace said to her son as they got out of the car.

"Yes Mom."

"You don't need to do your walks anymore. This isn't a punishment. I just think there's plenty to do here. And besides, I spoke to Xander yesterday and he said you've been an absolute godsend. He's very impressed with you."

Ollie couldn't help but smile at the compliment. "It's okay. I promise. I'll stay in the greenhouse until you come get me every day."

"Thanks Ollie." Samantha Trace smiled at her son as they walked towards the greenhouse.

§

"Binnneeee" Cassie yelled. "We need you."

The children had gotten to the shelter early despite staying out the night before. They were eager to recount their adventuring.

While the other kids recounted their favorite highlights, Binny had decided to relocate her box of notebooks from the upper ante-room to the command center of the shelter.

It was there she now sat writing furiously in the register trying to document everything their small team had accomplished. The pages were filling quickly as Binny would periodically add diagrams and small sketches to illustrate the events.

"We *need* you." Cassie yelled again.

"Come on Binny." The others chimed in.

Binny poked her head out stairwell. "When I'm done, I promise." And then without waiting for a response she had disappeared back up the stairs to continue her writing.

§

"Ollie my boy. So glad to see you. I missed you yesterday." Luce said after Samantha had dropped off her son.

"Thanks." Ollie was still a little nervous about getting in trouble for the events of the previous night.

"Your mother says you're back to full-time here at the greenhouse."

"Yeah."

"I hope that's not too disappointing." Luce teased.

Ollie forced a smile to show Xander he wasn't disappointed at having his independence curtailed.

"You know, I was thinking about your desire to have a place of your own. Somewhere to conduct your own experiments. Now that your mother prefers you stay here in the afternoons, I realize the other location won't necessarily work."

Ollie looked at Luce interested but held his tongue.

"Well, I was just thinking that I might have a solution that would work for you and your mother." Luce continued. "But I wouldn't want to bother you if you had a better solution." Luce held up his hands indicating he was happy to drop the matter if Ollie wasn't interested.

"No, it's okay. That could be good. What were you thinking?" Ollie tried to keep the eagerness from his voice.

"Well, it's my own private lab space, but I'm so busy with work here in the greenhouse that I rarely get time to use it. So you'd be on your own there. I'd help you of course with getting to know the equipment and such, only if you're interested of course."

"That sounds pretty good." Ollie remained casual as long as he could but finally let some of his excitement spill into his voice. "Where is this lab?"

"You'll never guess." Xander's eyes sparkled and his face broke into a wide smile.

§

"Seriously Binny, we need your help." Penny begged her best friend.

"OK. OK. I'm done for now anyway. What's so important?" Binny trailed Penny down the stairs into the cavernous concrete underground shelter.

"Well, we're playing capture the flag, but the other team has a bit of an unfair advantage." Penny pointed in the air as she explained.

Binny's gaze followed Penny's finger and saw Zoe directing traffic for her team from the air. Floating up by the ceiling she could see where everyone was and gave her, Zach, and Gabe an unfair advantage.

"Oh no. Forget that. I'm in!" Binny pledged. "I've got some tricks up my sleeve too."

"She's in. We've got a chance now." Penny yelled to Cassie who squealed in delight at the news.

§

"Mind if I come in?" Xander Luce poked his head into Samantha Trace's office.

"Of course, of course." Samantha pulled a chair over for her boss and mentor.

"I think Ollie's happy with the new arrangement." Xander reassured.

"Thank you so much. I'm indebted to you."

"No no. Not at all. Your son has been truly valuable to me. Not that I'm entirely surprised given his genetics." Xander winked.

Samantha came as close to blushing as she ever did. It wasn't much but the redness stood out on her relatively pale skin.

"In fact, just to plant a seed in your mind, I know Ollie's school isn't too far away, assuming he's doing well in his studies, I wonder if he would be available some afternoons after school is out? I'd pay him of course." Xander smiled.

"You're offering him a job?" Samantha laughed.

"Well, I didn't want to say anything to him until I talked to you first of course."

"You're serious?" Samantha said.

"Of course. The boy has a gift." Xander's eyes crinkled as he spoke.

"That's very kind of you."

"Don't be silly. You and your son are doing me a kindness. And since we're already on the subject of all the wonderful contributions the Trace family is making to our mission here at Luce Laboratories, let's talk about you." Xander said.

"You want to talk about me?" A hint of nervousness crept into Samantha's voice.

Xander continued, "Samantha, you've been my most loyal employee. I depend on you more than anyone and trust you with my life and my life's work. You've been working hard on multiple projects for years and on one in particular you've not gotten any credit as we've had to keep its nature somewhat *under wraps*."

"Under your supervision, your man Grater has done an excellent job documenting those children's activities. I think I have everything I need to continue our progress."

Samantha swallowed and started speaking quickly. "But we haven't gotten the documentation you wanted. We haven't seen them demonstrating any special powers."

"Well, I've been working on some strategies to tackle the problem from a slightly different angle. So I hope it's okay with you, I saw Gore this morning and told him he could pause the surveillance activities for now."

"Oh." Samantha thought for a moment. "So you want me to help with this new methodology?"

"Actually, no." Luce said.

Samantha was crushed. *Was she being fired?*

Luce continued, "I have something far more important I need your full attention on."

Samantha Trace's emotions were all over the place. "You do?" She looked at Luce hopefully.

"Sam, I'm not getting younger. I had hoped sometime we'd come up with a way to do that, but it currently seems a little out of our reach." Luce joked and then lowered his voice. "And as such, I can't run this company forever. I need someone to be my successor, and I am certain that person is you."

Samantha stared at her boss unsure of what to say.

"Only if you're interested in the role of course." Luce said.

"Of course. I'm flattered. I'm honored. But, I expect you to be here for quite a while longer. Isn't this a bit early to be considering?" Samantha hoped her excitement at the possibility of becoming CEO of Luce Labs didn't show in her voice.

"Oh, don't worry. I expect to be here for some time as well, but this transition will take a while. You will need to get up to speed on a variety of issues across the company that you typically haven't had to deal with."

"Of course. Anything you need." Samantha promised.

"It may mean more hours. Late nights. Out-of-town business trips – on the jet of course. All that."

"Not a problem. Whatever you need Xander. You know that."

"Thank you Sam. I knew I could count on you. You make an old man happy."

§

Henry Huitre wasn't sure exactly why he had snapped the picture. It wasn't like him to be up on all the latest trends. He'd had trouble sleeping the night before.

Rembrandt hadn't been a bother even though Henry had let him sleep on the edge of the bed. A special privilege. It was just that Henry kept waking up. He would look at Rembrandt's chest rising and falling and go back to sleep for a while until the next waking.

Rather than leave Rembrandt to his own devices, Henry had decided to spend some quality time with his dog. A trip to the park was in order. The park in Madrona had a special fenced in section where dogs could go without leashes. Huitre didn't want Rembrandt to have any more urges to roam freely on his own, so he thought some time off leash might make Rembrandt happy.

Sitting on the ground with Rembrandt nuzzling him, something came over him and he snapped what the kids were calling *a selfie* of him and the dog on his cell phone. He'd caught it just at the right moment as Rembrandt was licking his face. Another special privilege that Huitre had now granted his furry friend.

As if that wasn't enough like a teenager, Henry sent the image to Julie over text accompanied by the message "Thank you." Then completing his brush with teenage behavior Henry waited eagerly hoping for a response and regretting sending the text in the first place.

But he didn't have to wait long. Within a minute his phone buzzed and a message from Julie said simply, "You're very welcome." The message was followed by a little yellow smiley face.

Henry Huitre was smiling too.

❧ 44 ❧

THE ELUSIVE TRUTH

The day had gone by quickly and the kids were still in the shelter but winding down from their capture-the-flag marathon, reviewing the previous day's heroics, and planning for the future. Cassie, Penny, and Gabe had spent a significant chunk of the day having ultra-serious discussions on just what their superhero outfits would look like.

It was late afternoon and Jay had asked Zach to pick up some ingredients from Madrona Dry Goods before dinner. For some reason Zach hadn't bristled at the request.

They sat around a table set on the wood floor of the basketball court. Interrupting a momentary lull in the conversation, Zoe brought up a topic they'd discussed briefly before. "Where did Ollie get his powers? That thing he does where he froze us."

"He didn't just freeze us, he was able to move us." Penny added.

"Telekinesis." Zach said.

"Caleb said he only gave us powers." Binny frowned.

"But?" Zach prodded his sister, her face making it clear she wasn't sharing everything on her mind.

"But, I'm not sure he was telling the truth." Binny said.

"He wouldn't lie to us, would he?" Zoe said.

"I looked in his mind when he was talking. It was like the truth and the lie were mixed up together. I couldn't tell what was what." Binny said.

"I hate to say it as Caleb's been so nice to us, but I'm starting to wonder if we can really trust Caleb." Zach said.

"There are only two possibilities. Either Caleb gave Ollie his power, or there's someone else who can give kids super powers." Penny said.

"I'm tired. I think I'm gonna go home." Cassie said.

"Just wait for us, we'll go home together." Binny said.

"I kind of want to walk on my own. I promise I'll go straight home." Cassie said earnestly.

Binny watched Cassie head for the exit before continuing the conversation, "I have a feeling that even if Caleb didn't give Ollie his power, he knows who did. He's not being honest with us."

"And if he knew that Ollie had a power, and didn't tell us, then..." Zoe said.

Zach finished her sentence, "...then Caleb sent us to find Ollie without warning us that Ollie had powers too." Zach looked at the others before uttering his conclusion. "Caleb put us in danger."

Privately Zach thought that it might not have been the first time Caleb had done something like that. Caleb had after all encouraged them to go to Luce Labs the previous summer. He may not have known that Dr. Trace was a threat, but he sent them there to investigate their powers knowing full well that he himself had given them these amazing skills. Zach wasn't sure of the truth, but he was getting increasingly certain that he hadn't heard it from Caleb.

"So children? How did it go?" Caleb's deep voice rumbled through the shelter.

The children's heads swiveled around, to see their visitor, surprised by his sudden entrance.

"We found Rembrandt." Zach reported in a stony voice.

"That's excellent news Mr. Jordan. Was it the pool or the library?" Caleb asked.

"Neither of those places. Ollie had him in an abandoned old mansion." Zoe answered.

"Oh. But you still found him. Excellent work. Truly excellent teamwork." Caleb said. "And your canine friend is undamaged I hope?"

"Ollie did something to him, but he'll be okay." Zoe answered.

"Caleb?" Zach said. "There's something else."

"Oh?"

"Ollie had powers. These light powers, and telekinesis. We're not entirely sure about all of it. But it was pretty scary." Zach said.

Caleb's faced remained an impenetrable mask.

Zach glanced at Binny giving her a look before continuing to talk to Caleb. "Since you gave us our powers, we were just wondering where he got his powers from."

Caleb looked down at his hands and then back up at Zach. "That's an excellent question Mr. Jordan."

Seeing no answer forthcoming, Zach plowed forward. "Did you know Ollie had powers?"

The silence hung in the air for what seemed like a minute. Finally Caleb uttered one word, "No."

Zach immediately turned to Binny. "Well?"

Binny shook her head, and spoke with a sadness in her voice. "It's confusing. It's not an outright lie, but it's definitely not the truth."

The faces of the other four children got stonier as Binny rendered her verdict.

Zach stood up and faced the grandfatherly old man in the overalls that they had welcomed into their hideout and into their secret lives so readily. Zach spoke without malice or anger but with resolve, "Caleb, I'm sorry to say this, but it seems like we can't trust you anymore."

Caleb hung his head. "I understand."

"That's it? You understand?" Binny was angry.

"Yes. I do." Caleb said quietly.

"Well I don't understand. Why don't you just tell us what's going on?" Binny shouted.

"I am trying to..." Caleb started to respond, but Binny didn't hear him. Binny's eyes burned red, and her pulse beat loud in her ears. Binny's face was scrunched in anger.

Zach addressed Caleb, "I'm sorry Caleb. We're grateful for the times you've helped us. But, you shouldn't come here again."

On that note, Zach and the other children walked towards the staircase, and made the long trek out of the shelter towards the warmth and safety of home.

Caleb Adams stayed rooted to the spot as the kids exited the shelter. His face revealed nothing of his thoughts. He just stood and stood. He wondered for a moment if this was how the trees felt.

Out of the corner of Caleb's eye, he saw a brief flash of light. The white sparkling ivy disappeared as fast as it had appeared, and in the very same spot now stood Cassie Jordan, her face inscrutable.

Neither said anything or looked away for what seemed like a long time. And then suddenly, Cassie ran to Caleb and hugged him with the full force of her eight-year-old grip.

Caleb reached a hand down to pat Cassie on the back gently. Cassie's eyes were closed as she hugged Caleb even tighter. If she'd looked up she would have seen a tear rolling down Caleb's lined cheek.

§

"Oooh. I love how you drew Rembrandt jumping out of the dumpster. The kids look so surprised to find him there. Cassie looks like she's afraid he's gonna flatten her." Serena admired Jay's handiwork."

"Yes. That's exactly what I was going for." Jay said.

"It's great." Serena smiled.

"It should be. We've been working on it for a month. Tell me again why you made the parents so dopey?" Jay asked. It was a familiar argument he and Serena had discussed several times now.

"As I've said, in these stories, you've got two choices. You can either kill the parents, or make them so clueless that they might as well be dead." Serena repeated, sounding bored.

"Yeah yeah. I know. It's just seems so far-fetched that the parents would be so clueless as to not know their kids are running around the neighborhood with superpowers." Jay made his traditional case.

"Jay, it's a comic book, not literature."

"I know. I just think superhero stories should be as realistic as possible." Jay lamented.

"You mean totally realistic aside from the superpowers of course." Serena teased.

"Yeah. Aside from the superpowers." Jay knew when he was defeated.

"Well, let's see if anyone reads this one, and then we can add some more realism in the second one. Sound good?" Serena said.

"Sounds good." Jay replied with a smile.

§

"Penny, I'm not sure you and I have the same notion of what the word 'help' means." Quincy Yang said to his daughter.

Penny was reclining on the couch as Quincy and Jonathan were carrying it up the broad stairs to the second floor of the apartment building.

"Less whining. More lifting." Jonathan teased.

"I *am* helping. I'm testing out the couch. And so far, I'm finding it very comfy." Penny giggled.

"I'm worried you'll fall off and break something." Quincy told his daughter.

"Don't worry. I'm good at fixing stuff." Penny responded nonchalantly.

"That's not what I meant. Oh, never mind." Quincy said as he and Jonathan set the couch down in the relatively empty living room.

"Which one is my room again?" Penny hopped off the couch and was peering into the various rooms.

"The one on the left okay?" Jonathan said. "You can see your friend Binny's room across the courtyard when you're here and she's staying with her Mom."

"Oh yeah. Right. Cool." Penny said and stuck her head out the window imagining how she and Binny would signal each other.

Jonathan laughed at Penny's excitement.

Quincy laughed and added. "Yeah. Very cool."

§

"Zach, would you mind folding these napkins please." Melissa Flowers instructed, and then turning to her daughter, "and what are you doing to help at this moment?

"I'm photographing the opening." Zoe responded from behind the lens of her fancy new camera.

"I think I'd rather you set out silverware." Melissa said.

"In a minute. I promise." Zoe responded amidst a flurry of shutter sounds.

"PopPop." Gabe yelled.

Gabriel Walker walked through the door of the brand new restaurant for the first time.

"He tried to get out of coming." James Flowers told his wife.

"I'm here. I'm here." PopPop said grouchily.

"Hi Dad. I'm glad you're here. Melissa kissed her father on the cheek.

"You're here too huh?" PopPop said to Zach. "It's getting so I can't go anywhere without seeing you. You gonna move into my house too?"

"PopPop!" Zoe blushed.

Zach wasn't sure what to say.

"Dad, don't be rude. Zach is our guest. And he's been very helpful." Melissa smiled at Zach as she spoke. "Zach, is the rest of your family coming tonight? We want to get as big a crowd as we can for opening night."

"I was just kidding. Zach knows that. Right kid?" PopPop said as much to his daughter as to Zach.

"Yep, they're coming." Zach said and then smiled at PopPop as he continued to fold napkins.

"Okay everyone. It's time." Melissa Flowers gathered family and staff just outside the front of the restaurant. Gabriel Walker, better known as PopPop didn't want to go back out but Gabe and Zoe dragged him by the hands.

"Zoe, you head over there. Now I need your photography skills. I want you to capture PopPop's reaction." Melissa said to her daughter.

"My reaction to what?" PopPop said.

"Dad, you know, you've been an inspiration to me in so many ways, culinary and otherwise." Melissa Flowers' voice broke a little but she kept herself from tearing up. "You've been so generous with your home, your time, your wisdom, and of course, you're cooking. Everything I know I learned from you. And as such we wanted to honor you."

Melissa looked over to her son who was standing holding a rope attached to a sheet that had been hung over the sign above the restaurant's façade. "Now Gabe."

Gabe pulled the rope and the sheet floated gently to the sidewalk. PopPop looked up to see a beautiful new sign, riddled with lights, and looking like it was straight out of the 1960's saying "Gabriel's Southern."

"We named it after you Dad." Melissa said to her father.

Even PopPop couldn't help but smile.

§

The night had been fabulously successful. Zach had lost count of how many ribs he'd eaten, but everyone knew that Cassie was on her third slice of Bourbon Peach Crumble. Zach wasn't far behind as he was tackling his second helping.

"Now can I?" Gabe wheeled his sister who was sitting next to Zach at one of the picnic tables that served as tables for the restaurant.

"Gabe I don't want you to break it." Zoe replied to her little brother.

"I won't break it. And you promised I could take pictures and you still haven't let me." Gabe complained.

"Are your hands clean?" Zoe looked down her nose at her brother's proffered palms. "Fine, but just this once."

Zoe handed Gabe the camera. Gabe rounded the table and focused it back on Zoe and Zach and said, "Okay you guys. Smile."

And they did.

EPILOGUE

Cassie still spent loads of time at the shelter with the other kids. But like Binny, Cassie sometimes wanted some time to herself. With the new emphasis on trusting the children more, Jay and Julie had given Cassie permission to go on walks in the neighborhood on her own.

At first Cassie walked aimlessly, but one day she found herself at the entrance to the alley behind Soul Repair. Cassie had a lot on her mind, and on this day Cassie didn't just want to walk, she wanted a place to sit down and think.

Cassie looked both ways to see if anyone was looking and went to her invisible place. She walked the alley until she got to the gate behind the abandoned mansion. The chain was still broken.

Cassie walked around the house until she found the cellar doors that had eluded them the first time. If anyone could have seen over the shrubs and growth that lined the property, they would have seen one of the cellar doors appear to open and close all on their own.

Once inside, Cassie twinkled back into visibility sure that nobody could see her now that she was safely in the basement where they had confronted Ollie and rescued Rembrandt.

Cassie half hoped that Ollie would be there – without an animal of course. But he wasn't. The basement was exactly as they had left it that day several weeks earlier. Boxes, shelves, all manner of stuff, and the huge pile of bricks that Gabe had created when he smashed through the wall to rescue his sister.

Cassie wandered through the basement, hoping that maybe Ollie had just wandered over to a different spot in the sprawling space. When it was clear Ollie was nowhere to be found Cassie thought of leaving but an old staircase beckoned. She'd never seen what was upstairs and curiosity got the better of her.

Cassie walked up the stairs, and slowly nudged open the door at the top, listening to the creak of the hinges and waiting to see if anyone shouted. Silence.

The first floor was in much better shape than the basement. Ornate furniture decorated the living room. The walls were covered in wallpaper with fancy dark red designs that felt fuzzy to the touch. The kitchen looked to

Cassie like it was from an old black and white movie that she'd seen on TV. Everything was old, covered in dust, and frankly – looked kind of haunted.

Cassie was getting a little bit spooked and decided to reverse course to the relative safety of the outdoors. She headed through the hallway near the front door and a series of framed hanging photographs caught her eye. Cassie wiped some of the dust from the glass surface of the nearest one.

Cassie recognized the mansion in the photograph. The picture had been taken right outside the front door. A couple of dozen children of various ages were gathered standing and sitting on the porch. Each child held a sign with a number. All boys.

A hand-painted sign hung over the front door. The very same sign that hung there today. But in the photograph the words were visible: "Madrona Home for Wayward Boys."

Cassie wasn't sure what exactly that meant but she didn't think it was good. She traced the faces with her finger until she saw two boys in particular, one was tall and gangly. The other was shorter with rosy cheeks. They were the only boys in the picture with smiles on their faces.

They each had one arm around the other and with their spare hands held their signs. The taller boy held "27". Cassie thought that the shorter boy's smile seemed mischievous. He held "28". Cassie looked to the right of the photograph where a list of numbers and names had been superimposed.

She scanned the list from the top until she got to the names next to 27 and 28. The two names listed were: "Caleb Adams" and "Alexander Luce".

SOUNDTRACK

Normally, books don't have musical accompaniment. But The Madrona Heroes Register wasn't originally intended to be a book. It was going to be a screenplay, and maybe eventually, a film. But screenplays aren't consumed widely unless they're made into movies. I considered making it a graphic novel for awhile, but that seemed like an even more daunting challenge than a screenplay. Thus, out of sheer laziness (and fear?), The Madrona Heroes Register became the novels you have before you.

But just because the story is told as a novel doesn't mean the movie ever left my mind. There are several points during the story when I imagine the camera pulling back from the scene you're reading, and a particular song plays over beautiful imagery. I am listing these moments here, so if you choose, you too can experience the film that I saw in my head as I wrote the book.

Each of these musical interludes aren't really described in the book at length because a film would rely on the song and the visuals to set the mood. So you'll have to fill in a minute or two of 'movie' when you play the song to get the full effect.

To experience these musical moments you may need to spend a few dollars if the songs aren't already in your music collection. But I promise they are worth it.

Good Times Bad Times, Led Zeppelin – This song plays just as Chapter 1 ends and we get a view of Zach biking home through the entire neighborhood.

You Can't Always Get What you Want, The Rolling Stones – This song plays just as Chapter 7 ends and from above we see Penny and Binny talking and then just staring in mutual silence at the ceiling.

La Mer, Jacqueline François – This is the song to which Henry Huitre and Julie Jordan are slow dancing in Chapter 11.

All Along the Watchtower, Jimi Hendrix – This song plays as the kids are making their way through the abandoned subway tunnel going from Cherry Street station to Sick's Stadium station in Chapter 18

Helplessly Hoping (Demo) Stephen Stills – This song plays after Gabe and Cassie talk about their respective fears in Chapter 25.

Change Partners (Live Version) Stephen Stills – This song plays as the adults are posting signs around the neighborhood in Chapter 35.

Silver Springs, Fleetwood Mac – This song plays as Samantha Trace is searching for her son in the Madrona Park and remembering their early years together in chapter 39.

Can't Find My Way Home, Blind Faith – This song plays as the adults and kids carry Rembrandt home toward Dr. Huitre's house in Chapter 43.

ACKNOWLEDGEMENTS

Now that I have completed my second book, my appreciation for all those who have joined me in one way or another on this path has only increased. Writing can be a lonely task, and ultimately the entire point of giving life to the Madrona Heroes universe is that it be shared.

First and foremost I am so grateful to everyone who read the first book. Children, adults, people I accosted in stores who looked like they might like it, family members, friends, pretty much anyone I could convince to give it a try without annoying them too much. I am so appreciative of you climbing the rocky path that was my first novel. And those of you who read the earlier versions and had to avoid typos and some of my awkward first-time novelist sentence construction deserve hazard pay as well. No matter how much you read or when you read it (and that goes for those of you who read this book as well) thank you.

Collaborating with someone on a creative pursuit can be a dicey prospect. Sometimes it works, and sometimes the visions are just too disparate. I'm proud to say that once again, Caroline Hadilaksono's beautiful illustrations have, in my opinion, raised the quality of the overall experience of this book in countless ways. Now that it's our second book together, Caroline and I are both getting more confident in our understanding of the characters and the stories. She has brought her unique insight into the story through the dozens of chapter headers and the positively stunning cover. I'm so incredibly grateful for all her hard work, her patience and the love and care she's put into her art that graces these pages.

Researching a book like this can be a breeze at times as I just observe my kids and my neighborhood and fill in all the superpower stuff. But there are times when more in-depth knowledge that I can't just observe from my living room are required.

Dr. Quintard Taylor, the Scott and Dorothy Bullitt Professor of American History at the University of Washington, is the author of The Forging of A Black Community: Seattle's Central District from 1870 through the Civil Rights Era. Dr. Taylor has been a good friend to me. His book has been an invaluable source on the history of the African-American community in Seattle's Central District. And next time he and I go to lunch, I want him to try *my* favorite Chinese restaurant. Dr. Taylor is also the President of BlackPast.org which you should visit immediately.

Robert "Red" Robinson, Senior Vice President, Director of Underground Services (what an awesome title) at Shannon & Wilson, Inc. in Seattle, spent an hour or two with me explaining to me how tunnels have actually been historically dug under the city and what was and wasn't possible and/or likely. That was a super fun discussion for me.

Responding to a random request on Facebook, Danny Bain was nice enough to spend awhile educating me on what would and wouldn't be possible to do with a mid-twentieth century gas generators that hadn't been touched in decades. He was very patient as by my recollection I asked the same questions at least two to three times.

There's a gaggle of kids who need thanking for reading the books and giving me feedback. They also were good at bugging me for the sequel which helped up the pressure on days when I didn't feel like writing. I'm so grateful to all of them: Jude, Sarah, Sasha, Liane, Tamara, Natalie, Elisha, Ido, Elena, Laurel, Stephanie, Chloe, John, Evan, Alex, Ellie, and Kai. Thank you.

I especially want to thank my niece Gavi who not only totally plowed through the book in just a couple of days, but sent in important edits as well. Thank you.

I'm also grateful to my dad who in between reading dusty documents about the Jews of Livorno, takes the time to read about what his grandchildren are up to with their superpowers. Thanks Dad.

In the home stretch, my cousin Debra came to the rescue with a marathon two day proofreading pass. Not only was she a huge help, but she's been a steadfast supporter and fan. I'm so appreciative.

And then there are my kids to thank. It must be hard to live with someone that might use your every statement and action as fodder for their books. But my three children have endured this state for over two years with only periodic complaining. Sivan, Bella, and Rakefet, thank you for reading the books, thank you for your feedback. And thank you for not being too annoyed. I love each of you so much. And as I mentioned after the last book, please note that any of the embarrassing things the kids do in the book are wholly made up by me.

I also need to call out Sivan in particular on this book, as he served a critical editorial role. Sivan read the book in just a couple of weeks and generated over 200 thoughtful insights as to where it could improve. Everything from questions as to whether a particular character would say something, all the way to great detailed editing with specific recommendations on how to improve things. In addition to all the other responsibilities he has, Sivan really came through for me and for the book. I'm so grateful.

Debbie was of course back at the helm with this book. Not only has she provided me with three great children about which I get to write my books, but she also has been the primary editor, guiding my writing, helping me improve, and caring deeply that the books come out great. This time was no exception. In addition to all her numerous responsibilities she made huge swaths of time to edit this book, and I'm super appreciative.

And finally, I need to thank the two earliest ~~guinea pigs~~ readers of this book – Kira and Shelby. They actually read the chapters as I wrote them. Honestly, it's a bit of a rough go. They deal with all my idiosyncrasies, my calls begging for feedback, and wading through all the rough edges that later drafts and editing by Debbie and Sivan polished off. They don't always get to see the drawings as I'm usually a little bit ahead of Caroline.

Kira and Shelby are basically standing in front of an unfinished painting, parts painted, parts need repainting, and parts are only sketched in. And yet, they plow on, reading quickly and with a positive attitude. I couldn't be more appreciative as it makes the writing process a little bit less of a solitary exercise.

Kira, your enthusiasm for the book and the characters is unparalleled. I love how much ownership you've taken of them, often arguing with me about whether one of them would do a certain thing, and making it clear in no uncertain terms how annoyed you'll be if I screw this up. Thank you so so much.

Shelby, your support for me is unequalled and limitless. I can't think of anyone on this planet who would put up with as many discussions about these books as you do. You discuss the books with passion, and attention to detail, and care. Your support gives me the confidence to keep going when I'm nervous that it's never gonna be good enough. There's no one I'd rather be by my side pushing me to do better, and cheering me across the finish line. Thank you. I love you completely.

IF YOU LIKED THIS BOOK...

Thank you so much for reading this book. Sharing this story with you is immensely rewarding for me. Since you've already given me your time, I hesitate to ask you for something else. That said, I believe that the more people that read this book, the better future books will be. So if you have the inclination and the energy, I would ask you simply to spread the word. Here are some suggestions:

Suggest the book to a friend.

Suggest that a parent read the book to their child.

Suggest that a child read the book to their parent.

Suggest to a teacher that they read it to their class.

Visit the Madrona Heroes website at http://madronaheroes.com. That's the primary place where I post everything Madrona Heroes related.

'Like' and 'Share' Madrona Heroes on Facebook. http://facebook.com/madronaheroes

'Tweet' about the Madrona Heroes. (@madronaheroes)

Give the book an honest review on goodreads.com.

Give the book an honest review on amazon.com.

Make and share some Madrona Heroes art.

And most importantly, write me with your feedback – hillel@madronaheroes.com. I'll do my best to reply, and I promise that I will read everything that comes my way.

– Hillel

P.S. If you're a true super fan of the Madrona Heroes, then write to me at the above e-mail address, and you may get added to the Madrona Heroes Reserves. It's a secret group of the book's biggest fans who get early access to writing, and art, and help me get the word out about the books. Space is limited, so act soon.

ABOUT THE AUTHOR

Hillel Cooperman has pretended to be a superhero since he was a small child. He conceived of the story of the Madrona Heroes in the summer of 2012 on a trip abroad with his family. He lives in the Madrona neighborhood of Seattle with his three children, his long-time girlfriend, their ~~three~~ four cats, and tens of thousands of Lego bricks. His superpower is procrastination. *The Madrona Heroes Register - Underneath It All* is his second novel.

ABOUT THE ILLUSTRATOR

Caroline Hadilaksono is an Indonesian-born illustrator living in Brooklyn by way of Los Angeles. Her life goal is to make watercolor travel-sketches from as many different places in the world as possible. She dreams of living in a tree house one day. She enjoys watercoloring, eating, and laughing, preferably simultaneously. Her superpower is organizing things.

Thank you for reading "Underneath it All – Book No. 5 of The Madrona Heroes Register".

Made in the USA
San Bernardino, CA
22 August 2015